About the Authors

USA *TODAY* bestselling author **Jules Bennett** has penned more than fifty novels during her short career. She's married to her high school sweetheart, has two active girls, and is a former salon owner. Jules can be found on Twitter, Facebook (Fan Page), and her website julesbennett.com. She holds contests via these three outlets with each release and loves to hear from readers!

Maureen Child is the author of more than 130 romance novels and novellas that routinely appear on bestseller lists and have won numerous awards, including the National Reader's Choice Award. A seven-time nominee for the prestigious RITA® award from Romance Writers of America, one of her books was made into a CBS-TV movie called THE SOUL COLLECTER. Maureen recently moved from California to the mountains of Utah and is trying to get used to snow.

Caitlin Crews discovered her first romance novel at the age of twelve and has since conducted a life-long love affair with romance novels, many of which she insists on keeping near her at all times. She currently lives in the Pacific Northwest, with her animator/comic book artist husband and their menagerie of ridiculous animals.

A Cinderella Story

COLLECTION

Seducing His Cinderella

JULES BENNETT

MAUREEN CHILD

CAITLIN CREWS

MILLS & BOON

First Published in Great Britain 2020
By Mills & Boon, an imprint of HarperCollins*Publishers*
1 London Bridge Street, London, SE1 9GF

SEDUCING HIS CINDERELLA © 2020 Harlequin Books S.A.

Maid for a Magnate © 2015 Harlequin Books S.A.
The Lone Star Cinderella © 2013 Harlequin Books S.A.
Bride by Royal Decree © 2017 Caitlin Crews

Special thanks and acknowledgement to Jules Bennett for her contribution to the *Dynasties: The Montoros* series.

Special thanks and acknowledgement to Maureen Child for her contribution to *Texas Cattleman's Club: The Missing Mogul* series.

ISBN: 978-0-263-28121-7

MAID FOR A MAGNATE

JULES BENNETT

A huge thanks to the Desire team for including me in this amazing continuity. And a special thanks to Janice, Kat, Katherine, Andrea and Charlene. I loved working with you all on this project.

One

JUAN CARLOS SALAZAR II TRUE HEIR
TO THRONE

William Rowling stared at the blaring headline as he sipped his coffee and thanked every star in the sky that he'd dodged marrying into the royal family of Alma. Between the Montoro siblings and their cousin Juan Carlos, that was one seriously messed up group.

Of course his brother, James, had wedded the beautiful Bella Montoro. Will's father may have had hopes of Will and Bella joining forces, but those devious plans obviously had fallen through when James fell in love with Bella instead.

Love. Such a fickle thing that botched up nearly every best laid plan. Not that Will had ever been on board with the idea of marrying Bella. He'd rather remain single than marry just to advance his family's business interests.

The Montoros were a force to be reckoned with in Alma, now that the powerful royal family was being restored to the throne after more than seventy years in exile. And Patrick Rowling was all too eager to have his son marry into such prestige, but thankfully that son was not to be Will.

Bella's brother had been heading toward the throne, until shocking letters were discovered in an abandoned family farmhouse, calling into question the lineage of the Montoros and diverting the crown into the hands of their cousin.

Secrets, scandal, lies... Will was more than happy to turn the reins over to his twin.

And since Will was officially single, he could carry out his own devious plan in great detail—his plot didn't involve love but a whole lot of seduction.

First, though, he had to get through this meeting with his father. Fortunately, Will's main goal of taking back control of his life involved one very intriguing employee of his father's household so having this little meeting at the Rowling home in Playa del Onda instead of the Rowling Energy offices was perfectly fine with him. Now that James had married and moved out and Patrick was backing away from working as much, Patrick used his weekend home more often.

"Rather shocking news, isn't it?"

Still clutching the paper in one hand and the coffee mug in the other, Will turned to see his father breeze into the den. While Patrick leaned more toward the heavier side, Will prided himself on keeping fit. It was just another way he and his father were different though some around them felt Will was a chip off the old block.

At one time Will would've agreed with those people, but he was more than ready to show everyone, including his father, he was his own man and he was taking charge.

"This bombshell will certainly shake things up for Alma." Will tossed the newspaper onto the glossy mahogany desktop. "Think parliament will ratify his coronation?"

Patrick grunted as he sank into his leather desk chair. "It's just a different branch of the Montoro family that will be taking the throne, so it really doesn't matter."

Will clutched his coffee cup and shook his head. Anything to do with the Montoros was not his problem. He had his own battles to face, starting with his father right now.

"What did you need to see me so early about?" his father asked, leaning back so far in the chair it squeaked.

Will remained standing; he needed to keep the upper hand here, needed to stay in control. Even though he was going up against his father's wishes, Will had to take back control of his own life. Enough with worrying about what his father would say or do if Will made the wrong move.

James had never bowed to their father's wishes and Will always wondered why his twin was so against the grain. It may have taken a few years to come around, but Will was more than ready to prove himself as a formidable businessman.

Will was a master at multitasking and getting what he wanted. And since he'd kissed Cat a few weeks ago, he'd thought of little else. He wanted her…and he would have her. Their intense encounter would allow for nothing less.

But for right this moment, Will was focusing on his

new role with Rowling Energy and this meeting with his father. Conquering one milestone at a time.

"Up till now, you've had me dealing with the company's oil interests," Will stated. "I'm ready to take total control of the real estate division, too."

His father's chest puffed out as he took in a deep breath. "I've been waiting for you to come to me with this," Patrick said with a smile. "You're the obvious choice to take over. You've done a remarkable job increasing the oil profits. They're up twelve percent since you put your mark on the company."

Will intended to produce financial gains for all of the company's divisions. For years, he'd wanted to get out from under his father's thumb and take control, and now was his chance. And that was just the beginning of his plans where Rowling Energy was concerned.

Finally, now that Will was seeing clearly and standing on his own two feet, nothing would stand in his way. His father's semiretirement would just help ease the path to a beautiful life full of power and wealth... and a certain maid he'd set in his sights.

"I've already taken the liberty of contacting our main real estate clients in London," Will went on, sliding his hands into his pockets and shifting his weight. "I informed them they would be dealing with me."

Will held his father's gaze. He'd taken a risk contacting the other players, but Will figured his father would be proud and not question the move. Patrick had wanted Will to slide into the lead role of the family business for years. Slowly Will had taken over. Now he was ready to seal every deal and hold all the reins.

"Another man would think you're trying to sneak behind his back." Patrick leaned forward and laced his fingers together on the desktop. "I know better. You're taking charge and that's what I want. I'll make sure my assistant knows you will be handling the accounts from here on out. But I'm here anytime, Will. You've been focused on this for so long, your work has paid off."

Will nodded. Part one of his plan was done and had gone just as smoothly as he'd envisioned. Now he needed to start working on the second part of his plan. And both aspects involved the same tactic...trust. He needed to gain and keep the trust of both his father and Cat or everything would blow up in his face.

Will refused to tolerate failure on any level.

Especially where Cat was concerned. That kiss had spawned an onslaught of emotions he couldn't, wouldn't, ignore. Cat with her petite, curvy body that fit perfectly against his. She'd leaned into that kiss like a woman starved and he'd been all too happy to give her what she wanted.

Unfortunately, she'd dodged him ever since. He didn't take that as a sign of disinterest. Quite the opposite. If she wasn't interested, she'd act as if nothing had happened. But the way she kept avoiding him when he came to visit his father at the Playa del Onda estate only proved to Will that she was just as shaken as he was. There was no way she didn't feel something.

Just one kiss and he had her trembling. He'd use that to his advantage.

Seeing Cat was another reason he opted to come to his father's second home this morning. She couldn't avoid him if he cornered her at her workplace. She'd been the maid for his twin brother, James, but James had often been away playing football—or as the Yanks called it, soccer—so Cat hadn't been a temptation thrust right in Will's face. But now she worked directly under Patrick. Her parents had also worked for Patrick, so

Cat had grown up around Will and James. It wasn't that long ago that Will had set his sights on Cat. Just a few years ago, in fact, he'd made his move, and they'd even dated surreptitiously for a while. That had ended tragically when he'd backed down from a fight in a moment of weakness. Since their recent kiss had brought back their scorching chemistry, Will knew it was time for some action.

Will may have walked out on her four years ago, but she was about to meet the new Will…the one who fought for what he wanted. And he wanted Cat in his bed and this time he wouldn't walk away.

Will focused back on his father. "I'll let myself out," he stated, more than ready to be finished with this part of his day. "I'll be in touch once I hear back from the investors and companies I contacted."

Heading for the open double doors, Will stopped when his father called his name.

"You know, I really wanted the thing with you and Bella to work," Patrick stated, as he stared at the blaring, boldface headline.

"She found love with my brother. She and I never had any type of connection. You'd best get used to them together."

Patrick focused his attention back on Will. "Just keep your head on your shoulders and don't follow the path your brother has. Getting sidetracked isn't the way to make Rowling Energy grow and prosper. Just do what you've been doing."

Oh, he intended to do just that.

Will gave his father a brief nod before heading out into the hallway. Little did his father know, Will was fully capable of going after more than one goal at a time. He had no intention of letting the oil or real estate businesses slide. If anything, Will fully intended to expand both aspects of the business into new territory within the next year.

Will also intended to seduce Cat even sooner. Much sooner. And he would stop at nothing to see all of his desires fulfilled.

That familiar woodsy scent assaulted her...much like the man himself had when he'd kissed her a few weeks ago.

Could such a full-on assault of the senses be called something so simple as a kiss? He'd consumed her from the inside out. He'd had her body responding within seconds and left her aching and wanting more than she should.

Catalina kept her back turned, knowing full well who stood behind her. She'd managed to avoid running into him, though he visited his father more and more lately. At this point, a run-in was inevitable.

She much preferred working for James instead of Patrick, but now that James was married, he didn't stay here anymore and Patrick did. Catalina had zero tolerance for Patrick and the fact that she worked directly for him now only motivated her more to finish saving up to get out of Alma once and for all. And the only reason she was working for Patrick was because she needed the money. She knew she was well on her way to leaving, so going to work for another family for only a few months didn't seem fair.

Years ago her mother had moved on and still worked for a prestigious family in Alma. Cat prayed her time here with Patrick was coming to an end, too.

But for now, she was stuck here and she hadn't been able to stop thinking about that kiss. Will had silently taken control of her body and mind in the span of just a few heated moments, and he'd managed to thrust her directly into their past to the time when they'd dated.

Unfortunately, when he'd broken things off with her, he'd hurt her more than she cared to admit. Beyond leaving her when she hadn't even seen it coming, he'd gone so far as to say it had all been a mistake. His exact words, which had shocked her and left her wondering how she'd been so clueless. Catalina wouldn't be played for a fool and she would never be his "mistake" again. She had more pride than that...even if her heart was still bruised from the harsh rejection.

Even if her lips still tingled at the memory of their recent kiss.

Catalina continued to pick up random antique trinkets on the built-in bookshelves as she dusted. She couldn't face Will, not just yet. This was the first encounter since that night three weeks ago. She'd seen him, he'd purposely caught her eye a few times since then, but he'd not approached her until now. It was as if the man enjoyed the torture he inflicted upon her senses.

"You work too hard."

That voice. Will's low, sultry tone dripped with sex appeal. She didn't turn around. No doubt the sight of him would still give her that swift punch of lust to the gut, but she was stronger now than she used to be...or she'd been stronger before he'd weakened her defenses with one simple yet toe-curling kiss.

"Would that make you the pot or the kettle?" she asked, giving extra attention to one specific shelf because focusing on anything other than this man was all that was holding her sanity together.

His rich laughter washed over her, penetrating any

defense she'd surrounded herself with. Why did her body have to betray her? Why did she find herself drawn to the one man she shouldn't want? Because she hadn't forgotten that he'd recently been the chosen one to wed Bella Montoro. Bella's father had put out a false press release announcing their engagement, but of course Bella fell for James instead and Will ended up single. James had informed Cat that Bella and Will were never actually engaged, but still. With Will single now, and after that toe-curling kiss, Cat had to be on her guard. She had too much pride in herself to be anybody's Plan B.

"That spot is clean." His warm, solid hand slid easily onto her shoulder. "Turn around."

Pulling in a deep breath, Catalina turned, keeping her shoulders back and her chin high. She would not be intimidated by sexy good looks, flawless charm and that knowing twinkle in Will's eye. Chemistry wouldn't get her what she wanted out of life…all she'd end up with was another broken heart.

"I have a lot on my list today." She stared at his ear, trying to avoid those piercing aqua eyes. "Your dad should be in his den if you're looking for him."

"Our business is already taken care of." Will's hand dropped, but he didn't step back; if anything, he shifted closer. "Now you and I are going to talk."

"Which is just another area where we differ," she retorted, skirting around him to cross in front of the mantel and head to the other wall of built-in bookcases. "We have nothing to discuss."

Of course he was right behind her. The man had dropped her so easily four years ago yet in the past few weeks, he'd been relentless. Perhaps she just needed to be more firm, to let him know exactly where she stood.

"Listen." She spun back around, brandishing her feather duster at him. Maybe he'd start sneezing and she could make a run for it. "I've no doubt you want to talk about that kiss. We kissed. Nothing we hadn't done before."

Of course this kiss was so, so much more; it had penetrated to her very soul. Dammit.

"But I'm not the same girl you used to know," she continued, propping her hand on her hip. "I'm not looking for a relationship, I'm not looking for love. I'm not even interested in you anymore, Will."

Catalina nearly choked on that lie, but she mentally applauded herself for the firmness in her delivery and for stating all she needed to. She wasn't about to start playing whatever game Will had in mind because she knew one thing for certain…she'd lose.

Will stepped closer, took hold of her wrist and pulled her arm gently behind her back. Her body arched into his as she gripped her feather duster and tried to concentrate on the bite of the handle into her palm and not the way those mesmerizing eyes were full of passion and want.

"Not interested?" he asked with a smirk. "You may be able to lie to yourself, Cat, but you can never lie to me. I know you too well."

She swallowed. "You don't know me at all if you think I still like to be called Cat."

Will leaned in until his lips caressed the side of her ear. "I want to stand out in your mind," he whispered. "I won't call you what everyone else does because our relationship is different."

"We have nothing but a past that was a mistake." She purposely threw his words back in his face and she didn't care if that was childish or not.

Struggling against his hold only caused her body to respond even more as she rubbed against that hard, powerful build.

"You can fight this all you want," he said as he eased back just enough to look into her eyes. "You can deny you want me and you can even try to tell yourself you hate me. But know this. I'm also not the same man I used to be. I'm not going to let you get away this time."

Catalina narrowed her gaze. "I have goals, Will, and you're not on my list."

A sultry grin spread across his face an instant before he captured her lips. His body shifted so that she could feel just how much he wanted her. Catalina couldn't stop herself from opening her mouth for him and if her hands had been free, she probably would've fully embarrassed herself by gripping his hair and holding him even tighter.

Damn this man she wanted to hate, but couldn't.

He demanded her affection, demanded desire from her and she gave it. Mercy, she had no choice.

He nipped at her, their tongues tangling, before he finally, finally lifted his head and ran a thumb across her moist bottom lip.

"I have goals, too, Cat," he murmured against her mouth. "And you're on the top of *my* list."

The second he released her, she had to hurry to steady herself. By the time she'd processed that full-on arousing attack, Will was gone.

Typical of the man to get her ready for more and leave her hanging. She just wished she still wasn't tingling and aching all over for more of his touch.

Two

Will sat on his patio, staring down at his boat and contemplating another plan of action. Unfortunately his cell phone rang before he could fully appreciate the brilliant idea he'd just had.

His father's name popped up on the screen and Will knew without answering what this would be about. It looked as if Patrick Rowling had just got wind of Will's latest business actions.

"Afternoon," he greeted, purposely being more cheerful than he assumed his father was.

"What the hell are you doing with the Cortes Real Estate company?"

Will stared out onto the sparkling water and crossed his ankles as he leaned back in his cushioned patio chair. "I dropped them."

"I'm well aware of that seeing as how Dominic called me to raise hell. What were you thinking?" his father demanded. "When you steamrolled into the head position, I thought you'd make wise moves to further the family business and make it even more profitable into the next generation. I never expected you to sever ties with companies we've dealt with for decades."

"I'm not hanging on to business relationships based on tradition or some sense of loyalty," Will stated, refusing to back down. "We've not gained a thing in the past five years from the Corteses and it was time to cut our losses. If you and Dom want to be friends, then go play golf or something, but his family will no longer do business with mine. The bottom line here is money, not hurt feelings."

"You should've run this by me, Will. I won't tolerate you going behind my back."

Will came to his feet, pulled in a deep breath of ocean air and smiled because he was in charge now and his father was going to start seeing that the "good" twin wasn't always going to bend and bow to Patrick's wishes. Will was still doing the "right thing," it just so happened the decisions made were Will's version of right and not his father's.

"I'm not sneaking at all," Will replied, leaning against the scrolling wrought iron rail surrounding his deck. "I'll tell you anything you want to know, but since I'm in charge now, I'm not asking for permission, either."

"How many more phone calls can I expect like the one I got from Cortes?"

His father's sarcasm wasn't lost on Will.

"None for the time being. I only let one go, but that doesn't mean I won't cut more ties in the future if I see we aren't pulling any revenue in after a period of time."

"You run your decisions by me first."

Giving a shrug even though his father couldn't see him, Will replied, "You wanted the golden son to take over. That's exactly what I'm doing. Don't second-guess me and my decisions. I stand to gain or lose like you do and I don't intend to see our name tarnished. We'll come out on top if you stop questioning me and let me do this job the way it's meant to be done."

Patrick sighed. "I never thought you'd argue with me."

"I'm not arguing. I'm telling you how it is."

Will disconnected the call. He wasn't going to get into a verbal sparring match with his father. He didn't have time for such things and nothing would change Will's mind. He'd gone over the numbers and cross-referenced them for the past years. Though that was a job his assistant could easily do, Will wanted his eyes on every report since he was taking over. He needed to know exactly what he was dealing with and how to plan accordingly.

His gaze traveled back to his yacht nestled against his private dock. Speaking of planning accordingly, he had more personal issues to deal with right now. Issues that involved one very sexy maid.

It had taken a lifeless, arranged relationship with Bella to really wake Will up to the fact his father had his clutches so tight, Will had basically been a mar-ionette his entire life. Now Will was severing those strings, starting with the ridiculous notion of his mar-rying Bella.

Will was more than ready to move forward and take all the things he'd been craving: money and Cat. A beautiful combo to start this second stage of his life.

And it would be soon, he vowed to himself as he stalked around his outdoor seating area and headed inside. Very soon he would add to his millions, secure his place as head of the family business by cementing its leading position in the oil and real estate industries and have Cat right where he wanted her…begging.

Catalina couldn't wait to finish this day. So many things had come up that hadn't been on her regular schedule…just another perk of working for the Rowling patriarch. She had her sights set on getting home, taking off her ugly, sensible work shoes and digging into another sewing project that would give her hope, get her one step closer to her ultimate goal.

This next piece she'd designed late last night would be a brilliant, classy, yet fun outfit to add to her private collection. A collection she fully intended to take with her when she left Alma very soon.

Her own secret goal of becoming a fashion designer had her smiling. Maybe one day she could wear her own stylish clothes to work instead of boring black cotton pants and button-down shirt with hideous shoes. Other than her mother, nobody knew of Catalina's real dream, and she had every intention of keeping things that way. The last thing she needed was anyone trying to dissuade her from pursuing her ambitions or telling her that the odds were against her. She was fully aware of the odds and she intended to leap over them and claim her dream no matter how long it took. Determination was a hell of a motivator.

She came to work for the Rowlings and did her job— and that was about all the human contact she had lately. She'd been too wrapped up in materials, designs and fantasies of runway shows with her clothing draped on models who could fully do her stylish fashions justice.

Not that Catalina hated how she looked, but she

wasn't blind. She knew her curvy yet petite frame wasn't going to get her clothing noticed. She merely wanted to be behind the scenes. She didn't need all the limelight on her because she just wanted to design, no more.

As opposed to the Rowling men who seemed to crave the attention and thrive on the publicity and hoopla.

Adjusting the fresh arrangement of lilacs and white calla lilies in the tall, slender crystal vase, Catalina placed the beautiful display on the foyer table in the center of the open entryway. There were certain areas where Patrick didn't mind her doing her own thing, such as choosing the flowers for all the arrangements. She tended to lean toward the classy and elegant...which was the total opposite of the man she worked for.

James on the other hand had more fun with her working here and he actually acknowledged her presence. Patrick only summoned her when he wanted to demand something. She hated thinking how much Will was turning into his father, how business was ruling him and consuming his entire life.

Will wasn't in her personal life anymore, no matter how much she still daydreamed about their kisses. And Patrick would only be her employer for a short time longer. She was hoping to be able to leave Alma soon, leave behind this life of being a maid for a man she didn't care for. At least James was pleasant and a joy to work for. Granted, James hadn't betrayed Cat's mother the way Patrick had. And that was just another reason she wanted out of here, away from Patrick and the secret Cat knew about him.

Catalina shoved those thoughts aside. Thinking of all the sins from Patrick's past wouldn't help her mood.

Patrick had been deceitful many years ago and Catalina couldn't ignore her mother's warning about the Rowling men. Even if Will had no clue how his father had behaved, it was something Catalina would never forget. She was only glad she'd found out before she did something foolish like fall completely in love with Will.

Apparently the womanizing started with Patrick and trickled down to his sons. James had been a notorious player before Bella entered his life. After all, there was nothing like stealing your twin brother's girl, which is what James had done to Will. But all had worked out in the end because Bella and James truly did love each other even if the way they got there was hardly normal. Leave it to the Rowlings and the Montoros to keep life in Alma interesting.

Catalina just wished those recent kisses from Will weren't overriding her mother's sound advice and obvious common sense.

Once the arrangement was to her liking—because perfection was everything whether you were a maid or a CEO—Catalina made her way up the wide, curved staircase to the second floor. The arrangements upstairs most likely needed to be changed out. At the very least, she'd freshen them up with water and remove the wilting stems.

As she neared the closed door of the library, she heard the distinct sound of a woman sobbing. Catalina had no clue who was visiting. No women lived here, and she'd been in the back of the house most of the morning and hadn't seen anyone come in.

The nosy side of her wanted to know what was going on, but the employee side of her said she needed to mind her own business. She'd been around the Rowling family enough to know to keep her head down, do her job and remember she was only the help.

Inwardly she groaned. She hated that term. Yes, she was a maid, but she was damn good at her job. She took pride in what she did. No, cleaning toilets and washing sheets wasn't the most glam of jobs, but she knew what she did was important. Besides, the structure and discipline of her work was only training her for the dream job she hoped to have someday.

The rumble of male voices blended in with the female's weeping. Whatever was going on, it was something major. Catalina approached the circular table in the middle of the wide hall. As she plucked out wilted buds here and there, the door to the library creaked open. Catalina focused on the task at hand, though she was dying to turn to see who came from the room.

"Cat."

She cringed at the familiar voice. Well, part of her curiosity was answered, but suddenly she didn't care what was going on in that room. She didn't care who Will had in there, though Catalina already felt sorry for the poor woman. She herself had shed many tears over Will when he'd played her for a fool, getting her to think they could ignore their class differences and have a relationship. "I need to see you for a minute."

Of course he hadn't asked. Will Rowling didn't ask… he demanded.

Stiffening her back, she expected to see him standing close, but when she turned to face him, she noted he was holding onto the library door, with only the top half of his body peeking out of the room.

"I'm working," she informed him, making no move to go see whatever lover's spat he was having with the unknown woman.

"You need to talk to Bella."

Bella? Suddenly Catalina found herself moving down

the hall, but Will stepped out, blocking her entry into the library. Catalina glanced down to his hand gripping her bicep.

"Her aunt Isabella passed away in the middle of the night," he whispered.

Isabella Montoro was the grand matriarch of the entire Montoro clan. The woman had been around forever. Between Juan Carlos being named the true heir to the throne and now Isabella's death, the poor family was being dealt one blow after another.

Will rubbed his thumb back and forth over Catalina's arm. "You know Bella enough through James and I figured she'd want another woman to talk to. Plus, I thought she could relate to you because…"

Swallowing, she nodded. When she and Will had dated briefly, Catalina had just lost her grandmother, a woman who had been like a second mother to her. Will had seen her struggle with the loss…maybe the timing of the loss explained why she'd been so naïve to think she and Will could have a future together. For that moment in time, Catalina had clung to any hope of happiness and Will had shown her so much…but it had all been built on lies.

Catalina started to move by him, but his grip tightened. "I don't want to bring up bad memories for you." Those aqua eyes held her in place. "As much as Bella is hurting, I won't sacrifice you, so tell me if you can't go in there."

Catalina swallowed as she looked back into those eyes that held something other than lust. For once he wasn't staring at her as if he wanted to rip her clothes off. He genuinely cared or at least he was playing the part rather well. Then again, he'd played a rather impressive role four years ago pretending to be the doting boyfriend.

Catalina couldn't afford to let her guard down. Not again with this man who still had the power to cripple her. That kiss weeks ago only proved the control he still had and she'd never, ever let him in on that fact. She could never allow Will to know just how much she still ached for his touch.

"I'll be fine," she replied, pulling her arm back. "I'd like to be alone with her, though."

Will opened his mouth as if to argue, but finally closed it and nodded.

As soon as Catalina stepped inside, her heart broke. Bella sat in a wingback chair. James rested his hip on the arm and Bella was curled into his side sobbing.

"James." Will motioned for his twin to follow him out.

Leaning down, James muttered something to Bella. Dabbing her eyes with a tissue, Bella looked up and saw she had company.

Catalina crossed to the beautiful woman who had always been known for her wild side. Right now she was hurting over losing a woman who was as close as a mother to her.

The fact that Will thought Catalina could offer comfort, the fact that he cared enough to seek her out, shouldn't warm her heart. She couldn't let his moment of sweetness hinder her judgment of the man. Bella was the woman he'd been in a relationship with only a month ago. How could Catalina forget that? No matter the reasons behind the relationship, Catalina couldn't let go of the fact that Will would've said *I do* to Bella had James not come along.

Will had an agenda, he always did. Catalina had no

clue what he was up to now, but she had a feeling his newfound plans included her. After all this time, was he seriously going to pursue her? Did he honestly think they'd start over or pick up where they'd left off?

Catalina knew deep down he was only after one thing…and she truly feared if she wasn't careful, she'd end up giving in.

Three

Will lifted the bottle of scotch from the bar in the living room, waving it back and forth slightly in a silent invitation to his brother.

James blew out a breath. "Yeah. I could use a drink."

Neither mentioned the early time. Sometimes life's crises called for an emergency drink to take the edge off. And since they'd recently started building their relationship back up, Will wanted to be here for his brother because even though Bella was the one who'd suffered the loss, James was no doubt feeling helpless.

"Smart thinking asking Catalina to help." James took the tumbler with the amber liquid and eased back on the leather sofa. "Something going on there you want to talk about?"

Will remained standing, leaning an elbow back against the bar. "Nothing going on at all."

Not to say there wouldn't be something going on very

soon if he had his way about it. Those heated kisses only motivated him even more…not to mention the fact that his father would hate knowing "the good twin" had gone after what he wanted, which was the total opposite of Patrick's wishes.

James swirled the drink as he stared down into the glass. "I know Isabella has been sick for a while, but still, her death came as a shock. Knowing how strong-willed she was, I'd say she hung on until Juan Carlos was announced the rightful heir to the throne."

Will nodded, thankful they were off the topic of Cat. She was his and he wasn't willing to share her with anyone right now. Only a month ago, Bella had caught Will and Cat kissing, but at the time she'd thought it was James locking lips with the maid. The slight misunderstanding had nearly cost James the love of his life. "How is Bella dealing with the fact her brother was knocked off the throne before he could fully take control?"

The Montoro family was being restored to the Alma monarchy after decades of harsh dictatorship. First Rafael Montoro IV and then, when he abdicated, his brother Gabriel were thought to be the rightful heirs. However, their sister, Bella, had then uncovered damning letters in an old family farmhouse, indicating that because of a paternity secret going back to before World War II, Juan Carlos's line of the family were the only legitimate heirs.

"I don't think that title ever appealed to Gabriel or Bella, to be honest." James crossed his ankle over his knee and held onto his glass as he rested it on the arm of the sofa. "Personally, I'm glad the focus is on Juan Carlos right now. Bella and I have enough media attention as it is."

In addition to the fact that James had married a member of Alma's royal family, he was also a star football player who drew a lot of scrutiny from the tabloids. The newlyweds no doubt wanted some privacy to start building their life together, especially since James had also recently taken custody of his infant baby, Maisey—a child from a previous relationship.

"Isabella's passing will have the media all over the Montoros and Juan Carlos. I'm probably going to take Bella and Maisey back to the farmhouse to avoid the spotlight. The renovations aren't done yet, but we need the break."

"What can I do to help?" Will asked.

James tipped back the last of the scotch, and then leaned forward and set the empty tumbler on the coffee table. "Give me back that watch," he said with a half smile and a nod toward Will's wrist.

"Nah, I won this fair and square," Will joked. "I told you that you wouldn't be able to resist putting a ring on Bella's finger."

James had inherited the coveted watch from their English grandfather and wore it all the time. It was the way people told the twins apart. But Will had wanted the piece and had finally won it in a bet that James would fall for Bella and propose. Ironically, it had almost ended James and Bella's relationship because Will had been wearing the watch that night he'd kissed Cat in the gazebo. Bella had mistaken him for James and jumped to conclusions.

"Besides the watch, what else can I do?" Will asked.

"I have no idea." James shook his head and blew out a sigh. "Right now keeping Dad out of my business would be great."

Will laughed. "I don't think that will be a problem.

He's up in arms about some business decisions I've made, so the heat is off you for now."

"Are you saying the good twin is taking charge?"

"I'm saying I'm controlling my own life and this is only the first step in my plan."

Leaning forward, James placed his elbows on his knees. "Sounds like you may need my help. I am the black sheep, after all. Let me fill you in on all the ways to defy our father."

"I'm pretty sure I'm defying him all on my own." Will pushed off the bar and shoved his hands in his pockets. "I'll let you know if I need any tips."

James leveled his gaze at Will. "Why do I have a feeling this new plan of yours has something to do with the beautiful maid?"

Will shrugged, refusing to rise to the bait.

"You were kissing her a few weeks ago," James reminded him. "That little escapade nearly cost me Bella."

The entire night had been a mess, but thankfully things ultimately worked out the way they should have.

"So Catalina…"

Will sighed. "You won't drop it, will you?"

"We practically grew up together with her, you dated before, you were kissing a few weeks ago. I'm sure dear old Dad is about to explode if you are making business decisions that he isn't on board with and if you're seducing his maid."

"I'm not seducing anyone." Yet. "And what I do with my personal life is none of his concern."

"He'll say different once he knows you're after the maid. He'll not see her as an appropriate match for you," James countered, coming to his feet and glancing toward the ceiling as if he could figure out what was going on upstairs between the women. "What's taking them so long? Think it's safe to go back?"

Will nodded. "Let's go see. Hopefully Cat was able to calm Bella down."

"Cat, huh?" James smiled as he headed toward the foyer and the staircase. "You called her that years ago and she hated it. You still going with that?"

Will patted his brother on the shoulder. "I am going for whatever the hell I want lately."

And he was. From this point on, if he wanted it, he was taking it...that went for his business and his bedroom.

The fact that the maid was consoling a member of the royal family probably looked strange from the outside, and honestly it felt a bit weird. But Catalina had been around Bella enough to know how down-to-earth James's wife was. Bella never treated Catalina like a member of the staff. Not that they were friends by any means, but Catalina was comfortable with Bella and part of her was glad Will had asked her to come console Bella over the loss of her aunt.

"You're so sweet to come in here," Bella said with a sniff.

Catalina fought to keep her own emotions inside as she hugged Bella. Even though years had passed, Catalina still missed her grandmother every single day. Some days were just more of a struggle than others.

"I'm here anytime." Catalina squeezed the petite woman, knowing what just a simple touch could do to help ease a bit of the pain, to know you weren't alone in your grief. "There will be times memories sneak up on you and crush you all over again and there will be days you are just fine. Don't try to hide your emotions.

Everyone grieves differently so whatever your outlet is, it's normal."

Bella shifted back and patted her damp cheeks. "Thank you. I didn't mean to cry all over you and bring up a bad time in your life."

Pushing her own memories aside, Catalina offered a smile. "You didn't do anything but need a shoulder to cry on. I just hope I helped in some small way to ease the hurt and I'm glad I was here."

"Bella."

The sound of James's voice had Catalina stepping back as he came in to stand beside his wife. Tucking her short hair behind her ears, Catalina offered the couple a brief smile. James hugged Bella to his side and glanced at Catalina.

"I didn't want to interrupt, but I know you need to work, too," James said. "We really appreciate you."

Those striking Rowling eyes held hers. This man was a star athlete, wanted by women all over the world. Yet Catalina felt nothing. He looked exactly like Will, but in Catalina's heart…

No. Her heart wasn't involved. Her hormones were a jumbled mess, but her heart was sealed off and impenetrable…at least where Will was concerned. Maybe when she left Alma she'd settle somewhere new and find the man she was meant to be with, the man who wouldn't consider her a mistake.

Those damning words always seemed to be in the forefront of her mind.

"I'm here all day through the week," Catalina told Bella. "You can always call me, too. I'm happy to help any way I can."

"Thank you." Bella sniffed. She dabbed her eyes again and turned into James's embrace.

Catalina left the couple alone and pulled the door shut behind her. She leaned against the panel, closed her eyes and tipped her head back. Even though Catalina still had her mother, she missed her grandmother. There was just something special about a woman who enters your life in such a bold way that leaves a lasting impression.

Catalina knew Bella was hurting over the loss of her aunt, there was no way to avoid the pain. But Bella had a great support team and James would stay by her side.

A stab of remorse hit her. Bella's and Catalina's situations were so similar, yet so different. Will had comforted her over her loss when they'd first started dating and Catalina had taken his concern as a sign of pure interest. Unfortunately, her moments of weakness had led her to her first broken heart.

The only good thing to come out of it was that she hadn't given him her innocence. But she'd certainly been tempted on more than one occasion. The man still tempted her, but she was smarter now, less naïve, and she had her eyes wide open.

Pushing off the door, she shoved aside the thoughts of Will and their past relationship. She'd jumped from one mistake to another after he broke things off with her. Two unfortunate relationships were more than enough for her. Focusing on turning her hobby and passion for making clothes into a possible career had kept her head on straight and her life pointed in the right direction. She didn't have time for obstacles...no matter how sexy.

She made her way down the hall toward the main bathroom on the second floor. This bathroom was nearly the size of her little flat across town. She could afford something bigger, but she'd opted to keep her place small because she lived alone and she'd rather save her money for fabrics, new sewing machines, investing in her future and ultimately her move. One day that nest egg she'd set aside would come in handy and she couldn't wait to leave Alma and see how far her dreams could take her. Another couple months and she truly believed she would be ready. She still couldn't pinpoint her exact destination, though. Milan was by far the hot spot for fashion and she could head there and aim straight for the top. New York was also an option, or Paris.

Catalina smiled at the possibilities as she reached beneath the sink and pulled out fresh white hand towels. Just as she turned, she collided with a very hard, very familiar chest.

Will gripped her arms to steady her, but she wasn't going anywhere, not when she was wedged between his solid frame and the vanity biting into her back.

"Excuse me," she said, gripping the terrycloth next to her chest and tipping her chin up. "I'm running behind."

"Then a few more minutes won't matter." He didn't let up on his hold, but instead leaned back and kicked the door shut with his foot. "You're avoiding me."

Hadn't she thought this bathroom was spacious just moments ago? Because now it seemed even smaller than the closet in her bedroom.

"Your ego is getting in the way of common sense," she countered. "I'm working. Why are you always here lately anyway? Don't you have an office to run on the other side of town?"

The edge of his mouth kicked up in a cocky half smile. "You've noticed. I was beginning to think you were immune."

"I've been vaccinated."

Will's rich laugh washed over her and she cursed the goose bumps that covered her skin. Between his touch, his masculine scent and feeling his warm breath on her, her defenses were slipping. She couldn't get sucked back into his spell, not when she was so close to breaking free once and for all.

"Come to dinner with me," he told her, smile still in place as if he truly thought she'd jump at the chance. "Your choice of places."

Now Catalina laughed. "You're delusional. I'm not going anywhere with you."

His eyes darkened as they slid to her lips. "You will."

Catalina pushed against him, surprised when he released her and stepped back. She busied herself with changing out the hand towels on the heated rack. Why wouldn't he leave? Did he not take a hint? Why suddenly was he so interested in her when a few years ago she'd been "a mistake"? Plus, a month ago he'd almost been engaged to another woman.

Being a backup plan for anybody was never an option. She'd rather be alone.

Taking more care than normal, Catalina focused on making sure the edges of the towels were perfectly lined up. She needed to keep her shaking hands busy.

"You can't avoid this forever." Will's bold words sliced through the tension. "I want you, Cat. I think you know me well enough to realize I get what I want."

Anger rolled through her as she spun around to face him. "For once in your life, you're not going to be able to have something just because you say so. I'm not just a possession, Will. You can't buy me or even work your charm on me. I've told you I'm not the same naïve girl I used to be."

In two swift steps, he'd closed the gap between them

and had her backed against the wall. His hands settled on her hips, gripping them and pulling them flush with his. This time she didn't have the towels to form a barrier and his chest molded with hers. Catalina forced herself to look up into his eyes, gritted her teeth and prayed for strength.

Leaning in close, Will whispered, "I'm not the man I used to be, either."

A shiver rippled through her. No, no he wasn't. Now he was all take-charge and demanding. He hadn't been like this before. He also hadn't been as broad, as hard. He'd definitely bulked up in all the right ways...not that she cared.

"What would your father say if he knew you were hiding in the bathroom with the maid?" she asked, hoping the words would penetrate through his hormones. He'd always been yanked around by Daddy's wishes... hence their breakup, she had no doubt.

Will shifted his face so his lips were a breath away from hers as his hands slid up to her waist, his thumbs barely brushing the underside of her breasts. "My father is smart enough to know what I'd be doing behind a closed door with a sexy woman."

Oh, man. Why did she have to find his arrogance so appealing? Hadn't she learned her lesson the first time? Wanting Will was a mistake, one she may never recover from if she jumped in again.

"Are you saying you're not bowing down to your father's commands anymore? How very grown up of you."

Why was she goading him? She needed to get out of here because the more he leaned against her, the longer he spoke with that kissable mouth so close to hers, the harder he was making her life. Taunting her, making her ache for things she could never have.

"I told you, I'm a different man." His lips grazed hers as he murmured, "But I still want you and nobody is going to stand in my way."

Why did her hormones and need for his touch override common sense? Letting Will kiss her again was a bad, bad idea. But she couldn't stop herself and she'd nearly arched her body into his just as he stepped back. The heat in his eyes did nothing to suppress the tremors racing through her, but he was easing backward toward the closed door.

"You're leaving?" she asked. "What is this, Will? A game? Corner the staff and see how far she'll let me take things?"

He froze. "This isn't a game, Cat. I'm aching for you, to strip you down and show you exactly what I want. But I need you to literally hurt for wanting me and I want you to be ready. Because the second I think we're on the same level, you're mine."

And with that, he turned and walked out, leaving the door open.

Catalina released a breath she hadn't realized she'd been holding. How dare he disrupt her work and get her all hot and bothered? Did he truly think she'd run to him begging to whisk her off to bed?

As much as her body craved his touch, she wouldn't fall into his bed simply because he turned on the sex appeal. If he wanted her, then that was his problem.

Unfortunately, he'd just made his wants her problem as well because now she couldn't think of anything else but how amazing he felt pressed against her.

Catalina cursed herself as she gathered the dirty towels. If he was set on playing games, he'd chosen the wrong opponent.

Four

Catalina lived for her weekends. Two full days for her to devote to her true love of designing and sewing. There was nothing like creating your own masterpieces from scratch. Her thick portfolio binder overflowed with ideas from the past four years. She'd sketched designs for every season, some sexy, some conservative, but everything was timeless and classy in her opinion.

She supposed something more than just heartache and angst had come from Will's exiting her life so harshly. She'd woken up, finally figured out what she truly wanted and opted to put herself, her dreams as top priority. And once she started achieving her career goals, she'd work on her personal dreams of a family. All of those were things she couldn't find in Alma. This place had nothing for her anymore other than her mother, who worked for another family. But her mother had already said she'd follow Catalina wherever she decided to go.

Glancing around, Catalina couldn't remember where she put that lacy fabric she'd picked up in town a few weeks ago. She'd seen it on the clearance table and had nothing in mind for it at the time, but she couldn't pass up the bargain.

Now she knew exactly what she'd use the material for. She had the perfect wrap-style dress in mind. Something light and comfortable, yet sexy and alluring with a lace overlay. The time would come when Catalina would be able to wear things like that every single day. She could ditch her drab black button-down shirt and plain black pants. When she dressed for work every morning, she always felt she was preparing for a funeral.

And those shoes? She couldn't wait to burn those hideous things.

Catalina moved around the edge of the small sofa and thumbed through the stack of folded materials on the makeshift shelving against the wall. She'd transformed this spare room into her sewing room just last year and since then she'd spent nearly all of her spare time in the cramped space. One day, though… One day she'd have a glorious sewing room with all the top-notch equipment and she would bask in the happiness of her creations.

As she scanned the colorful materials folded neatly on the shelves, her cell rang. Catalina glanced at the arm of the sofa where her phone lay. Her mother's name lit up the screen.

Lunging across the mess of fabrics on the cushions, Catalina grabbed her phone and came back to her feet as she answered.

"Hey, Mum."

"Sweetheart. I'm sorry I didn't call earlier. I went out to breakfast with a friend."

Catalina stepped from her bedroom and into the cozy

living area. "No problem. I've been sewing all morning and lost track of time."

"New designs?" her mother asked.

"Of course." Catalina sank down onto her cushy sofa and curled her feet beneath her. "I actually have a new summery beach theme I'm working on. Trying to stay tropical and classy at the same time has proven to be more challenging than I thought."

"Well, I know you can do it," her mother said. "I wore that navy-and-gray-print skirt you made for me to breakfast this morning and my friend absolutely loved it. I was so proud to be wearing your design, darling."

Catalina sat up straighter. "You didn't tell her—"

"I did not," her mother confirmed. "But I may have said it was from a new up-and-coming designer. I couldn't help it, honey. I'm just so proud of you and I know you'll take the fashion world by storm once you leave Alma."

Just the thought of venturing out on her own, taking her secret designs and her life dream and putting herself out there had a smile spreading across her face as nerves danced in her belly. The thought of someone looking over her designs with a critical eye nearly crippled her, but she wouldn't be wielding toilet wands for the rest of her life.

"I really think I'll be ready in a couple of months," Catalina stated, crossing back to survey her inventory on the shelves. "Saying a timeframe out loud makes this seem so real."

Her mother laughed. "This is your dream, baby girl. You go after it and I'll support you all the way. You know I want you out from under the Rowlings' thumb."

Catalina swallowed as she zeroed in on the lace and

pulled it from the pile. "I know. Don't dwell on that, though. I'm closer to leaving every day."

"Not soon enough for me," her mother muttered.

Catalina knew her mother hated Patrick Rowling. Their affair years ago was still a secret and the only reason Catalina knew was because when she'd been dumped by Will and was sobbing like an adolescent schoolgirl, her mother had confessed. Maria Iberra was a proud woman and Catalina knew it had taken courage to disclose the affair, but Maria was dead set on her daughter truly understanding that the Rowling men were only after one thing and they were ruthless heartbreakers. Feelings didn't exist for those men, save for James, who seemed to be truly in love and determined to make Bella happy.

But Patrick was ruthless in everything and Will had followed suit. So why was he still pursuing her? She just wanted a straight answer. If he just wanted sex, she'd almost wish he'd just come out and say it. She'd take honesty over adult games any day.

Before she could respond to her mother, Catalina's doorbell rang. "Mum, I'll call you back. Someone is at my door."

She disconnected the call and pocketed her cell in her smock pocket. She'd taken to wearing a smock around her waist to keep pins, thread, tiny scissors and random sewing items easily accessible. Peeking through the peephole, Catalina only saw a vibrant display of flowers.

Flicking the deadbolt, she eased the door open slightly. "Yes?"

"Catalina Iberra?"

"That's me."

The young boy held onto the crystal vase with two hands and extended it toward her. "Delivery for you."

Opening the door fully, she took the bouquet and soon realized why this boy had two hands on it. This thing was massive and heavy.

"Hold on," she called around the obscene arrangement. "Let me give you a tip."

"Thank you, ma'am, but that was already taken care of. You have a nice day."

Catalina stepped back into her apartment, kicked the door shut with her foot and crossed the space to put the vase on her coffee table. She stood back and checked out various shades and types of flowers. Every color seemed to be represented in the beautiful arrangement. Catalina couldn't even imagine what this cost. The vase alone, made of thick, etched glass, appeared to be rather precious.

A white envelope hung from a perfectly tied ribbon around the top of the vase. She tugged on the ribbon until it fell free and then slid the small envelope off. Pulling the card out and reading it, her heart literally leapt up into her throat. *Think of me. W.*

Catalina stared at the card, and then back at the flowers. Suddenly they weren't as pretty as they'd been two minutes ago. Did he seriously think she'd fall for something as cliché as flowers? Please. And that arrogant message on the card was utterly ridiculous.

Think of him? Lately she'd done little else, but she'd certainly never tell him that. What an ego he'd grown since they were last together. And she thought it had been inflated then.

But because no one was around to see her, she bent down and buried her face in the fresh lilacs. They smelled so wonderful and in two days they would still look amazing.

A smile spread across her face as her plan took shape. Will had no idea who he was up against if he thought an expensive floral arrangement was going to get her to drop her panties or common sense.

As much as she was confused and a bit hurt by his newfound interest in her now that he wasn't involved with Bella, she had to admit, toying with him was going to be fun. Only one person could win this battle…she just prayed her strength held out and she didn't go down in the first round.

Will slid his cell back into his pocket and leaned against the window seat in his father's office at his Playa del Onda home. "We've got them."

Patrick blinked once, twice, and then a wide smile spread across his face. "I didn't think you could do it."

Will shrugged. "I didn't have a doubt."

"I've been trying to sign with the Cherringtons for over a year." Patrick shook his head and pushed off the top of his desk to come to his feet. "You're really making a mark here, Will. I wondered how things would fair after Bella, but business is definitely your area of expertise."

Will didn't tell his father that Mrs. Cherrington had tried to make a pass at Will at a charity event a few months back. Blackmail in business was sometimes not a bad thing. It seemed that Mrs. Cherrington would do anything to keep her husband from learning she'd had too much to drink and gotten a little frisky. She apparently went so far as to talk him into doing business with the Rowlings, but considering both families would prosper, Will would keep her little secret.

In Will's defense, he didn't let her advances go far. Even if she weren't old enough to be his mother and if she hadn't smelled as if she bathed in a distillery, she was married. He may not want any part of marriage for himself, but that didn't mean he was going to home in on anybody else's, either.

Before he could say anything further, Cat appeared in the doorway with an enormous bouquet. The arrangement reminded him of the gift he'd sent her. He'd wondered all weekend what she'd thought of the arrangement. Had she smiled? Had she thought about calling him?

He'd end this meeting with his father and make sure to track her down before he headed back to the Rowling Energy offices for an afternoon meeting. He had an ache that wasn't going away anytime soon and he was starting to schedule his work around opportunities to see Cat. His control and priorities were becoming skewed.

"I'm sorry to interrupt," she stated, not glancing Will's way even for a second. "I thought I'd freshen up your office."

Patrick glanced down at some papers on his desk and motioned her in without a word. Will kept his eyes on Cat, on her petite, curvy frame tucked so neatly into her black button-down shirt and hip-hugging dress pants. His hands ached to run over her, *sans* clothing.

She was sporting quite a smirk, though. She was up to something, which only put him on full alert.

"I don't always keep flowers in here, but I thought this bouquet was lovely." She set it on the accent table nestled between two leather wingback chairs against the far wall. "I received these the other day and they just did a number on my allergies. I thought about trashing them, but then realized that you may want something fresh for your office, Mr. Rowling."

Will stood straight up. She'd received those the other day? She'd brought his bouquet into his father's office and was giving it away?

Apparently his little Cat had gotten feisty.

"I didn't realize you had allergies," Will stated, drawing her attention to him.

She tucked her short black hair behind her ears and smiled. "And why should you?" she countered with a bit more sass than he was used to from her. "I'll leave you two to talk."

As she breezed out just as quickly as she'd come, Will looked at his father, who was staring right back at him with a narrowed gaze. Why did Will feel as if he'd been caught doing something wrong?

"Keep your hands off my staff," his father warned. "You already tried that once. I hesitated keeping her on, but James swore she was the best worker he'd ever had. Her mother had been a hard worker, too, so don't make me regret that decision."

No way in hell was he letting his father, or anybody else for that matter, dictate what he could and couldn't do with Cat. Listening to his father's instructions about his personal life was what got Will into this mess in the first place.

"Once we've officially signed with the Cherringtons, I'll be sure to send them a nice vintage wine with a personalized note."

Patrick came to his feet, rested his hands on his desk and leaned forward. "You're changing the subject."

"The subject of your staff or my personal life has no relevance in this meeting," Will countered. "I'll be sure to keep you updated if anything changes, but my assistant should have all the proper paperwork emailed by the end of the day."

Will started to head out the door, but turned to glance over his shoulder. "Oh, and the next time Cat talks to you, I suggest you are polite in return and at least look her in the eye."

Leaving his father with his mouth wide open, Will turned and left the office. Perhaps he shouldn't have added that last bit, but Will wasn't going to stand by and watch his father dismiss Cat like that. She was a person, too—just because she cleaned for Patrick and he signed her checks didn't mean he was more important than she. Will had no doubt that when Cat worked for James, he at least treated her with respect.

Dammit. Why was he getting so defensive? He should be pissed she'd dumped his flowers onto his father. There was a twisted irony in there somewhere, but Will was too keyed up to figure it out. What was it about her blatantly throwing his gift back in his face that had him so turned on?

Will searched the entire first and second floors, but Cat was nowhere to be found. Granted, the house was twelve thousand square feet, but there weren't that many people on staff. How could one petite woman go missing?

Will went back to the first floor and into the back of the house where the utility room was. The door was closed and when he tried to turn the knob, he found it locked. That was odd. Why lock a door to the laundry? He heard movement, so someone was in there.

He tapped his knuckles on the thick wood door and waited. Finally the click of a lock sounded and the door eased open. Cat's dark eyes met his.

"What do you want?" she asked.

"Can I come in?"

"This isn't a good time."

He didn't care if this was good or bad. He was here and she was going to talk to him. He had to get to another meeting and wasn't wasting time playing games.

Will pushed the door, causing her to step back. Squeezing in, he shut the door behind him and flicked the lock into place.

Cat had her back to him, her shoulders hunched. "What do you want, Will?"

"You didn't like the flowers?" he asked, crossing his arms over his chest and leaning against the door.

"I love flowers. I don't like your clichéd way of getting my attention or trying to buy me."

He reached out, grabbed her shoulder and spun her around. "Look at me, dammit."

In an instant he realized why she'd been turned away. She was clutching her shirt together, but the swell of her breasts and the hint of a red lacy bra had him stunned speechless.

"I was trying to carry a small shelf into the storage area and it got caught on my shirt," she explained, looking anywhere but at his face as she continued to hold her shirt. "I ran in here because I knew there was a sewing kit or maybe even another shirt."

Everything he'd wanted to say to her vanished from his mind. He couldn't form a coherent thought at this point, not when she was failing at keeping her creamy skin covered.

"I'd appreciate it if you'd stop staring," she told him, her eyes narrowing. "I don't have time for games or a pep talk or whatever else you came to confront me about. I have work to do and boobs to cover."

Her snarky joke was most likely meant to lighten the mood, but he'd wanted her for too long to let anything deter him. He took a step forward, then another, until he'd backed her up against the opposite wall. With her hands holding tight onto her shirt, her eyes wide and her cheeks flushed, there was something so wanton yet innocent about her.

"What do you like?" he asked.

Cat licked her lips. "What?" she whispered.

Will placed a hand on the wall, just beside her head, and leaned in slightly. "You don't like flowers. What do you like?"

"Actually, I love flowers. I just took you for someone who didn't fall into clichés." She offered a slight smile, overriding the fear he'd seen flash through her eyes moments ago. "But you're trying to seduce the maid, so maybe a cliché is all we are."

Will slid his other hand across her cheek and into her hair as he brought his mouth closer. "I don't care if you're the queen or the maid or the homeless person on the corner. I know what I want and I want you, Cat."

She turned her palms to his chest, pushing slightly, but not enough for him to think she really meant for him to step back…not when she was breathless and her eyes were on his mouth.

"I'm not for sale," she argued with little heat behind her words.

He rubbed his lips across hers in a featherlight touch that instantly caused her to tremble. That had to be her body, no way would he admit those tremors were from him.

"Maybe I'll just sample, then."

Fully covering her mouth, Will kept his hand fisted in her hair as he angled her head just where he wanted it. If she didn't want him at all, why did she instantly open for him?

The sweetest taste he'd ever had was Cat. No woman compared to this one. As much as he wanted to strip her naked right here, he wanted to savor this moment and simply savor her. He wanted that familiar taste only Cat could provide, he wanted to reacquaint himself with every minute sexy detail.

Delicate hands slid up his chest and gripped his shoulders, which meant she had to have released her hold on her shirt. Will removed his hand from the wall and gripped her waist as he slid his hand beneath the hem of her shirt and encountered smooth, warm skin. His thumb caressed back and forth beneath the lacy bra.

Cat arched into him with a slight moan. Her words may have told him she wasn't interested, but her body had something else in mind…something much more in tune with what he wanted.

Will shifted his body back just enough to finish unbuttoning her shirt. He parted the material with both hands and took hold of her breasts. The lace slid beneath his palm and set something off in him. His Cat may be sweet, somewhat innocent, but she loved the sexy lingerie. Good to know.

Reluctantly breaking the kiss, Will ached to explore other areas. He moved down the column of her throat and continued to the swell of her breasts. Her hands slid into his hair as if she were holding him in place. He sure as hell wasn't going anywhere.

Will had wanted this, wanted her, four years ago. He'd wanted her with a need that had only grown over the years. She'd been a virgin then; he'd known it and respected her for her decisions. He would've waited for her because she'd been so special to him.

Then his father had issued an ultimatum and Will had made the wrong choice. He didn't fight for what he wanted and he'd damn well never make that mistake again.

Now Cat was in his arms again and he'd let absolutely nothing stand in the way of his claiming her.

"Tell me you want this," he muttered against her heated skin. "Tell me."

His hands encircled her waist as he tugged her harder against his body. Will lifted his head long enough to catch the heat in her eyes, the passion.

A jiggling of the door handle broke the spell. Will stepped back as Cat blinked, glanced down and yanked her shirt together.

"Is someone in there?" a male voice called.

Cat cleared her throat. "I got something on my shirt," she called back. "Just changing. I'll be out shortly, Raul."

Will stared down at her. "Raul?" he whispered.

Cat jerked her shirt off and stalked across the room. Yanking open a floor-to-ceiling cabinet, she snagged another black shirt and slid into it. As she secured the buttons, she spun back around.

"He's a new employee, not that it's any of your business." When she was done with the last button, she crossed her arms over her chest. "What just happened here, as well as in the bathroom the other day, will not happen again. You can't come in to where I work and manhandle me. I don't care if I work for your family. That just makes this even more wrong."

Will couldn't suppress the grin. "From the moaning, I'd say you liked being manhandled."

He started to take a step forward but she held up her hand. "Don't come closer. You can't just toy with me, Will. I am not interested in a replay of four years ago. I have no idea what your agenda is, but I won't be part of it."

"Who says I have an agenda?"

Her eyes narrowed. "You're a Rowling. You all have agendas."

So she was a bit feistier than before. He always loved a challenge—it was impossible to resist.

"Are you still a virgin?"

Cat gasped, her face flushed. "How dare you. You have no right to ask."

"Considering I'm going to take you to bed, I have every right."

Cat moved around him, flicked the lock and jerked the door open. "Get the hell out. I don't care if this is your father's house. I'm working and we are finished. For good."

Will glanced out the door at a wide-eyed Raul. Before he passed, he stopped directly in front of Cat. "We're not finished. We've barely gotten started."

Crossing into the hall, Will met Raul's questioning stare. "You saw and heard nothing. Are we clear?"

Will waited until the other man silently nodded before walking away. No way in hell did he need his father knowing he'd been caught making out in the damn laundry room with the maid.

Next time, and there would be a next time, Will vowed she'd be in his bed. She was a willing participant every time he'd kissed her. Hell, if the knock hadn't interrupted them, they'd probably both be a lot happier right now.

Regardless of what Cat had just said, he knew full well she wanted him. Her body wasn't lying. What kind of man would he be if he ignored her needs? Because he sure as hell wasn't going to sit back and wait for another man to come along and explore that sexual side.

She was his.

Five

Alma was a beautiful country. Catalina was going to miss the island's beautiful water and white sandy beaches when she left. Swimming was her first love. Being one with the water, letting loose and not caring about anything was the best source of therapy.

And tonight she needed the release.

For three days she'd managed to dodge Will. He had come to Patrick's house every morning, holed himself up in the office with his father and then left, assumedly to head into the Rowling Energy offices.

Will may say he'd changed, but to her he still looked as if he was playing the perfect son, dead set on taking over the family business. Apparently he thought he could take her over as well. But she wasn't a business deal to close and she certainly wouldn't lose her mind again and let him devour her so thoroughly no matter how much she enjoyed it.

Lust was something that would only get her into trouble. The repercussions of lust would last a lifetime; a few moments of pleasure wouldn't be worth the inevitable heartache in the end.

Catalina sliced her arms through the water, cursing herself for allowing thoughts of Will to infringe on her downtime when she only wanted to relax. The man wanted to control her and she was letting him because she had no clue how to stop this emotional roller coaster he'd strapped her into.

Heading toward the shoreline, Catalina pushed herself the last few feet until she could stand. Shoving her short hair back from her face, she took deep breaths as she sloshed through the water. With the sun starting to sink behind her, she crossed the sand and scooped up her towel to mop her face.

He'd seriously crossed the line when he'd asked about her virginity. Yes, she'd gotten carried away with him, even if she did enjoy those stolen moments, but her sexual past was none of his concern because she had no intention of letting him have any more power over her. And she sure as hell didn't want to know about all of his trysts since they'd been together.

Cat wrapped the towel around her body and tucked the edge in to secure the cloth in place. This small stretch of beach wasn't far from her apartment, only a five-minute walk, and rarely had many visitors in the evening. Most people came during the day or on weekends. On occasion, Catalina would see families playing together. Her heart would always seize up a bit then. She longed for the day when she could have a family of her own, but for now, she had her sights set on fashion.

Giving up one dream for another wasn't an option. Who said she couldn't have it all? She could have her ideal career and then her family. She was still young. At twenty-four some women were already married and had children, but she wasn't like most women.

And if Will Rowling thought he could deter her from going after what she wanted, he was delusional. And sexy. Mercy, was the man ever sexy.

No, no, no.

Will and his sexiness had no room in her life, especially her bed, which he'd work his way into if she wasn't on guard constantly.

Catalina pulled out her tank-style sundress and exchanged the towel for the modest coverup. After shoving the towel into her bag, she slid into her sandals and started her walk home. The soft ocean breeze always made her smile. Wherever she moved, she was going to need to be close to water or at least close enough that she could make weekend trips.

This was the only form of exercise she enjoyed, and being so short, every pound really showed. Not that she worried about her weight, but she wanted to feel good about herself and she felt her best when she'd been swimming and her muscles were burning from the strain. She wanted to be able to throw on anything in her closet and have confidence. For her, confidence came with a healthy body.

Catalina crossed the street to her apartment building and smiled at a little girl clutching her mother's hand. Once she reached the stoop leading up to her flat, she dug into her bag for her keys. A movement from the corner of her eye caught her attention. She knew who was there before she fully turned, though.

"What are you doing here, Will?"

She didn't look over her shoulder, but she knew he

followed her. Arguing that he wasn't invited was a moot point; the man did whatever he wanted anyway.

"I came to see you."

When she got to the second floor, she stopped outside her door and slid her key into the lock. "I figured you'd given up."

His rich laughter washed over her chilled skin. Between the warm water and the breezy air, she was going to have to get some clothes on to get warm.

"When have you known me to give up?" he asked.

Throwing a glance over her shoulder, she raised a brow. "Four years ago. You chose your career over a relationship. Seeing me was the big mistake. Ring any bells?"

Will's bright aqua-blue eyes narrowed. "I didn't give up. I'm here now, aren't I?"

"Oh, so I was just put on hold until you were ready," she mocked. "How silly of me not to realize."

"Can I come in?" he asked. "I promise I'll only be a couple minutes."

"You can do a lot of damage in a couple minutes," she muttered, but figured the sooner she let him in, the sooner he'd leave…she hoped.

Catalina pushed the door open and started toward her bedroom. Thankfully the door to the spare room was closed. The last thing she needed was for Will to see everything she'd been working on. Her personal life was none of his concern.

"I'm changing and you're staying out here."

She slammed her bedroom door, hoping he'd get the hint he wasn't welcome. What was he doing here? Did he think she'd love how he came to her turf? Did he think she'd be more comfortable and melt into a puddle at his feet, and then invite him into her bed?

Oh, that man was infuriating. Catalina jerked off

her wet clothes and draped them over her shower rod in her bathroom. Quickly she threw on a bra, panties and another sundress, one of her own designs she liked to wear out. It was simple, but it was hers, and her confidence was always lifted when she wore her own pieces.

Her damp hair wasn't an issue right now. All she wanted to know was why he was here. If he only came for another make-out scene that was going to leave her frustrated and angry, she wanted no part of it. She smoothed back a headband to keep her hair from her face. It was so short it would be air-dried in less than an hour.

Padding barefoot back into her living room, she found Will standing near the door where she'd left him. He held a small package in his hands that she hadn't noticed before. Granted she'd had her back to him most of the time because she didn't want to face him.

"Come bearing gifts?" she asked. "Didn't you learn your lesson after the flowers?"

Will's smile spread across his face. "Thought I'd try a different tactic."

On a sigh, Catalina crossed the room and sank into her favorite cushy chair. "Why try at all? Honestly. Is this just a game to see if you can get the one who got away? Are you trying to prove to yourself that you can conquer me? Is it a slumming thing? What is it, Will? I'm trying to understand this."

He set the box on the coffee table next to a stack of the latest fashion magazines. After taking a seat on her couch, Will rested his elbows on his knees and leaned forward.

Silence enveloped them and the longer he sat there, the more Catalina wondered what was going through his mind. Was he planning on lying? Was he trying to figure out how to tell her the truth? Or perhaps he was second-guessing himself.

She studied him—his strong jawline, his broad frame taking up so much space in her tiny apartment. She'd never brought a man here. Not that she'd purposely brought Will here, but having such a powerful man in her living room was a new experience for her.

Maybe she was out of her league. Maybe she couldn't fight a force like Will Rowling. But she was sure as hell going to try because she couldn't stand to have her heart crushed so easily again.

Catalina curled her feet beside her in the spacious chair as Will met her gaze. Those piercing aqua eyes forced her to go still.

"What if I'm here because I've never gotten over you?"

Dammit. Why did he let that out? He wasn't here to make some grand declaration. He was here to soften her, to get her to let down that guard a little more because he was not giving up. He'd jump through whatever hoop she threw in front of him, but Cat would be his for a while. A steamy affair that no one knew about was exactly what they needed whether she wanted to admit it or not.

When he'd been given the ultimatum by his father to give up Cat or lose his place in Rowling Energy, Will hadn't had much choice. Oh, and his father had also stated that he'd make sure Catalina Iberra would never work anywhere in Alma again if Will didn't let her go.

He'd had to protect her, even though she hated him at the time. He'd do it all over again. But he didn't want to tell her what had happened. He didn't want her to feel guilty or to pity him. Will would win her back just as he'd won her the first time. He'd be charming and wouldn't take no for an answer.

His quiet, almost vulnerable question still hung heavy in the space between them as he waited for her response. She hadn't kicked him out of her flat, so he was making progress. Granted, he'd been making progress since that spur-of-the-moment kiss a month ago, but he'd rather speed things along. A man only had so much control over his emotions.

"You can have any woman you want." Catalina toyed with the edge of the hem on her dress, not making eye contact. "You let me go, you called me a mistake."

He'd regret those words until he died. To know he'd made Cat feel less than valuable to him was not what he'd wanted to leave her with, but once the damning words were out, he couldn't take them back. Anything he said after that point would have been moot. The damage had been done and he'd moved on…or tried to. He'd said hurtful things to get her to back away from him; he'd needed her to stay away at the time because he couldn't afford to let her in, not when his father had such a heavy hand.

Will had been devastated when she'd started dating another man. What had he expected? Did he think a beautiful, vibrant woman was just going to sit at home and sulk about being single? Obviously she had taken the breakup better than he had. And how sick was that, that he wished she'd been more upset? He wanted her to be happy…he just wanted it to be with him.

"I can't have any woman," he countered. "You're still avoiding me."

She lifted her dark eyes, framed by even darker lashes, and focused on him. Every time she looked at him, Will felt that punch to the gut. Lust. It had to be lust because he wouldn't even contemplate anything else. They'd been apart too long for any other emotion to have settled in. They were two different people now and he just wanted to get to know her all over again, to prove himself to her. She deserved everything he had to give.

Will came to his feet. He couldn't stay here because the longer he was around her, the more he wanted her. Cat was going to be a tough opponent and he knew all too well that the best things came from patience and outlasting your opponent. Hadn't it taken him four years to best his father? And he was still in the process of doing that.

"Where are you going?" she asked, looking up at him.

"You want me to stay?" He stepped forward, easing closer to the chair she sat in. "Because if I stay, I'm going to want more than just talking."

"Did you just come to see where I lived? Did you need this reminder of how opposite we are? How I'm just—"

Will put his hand over her mouth. Leaning down, he gripped the arm of her chair and rested his weight there. He eased in closer until he could see the black rim around her dark eyes.

"We've been over this. I don't care what you are. I know what I want, what I need, and that's you."

Her eyes remained locked on his. Slowly he drew his hand away and trailed his fingertips along the thin tan line coming down from behind her neck.

"You're getting red here," he murmured, watching her shiver beneath his touch. "I haven't seen you out of work clothes in years. You need to take better care of your skin."

Cat reached up, grabbed his hand and halted his movements. "Don't do this, Will. There's nothing for you here and I have nothing to give. Even if I gave you my body, I'd regret it because you wouldn't give me any more and I deserve so much. I see that now and I won't lose sight of my goals just because we have amazing chemistry."

Her pleading tone had him easing back. She wanted him. He'd broken her down enough for her to fully admit it.

What goals was she referring to? He wanted to know what her plans were because he wouldn't let this go. He'd waited too long for this second chance and to finally have her, to finally show his father he was in control now, was his ultimate goal.

"I'm not about to give up, Cat." Will stood straight up and kept his eyes on hers. "You have your goals, I have mine."

As he turned and started walking toward the door, he glanced back and nodded toward the package on the table. "You didn't like flowers. This may be more practical for you."

Before she could say a word, he let himself out. Leaving her flat was one of the hardest things he'd done. He knew if he'd hung around a bit longer she would give in to his advances, but he wanted her to come to him. He wanted her to be aching for him, not reluctant.

Cat would come around. They had too much of a history and a physical connection now for her to ignore her body. He had plenty to keep him occupied until she decided to come to him.

Starting with dropping another bomb on his father where their investments and loyalties lay.

Six

Damn that man.

Catalina resisted the urge to march into the Rowling Energy offices and throw Will's gift back in his face.

But she'd used the thing all weekend. Now she was back at the Playa del Onda estate cleaning for his father. Same old thing, different day.

Still, the fact that Will had brought her a sewing kit, a really nice, really expensive sewing kit, had her smiling. She didn't want to smile at his gestures. She wanted to be grouchy and hate them. The flowers had been easy to cast aside, but something as personal as the sewing kit was much harder to ignore.

Will had no idea about her love of sewing, he'd merely gotten the present because of the shirt she'd ripped the other day. Even though he had no clue of her true passion, he thought outside the proverbial box and took the time to find something to catch her attention… as if he hadn't been on her radar already.

Catalina shoved a curtain rod through the grommets and slid it back into place on the hook. She'd long put off laundering the curtains in the glass-enclosed patio room. She'd been too distracted since that initial kiss nearly a month ago.

Why, after four years, why did Will have to reawaken those feelings? Why did he have to be so bold, so powerful, making her face those desires that had never fully disappeared?

The cell in her pocket vibrated. Pulling the phone out, she glanced down to see Patrick's name on the screen. She wasn't afraid of her boss, but she never liked getting a call from him. Either she'd done something wrong or he was about to unload a project on her. He'd been so much more demanding than James had. Granted James had traveled all over the world for football and had rarely been home, but even when he was, he treated Catalina with respect.

Patrick acted as if the dirt on his shoe had a higher position in the social order than she did.

But she needed every dime she could save so that she could leave once she'd finished all her designs. She made a good income for a maid, but she had no idea how much she'd need to start over in a new country and get by until she got her big break.

"Hello?" she answered.

"Come to my office."

She stared at the phone as he hung up. So demanding, so controlling...much like his son.

Catalina made her way through the house and down the wide hall toward Patrick's office. Was Will here today? She didn't want to pry or ask, but she had a feeling Patrick was handing over the reins to the twin he'd groomed for the position.

The office door stood slightly ajar, so Catalina tapped her knuckles against the thick wood before entering.

"Sir," she said, coming to stand in front of Patrick's wide mahogany desk.

The floral arrangement she'd brought a few days ago still sat on the edge. Catalina had to suppress her grin at the fact that the gift a billionaire purchased for a maid now sat on said billionaire's father's desk.

When Patrick glanced up at her, she swallowed. Why did he always make her feel as if she was in the principal's office? She'd done nothing wrong and had no reason to worry.

Oh, wait. She'd made out with his son in the laundry room and there had been a witness outside the door. There was that minor hiccup in her performance.

"I'm going to have the Montoro family over for a dinner," Patrick stated without preamble. "With the passing of Isabella, it's fitting we extend our condolences and reach out to them during this difficult time."

Catalina nodded. "Of course. Tell me what we need."

"The funeral will be Wednesday and I know they will have their own gathering. I'd like to have the dinner Friday night."

Catalina pulled out her cell and started typing in the notes as he rattled off the details. Only the Montoros and the Rowlings would be in attendance. Patrick expected her to work that day preparing the house and that evening cleaning up after the party... Long days like that were a killer for her back and feet. But the double time pay more than made up for the aches and pains.

"Is that all?" she asked when he stopped talking.

He nodded. "There is one more thing."

Catalina swallowed, slid her phone into her pocket and clasped her hands in front of her body. "Yes, sir?"

"If you have a notion of vying for my son's attention, it's best you stop." Patrick eased back in his chair as if he had all the power and not a worry in the world. "He may not be marrying Bella as I'd hoped, but that doesn't mean he's on the market for you. Will is a billionaire. He's handling multimillion dollar deals on a daily basis and the last thing he has time for is to get tangled up in the charms of my maid."

The threat hung between them. Patrick wasn't stupid; he knew exactly what was going on with his own son. Catalina wasn't going to be a pawn in their little family feud. She had a job to do. She'd do it and be on her way in just a few months. Patrick and Will would still be bringing in money and she'd be long forgotten.

"I have no claim on your son, Mr. Rowling," she stated, thankful her voice was calm and not shaky. "I apologize if you think I do. We dated years ago but that's over."

Patrick nodded. "Let's make sure it stays that way. You have a place here and it's not in Will's life."

Even though he spoke the truth, a piece of her heart cracked a bit more over the fact.

"I'll get to work on these arrangements right away," she told Patrick, purposely dropping the topic of his son.

Catalina escaped the office, making it out to the hall before she leaned back against the wall and closed her eyes. Deep breaths in and out. She forced herself to remain calm.

If Patrick had known what happened in the laundry room days ago, he would've outright said so. He wasn't a man known for mincing words. But he knew something was up, which was all the more reason for her to stay clear of Will and his potent touch, his hypnotizing kisses and his spellbinding aqua eyes.

Pushing off the wall, Catalina made her way to the kitchen to speak to the head chef. They had a dinner to discuss and Catalina needed to focus on work, not the man who had the ability to destroy her heart for a second time.

He'd watched her bustle around for the past hour. She moved like a woman on a mission and she hadn't given him one passing glance.

Will wouldn't tolerate being ignored, especially by a woman he was so wrapped up in.

Slipping from the open living area where Cat was rearranging seating and helping the florist with new arrangements, Will snuck into the hallway and pulled his phone from his pocket. Shooting off a quick text, he stood in a doorway to the library and waited for a reply.

And waited. And waited.

Finally after nearly ten minutes, his phone vibrated in his hand. Cat hadn't dismissed him completely, but she wasn't accepting his offer of a private talk. What the hell? She was just outright saying no?

Unacceptable.

He sent another message.

Meet me once the guests arrive. You'll have a few minutes to spare once you're done setting up.

Will read over his message and quickly typed another. I'll be in the library.

Since he hadn't seen his father yet, Will shot his dad a message stating he may be a few minutes late. There was no way he could let another opportunity pass him by to be alone with Cat.

He'd worked like a madman these past few days and

hadn't even had a chance to stop by for a brief glimpse of her. He knew his desires ran deep, but he hadn't realized how deep until he had to go this long without seeing her, touching her, kissing her.

In the past two days Will had severed longstanding ties with another company that wasn't producing the results he wanted. Again he'd faced the wrath of his father, but yet again, Will didn't care. This was his time to reign over Rowling Energy and he was doing so by pushing forward, hard and fast. He wasn't tied to these companies the way his father was and Will intended to see the real estate division double its revenues in the next year.

But right now, he didn't want to think about finances, investments, real estate or oil. He wanted to focus on how fast he could get Cat in his arms once she entered the room. His body responded to the thought.

She wasn't even in the same room and he was aching for her.

Will had plans for the weekend, plans that involved her. He wanted to take her away somewhere she wouldn't expect, somewhere they could be alone and stop tiptoeing around the chemistry. Stolen kisses here and there were getting old. He felt like a horny teenager sneaking around his father's house copping a feel of his girl.

Will took a seat on the leather sofa near the floor-to-ceiling windows. He kept the lights off, save for a small lamp on the table near the entryway. That soft glow was enough; he didn't want to alert anyone who might be wandering outside that there was a rendezvous going on in here.

Finally after he felt as if he'd waited for an hour,

the door clicked softly and Cat appeared. She shut the door at her back, but didn't step farther into the room.

"I don't have much time," she told him.

He didn't need much…yet. Right now all he needed was one touch, just something to last until he could execute his weekend plans.

Will stood and crossed the spacious room, keeping his eyes locked on hers the entire time. With her back to the door, he placed a hand on either side of her face and leaned in.

His lips grazed over hers softly. "I've missed kissing you."

Cat's body trembled. When her hands came up to his chest, he thought she'd take the initiative and kiss him, but she pushed him away.

"I know I've given mixed signals," she whispered. "But this has to end. No matter how much I enjoy kissing you, no matter how I want you, I don't have the energy for this and I can't lose my j—"

Cat put a hand over her mouth, shook her head and glanced away.

"Your job?" he asked, taking hold of her wrist and prying her hand from her lips. "You think you're going to lose your job over what we have going?"

Her deep eyes jerked back to his. "We have nothing going, Will. Don't you get that? You can afford to mess around. You have nothing at stake here."

He had more than she realized.

"I need to get back to the guests. Bella and James just arrived."

He gripped her elbow before she could turn from him. "Stop. Give me two minutes."

Tucking her hair behind her ears, she nodded. "No more."

Will slid his thumb beneath her eyes. "You're exhausted. I don't like you working so hard, Cat."

"Some of us don't have a choice."

If she were his woman, she'd never work a day in her life.

Wait. What was he saying? She wasn't his woman and he wasn't looking to make her his lifelong partner, either. Marriage or any type of committed relationship was sure as hell not something he was ready to get into. Yes, he wanted her and wanted to spend time with her, but anything beyond that wasn't on his radar just yet.

Gliding his hands over her shoulders, he started to massage the tense muscles. His thumbs grazed the sides of her neck. Cat let out a soft moan as she let her head fall back against the door.

"What are you doing to me?" she groaned.

"Giving you the break you've needed."

Will couldn't tear his gaze from her parted lips, couldn't stop himself from fantasizing how she would look when he made love to her…when, not if.

"I really need to get back." Cat lifted her head and her lids fluttered open. "But this feels so good."

Will kept massaging. "I want to make you feel better," he muttered against her lips. "Let me take you home tonight, Cat."

On a sigh, she shook her head and reached up to squeeze his hands, halting his movements. "You have to know your father thinks something is going on with us."

Will stilled. "Did he say something to you?"

Her eyes darted away. "It doesn't matter. What matters is I'm a maid. You're a billionaire ready to take on the world. We have different goals, Will."

Yeah, and the object of his main goal was plastered against his body.

Will gripped her face between his palms and forced her to look straight at him. "What did he say?"

"I'm just fully aware of my role in this family and it's not as your mistress."

Fury bubbled through Will. "Patrick Rowling does not dictate my sex life and he sure as hell doesn't have a clue what's going on with us."

The sheen in her eyes only made Will that much angrier. How dare his father say anything? He'd done that years ago when Will had let him steamroll over his happiness before. Not again.

"There's nothing going on between us," she whispered.

Will lightened his touch, stroked her bottom lip with the pads of his thumbs. "Not yet, but there will be."

Capturing her lips beneath his, Will relaxed when Cat sighed into his mouth. Will pulled back because if he kept kissing her, he was going to want more and he'd be damned if he had Cat for the first time in his father's library.

When he took Cat to bed, it would be nowhere near Patrick Rowling or his house.

"Get back to work," he muttered against her lips. "We'll talk later."

"Will—"

"Later," he promised with another kiss. "I'm not done with you, Cat. I told you once, I've barely started."

He released her and let her leave while he stayed behind.

If he walked out now, people would know he'd been hiding with Cat. The last thing he ever intended was to get her in trouble or risk her job. He knew she took pride in what she did and the fact she was a perfection-ist only made Will respect her more. She was so much more, though. She was loyal and determined. Qualities he admired.

Well, he was just as determined and his father would never interfere with his personal life again. They'd gone that round once before and Patrick had won. This time, Will intended to come out, not only on top, but with Rowling Energy and Cat both belonging to him.

Seven

Will stared over the rim of his tumbler as he sipped his scotch. The way Cat worked the room was something he'd seen in the past, but he hadn't fully appreciated the charm she portrayed toward others during such a difficult time.

There were moments where she'd been stealthy as she slipped in and out of the room, removing empty glasses and keeping the hors d'oeuvre trays filled. Will was positive others hadn't even noticed her, but he did. He noticed every single thing about her.

The dinner was due to be served in thirty minutes and the guests had mostly arrived. Bella stood off to the side with her brother Gabriel, his arm wrapped around her shoulders.

"Your maid is going to get a complex if you keep drilling holes into her."

Will stiffened at James's words. His brother came to stand beside him, holding his own tumbler of scotch.

"I'm not drilling holes," Will replied, tossing back the last of his drink. He welcomed the burn and turned to set the glass on the accent table. "I'm making sure she's okay."

James's brief laugh had Will gritting his teeth to remain quiet and to prevent himself from spewing more defensive reasons as to why he'd been staring at Cat.

"She's used to working, Will. I'd say she's just fine."

Will turned to face his twin. "Did you come over here to hassle me or did you actually want to say something important?"

James's smile spread across his face. Will knew that smile, dammit. He'd thrown it James's way when he'd been in knots over Bella.

"Shut up," Will said as he turned back to watch Cat.

If his brother already had that knowing grin, then Will's watching Cat wouldn't matter at this point. She was working too damn hard. She'd been here all day to make sure the house was perfect for the Montoros and she was still busting her butt to make everyone happy. The chef was really busting it, too, behind the scenes. Cat was definitely due for a much needed relaxing day away from all of this.

"You appear to be plotting," James commented. "But right now I want to discuss what Dad is in such a mood about."

Will threw his brother a glance. "He's Patrick Rowling. Does he need a reason?"

"Not necessarily, but he was a bit gruffer than usual when I spoke with him earlier."

Will watched his father across the room as the man approached Bella and Gabriel. As they all spoke, Will knew his father was diplomatic enough to put on a front of being compassionate. He wouldn't be his stiff, grouchy self with those two.

"I may have made some business decisions he wasn't happy with," Will stated simply.

"Business? Yeah, that will do it." James sighed and finished his scotch. "He put you in charge, so he can't expect you to run every decision by him."

"That's what I told him. I'm not one of his employees, I'm his son and I'm the CEO of Rowling Energy now."

"Plus you're trying to seduce his maid," James added with a chuckle. "You're going to get grounded."

Will couldn't help but smile. "You're such an ass."

"It's fun to see the tables turned and you squirming over a woman for once."

"I'm not squirming, dammit," Will muttered.

But he wouldn't deny he was using Cat as another jab at his father. Yes, he wanted Cat and always had, but if being with her still irritated the old man, so much the better.

Part of him felt guilty for the lack of respect for his father, but that went both ways and the moment Patrick had issued his ultimatum years ago, Will had vowed then and there to gain back everything he deserved, no matter what the cost to his relationship with his father.

Bella's oldest brother, Rafe, and his very pregnant wife, Emily, crossed the room, heading for Will and James. Since he'd abdicated, Rafe and Emily had lived in Key West. But they'd traveled back to be with the family during this difficult time.

"This was a really nice thing for Patrick to do," Rafe stated as he wrapped an arm around his wife's waist. "Losing Isabella has been hard."

"I'm sorry for your loss," Will said. "She was definitely a fighter and Alma is a better place because of her."

"She was quite stubborn," Emily chimed in with a smile. "But we'll get through this because the Montoros are strong."

Will didn't think this was the appropriate time to bring up the subject of Rafe resigning from his duties before his coronation. It was the proverbial elephant in the room.

"I'm going to save my wife from my father," James told them. "Excuse me."

Rafe and Emily were talking about the funeral—how many people had turned out and how supportive the country was in respecting their time of mourning. But Will was only half listening. Cat glanced his way once and that's all it took for his heart to kick up and his body to respond. She didn't smile, she merely locked those dark eyes on him as if she knew his every thought.

Tension crackled between them and everyone else in the room disappeared from his world. Nobody existed but Cat and he knew without a doubt she would agree to his proposal.

He wouldn't accept no for an answer.

Her feet were absolutely screaming. Her back wasn't faring much better. The Montoros lingered longer than she'd expected and Catalina had stuck around an hour after the guests had left.

This fourteen-hour workday would certainly yield a nice chunk of change, but right now all Catalina could think of was her bed, which she hoped to fall into the moment she got home. She may not even take the time to peel out of her clothes.

Catalina nearly wept as she walked toward her car.

She'd parked in the back of the estate near the detached garage where Patrick kept his sporty cars that he only brought out on special occasions. The motion light popped on as she approached her vehicle.

Instantly she spotted Will sitting on a decorative bench along the garage wall. Catalina stopped and couldn't help but smile.

"Are you hiding?" she asked as she started forward again.

"Waiting." He unfolded that tall, broad frame and started coming toward her. "I know you're exhausted, but I just wanted to ask something."

Catalina crossed her arms and stared up at him. "You could've called or texted me your question."

"I could've," he agreed with a slight nod. "But you could say no too easily. I figure if you're looking me in the eye—"

"You think I can't resist you?" she laughed.

Exhaustion might have been consuming her and clouding her judgment, but there was still something so irresistible and charming about this overbearing man...and something calculating as well. He'd purposely waited for her, to catch her at a weak moment. He must really want something major.

"I'm hoping." He reached out, tucking her hair behind her ears before his fingertips trailed down her jawline. "I want to take you somewhere tomorrow afternoon. Just us, on my yacht for a day out."

Catalina wanted to give in to him, she wanted to forget all the reasons they shouldn't be together in any way. She wished her head and her heart would get on the same page where Will Rowling was concerned. She had goals, she had a job she needed to keep in order to reach those goals...yet everything about Will made her want to entertain the idea of letting him in, even if just for one night.

"I even have the perfect spot chosen for a swim," he added, resting his hands on her shoulders. Squeezing her tense muscles, Will smiled. "I'll be a total gentleman."

"A total gentleman?" Catalina couldn't help but laugh. "Then why are you so eager to go?"

"Maybe I think it's time someone gives back to you." His hands stilled as he held her gaze and she realized he wasn't joking at all. "And maybe it's time you see that I'm a changed man."

Her heart tumbled in her chest. "I'm so tired, Will. I'm pretty sure I'm going to spend the next two days sleeping."

"You won't have to do a thing," he promised. "I'll bring the food. All you have to do is wear a swimsuit. I promise this will be a day of total relaxation and pampering."

Catalina sighed. "Will, your father—"

"He's not invited."

She laughed again. "I'm serious."

"I am, too."

Will backed her up to her car and towered over her with such an intense gaze, Catalina knew she was fighting a losing battle.

"This has nothing to do with my father, your job or our differences." His strong jaw set firm, he pressed his gloriously hard body against hers as he stared into her eyes. "I want to spend time with you, Cat. I've finally got my sights set on what is important to me and I'm not letting you get away again. Not without a fight."

"That's what scares me." She whispered the confession.

"There's nothing to be afraid of."

"Said the big bad wolf."

Will smiled, dropped his hands and eased back. "No pressure, Cat. I want to spend time with you, but if you're not ready, I understand. I'm not going anywhere."

The man knew exactly what to say and his delivery was flawless. In his line of work, Will was a master at getting people to see things his way, to ensure he got what he wanted at the end of the day.

No matter what common sense tried to tell her, Catalina wasn't about to start in on a battle she had no chance of winning.

"I'll go," she told him.

The smile that spread across his face was half shadowed by the slant of the motion lights, but she knew all too well how beautiful and sexy the gesture was.

"I'll pick you up at your apartment around noon," he told her. "Now, go home. I'm going to follow you to make sure you get there safely since you're so tired."

"That's not necessary."

Will shrugged. "Maybe not, but I wasn't kidding when I said someone needed to take care of you and pamper you for a change. I'm not coming in. I'll just follow, and then be on my way home."

"I live in the opposite direction from your house," she argued.

"We could've been halfway to your flat by now." He slid his arm around her and tugged on her door handle. "Get in, stop fighting me and let's just save time. You know I'll win in the end anyway."

That's precisely what she feared the most. Will having a win over her could prove more damaging than the last time she'd let him in, but she wanted to see this new side of him. She wanted to take a day and do absolutely nothing but be catered to.

Catalina eased behind the wheel and let Will shut her door. Tomorrow would tell her one of two things: either she was ready to move on and just be his friend or she wanted more with him than stolen kisses behind closed doors.

Worry and panic flooded Catalina as she realized she already knew what tomorrow would bring.

Will had been meaning to see his niece, Maisey, and this morning he was making her his top priority. Before he went to pick up Cat for their outing, he wanted to surprise his adorable niece with a gift...the first of many. He had a feeling this little girl was going to be spoiled, which was better than a child being ignored.

Maisey Rowling would want for nothing. Will's brother had given up being a playboy and was growing into his family-man role rather nicely, and Bella was the perfect stepmother to the infant. Will figured since he and his twin were growing closer, he'd stop in and offer support to James. This complete one-eighty in lifestyles had to be a rough transition for James, but he had Bella and the two were completely in love. And they both loved sweet Maisey.

A slight twinge of jealousy speared through Will, but not over the fact that his brother had married Bella. There had been no chemistry between Will and Bella. She was sweet and stunning, but Will only had eyes for one woman.

The jealousy stemmed from the thought of his brother settling down with his own family. Will hadn't given much thought to family before. He'd been raised to focus solely on taking over Rowling Energy one day.

Will tapped on the etched glass front door to James and Bella's temporary home. They were living here until they knew for sure where they wanted to be permanently. They were in the middle of renovating the old farmhouse that belonged to the Montoros and James had mentioned that they'd probably end up there.

But for now, this house was ideal. It was near the beach, near the park and near Bella's family. Family was important to the Montoros...and yet Will was still thrilled he'd dodged that clan.

The door swung open and Bella greeted him with a smile. "Will, this is a surprise. Come on in."

Clutching the doll he'd brought as a present, Will stepped over the threshold. "I should've called, but I really thought of this last-minute."

Bella smoothed her blond hair behind her shoulders. "This is fine. Maisey and James are in the living room. They just finished breakfast and they're watching a movie."

Her blue eyes darted down to his hands. "I'm assuming that's for Maisey?"

Will nodded. "I haven't played the good uncle yet. Figured it was time I started spoiling her."

Bella's smile lit up her face. "She's going to love it."

The thought of being married to this woman did nothing for Will. Yes, she was stunning, but he'd never felt the stirrings of lust or need when he'd been around her. Their fathers never should have attempted to arrange their engagement, but thankfully everything had worked out for the best...at least where Bella and James were concerned. They were a unified family now.

The thought of his black sheep, playboy brother snuggling up with a baby girl and watching some kid flick was nearly laughable. But Will also knew that once James had learned he had a child, his entire life had changed and his priorities had taken on a whole new order, Maisey being at the top.

Bella led Will through a wide, open-arched doorway to a spacious living room. Two pale yellow sofas sat facing each other with a squat, oversized table between them. An array of coloring books and crayons were scattered over the top of the glossy surface.

James sat on one of the sofas, legs sprawled out before him with Maisey on his lap. James's short hair was all in disarray. He still wore his pajama bottoms and no shirt, and Maisey had a little pink nightgown on; it was obvious they were enjoying a morning of laziness.

As Will stepped farther into the room, James glanced over and smiled. "Hey, brother. What brings you out?"

Bella sat at the end of the couch at her husband's feet. Maisey crawled over her father's legs and settled herself onto Bella's lap. Will looked at his niece and found himself staring into those signature Rowling aqua eyes. No denying who this baby's father was.

"I brought something for Maisey." Will crossed the room and sat on the edge of the coffee table. "Hey, sweetheart. Do you like dolls?"

What if she didn't like it? What if she didn't like him? Dammit. He should've planned better and called to see what Maisey actually played with. He'd just assumed a little girl would like a tiny stuffed doll.

"Her dress matches your nightgown," Bella said softly to the little girl.

Maisey kept her eyes on him as she reached for the toy. Instantly the blond hair went into Maisey's mouth.

"She likes it." James laughed. "Everything goes into her mouth these days."

Will continued to stare at his niece. Children were

one area where he had no clue, but if James said Maisey liked it, then Will had to assume she did.

James swung his legs to the floor and leaned forward. "You hungry?" he asked. "We still have some pancakes and bacon in the kitchen."

"No, I'm good. I'm getting ready to pick up Cat, so I can't stay anyway."

James's brows lifted as he shot Bella a look. "Is this a date?"

Will hadn't intended on telling anyone, but in growing closer with James over the past couple months, he realized he wanted this bond with his twin. Besides, after their conversation last night, James pretty much knew exactly where Will stood in regards to Cat.

He trusted James, that had never been an issue. The issue they'd had wedged between them stemmed from their father always doting on one brother, molding him into a disciple, while ostracizing the other one.

"I'm taking her out on my yacht," Will told him. "We're headed to one of the islands for the day. I'm hoping for total seclusion. Most tourists don't know about them."

There was a small cluster of islands off the coast of Alma. He planned on taking her to Isla de Descanso. The island's name literally meant Island of Relaxation. Cat deserved to be properly pampered and he was going to be the man to give her all of her needs...every single one.

"Sounds romantic." Bella shifted Maisey on her lap as she stared at Will. "I wasn't aware you and Catalina were getting more serious."

James laughed. "I think they've been sneaking."

"We're not serious and we're not sneaking," Will

defended himself. "Okay, fine. We were sneaking, but she's private and she's still leery of me."

"You can't blame her," James added.

Will nodded. "I don't, which is why we need this time away from everything. Plus she's working like crazy for Dad and she's never appreciated."

James snorted. "He barely appreciates his sons. You think he appreciates a maid? I was worried when he moved into my old house. I tried to warn her, but she said she could handle it and she needed the job."

Will hated the thought of her having to work. Hated how much she pushed herself for little to no praise and recognition.

"Well, I appreciate her," Bella chimed in. "I saw how hard she worked the dinner last night. I can't imagine the prep that she and the cooks went through, plus the cleanup after. Catalina is a dedicated, hard worker."

"She won't stay forever," James stated as he leaned over and ruffled Maisey's hair.

Will sat up straighter. "What do you mean?"

His brother's eyes came back to meet his. "I'm just saying someone who is such a perfectionist and self-disciplined surely has a long-term goal in mind. I can't imagine she'll want to play maid until she's old and gray. She hinted a few times when she worked for me that she hoped to one day leave Alma."

Leave Alma? The thought hadn't even crossed Will's mind. Would Cat really go somewhere else? Surely not. Her mother still worked here. She used to work for Patrick, but years ago she had suddenly quit and gone to work for another prominent family. Cat had been with the Rowlings for five years, but James was right. Someone as vibrant as Cat wouldn't want to dust and wash sheets her entire life. He'd already seen the toll her end-less hours were taking on her.

Will came to his feet, suddenly more eager than ever to see her, to be alone with her. "I better get going. I just wanted to stop by and see Maisey before I headed out."

James stood as well. "I'll walk you to the door."

Bidding a goodbye to Bella and Maisey, Will fol-lowed his brother to the foyer.

"Don't say a word about Cat and me," Will said.

Gripping the doorknob, James nodded. "I'm not say-ing a word. I already know Dad would hate the idea and he's interfered enough in our personal lives lately. And I'm not judging you and Catalina. I actually think you two are a good match."

"Thanks, man, but don't let this happily-ever-after stuff you have going on filter into my world. I'm just spending time with Cat. That's all." Will gave his brother a one-armed man hug. "I'll talk to you next week."

Will headed toward his car, more than ready to pick up Cat and get this afternoon started. He planned to be in complete control, but he'd let her set the tone. As much as he wanted her, he wasn't going to pressure her and he wasn't going to deceive her.

Yes, there was the obvious appeal of the fact that his father would hate Will bedding the maid, but he wouldn't risk her job that way even to get petty revenge on his domineering father.

Besides, Cat was so much more than a romp. He couldn't figure out exactly what she was…and that ir-ritated him.

But now he had another worry. What was Cat's ul-timate goal in life? Would she leave Alma and pursue something more meaningful? And why did he care? He wasn't looking for a ring on his finger and he wasn't about to place one on hers, either.

Still, the fact that she could leave bothered him more than he cared to admit.

Will pushed those thoughts aside. Right now, for today, all he was concerned with was Cat and being alone with her. All other world problems would have to wait.

[faint text showing through from previous page]

Eight

Nerves kicked around in Catalina's belly as she boarded the yacht. Which seemed like such a simple word for this pristine, massive floating vessel. The fact that the Rowlings had money was an understatement, but to think that Will could own something this amazing…it boggled her mind. She knew he would make a name for himself, knew he'd climb to the top of Rowling Energy. There was never any doubt which twin Patrick was grooming for the position.

But she wasn't focusing on or even thinking of Patrick today. Will wanted her to relax, wanted her to enjoy her day off, and she was going to take full advantage.

Turning toward Will, Catalina laughed as he stepped on board. "I'm pretty sure my entire flat would fit on this deck."

Near the bow, she surveyed the wide, curved outdoor seating complete with plush white pillows. There was even a hot tub off to the side. Catalina couldn't even imagine soaking in that warm water out under the stars. This yacht screamed money, relaxation…and seduction.

She'd voluntarily walked right into the lion's den.

"Let me show you around." Will took hold of her elbow and led her to the set of steps that went below deck. "The living quarters are even more impressive."

Catalina clutched her bag and stepped down as Will gestured for her to go first. The amount of space in the open floor plan below was shocking. It was even grander than she'd envisioned. A large king-sized bed sat in the distance and faced a wall of curved windows that overlooked the sparkling water. Waking up to a sunrise every morning would be heavenly. Waking up with your lover beside you would simply be the proverbial icing on the cake.

No. She couldn't think of Will as her lover or icing on her cake. She was here for a restful day and nothing else. Nookie could not play a part in this because she had no doubt the second he got her out of her clothes, she'd have no defense against him. She needed to stay on guard.

A deep, glossy mahogany bar with high stools separated the kitchen from a living area. The living area had a mounted flat-screen television and leather chairs that looked wide enough for at least two people.

The glossy fixtures and lighting only added to the perfection of the yacht. It all screamed bachelor and money…perfect for Will Rowling.

"You've done well for yourself," she told him as she placed her tote bag on a barstool. "I'm impressed."

Will's sidelong smile kicked up her heart rate. They hadn't even pulled away from the dock and he was already getting to her. This was going to be a day full of her willpower battling her emotions and she didn't know if she'd have the strength to fight off Will's advances.

Who was she kidding? Catalina already knew that if Will tried anything she would succumb to his charms. She'd known this the moment she'd accepted his invitation. But that didn't mean she'd drop her wall of defenses so easily. He'd seriously hurt her before and if he wanted to show her what a changed man he was now, she was going to make him work for it.

"Did you think I was taking you out in a canoe for the day?"

"I guess I hadn't given much thought to the actual boat," she replied, resting her arm on the smooth, curved edge of the bar. "I was too worried about your actions."

"Worried you'd enjoy them too much?" he asked with a naughty grin.

"More like concerned I'd have to deflate your ego," she countered with a matching smile. "You're not seriously going to start putting the moves on me now, are you?"

Will placed a hand over his heart. "You wound me, Cat. I'm at least going to get this boat on course before I rip your clothes off."

Catalina's breath caught in her throat.

Will turned and mounted the steps to go above deck, and then froze and threw a sexy grin over his shoulder. "Relax, Cat. I won't do anything you don't want."

The playful banter had just taken a turn, a sharp turn that sent shivers racing through her entire body. Was she prepared for sex with this man? That's what everything leading up to this moment boiled down to.

Cat would be lying to herself if she tried to say she

didn't want Will physically. That had been proven each time he'd kissed her recently.

I won't do anything you don't want, he'd said.

And that was precisely what scared her the most.

With the ocean breeze sliding across his face, Will welcomed the spittle of spray, the taste of salt on his lips. He needed to get a damn grip. He hadn't meant to be so teasing with Cat.

Okay, he had, but he hadn't meant for her to get that panicked look on her face. He knew full well she was battling with herself where he was concerned. There wasn't a doubt in his mind she wanted him physically and that was easy to obtain. But there was part of Will that wanted her to see that he wasn't at all the same man he used to be.

She would get to see that side of him today. He intended to do everything for her, to prove to her just how appreciated she was and how valued. Will had fully stocked the yacht when he'd had this idea a couple days ago. He'd known he would take her out at some point, but it wasn't until he saw her working the crowd, with circles under her eyes and a smile on her face at the dinner last night, that he decided to invite her right away.

With all of the recent upheaval in Alma—the Montoro monarchy drama and Isabella's passing, not to mention Will's taking the reins of Rowling Energy—there was just too much life getting in the way of what he wanted. Too many distractions interfering with his main goal...and his goal was to have Cat.

He may be the good son, the twin who was raised to follow the rules and not question authority. But Will wasn't about to make the same mistake with Cat as he had in the past. The moment he'd let her walk away years ago, he'd already started plotting to get her back. Then the whole debacle with Bella had happened and Will knew more than ever that it was time to make his move with Rowling Energy and Cat.

Spending the day together on his yacht, however, was something totally unrelated to everything else that had happened in their past. Today was all about them and nothing or nobody else. Everything that happened with Cat from here on out was going to be her call…he may just silently nudge and steer her in the right direction. Those initial kisses had reignited the spark they'd left burning long ago and he knew without a doubt that she felt just as passionate as he did.

He didn't blame her one bit for being leery. He'd done some major damage before and she wouldn't let him forget it anytime soon. Not that he could. He'd never forget that look on her face when he'd told her they'd been a mistake and then walked away. That moment had played over and over in his mind for the past several years. Knowing he'd purposely hurt Cat wasn't something he was likely to ever forget.

Still, if she ever discovered the truth, would she see that he'd done it for her? He'd best keep that secret to himself and just stay on course with his plan now. At least she was here, she was talking and she was coming around. The last thing Will wanted to do was rehash the past when they could be spending their time concentrating on the here and now.

Will steered the yacht toward the private island not too far from Alma. In just under an hour he'd have Cat on a beach with a picnic. He wondered when the last time was that she'd had someone do something like that for her, but quickly dismissed the thought. If another man had pampered her, Will sure as hell didn't want to know.

Of course, there was no man in her life now. Will was the one kissing her, touching her. She was his for at least today so he needed to make the most of every moment they were alone. He truly hoped the tiny island was deserted. He'd come here a few times to think, to get away from all the pressure and stress. Only once had he run into other people.

Cat stayed below for the duration of the trip. Perhaps she was trying to gather her own thoughts as well. Maybe she was avoiding him because she thought that taking her out to a private island for sex was so cliché, so easy to read into.

But for reasons Will didn't want to admit or even think about, this day was so much more than sex. *Cat* was more than sex. Yes, he wanted her in the fiercest way imaginable, but he also wanted more from her... he just didn't know what.

No, that was wrong. The first thing he wanted was for her to see him in a different light. He wanted her to see the good in him she'd seen when they'd grown up together, when they'd laughed and shared secrets with each other. He wanted her to see that he wasn't the monster who had ripped her heart out and diminished their relationship into ashes with just a few damning words.

Perhaps this outing wasn't just about him proving to her what a changed man he was, but for him to try to figure out what the hell to do next and how far he wanted to take things with her once they got back to reality.

When he finally pulled up to the dock and secured the yacht, he went below deck. He hoped the last forty-five minutes had given Cat enough time to see that he

wasn't going to literally jump her. The playful banter
had taken a sexual turn, but he wasn't sorry. He was
only sorry Cat hadn't come up once to see him. This initial space was probably for the best. After all, today was
the first time they'd been fully alone and not sneaking
into the bathroom or laundry area of his father's home
for a make-out session.

Yeah, his seduction techniques needed a bit of work
to say the least. But he'd had four years to get control
over just how he wanted to approach things once he finally got his Cat alone. And now he was ready.

As he stepped below, Will braced his hands on the
trim overhead and froze on the last step. Cat lay side-
ways, curled into a ball on his bed. The innocent pose
shouldn't have his body responding, but...well, he was a
guy and this woman had had him tied in knots for years.

Will had wanted Cat in his bed for too long. All his
fantasies involved the bed in his house, but the yacht
would do. At this point he sure as hell wasn't going to
be picky. He'd waited too damn long for this and he
was going to take each moment he could get, no matter the surroundings.

And the fact that she was comfortable enough to
rest here spoke volumes for how far they'd come. Just
a few weeks ago he'd kissed her as if she was his next
breath and she'd run away angry. Though Will was
smart enough to know her anger stemmed from arousal.

Passion and hate...there was such a fine line between the two.

Slowly, Will crossed the open area and pulled a small
throw from the narrow linen closet. Gently placing the
thin blanket over her bare legs and settling it around her
waist, Will watched the calm rise and fall of her chest.
She was so peaceful, so relaxed and not on her guard.

For the first time in a long time, Will was finally seeing the woman he knew years ago, the woman who was more trusting, less cautious.

Of course, he'd helped shape her into the vigilant person she was today. Had he not made such bad choices when they'd been together the first time, perhaps she wouldn't have to feel so guarded all the time. Perhaps she'd smile more and laugh the way she used to.

Cat shifted, let out a throaty moan and blinked up at Will. Then her eyes widened as she sat straight up.

"Oh my. Was I asleep?"

Will laughed, crossing his arms over his chest. "Or you were playing dead."

Cat smoothed her short hair away from her face and glanced toward the wall of windows. "I was watching the water. I was so tired, so I thought I'd just lie here and enjoy the scenery."

"That was the whole point in having my bed right there. It's a breathtaking view."

When she turned her attention back to him, she gasped. That's right, he hadn't been discussing the water. The view of the woman was much more enticing.

"Why don't you use the restroom to freshen up and change into your suit?" he suggested. "I'll get our lunch set up."

The bright smile spreading across her face had something unfamiliar tugging on his heart. He may not be able to label what was going on between them, but he couldn't afford to be emotional about it.

Dammit. He didn't even know what to feel, how to act anymore. He wanted her, but he wasn't thinking of forever. He wanted now. He needed her to see he was a different man, yet he was more than ready to throw this relationship into his father's face.

Sticking to business would have been best; at least he knew exactly what he was getting into with real estate and oil. With Cat, he had no clue and the fact that she had him so tied in knots without even trying was terrifying.

Once his mission had been clear—to win back Cat to prove he could and to show his father who was in charge. But then, somewhere along the way, Will had shifted into needing Cat to see the true person he'd come to be, the man who still had feelings for her and cared for her on a level even he couldn't understand.

Cat came to her feet and started folding the throw. "I'm sorry I fell asleep on you."

Stepping forward and closing the space between them, Will pulled the blanket from her hands, wadded it up and threw it into the corner. "You aren't cleaning. You aren't folding, dusting, doing dishes. Your only job is to relax. If you want a nap, take a nap. The day is yours. The cleaning is up to me. Got it?"

Her eyes widened as she glanced at the crumpled blanket. "Are you just going to leave that there?"

Will took her chin between his thumb and finger, forcing her to look only at him. "You didn't answer my question."

Her wide, dark eyes drew him in as she merely nodded. "I can't promise, but I'll try."

Unable to help himself, Will smacked a kiss on her lips and pulled back as a grin spread across his face. "Go freshen up and meet me on the top deck."

Will watched as Cat grabbed her bag off the barstool and crossed to the bathroom. Once the door clicked shut, he let out a breath.

He'd sworn nobody would ever control him or hold any power over him again. Yet here was a petite, doe-eyed maid who had more power over him than any business magnate or his father ever could.

Will raked a hand through his hair. He'd promised Cat a day of relaxation and he intended to deliver just that. If she wasn't ready for more, then he'd have to pull all of his self-control to the surface and honor her wishes.

What had he gotten himself into?

Nine

Maybe bringing this particular swimsuit had been a bad idea. When she'd grabbed the two-piece black bikini, Catalina had figured she'd make Will suffer a little. But, by wearing so little and having him so close, she was the one suffering.

Catalina pulled on a simple red wrap dress from her own collection and slipped on her silver flip-flops.

One glance in the mirror and she laughed. The bikini would at least draw attention away from the haggard lines beneath her eyes and the pallor of her skin. Over the past few months, if she wasn't working for James or Patrick, she was working for herself getting her stock ready to showcase when the opportunity presented itself. She believed in being prepared and the moment she saw an opening with any fashion design firm, she was going to be beating down their doors and promoting her unique styles.

Catalina tossed her discarded clothes back into her tote and looked around to make sure she hadn't left anything lying around in the bathroom. Could such a magnificent room be a simple, mundane bathroom?

With the polished silver fixtures, the glass wall shower and sparkling white tile throughout, Catalina had taken a moment to appreciate all the beauty before she'd started changing. The space screamed dominance...male dominance.

Will was pulling out all the stops today. He'd purposely invited her aboard his yacht because he knew that given her love of water she'd never be able to say no. He was right. Anything that got her away from her daily life and into the refreshing ocean was a no-brainer.

Exiting the bathroom, Catalina dropped her bag next to the door and headed up to the top deck. The sun warmed her skin instantly as she turned and spotted Will in a pair of khaki board shorts and a navy shirt he'd left completely unbuttoned. The man wasn't playing fair...which she assumed was his whole plan from the start.

Fine. She had a bikini and boobs. Catalina figured she'd already won this battle before it began. Men were the simplest of creatures.

Will had transformed the seating area into a picnic. A red throw covered the floor, a bucket with ice and wine sat to one side and Will was pulling fruit from a basket.

"Wow. You really know how to set the stage."

He threw her a smile. "Depends on the audience."

"It's just me, so no need to go to all the trouble." She edged around the curving seats and stood just to the side of the blanket. "I'd be happy with a simple salad."

"There is a need to go to all this trouble," he corrected her as he continued to pull more food from the basket. "Have a seat. The strawberries are fresh, the wine is chilled and I have some amazing dishes for us."

Catalina couldn't turn down an invitation like that. She eased down onto the thick blanket and reached for a strawberry. She'd eaten three by the time Will came to sit beside her.

With his back resting against the sofa, he lifted his knee and wrapped his arm around it. "I have a variety of cheese, salmon, baguettes, a tangy salad my chef makes that will make you weep and for dessert…"

He reached over and pulled the silver lid from the dish. "Your favorite."

Catalina gasped as she stared at the pineapple upside-down cheesecake. "You remembered?"

"Of course I did." He set the lid back down. "There's not a detail about you that I've forgotten, Cat."

When she glanced over at him, she found his eyes locked on hers and a small smile dancing around his lips. "I remembered how much you love strawberries and that you will always pick a fruity dessert over a chocolate one. I also recall how much you love salmon, so I tried to incorporate all of your favorites into this lunch."

Strawberry in hand, she froze. "But you just asked me last night. How did you get all of this together?"

Will shrugged and made up a plate for her. "I knew I wanted to take you out on my yacht at some point. I was hoping for soon, but it wasn't until yesterday that I realized how hard you've been working."

He passed her the plate with a napkin. "You need this break and I want to be the one to give it to you. Besides, there's a lot I can do with a few hours and the right connections."

Catalina smiled as she picked up a cube of cheese.

"I'm sure your chef was making the cheesecake before the crack of dawn this morning."

Will shrugged. "Maybe. He did have nearly everything else done by the time I headed out to James and Bella's house this morning."

"You visited James already, too?"

Will settled back with his own plate and forked up a bite of salmon before answering. "I wanted to see Maisey before James heads back out on the road for football. I haven't really bonded with her much, especially with the strain on my relationship with James. But we're getting there and I wanted to see my niece. I'm sure she and Bella will accompany James on the road when they can."

Something inside Catalina warmed at the image of Will playing the doting, spoiling uncle. A family was definitely in her future plans, but knowing Will was taking an active part in little Maisey's life awakened something in her she hadn't yet uncovered.

But no. Will couldn't be father material. He wasn't even husband material. No matter how much, at one time, she'd wished he was. Will was a career-minded, power-driven man who valued family, but he didn't scream minivan and family portraits.

"How did the bonding go?" she asked, trying to concentrate on her food and not the fact that the image had been placed in her head of Will with a baby. Was there anything sexier than a big, powerful man holding an innocent child?

"She seemed to like the doll I brought her."

Of course he'd brought a doll. Now his "aww" level just exploded. Why did the man have to be so appealing on every single level? She didn't want to find him even more irresistible. She couldn't afford to let her heart get tangled up with him again.

Catalina couldn't handle the struggle within her. "You took her a doll? Did your assistant or someone on your staff go buy it?"

Will glanced at her, brows drawn in. "No, I bought it the other day when I was out and just got the chance to take it to her this morning. Why?"

The man was gaining ground and scaling that wall of defenses she'd so carefully erected. And in unexpected ways. He'd wanted to have a special moment with his niece, which had nothing to do with Catalina. Yet here she sat, on his boat, eating her favorite foods that he'd remembered while listening to him talk of his love for his baby niece.

Why was she keeping him at a distance again?

Oh, yeah. That broken heart four years ago.

They ate the rest of their lunch in silence, except when she groaned like a starved woman as she inhaled her piece of cheesecake. As promised, Will cleaned up the mess and took everything back down to the galley. Once he returned, he extended his hand to her.

"Ready to go for a walk?" he asked.

Catalina placed her hand in his, allowing him to pull her up. "I'm not sure I can walk after that, but I can waddle. I'm pretty stuffed."

Will laughed as he led her from the boat. Once they stepped off the wooden dock, Catalina slipped out of her sandals to walk on the warm, sandy beach. The sand wasn't too hot to burn her feet and as the soft grains shifted beneath her, she found herself smiling. She couldn't remember the last time she'd done absolutely nothing by way of working in one form or another.

"I hope that smile has something to do with me,"

Will stated, again slipping his hand into hers as they walked along the shoreline.

"I'm just happy today. I needed a break and I guess I didn't realize it."

"From one workaholic to another, I recognized the signs."

His confession had her focusing on the words and not how powerful and wonderful his fingers felt laced with hers.

"I never thought you took a break," she replied.

Catalina looked at all the tiny seashells lining the shore and made a mental note to find some beautiful ones to take back with her.

"I've had breaks," he replied. "Not many, mind you, but I know when I need to step back so I don't get burnt out."

Catalina turned her face toward the ocean. She'd been burnt out on cleaning since she started. But sewing and designing, she could never imagine falling out of love with her passion.

They walked along in silence and Catalina let her thoughts run wild. What would've happened between them had Will not succumbed to his father's demands that he drop her? Would they have these romantic moments often? Would he make her take breaks from life and put work on hold for her?

She really couldn't see any of that, to be honest. Will was still under his father's thumb, whether he admitted it or not. He'd been at the house most mornings going over Rowling Energy stuff, which Catalina assumed was really just Will checking in.

"Why did you give up on us before?" she asked before she could think better of it.

Will stopped, causing Catalina to stop as well. She dropped his hand and turned to fully face him.

"Never mind," she said, shaking her head. "It doesn't matter now."

The muscle in Will's jaw ticked as he stared back at her. "It does matter. Our breakup damaged both of us."

Catalina pushed her hair behind her ears, which was useless as the wind kept whipping it out. "I'm pretty sure you weren't damaged, seeing as how ending our relationship was your decision."

When she started to walk on, Will gripped her elbow. "You think seeing you move on and dating another man wasn't crushing to me? You think knowing you were in another man's arms, maybe even in his bed, didn't tear me up?"

She'd tried not to think about Will when she threw herself into another relationship to mask the hurt. From the angst in his tone and the fire in his eyes, though... *had* Will been hurt over the breakup? How could that be when he was the one who had ultimately ended things? Did he not want the split? Was he doing it to appease his father? If that was the case then she was doubly angry that he hadn't fought for them.

"You thought I'd sit around and cry myself to sleep over you?" she retorted, refusing to feel guilt over a decision he'd made for both of them.

And so what if she'd shed tears over him? Many tears, in fact, but there was no way she'd admit such a thing. As far as he knew she was made of steel and stronger than her emotions.

"Besides, you had moved on quite nicely. You ended up in a relationship with a Montoro princess."

Dammit. She hadn't meant for that little green monster to slip out. Catalina knew just how much Bella and

James loved each other, yet there was that sliver of jealousy at the fact that Will had been all ready to put a ring on Bella's finger first.

Will laughed. "That fake engagement was a mistake from all angles. James and Bella have found something she never would've had with me."

"But you would've married her."

And that fact still bothered Catalina. She hated the jealousy she'd experienced when she'd discovered Will was engaged. Not that she ever thought she stood a chance, but how could anyone compete with someone as beautiful and sexy as Bella Montoro? She was not only royalty, she was a humanitarian with a good heart.

On a sigh, Catalina started walking again, concentrating on the shells lining the shore. "It doesn't matter, honestly. I shouldn't have brought it up."

She reached down to pick up an iridescent shell, smoothing her finger over the surface to swipe away the wet sand. Catalina slid the shell into the small hidden pocket on the side of her dress and kept walking, very much aware of Will at her side. He was a smart man not to deny her last statement. They both knew he would've married Bella because that's what his father had wanted. Joining the fortunes of the two dynamic families was Patrick's dream...the wrong son had fallen for the beauty, though.

They walked a good bit down the deserted beach. Catalina had no idea how Will had managed to find such a perfect place with total privacy, but he had no doubt planned this for a while. On occasion he would stop and find a shell for her, wordlessly handing it to her as they walked on. The tension was heavier now that she'd opened up the can of worms. She wished she'd kept her feelings to herself.

What did it matter if he was going to marry Bella? What man wouldn't want to spend his life with her? Not only that, had Catalina truly thought Will would remain single? Had she believed he was so exclusively focused on work that he wouldn't want to settle down and start the next generation of Rowling heirs?

The warm sun disappeared behind a dark cloud as the wind kicked into high gear. Catalina looked up and suppressed a groan. Of course a dark cloud would hover over her. The ominous sky was starting to match her mood.

"Should we head back to the yacht?" she asked, trying to tuck her wayward strands of hair behind her ears as she fought against the wind.

"I don't think it's going to do anything major. The forecast didn't show rain."

That nasty cloud seemed to indicate otherwise, but she wasn't going to argue. They already had enough on their plate.

Catalina glanced through the foliage, squinting as something caught her eye. "What's that?"

Will stopped and looked in the direction she'd indicated. "Looks like a cabin of sorts. I've not come this far inland before. Let's check it out."

Without waiting for her, Will took off toward the small building. Catalina followed, stepping over a piece of driftwood and trailing through the lush plants that had nearly overtaken the property.

"I wonder who had this cabin built," he muttered as he examined the old wood shack. "The island belongs to Alma from what I could tell when I first started coming here."

The covered porch leaned to one side, the old tin roof had certainly seen better days and some of the wood around the door and single window had warped. But the place had charm and someone had once cared enough to put it here. A private getaway for a couple in love? A hideout for someone seeking refuge from life? There was a story behind this place.

Will pushed on the door and eased inside. Catalina couldn't resist following him. The musty smell wasn't as bad as she'd expected, but the place was rather dusty. Only a bit of light from outside crept in through the single window, but even that wasn't bright because of the dark cloud covering.

"Careful," he cautioned when she stepped in. "Some of those boards feel loose."

There was enough dim light coming in the front window for them to see a few tarps, buckets and one old chair sitting against the wall.

"Looks like someone was working on this and it was forgotten," Catalina said as she walked around the room. "It's actually quite cozy."

Will laughed. "If you like the rustic, no-indoor-plumbing feel."

Crossing her arms over her chest, she turned around. "Some of us don't need to be pampered with amenities. I personally enjoy the basics."

"This is basic," he muttered, glancing around.

The sudden sound of rain splattering on the tin roof had Catalina freezing in place. "So much for that forecast."

Will offered her a wide smile. "Looks like you get to enjoy the basics a bit longer unless you want to run back to the yacht in the rain."

Crossing the room, Catalina sank down onto the old, sheet-covered chair. "I'm good right here. Will you be able to handle it?"

His aqua eyes raked over her, heating her skin just as effectively as if he'd touched her with his bare hands. "Oh, baby, I can handle it."

Maybe running back to the yacht was the better option after all. How long would she be stranded in an old shack with Will while waiting out this storm?

Catalina wasn't naïve. She knew full well there were only so many things they could talk about and nearly every topic between them circled back to the sexual tension that had seemed to envelop them and bind them together for the past several weeks.

Her body trembled as she kept her gaze locked onto his.

There was only one way this day would end.

Ten

Will stared out the window at the sheets of rain coming down. He didn't need to look, though; the pounding on the roof told him how intense this storm was.

So much for that flawless forecast.

Still, staying across the room from Cat was best for now. He didn't need another invisible push in her direction. He glanced over his shoulder toward the woman he ached for. She sat as casual as you please with her legs crossed, one foot bouncing to a silent beat as her flip-flop dangled off her toes. Those bare legs mocked him. The strings of her bikini top peeking out of her dress mocked him as well. Every damn thing about this entire situation mocked him.

What had he been thinking, inviting her for a day out? Why purposely resurrect all of those old, unresolved feelings? They'd gone four years without bringing up their past, but Will had reached his breaking

point. He needed to know if they had a chance at…
what? What exactly did he want from her?

He had no clue, but he did know the need for Cat had
never lessened. If anything, the emptiness had grown
without her in his life. He'd let her go once to save her,
but he should've fought for them, fought for what he
wanted and found another way to keep her safe. He'd
been a coward. As humiliating as that was to admit,
there was no sugarcoating the truth of the boy he used
to be.

"You might as well have a seat," she told him, meeting his gaze. "The way you're standing across the room
is only making the tension worse. You're making me
twitchy."

Will laughed. Leave it to Cat to call him on his actions, though he didn't think the tension could get worse.

He crossed the room and took a seat on the floor in
front of the chair.

"This reminds me of that time James, you and I were
playing hide-and-seek when it started raining," she said.
"You guys were home from school on break and I had
come in to work with my mum."

Will smiled as the memory flooded his mind. "We
were around eight or nine, weren't we?"

Cat nodded. "James kept trying to hold my hand
when we both ran into the garage to hide and get dry."

Will sat up straighter. "You never told me that."

"Seriously?" she asked, quirking a brow. "You're
going to get grouchy over the actions of a nine-year-old?"

"I'm not grouchy. Surprised, but not grouchy."

"James was only doing it because he knew I had a
thing for you."

The corner of Will's mouth kicked up. "You had a
thing for me when you were that young?"

Cat shrugged, toying with the edge of her dress. "You were an older man. Practically worldly in all of your knowledge."

"It was the Spanish, wasn't it?" he asked with a grin.

Cat rolled her eyes and laughed. "James was fluent in Spanish as well. You two both had the same hoity-toity schooling."

Will lifted his knee and rested his arm on it as he returned her smile. "Nah. I was better. We would sometimes swap out in class because the teacher couldn't tell us apart. She just knew a quiet blond boy sat in the back. As long as one of us showed up, she didn't pay much attention to the fact there were really supposed to be two."

"Sneaky boys. But, I bet if I asked James about the Spanish speaking skills he'd say he was better," she countered.

"He'd be wrong."

Cat tipped her head, shifting in her seat, which only brought her bare legs within touching distance. "You tricked your teachers and got away with it. Makes me wonder how many times you two swapped out when it came to women."

Will shook his head. "I'm not answering that."

"Well, I know that watch nearly cost James the love of his life," Cat said, nodding toward the gold timepiece on his wrist.

"It was unfortunate Bella saw you and me kissing. I truly thought we were secluded." Will sighed and shifted on the wood floor. "She had every right to think James was kissing someone else because she had no clue about the bet."

The rain beat against the window as the wind kicked up. Cat tensed and her eyes widened.

"Hope this old place holds up," she said. "Maybe running back to the yacht would have been a better idea."

"Too late now." Will reached over, laying his hand on her knee. "We're fine. It's just a pop-up storm. You know these things pass fast."

With a subtle nod, she settled deeper into the seat and rested her head on the back cushion. Guilt rolled through Will. He'd planned a day for her, and had been hopeful that seduction would be the outcome. Yet here they sat in some abandoned old shack waiting out some freak storm. Even Mother Nature was mocking him.

But there was a reason they were here right now, during this storm, and Will wasn't going to turn this chance away. He planned on taking full advantage and letting Cat know just how much he wanted her.

Shifting closer to her chair, Will took Cat's foot and slid her shoe off. He picked up her other foot and did the same, all while knowing she had those dark, intoxicating eyes focused on his actions. It was her exotic eyes that hypnotized him.

Taking one of her delicate feet between his hands, Will started to massage, stroking his thumb up her arch.

"I'll give you ten minutes to stop that," she told him with a smile.

The radiant smile on her face was something he hadn't realized he'd missed so much. Right now, all relaxed and calm, even with the storm raging outside, Cat looked like the girl he once knew…the girl he'd wanted something more with.

But they were different people now. They had different goals. Well, he did; her goals were still unclear to him. He suddenly found himself wanting to know about those dreams of hers, and the fact that she'd hinted to James that she wouldn't stay in Alma forever.

But all of those questions could come later. Right now, Cat's comfort and happiness were all that mattered. Tomorrow's worries, issues and questions could be dealt with later. He planned on enjoying Cat for as long as she would allow.

Damn. When had this petite woman taken control over him? When had he allowed it? There wasn't one moment he could pinpoint, but there were several tiny instances where he could see in hindsight the stealthy buildup of her power over him.

Cat laughed as she slid down a bit further in the chair and gazed down at him beneath heavy lids. "If your father could see you on the floor rubbing his maid's feet, you'd lose your prestigious position at Rowling Energy."

Will froze, holding her gaze. It may have been a lighthearted joke, but there was so much truth to her statement about how angry this would make his father. But Will had already set in motion his plan to freeze his father out of the company.

Besides, right now, Will didn't care about Patrick or Rowling Energy. What he did care about was the woman who was literally turning to putty in his hands. Finally, he was going to show her exactly what they could be together and anticipation had his heart beating faster than ever.

"Does this feel good?" he asked.

Her reply was a throaty moan, sexy enough to have his body responding.

"Then all of the other stuff outside of this cabin doesn't matter."

Blinking down at him, Cat replied, "Not to me, but I bet if your father made you choose, you'd be singing a different tune."

Just like last time.

The unspoken words were so deafening, they actually drowned out the beating of the rain and the wind against the small shelter.

Will's best option was to keep any answer to himself. He could deny the fact, but he'd be lying. He'd worked too hard to get where he was to just throw it all away because of hormones.

At the same time, he planned on working equally as hard to win over Cat. There was no reason he had to give up anything.

His hand glided up to her ankle, then her calf. She said nothing as her eyes continued to hold his. He purposely watched her face, waiting for a sign of retreat, but all that was staring back at him was desire.

There was a silent message bouncing between them, that things were about to get very intimate, very fast.

The old cabin creaked and groaned against the wind's force. Cat tensed beneath him.

"You're safe," he assured her softly, not wanting to break this moment of trust she'd settled into with him. "This place is so old. I know it has withstood hurricanes. This little storm won't harm the cabin or us."

And there weren't any huge trees around, just thick bushes and flowers, so they weren't at risk for anything falling on them.

Right now, the only thing he needed to be doing was pushing through that line of defense Cat had built up. And from her sultry grin and heavy lids, he'd say he was doing a damn fine job.

Catalina should tell him to stop. Well, the common sense side of her told her she should. But the female side, the side that hadn't been touched or treasured in

more time than she cared to admit, told her common
sense to shut up.

Will had quite the touch. She had no idea the nerves
in your feet could be so tied into all the girly parts. She
certainly knew it now. Every part of her was zipping
with ache and need. If he commanded her to strip and
dance around the room naked, she would. The power
he held over her was all-consuming and she was dying
to know when he was going to do more.

She'd walked straight into this with her eyes wide
open. So if she was having doubts or regrets already,
she had no one to blame but herself. Though Catalina
wasn't doubting or regretting. She was aching, on the
verge of begging him to take this to the next level.

Catalina's head fell back against the chair as his
hands moved to her other calf, quickly traveling up
to her knee, then her thigh. She wanted to inch down
further and part her legs just a tad, but that would be
a silent invitation she wasn't quite brave enough for.

Yet.

"I've wanted to touch you for so long," he muttered,
barely loud enough for her to hear over the storm. "I've
watched you for the past four years, wondering if you
ever thought of me. Wondering if you ever fantasized
about me the way I did you."

Every. Single. Night.

Which was a confession she wasn't ready to share.
The ball was in his court for now and she planned on
just waiting to see how this played out.

He massaged her muscles with the tips of his fingers
and the room became hotter with each stroke. If the
man could have such power over her with something
so simple as a foot massage, how would her body react
once Will really started showing her affection?

"Do you remember that time your mother caught us making out?" he asked with a half laugh.

At the time, Catalina had been mortified that her mother caught them. But it wasn't until after the breakup that she realized why her mother had been so disappointed.

Patrick Rowling had really done a number on Catalina's mum. And it was those thoughts that could quickly put a bucket of cold water on this encounter, but she refused to allow Patrick to steal one more moment of happiness from her life…he'd already taken enough from her.

Will may not be down on his knees proposing marriage, but he was down on his knees showing her affection. And maybe she hoped that would be a stepping-stone to something more… But right now, that was all she wanted. She'd fought this pull toward him for too long. She hadn't wanted to let herself believe they could be more, but now she couldn't deny herself. She couldn't avoid the inevitable…she was falling for Will all over again.

"She didn't even know we were dating," Catalina murmured, her euphoric state suddenly overtaking her ability to speak coherently.

"Not many people did. That's when I realized I didn't want to keep us a secret anymore."

And that had been the start of their spiral toward the heartbreak she'd barely recovered from.

Once they were an "official" item, Patrick had intervened and put a stop to his good son turning to the maid. Shocking, since turning to the staff for pleasure certainly hadn't been below Patrick at one time. Not that what Catalina and Will shared had been anything like that. But the idea that Patrick could act as if he were so far above people was absolutely absurd.

"Don't tense on me now," Will warned. "You're supposed to be relaxing."

Catalina blew out a breath. "I'm trying. It's just hard when I'm stuck between the past and whatever is happening to us now."

Will came up to his knees, easing his way between her parted legs, his hands resting on the tops of her thighs, his fingertips brushing just beneath the hem of her dress.

"It's two different times. We're two different people. There's nothing to compare. Focus on now."

She stared down at those bright blue eyes, the wide open shirt and something dark against his chest. Was that…

"Do you have a tattoo?" she asked, reaching to pull back the shirt.

He said nothing as she eased the material aside. The glimpse she got wasn't enough. Catalina didn't ask, she merely gripped the shirt and pushed it off his shoulders. Will shifted until it fell to the floor.

Sure enough, black ink swirled over the left side of his chest and over his shoulder. She had no idea what the design was. All she knew was that it was sexy.

Without asking, she reached out and traced a thin line over his heart, then on up. The line thickened as it curled around his shoulder. Taut muscles tensed beneath her featherlight touch.

Catalina brought her gaze up to Will's. The intensity of his stare made her breath catch in her throat and stilled her hand.

"Don't stop," he whispered through clenched teeth.

"Will…"

His hand came up to cover hers. "Touch me, Cat."

He'd just handed her the reins.

With just enough pressure, he flattened her hand between his palm and his shoulder. The warmth of his skin penetrated her own, the heat sliding through her entire body.

"I—I want to but—"

She shook her head, killing the rest of her fears before they could be released and never taken back.

"But what?" he muttered, pushing her hair behind her ear, letting his fingertips trail over her cheek, her jawline and down her neck until she trembled.

"I'm not sure I can go any farther than that," she confessed. "I don't want to tease you."

"I've fantasized about you touching me like this for years. You're not teasing, you're fulfilling a fantasy."

Catalina stared into those aqua eyes and knew without a doubt he was serious. The fact that he'd been dreaming of her for this long confused her further, brought on even more questions than answers.

"Don't go there," he warned as if he knew where her thoughts were headed. "Keep touching me, Cat. Whatever happens here is about you and me and right this moment. Don't let past memories rob us of this time together."

Catalina opened her mouth, but Will placed one finger over her lips. "I have no expectations. Close your eyes."

Even though her heart beat out of control from anticipation and a slither of fear of the unknown, she did as he commanded.

"Now touch me. Just feel me, feel this moment and nothing else."

His tone might have been soft, but everything about

his words demanded that she obey. Not that he had to do much convincing. With her eyes closed, she wasn't forced to look at the face of the man who'd broken her heart. She wanted this chance to touch him, to ignore all the reasons why this was such a bad idea. But she couldn't look into those eyes and pretend that this was normal, that they were just two regular people stranded in an old shack.

With her eyes closed she actually felt as if they were regular people. She could pretend this was just a man she ached for, not a man who was a billionaire with more power than she'd ever see.

With her eyes closed she could pretend he wanted her for who she was and not just because she was a challenge.

Catalina brought her other hand up and over his chest. If she was given the green light to explore, she sure as hell wanted both hands doing the job. Just as she smoothed her palms up and over his shoulders, over his thick biceps, she felt the knot on her wrap dress loosen at her side.

Her eyes flew open. "What are you doing?"

"Feeling the moment."

The dress parted, leaving her torso fully exposed. "You don't play fair."

The heat in his eyes was more powerful than any passion she'd ever seen. "I never will when it comes to something I want."

"You said—"

"I'd never force you," he interrupted, gliding his fingertips over the straps of her bikini that stretched from behind her neck to the slopes of her breasts. "But that doesn't mean I won't try to persuade you."

As the rain continued to beat against the side of the

shack, Catalina actually found herself happy that she was stuck here. Perhaps this was the push she needed to follow through with what she truly wanted. No, she wasn't looking for happily-ever-after, she'd never be that naïve again where Will was concerned. But she was older now, was going into this with both eyes wide open.

And within the next couple months, hopefully she'd be out of Alma and starting her new life. So why not take the plunge now with a man she'd always wanted? Because he was right. This was all about them, here and now. Everything else could wait outside that door.

For now, Catalina was taking what she'd wanted for years.

Eleven

Catalina came to her feet. From here on out she was taking charge of what she'd been deprived of and what she wanted…and she wanted Will. Whatever doubts she had about sleeping with him wouldn't be near as consuming as the regret she'd have if she moved away and ignored this opportunity.

The moment she stood before him, Will sank back down on the floor and stared up at her as her dress fell into a puddle around her feet. As she stepped away and kicked the garment aside, his eyes roamed over her, taking in the sight of the bikini and nothing else.

The image of him sitting at her feet was enough to give her a sense of control, a sense of dominance. The one time when it counted most, she didn't feel inferior.

Will could've immediately taken over, he could've stood before her and taken charge, but he'd given her the reins.

"That bikini does some sinful things to your body." He reached out, trailed his fingertips over the sensitive area behind her knee and on up to her thigh. "Your curves are stunning, Cat. Your body was made to be uncovered."

"How long have you wanted me, Will?" she asked, needing to know this much. "Did you want me when we were together before?"

"More than anything," he rasped out, still sliding his fingers up and down the backs of her legs. "But I knew you were a virgin and I respected you."

"What if I were a virgin now?" she asked, getting off track. "Would you still respect me?"

"I've always respected you." He came up to his knees, putting his face level with her stomach. He placed a kiss just above her bikini bottoms before glancing up at her. "And I don't want to discuss if there's been another man in your bed."

With a move she hadn't expected, he tossed her back into the chair and stood over her, his hands resting on either side of her head. "Because I'm the only man you're going to be thinking of right now."

"I've only been with one other, but you're the only man I've ever wanted in my bed," she admitted. "I need you to know that."

Maybe she was naïve for letting him in on that little piece of information she'd kept locked in her heart for so long, but right now, something more than desire was sparking between them. He was too possessive for this to just be something quick and easy.

They weren't just scratching an itch, but she had no clue what label to put on what was about to happen. Which was why she planned on not thinking and just feeling. This bond that was forming here was something she'd have to figure out later...much later.

"All I need to know is that you want this as much as I do," he told her. "That you're ready for anything that happens because I can't promise soft and gentle. I've wanted you too long."

A shiver of arousal speared through her. "I don't need gentle, Will. I just need you."

In an instant his lips crushed hers. She didn't know when things had shifted, but in the span of about two minutes, she'd gone from questioning sex with Will to nearly ripping his shorts off so she could have him.

Will's strong hands gripped her hips as he shifted the angle of his head for a deeper kiss. Cat arched her body, needing to feel as much of him as possible. There still didn't seem to be enough contact. She wanted more... she wanted it all. The need to have everything she'd deprived herself of was now an all-consuming ache.

"Keep moaning like that, sweetheart," he muttered against her lips. "You're all mine."

She hadn't even realized she'd moaned, which just proved how much control this man had over her actions.

Gripping his shoulders, she tried to pull him down further, but he eased back. With his eyes locked onto hers, he hooked his thumbs in the waistband of his board shorts and shoved them to the floor. Stepping out of them he reached down, took her hand and pulled her to her feet.

Keeping her eyes on his, she reached behind her neck and untied her top. It fell forward as she worked on the knot. Soon they'd flung the entire scrap of fabric across the room. Will's eyes widened and his nostrils flared.

Excitement and anticipation roiled through her as she shoved her bottoms down without a care. She had no clue who reached for whom first, but the next second she was in his arms, skin to skin from torso to knees and she'd never felt anything better in her entire life.

Will's arms wrapped around her waist, his hands splaying across her bare back. He spun her around and sank down into the chair, pulling her down with him. Instinctively her legs straddled his hips. Catalina fisted her fingers in his hair as his lips trailed down her throat.

"So sexy," he murmured against her heated skin. "So mine."

Yes. She was his for now...maybe she always had been.

When his mouth found her breast, his hands encircled her hips. She waited, aching with need.

"Will," she panted, not recognizing her own voice. "Protection."

With his hair mussed, his lids heavy, he looked up. "I don't have any with me. Dammit, they're on the yacht. I didn't expect to get caught out here like this." Cursing beneath his breath, he shook his head. "I'm clean. I swear I wouldn't lie about something like that. I haven't been with a woman in...too long, and I recently had a physical."

"I know I'm clean and I'm on birth control."

He gave her a look, silently asking what she wanted to do. Without another word she slowly sank down onto him, so that they were finally, fully joined after years of wanting, years of fantasizing.

Their sighs and groans filled the small room. Wind continued to beat against the window as rain pelted the tin roof. Everything about this scenario was perfect. Even if they were in a rundown shed, she didn't care. The ambiance was amazingly right. The storm that had swept through them over the years only matched Mother

Nature's fury outside the door. This was the moment they were supposed to be together, this was what they'd both waited for so long.

"Look at me," he demanded, his fingertips pressing into her hips.

Catalina hadn't realized she'd closed her eyes, but she opened them and found herself looking into Will's bright, expressive aqua eyes. He may be able to hold back his words, but those eyes told her so much. Like the fact that he cared for her. This was sex, but there was so much more going on...so much more they'd discuss later.

As her hips rocked back and forth against his, Will continued to watch her face. Catalina leaned down, resting her hands on his shoulders. The need inside her built so fast, she dropped her forehead against his.

"No," he stated. "Keep watching me. I want to see your face."

As she looked back into his eyes, her body responded to every touch, every kiss, every heated glance. Tremors raced through her at the same time his body stilled, the cords in his neck tightened and his fingertips dug even further into her hips.

His body stiffened against hers, his lips thinned as his own climax took control. Catalina couldn't look away. She wanted to see him come undone, knowing she caused this powerful man to fall at the mercy of her touch.

Once their bodies eased out of the euphoric state, Catalina leaned down, rested her head on his shoulder and tried to regain some sense of normal breathing. She didn't know what to say now, how to act. They'd taken this awkward, broken relationship and put another speed bump in it. Now all they had to do was figure out how to maneuver over this new hurdle since they'd moved to a whole new, unfamiliar level.

Will trailed his hand up and down Cat's back, which was smooth and damp with sweat. Damn, she was sexier than he'd ever, *ever* imagined. She'd taken him without a second thought and with such confidence. Yet she'd been so tight…had she not slept with anyone? How had that not happened? Surely she wasn't still a virgin.

Had Cat kept her sexuality penned up all this time? For completely selfish reasons, this thought pleased him.

As much as Will wanted to know, he didn't want to say a word, didn't want to break the silence with anything that would kill the mood. The storm raged on outside, the cabin creaked and continued to groan under the pressure, but Cat was in his arms, her heart beating against his chest, and nothing could pull him from this moment.

The fact that he was concentrating on her heartbeat was a bit disconcerting. He didn't want to be in tune with her heart, he couldn't get that caught up with her, no matter how strong this invisible force was that was tugging him to her. Having her in his arms, finally making love to her was enough.

So why did he feel as if there was more to be had?

Because when he'd originally been thinking of the here and now, he'd somehow started falling into the zone of wanting more than this moment. He wanted Cat much longer than this day, this week, even. Will wanted more and now he had to figure out just how the hell that would work.

"Tell me I wasn't a substitute for Bella."

Will jerked beneath her, forcing her to sit up and meet his gaze. "What?"

Cat shook her head, smoothing her short hair away from her face. "Nothing," she said, coming to her feet. "That was stupid of me to say. We had sex. I'm not expecting you to give me anything more."

As she rummaged around the small space searching for her bikini and dress, Will sat there dumbfounded. So much for not letting words break the beauty of the moment.

What was that about Bella? Seriously? Did Cat honestly think that Will had had a thing for his brother's fiancée?

"Look at me," he demanded, waiting until Cat spun around, gripping her clothing to her chest. "Bella is married to James. I have no claim to her."

"It's none of my business."

Will watched as she tied her top on and slid the bikini bottoms up her toned legs. "It is your business after what we just did. I don't sleep with one woman and think of another."

Cat's dark eyes came up to his. A lock of her inky black hair fell over her forehead and slashed across her cheek.

"You owe me no explanations, Will." Hands on her hips, she blew the rogue strand from her face. "I know this wasn't a declaration of anything to come. I'm grown up now and I have no delusions that things will be any different than what they are. We slept together, it's over."

Okay, that had originally been his mindset when he'd gone into this, but when the cold words came from her mouth, Will suddenly didn't like the sound of it. She wasn't seeing how he'd changed at all and that was his fault. She still believed he was a jerk who had no cares at all for her feelings. But he did care…too damn much.

"I know you saw me as a challenge," she went on as she yanked the ties together to secure her dress. "A conquest, if you will. It's fine, really. I could've stopped you, but I was selfish and wanted you. So, thanks for—"

"Do not say another word." Pushing to his feet, Will jerked his shorts from the floor and tugged them on before crossing to her. "You can't lie to me, Cat. I know you too well. Whatever defense mechanism you're using here with ugly words isn't you. You're afraid of what you just felt, of what just happened. This wasn't just sex and you damn well know it."

Her eyes widened, her lips parted, but she immediately shut down any emotion he'd just seen flash across her face. No doubt about it, she was trying to cut him off before he did anything to hurt her…again. He should have seen this coming.

Guilt slammed into him. Not over sleeping with her just now, but for how she felt she had to handle the situation to avoid any more heartache.

"Will, I'm the maid," she said softly. "While I'm not ashamed of my position, I also know that this was just a onetime thing. A man like you would never think twice about a woman like me for anything more than sex."

Will gripped her arms, giving her a slight shake. "Why are you putting yourself into this demeaning little package and delivering it to me? I've told you more than once I don't care if you're a maid or a damn CEO. What just happened has nothing to do with anything other than us and what we feel."

"There is no us," she corrected him.

"There sure as hell was just a minute ago."

Why was he so dead set on correcting her? Here he

stood arguing with her when she was saying the same exact thing he'd been thinking earlier.

"And I have no clue why you're bringing Bella into this," he added.

Cat lifted her chin in a defiant gesture. "I'm a woman. Sometimes my insecurities come out."

"Why are you insecure about her?"

Cat laughed and broke free from his hold, taking a step back. "You were with one of the most beautiful women I've ever seen. Suddenly when that relationship is severed, you turn to me. You haven't given me any attention in nearly four years, Will. Forgive me if suddenly I feel like leftovers."

"Don't downgrade what just happened between us," he demanded. "Just because I didn't seek you out in the past few years doesn't mean I didn't want you. I wanted the hell out of you. And I was fighting my way back to you, dammit."

He eased closer, watching as her eyes widened when he closed the gap and loomed over her. "Seeing you all the time, being within touching distance but knowing I had no right was hell."

"You put yourself there."

As if he needed the reminder of the fool he'd been.

Will smoothed her hair back from her forehead, allowing his hand to linger on her jawline. "I can admit when I was wrong, stubborn and a jerk. I can also admit that I have no clue what just happened between us because it was much more than just sex. You felt it, I felt it, and if we deny that fact we'd just be lying to ourselves. Let's get past that. Honesty is all we can have here. We deserve more than something cheap, Cat."

Cat closed her eyes and sighed. When her lids lifted,

she glanced toward the window. "The rain has let up. We should head back to the yacht."

Without another word, without caring that he was standing here more vulnerable than he'd ever been, Cat turned, opened the door and walked out.

Nobody walked out on Will Rowling and he sure as hell wasn't going to let the woman he was so wrapped up in and had just made love to be the first.

Twelve

Catalina had known going into this day that they'd most likely end up naked and finally giving into desires from years ago.

And she hadn't been able to stop herself.

No matter what she felt now, no matter what insecurities crept up, she didn't regret sleeping with Will.

This was a one and done thing—it had to be. She couldn't afford to fall any harder for this man whom she couldn't have. She was planning on leaving Alma anyway, so best to cut ties now and start gearing up for her fresh start. Letting her heart interfere with the dreams she'd had for so long would only have her working backward. She was so close, she'd mentally geared up for the break from Alma, from Will…but that was before she'd given herself to him.

But what had just transpired between them was only closure. Yes, that was the term she'd been looking for.

Closure. Nothing else could come from their intimacy and finally getting each other out of their systems was the right thing to do...wasn't it?

While the rain hadn't fully stopped, Catalina welcomed the refreshing mist hitting her face. She had no clue of the amount of time that had passed while they'd been inside the cabin lost in each other. An hour? Three hours?

The sand shifted beneath her bare feet as she marched down the shore toward the dock. Sandals in her hand, she kept her focus on the yacht in the distance and not the sound of Will running behind her. She should've known he'd come chasing after her, and not just because he wanted to get back to the yacht.

She'd left no room for argument when she'd walked out, and Will Rowling wouldn't put up with that. Too bad. She was done talking. It was time to move on.

Too bad her body was still humming a happy tune and tingling in all the areas he'd touched, tasted.

Figuring he'd grab her when he caught up to her, Catalina turned, ready to face down whatever he threw her way. Will took a few more steps, stopping just in front of her. He was clutching his wadded up shirt at his side. Catalina couldn't help but stare at his bare chest and the mesmerizing tattoo as he pulled in deep breaths.

"You think we're done?" he asked as he stared her down. "Like we're just heading back to the yacht, setting off to Alma and that's it? You think this topic is actually closed? That I would accept this?"

Shrugging, Catalina forced herself to meet his angry gaze. "You brought me here to seduce me. Wasn't that the whole plan for getting me alone? Well, mission accomplished. The storm has passed and it'll start getting dark in a couple hours. Why wait to head back?"

"Maybe because I want to spend more time with you," he shouted. "Maybe because I want more here than something cheap and easy."

As the misty rain continued to hit her face, Catalina wanted to let that sliver of hope into her heart, but she couldn't allow it…not just yet. "And what do you want, Will? An encore performance? Maybe in your bed on the yacht so you can have a more pampered experience?"

His lips thinned, the muscle in his jaw tightened. "What made you so harsh, Cat? You weren't like this before."

Before when she'd been naïve, before when she'd actually thought he may love her and choose her over his career. And before she discovered a secret that he still knew nothing about.

Beyond all of that, she was angry with herself for allowing her emotions to get so caught up in this moment. She should've known better. She'd never been someone to sleep around, but she thought for sure she could let herself go with Will and then walk away. She'd been wrong and now because of her roller coaster of emotions, she was taking her anger out on him.

Shaking her head, Catalina turned. Before she could take a step, she tripped over a piece of driftwood she hadn't seen earlier. Landing hard in the sand, she hated how the instant humiliation took over.

Before she could become too mortified, a spearing pain shot through her ankle. She gasped just as Will crouched down by her side.

"Where are you hurt?" he asked, his eyes raking over her body.

"My ankle," she muttered, sitting up so she could look at her injury.

"Anywhere else?" Will asked.

Catalina shook her head as she tried to wiggle her ankle back and forth. Bad idea. She was positive it wasn't broken—she'd broken her arm as a little girl and that pain had been much worse—but she was also sure she wouldn't be able to apply any pressure on it and walk. The piercing pain shot up her leg and had her wincing. She hoped she didn't burst into tears and look even more pathetic.

So much for her storming off in her dramatic fit of anger.

Will laid his shirt on her stomach.

"What—?"

Before she could finish her question, he'd scooped her up in his arms and set off across the sand. Catalina hated how she instantly melted against his warm, bare chest. Hated how the image of them in her mind seemed way more romantic than what it was, with Will's muscles straining as he carried her in his arms—yeah, they no doubt looked like something straight out of a movie.

"You can't carry me all the way to the yacht," she argued. "This sand is hard enough to walk in without my added weight."

"Your weight is perfect." He threw her a glance, silently leaving her no room for argument. "Relax and we'll see what we're dealing with once I can get you on the bed in the cabin."

Those words sent a shiver of arousal through her that she seriously did not want. Hadn't she learned from the last set of shivers? Hadn't she told herself that after they slept together she'd cut ties? She had no other choice, not if she wanted to maintain any dignity and sanity on her way out of his life for good.

As they neared the dock, Will was breathing hard,

but he didn't say a word as he trudged forward. Her ankle throbbed, which should have helped shift her focus, but being wrapped in Will's strong arms pretty much overrode any other emotion.

Catalina had a sinking feeling that in all her pep talks to herself, she'd overlooked the silent power Will had over her. She may have wanted to have this sexcapade with him and then move on, but she'd seriously underestimated how involved her heart would become.

And this hero routine he was pulling was flat-out sexy…as if she needed another reason to pull her toward him.

Will quickly crossed toward the dock, picking up his pace now that he was on even ground. When he muttered a curse, Catalina lifted her head to see what the problem was. Quickly she noted the damage to the yacht and the dock. Apparently the two had not played nice during the freak storm.

"Oh, Will," she whispered.

He slowed his pace as he carefully tested the weight of the dock. Once his footing was secure, and it was clear that the planks would hold them, he cautiously stepped forward.

"I need to set you down for a second to climb on board, but just keep pressure off that ankle and hold onto my shoulders."

She did as he asked and tried not to consider just what this damage meant for their return trip home. When Will was on deck, he reached out, proceeded to scoop her up again and lifted her onto the yacht.

"I can get down the steps," she told him, really having no clue if she could or not. But there was no way they could both fit through that narrow doorway to get below deck. "Go figure out what happened."

He kept his hold firm. "I'm going to get you settled, assess your ankle and then go see what damage was done to the yacht."

Somehow he managed to get her down the steps and onto the bed without bumping her sore, now swollen ankle along the way. As he adjusted the pillows behind her, she slid back to lean against the fluffy backdrop. Will took a spare pillow and carefully lifted her leg to elevate her injury.

"It's pretty swollen," he muttered as he stalked toward the galley kitchen and returned with a baggie full of ice wrapped in a towel. "Keep this on it and I'll go see if I can find some pain reliever."

"Really, it'll be fine," she lied. The pain was bad, but she wanted him to check on the damage so they could get back to Alma... She prayed they could safely get back. "Go see how bad the destruction is. I'm not going anywhere."

Will's brows drew in. With his hands on his hips, that sexy black ink scrolling over his bare chest and the taut muscles, he personified sex appeal.

"Staring at my ankle won't make it any better," she told him, suddenly feeling uncomfortable.

His unique blue eyes shifted and held her gaze. "I hate that I hurt you," he muttered.

So much could be read from such a simple statement. Was he referring to four years ago? Did he mean the sexual encounter they'd just had or was he referencing her fall?

No matter what he was talking about, Catalina didn't want to get into another discussion that would only take them in circles again. They were truly getting nowhere...well, they'd ended up naked, but other than that, they'd gotten nowhere.

"Go on," she insisted. "Don't worry about me."

He looked as if he wanted to argue, but ended up nodding. "I'll be right back. If you need something, just yell for me. I'll hear you."

Catalina watched as he ascended the steps back up to the deck. Closing her eyes, she dropped her head against the pillows and pulled in a deep breath. If the storm had done too much damage to the yacht, she was stuck. Stuck on a glamorous yacht with an injured ankle with the last person she should be locked down with.

The groan escaped before she could stop it. Then laughter followed. Uncontrollable laughter, because could they be anymore clichéd? The maid and the millionaire, stranded on a desert island. Yeah, they had the makings for a really ridiculous story or some skewed reality show.

Once upon a time she would've loved to have been stranded with Will. To know that nothing would interrupt them. They could be who they wanted to be without pretenses. Just Will and Catalina, two people who l—

No. They didn't love each other. That was absurd to even think. Years ago she had thought they were in love, but they couldn't have been. If they'd truly been in love, wouldn't he have fought for everything they'd discussed and dreamed of?

Maybe he'd been playing her the entire time. A twenty-year-old boy moving up the ladder of success really didn't have much use for a poor staff member. She was a virgin and an easy target. Maybe that's all he'd been after.

But she really didn't think so. She'd grown up around Will and James. James was the player, not Will. Will had always been more on the straight and narrow, the rule follower.

And he'd followed those rules right to the point of breaking her heart. She should have seen it coming, really. After their mother passed away, Will did every single thing he could to please his father, as if overcompensating for the loss of a parent.

Yet there was that little girl fantasy in her that had held out hope that Will would see her as more, that he would fall in love with her and they could live happily ever after.

Catalina sighed. That was long ago; they were different people now and the past couldn't be redone...and all those other stupid sayings that really didn't help in the grand scheme of things.

And it was because she was still so tied up in knots over this man that she needed to escape Alma, fulfill her own dreams and forget her life here. She was damn good at designing and she couldn't wait to burn her uniforms and sensible shoes, roast a marshmallow over them and move on.

"We're not going anywhere for a while."

Catalina jerked her head around. Will was standing on the bottom step, his hands braced above him on the doorframe. The muscles in his biceps flexed, drawing her attention to his raw masculinity. No matter how much the inner turmoil was caused by their rocky relationship, Catalina couldn't deny that the sight of his body turned her on like no other man had ever been able to do.

"There's some major damage to the starboard side. I thought maybe I could get it moving, but the mechanics are fried. I can only assume the boat was hit by lightning as well as banging into the dock repeatedly."

Catalina gripped the plush comforter beneath her palms. "How long will we be stuck here?"

"I have no clue."

He stepped farther into the room and raked a hand over his messy hair. Will always had perfectly placed hair, but something about that rumpled state made her hotter for him.

"The radio isn't working, either," he added as he sank down on the edge of the bed, facing her. "Are you ready for some pain medicine since we're going to be here awhile?"

She was going to need something a lot stronger if she was going to be forced to stick this out with him for too long. Hours? Days? How long would she have to keep her willpower on high alert?

"I probably better," she admitted. "My ankle's throbbing pretty good now."

Will went to the bathroom. She heard him rummaging around in a cabinet, then the faucet. When he strode back across the open room, Catalina couldn't keep her eyes off his bare chest. Why did he have to be so beautiful and enticing? She wanted to be over her attraction for this man. Anything beyond what happened in that cabin would only lead to more heartache because Will would never choose anyone over his father and Rowling Energy and she sure as hell wasn't staying in Alma to clean toilets the rest of her life waiting to gain his attention.

Catalina took the pills and the small paper cup of water he offered. Hoping the medicine kicked in soon, she swallowed it as Will eased back down beside her on the bed.

"Dammit," he muttered, placing his hand on the shin of her good leg. "If we hadn't been arguing—"

"We've argued for weeks," she told him with a half smile. "It was an accident. If anyone is to blame it's me for not watching where I was going and for trying to stomp off in a fit."

"Were you throwing a fit?" he asked. "I don't remember."

Catalina lifted an eyebrow. "You're mocking me now."

Shaking his head, he slid his hand up and down her shin. "Not at all. I just remember thinking how sexy you looked when you were angry. You have this red tint to your cheeks. Or it could've been the great sex. Either way, you looked hot."

"Was that before or after I was sprawled face first in the sand?" she joked, trying to lighten the mood.

"You can't kill sexy, Cat, even if you're eating sand."

The slight grin he offered her eased her worry. Maybe they could spend the day here and actually be civil without worrying about the sexual tension consuming them. Maybe they had taken the edge off and could move on.

Well, they could obviously move on, but would this feeling of want ever go away? Because if anything, since they'd been intimate, Catalina craved him even more.

So now what could she do? There was nowhere to hide and definitely nowhere to run in her current state.

As she looked into Will's mesmerizing eyes, her worry spiked once again because he stared back at her like a man starved...and she was the main course.

Thirteen

Thankfully the kitchen was fully stocked and the electricity that fed the appliances hadn't been fried because right now Will needed to concentrate on something other than how perfect Cat looked in his bed.

He'd come to the kitchen a while ago to figure out what they should do for dinner. Apparently the pain pills had kicked in because Cat was resting peacefully, even letting out soft moans every now and then as she slept.

It was those damn moans that had his shorts growing tighter and his teeth grinding as he attempted to control himself. He'd heard those groans earlier, up close and personal in his ear as she'd wrapped her body around his.

The experience was one he would never forget.

Will put together the chicken and rice casserole that his mother used to make. Yes, they'd had a chef when he was a child, but James and Will had always loved this dish and every now and then, Will threw it together just to remember his mother. He still missed her, but it was the little things that would remind him of her and make him smile.

Setting the timer on the oven, Will glanced back to the sleeping beauty in his bed. His mother would have loved Cat. She wouldn't have cared if she was the maid or—

What the hell? How did that thought sneak right in without his realizing the path his mind was taking? It didn't matter what his mother would have thought of Cat. He wasn't getting down on one knee and asking her into the family.

He needed to get a grip because his hormones and his mind were jumbling up all together and he was damn confused. Sleeping with Cat should have satisfied this urge to claim her, but instead of passing, the longing only grew.

With the casserole baking for a good bit, Will opted to grab a shower. He smelled like sex, sand and sweat. Maybe a cold shower would help wake him up to the reality that he'd let Cat go once. Just because they slept together didn't mean she was ready to give this a go again. And was that what he wanted? In all honesty did he want to try for this once more and risk hurting her, hurting himself, further?

He was making a damn casserole for pity's sake. What type of man had he become? He'd turned into some warped version of a homemaker and, even worse, he was perfectly okay with this feeling.

Before he went to the shower, he wanted to try the radio one more time. There had to be a way to communicate back to the mainland. Unfortunately, no matter which knobs he turned, which buttons he hit, nothing sparked to life. Resigned to the fact they were indeed stuck, Will went to his master suite bathroom.

As he stripped from his shorts and stepped into the spacious, open shower, he wondered if maybe being stranded with Cat wasn't some type of sign. Maybe they were supposed to be together with no outside forces hindering their feelings or judgment.

And honestly, Will wanted to see what happened with Cat. He wanted to give this another chance because they were completely different people than they were before and he was in total control of his life. She was that sliver of happiness that kept him smiling and their verbal sparring never failed to get him worked up.

No other woman matched him the way she did and he was going to take this opportunity of being stranded and use every minute to his advantage. He'd prove to her he was different because just telling her he was really wouldn't convince her. He needed to show her, to let her see for herself that he valued her, that he wanted her. He'd never stopped wanting her.

While he may want to use this private time to seduce the hell out of her, Will knew those hormones were going to have to take a back seat because Cat was worth more and they were long overdue for some relaxing, laid back time. And then maybe they could discuss just what the hell was happening between them.

Whatever that smell was, Catalina really hoped she wasn't just dreaming about it. As soon as she opened her eyes, she was greeted with a beautiful orange glow across the horizon. The sun was setting, and lying in this bed, Will's bed, watching such beauty was a moment she wanted to lock in her mind forever.

She rolled over, wincing as the pain in her ankle reminded her she was injured. The ice bag had melted and slid off the pillow she'd propped it on. As soon as she sat up, she examined her injury, pleased to see the swelling had gone down some.

"Oh, good. Dinner is almost ready."

Catalina smoothed her hair away from her face and smiled as Will scooped up something from a glass pan.

"I tried the radio again," he told her. "It didn't work. The whole system is fried."

Catalina sighed. As much as she wanted to get back home, she couldn't deny the pleasure she'd experienced here, despite the injury. She had a feeling she was seeing the true Will, the man who wasn't all business and power trips, but a man who cared for her whether he was ready to admit it or not.

"Someone will come for us," she told him. "Besides, with you cooking and letting me nap, you're spoiling me. Dinner smells a lot like that chicken dish you made me for our first date."

Will grinned back at her and winked. *Winked.* What had she woken to? Will in the kitchen cooking and actually relaxed enough to wink and smile as if he hadn't a care in the world.

"It is," he confirmed. "I'll bring it to you so don't worry about getting up."

"I actually need to go to the restroom."

In seconds, Will was at her side helping her up. When he went to lift her in his arms, she pushed against him.

"Just let me lean on you, okay? No need to carry me."

Wrapping an arm around her waist, Will helped her stand. "How's the ankle feeling?"

"Really sore, but better than it was." She tested it, pulling back when the sharp throbbing started again.

"Putting weight on it still isn't a smart move, but hopefully it will be much better by tomorrow."

Will assisted her across the room, but when they reached the bathroom doorway, she placed a hand on his chest. "I can take it from here."

No way was he assisting her in the bathroom. She'd like to hold onto some shred of dignity. Besides, she needed a few moments to herself to regain mental footing since she was stuck playing house with the only man she'd ever envisioned spending forever with.

"I'll wait right here in case you need something," he told her. "Don't lock the door."

With a mock salute, Catalina hobbled into the bathroom and closed the door. The scent of some kind of masculine soap assaulted her senses. A damp towel hung over the bar near the shower. He'd made use of the time she'd been asleep. Her eyes darted to the bathtub that looked as if it could seat about four people. What she wouldn't give to crawl into that and relax in some hot water, with maybe a good book or a glass of wine. When was the last time she'd indulged in such utterly selfish desires?

Oh, yeah, when she'd stripped Will naked and had her way with him in the old cabin earlier today.

A tap on the door jerked her from her thoughts. "Are you okay?"

"Yeah. Give me a minute."

A girl couldn't even fantasize in peace around here. She still needed time to process what their intimacy meant and the new, unexpected path their relationship had taken. Will had most likely thought of what happened the entire time she'd been asleep. Of course he was a man, so he probably wasn't giving their encounter the amount of mind space she would.

Minutes later, Catalina opened the door to find Will leaning against the frame. Once again he wrapped an arm around her and steered her toward the bed.

"I can eat at the table." She hated leaning on him, touching him when her nerves were still a jumbled up mess. "I'm already up. That bed is too beautiful to eat on."

In no time he'd placed their plates on the table with two glasses of wine…again, her favorite. A red Riesling.

"If I didn't know better, I'd say you stocked this kitchen just for me," she joked as she took her first sip and knew it wasn't the cheap stuff she kept stocked in her fridge.

"I did buy a lot of things I knew you liked." His fork froze midway to his mouth as he looked up at her. "At least, you liked this stuff four years ago."

For a split second, he seemed unsure. Will was always confident in everything, but when discussing her tastes, he suddenly doubted himself. Why did she find that so adorable?

She felt a shiver travel up her spine. She didn't have time for these adorable moments and couldn't allow them to influence her where this man was concerned. That clean break she wanted couldn't happen if she let herself be charmed like that.

They ate in silence, but Catalina was surprised the strain wasn't there. Everything seemed…normal. Something was up. He wasn't trying to seduce her, he wasn't bringing up the past or any other hot topic.

What had happened while she'd been asleep? Will had suddenly transformed into some sort of caretaker with husbandlike qualities.

But after a while she couldn't take the silence anymore. Catalina dropped her fork to her empty plate.

"That was amazing. Now, tell me what's going through your mind."

Will drained his glass before setting it back down and focusing on her. "Right now I'm thinking I could use dessert."

"I mean why are you so quiet?"

Shrugging, he picked up their plates and put them in the kitchen. When he brought back the wine bottle, she put a hand over hers to stop him from filling her glass back up.

"If I need more pain pills later, it's best I don't have any more even though I only took a half pill."

Nodding, he set the bottle on the table and sat across from her again.

"Don't ignore the question."

A smile kicked up at the corners of his mouth. "I'm plotting."

Catalina eased back in her seat, crossing her arms over her chest. "You're always plotting. I take it I'm still in the crosshairs?"

His eyes narrowed in that sexy, toe-curling way that demanded a woman take notice. "You've never been anywhere else."

Her heart beat faster. When he said those things she wanted to believe him. She wanted to be the object of his every desire and fantasy. And when he looked at her as if nothing else in the world mattered, she wanted to stay in that line of sight forever, though she knew all of that was a very naïve way of thinking.

"I only set out to seduce you," he went on, toying with the stem on his glass. "I wanted you in my bed more than anything. And now that I've had you…"

Catalina wished she'd had that second glass of wine after all. "What are you saying?"

His intense stare locked onto her. "We're different people. Maybe we're at a stage where we can learn from the past and see..."

It took every ounce of her willpower not to lean forward in anticipation as his words trailed off yet again. "And see what?" she finally asked.

"Maybe I want to see where we could go."

Catalina gasped. "You're not serious."

Those heavy-lidded eyes locked onto her. "I can't let you go now that I know how right we are together."

Her eyes shifted away and focused on the posh living space while she tried to process all he was saying.

Her mother's words of warning from years ago echoed in Catalina's mind. How could she fall for this man with his smooth words and irresistible charm? Hadn't her mother done the same thing with Patrick?

No. Will wasn't Patrick and Catalina was not her mother.

To her knowledge, Will, even to this day, had absolutely no idea what had transpired when he'd been a young boy right around the time of his mother's death. That hollow pit in Catalina's stomach deepened. Had the affair been the catalyst in Mrs. Rowling's death?

"Why now?" she asked, turning back to face him. "Why should I let you in now after all this time? Is it because I'm convenient? Because I'm still single or because you're settling?"

Why was fate dangling this right in front of her face when she'd finally decided to move on? It had taken her years to get up the nerve to really move forward with her dream and now that she'd decided to take a chance, Will wanted back in?

"Trust me, you're anything but convenient," he laughed.

"I've busted my butt trying to think of ways to get your attention."

Catalina swallowed. "But why?"

"Because you want this just as much as I do," he whispered.

Catalina stared down at her hands clasped in her lap. "We're at the age now that our wants don't always matter." Letting her attention drift back up, she locked her eyes on him. "We both have different goals, Will. In the end, nothing has really changed."

"On that we can agree." Will came to his feet, crossed to her side of the table and loomed over her. His hands came to rest on the back of her chair on either side of her shoulders. "In the end, I'll still want you and you'll still want me. The rest can be figured out later."

Before she could say anything, he'd scooped her up in his arms. "Don't say a word," he chided. "I want to carry you, so just let me. Enjoy this moment, that's all I'm asking. Don't think about who we are away from here. Let me care for you the way you deserve."

His warm breath washed over her face as she stared back at him. He didn't move, he just waited for her reply.

What could she say? He was right. They both wanted each other, but was that all this boiled down to? There were so many other outside factors driving a wedge between them. Did she honestly believe that just because he said so things would be different?

Catalina stared into those eyes and for once she saw hope; she saw a need that had nothing to do with sex.

Resting her head on his shoulder, Catalina whispered, "One of us is going to get hurt."

Fourteen

Catalina leaned back against Will's chest as they settled onto the oversized plush sofa on the top deck. The full moon provided enough light and just the perfect ambiance; even Will couldn't have planned it better.

Granted he didn't like that the yacht was damaged or that Catalina had been injured, but the feel of her wrapped in his arms, their legs intertwined, even as he was careful of her ankle, was everything he'd wanted since he let her walk away so long ago.

Will laced his hands over her stomach and smiled when she laid her hands atop his.

"It's so quiet and peaceful," she murmured. "The stars are so vibrant here. I guess I never pay much attention in Alma."

"One of these days you're going to have your own maid, your own staff," he stated firmly. "You deserve to be pampered for all the hours you work without asking for anything in return. You work too hard."

"I do," she agreed. "I have so many things I want to do with my life and working is what keeps me motivated."

A strand of her hair danced in the breeze, tickling his cheek, but he didn't mind. Any way he could touch her and be closer was fine with him. She wasn't trying to ignore this pull and she'd actually relaxed fully against him. This is what they needed. The simplicity, the privacy.

"What are your goals, Cat?"

"I'd love a family someday."

The wistfulness in her tone had him wanting to fulfill those wishes. Will knew he'd never be able to sit back and watch her be with someone else, make a life and a family with another man.

"What else?" he urged. "I want to know all of your dreams."

She stiffened in his arms. Will stroked her fingers with his, wanting to keep her relaxed, keep her locked into this euphoric moment.

"It's just me, Cat." He purposely softened his tone. "Once upon a time we shared everything with each other."

"We did. I'm just more cautious now."

Because of him. He knew he'd damaged that innocence in her, he knew full well that she was a totally different woman because of his selfish actions. And that fact was something he'd have to live with for the rest of his life. All he could do was try to make things better now and move forward.

"I shouldn't have let you go," he muttered before he could think.

"Everything happens for a reason."

Will didn't miss the hint of pain in her tone. "Maybe so, but I should've fought for you, for us."

"Family has always been your top priority, Will. You've been that way since your mother passed. You threw yourself into pleasing your father and James ran wild. Everyone grieves differently and it's affected your relationships over the years."

Will shouldn't have been surprised that she'd analyzed him and his brother so well. Cat had always been so in tune with other people's feelings. Had he ever done that for her? Had he ever thought of her feelings if they didn't coincide with his own wants and needs?

"I never wanted you hurt." Yet he'd killed her spirit anyway. "I have no excuse for what I did. Nothing I say can reverse time or knock sense into the man I was four years ago."

"Everything that happened made me a better person." She shifted a bit and lifted her ankle to resettle it over the edge of the sofa. "I poured myself into new things, found out who I really am on my own. I never would've done that had I been with you."

Will squeezed her tighter. "I wouldn't have let you lose yourself, Cat. Had you been with me I would've pushed you to do whatever you wanted."

She tipped her head back and met his gaze. "You wouldn't have let me work. You would've wanted the perfect, doting wife."

There was a ring of truth to her words. He most likely would have tried to push her into doing what he thought was best.

"I wasn't good to you." He swallowed. "You were better off without me, but it killed me to let you go, knowing you'd be fine once you moved on."

Silence settled heavily around them before she finally said, "I wasn't fine."

"You were dating a man two months after we broke up."

Cat turned back around, facing the water. "I needed to date, I needed to move on in any way that I could and try to forget you. When I was alone my mind would wander and I'd start to remember how happy I was with you. I needed to fill that void in any way I possibly could."

Will swallowed. He'd hated seeing her with another man, hated knowing he was the one who drove her into another's arms.

"I slept with him."

Her words cut through the darkness and straight to his heart. "I don't want—"

"I slept with him because I was trying to forget you," she went on as if he hadn't said a word. "I was ready to give myself to you, then you chose to obey your father once again at my expense. When I started dating Bryce, I mistook his affection for love. I knew I was on the rebound, but I wanted so badly to be with someone who valued me, who wanted to be with me and put me first."

Those raw, heartfelt words crippled him. He'd had no idea just how much damage he'd caused. All this time, she'd been searching for anyone to put her at the top of their priority list when he'd shoved her to the bottom of his.

"Afterward I cried," she whispered. "I hated that I'd given away something so precious and I hated even more that I still wished I'd given it to you."

Her honesty gutted him. Will wished more than anything he could go back and make changes, wished he could go back and be the man she needed him to be.

But he could be honest now, he could open up. She'd shared such a deep, personal secret, he knew she deserved to know why he'd let her go so easily.

"I had to let you go."

"I know, your father—"

"No." Will adjusted himself in the seat so he could face her better. "I need you to know this, I need you to listen to what I'm saying. I let you go because of my father, but not for the reasons you think."

The moon cast enough of a glow for Will to see Cat's dark eyes widen. "What?"

"I let you go to save you. My father's threats…" Will shook his head, still angry over the way he'd let his father manipulate him. "As soon as I let you go, I was plotting to get you back, to put my father in his place. I didn't care how long it took, didn't care what I had to do."

Cat stared back at him, and he desperately wanted to know what was swirling around in her head. There was so much hurt between them, so many questions and years of resentment. Will hated his father for putting him in this position, but he hated even more the way Cat had been the victim in all of this.

"Your father threatened me, didn't he?" Cat asked, her voice low, yet firm. "He held me over your head? Is that why you let me go?"

Swallowing the lump of guilt, Will nodded.

Cat sat up, swung her feet over the side and braced her hands on either side of her hips. Will lifted his leg out of her way and brought his knee up to give her enough room to sit. He waited while she stared down at the deck. Silence and moonlight surrounded them, bathing them in a peace that he knew neither of them felt.

"Talk to me." He couldn't handle the uncertainty. "I don't want you going through this alone."

A soft laugh escaped her as she kept her gaze averted. "But you didn't care that I went through this alone four years ago."

"Dammit, Cat. I couldn't let you get hurt. He had the ability to ruin you and I wasn't going to put my needs ahead of yours."

When she threw him a glance over her shoulder, Will's gut tightened at the moisture gathered in her eyes. "You didn't put my needs first at all. You didn't give me a chance to fight for us and you took the easy way out."

Raking a hand over his hair, Will blew out a breath. "I didn't take the easy way," he retorted. "I took the hardest way straight through hell to keep you safe and to work on getting you back."

She continued to stare, saying nothing. Moments later her eyes widened. "Wait," she whispered. "How did Bella come into play?"

"You know I never would've married her. That was all a farce to begin with." Will shifted closer, reaching out to smooth her hair back behind her ear. "And once I kissed you, I knew exactly who I wanted, who I needed."

Cat started to stand, winced and sat back down. Will said nothing as he pushed his leg around her, once again straddling her from behind. He pulled her back against his chest and leaned on the plush cushions. Even though she remained rigid, he knew the only way to get her to soften was for him to be patient. He'd waited four years; he was the epitome of patient.

Wrapping his arms around her, he whispered in her ear. "I messed up," he admitted. "I only wanted to protect you and went about it the wrong way. Don't shut me out now, Cat. We have too much between us. This goes so much deeper than either of us realizes and I won't let my father continue to ruin what we have."

Dammit, somewhere along the way to a heated affair Will had developed stronger feelings, a deeper bond with Cat than he'd anticipated. And now that he knew he wanted more from her, he was close to losing it all.

"And what do we have, Will?" Her words came out on a choked sob.

"What do you want?"

What do you want?

Catalina couldn't hold in the tension another second. There was only so much one person could handle and Will's simple question absolutely deflated her. Melting back against his body once more, she swallowed the emotion burning her throat.

"I want…" Catalina shut her eyes, trying to figure out all the thoughts fighting for head space. "I don't know now. Yesterday I knew exactly what I wanted. I was ready to leave Alma to get it."

Will's fingertips slid up and down her bare arms, causing her body to tremble beneath his delicate touch. "And now? What do you want now, Cat?"

Everything.

"I don't want to make things harder for you," he went on. "But I'm not backing down. Not this time."

And there was a portion of her heart that didn't want him to. How could she be so torn? How could two dreams be pulling her in completely different directions?

Because the harder she'd tried to distance herself from him, the more she was being pulled back in.

"I'm afraid," she whispered. "I can't make promises and I'm not ready to accept them from you, either."

His hands stilled for the briefest of moments before he kissed the top of her head. Catalina turned her cheek to rest against his chest, relishing the warmth of his body, the strong steady heartbeat beneath her. Part of her wanted to hate him for his actions years ago, the other part of her wanted to cry for the injustice of it all.

But a good portion of her wanted to forgive him, to believe him when he said that he'd sacrificed himself to keep her safe. Why did he have to be so damn noble and why hadn't he told her to begin with? He didn't have to fight that battle all on his own. Maybe she could have saved him, too.

Catalina closed her eyes as the yacht rocked steadily to the soothing rhythm of the waves. She wanted to lock this moment in time and live here forever. Where there were no outside forces trying to throw obstacles in their way and the raw honesty...

No. She still carried a secret that he didn't know and how could she ever tell him? How could she ever reveal the fact that his father had had an affair with her mother? Would he hate her for knowing?

"Will, I need—"

"We're done talking. I just want to hold you. Nothing else matters right now."

Turning a bit more in his arms, Catalina looked up into those vibrant eyes that had haunted her dreams for years. "Make love to me, Will. I don't care about anything else. Not when I can be with you."

In one swift, powerful move, he had her straddling his lap. Catalina hissed a breath when her ankle bumped his thigh.

"Dammit. Sorry, Cat."

She offered him a smile, stroking the pad of her thumb along the worry lines between his brows. "I'm fine," she assured him as she slid the ties at the side of her dress free. "I don't want to think about my injury, why we're stuck here or what's waiting for us when we get back. All I want is to feel you against me."

Will took in the sight of her as she continued to work out of her clothing. When his hands spanned her waist, she arched against his touch.

He leaned forward, resting his forehead against her chest as he whispered, "You're more than I deserve and everything I've ever wanted."

Framing his face with her hands, Catalina lifted his head until she could look him in the eyes. "No more talking," she reminded him with a soft kiss to his lips. "No more talking tonight."

Tomorrow, or whenever they were able to get off this island, she'd tell him about his father. But for now, she'd take this gift she'd been given and worry about the ugly truth, and how they would handle it, later.

Fifteen

By the second day, Catalina still hadn't told Will the truth. How could she reveal such a harsh reality when they'd been living in passionate bliss on a beautiful island in some fantasy?

They'd both fiddled with the radio and tried their cell phones from various spots on the island, but nothing was going through. She wasn't going to panic quite yet. They had plenty of food and for a bit, she could pretend this was a dream vacation with the man she'd fallen in love with.

Will rolled over in bed, wrapping his arm around her and settling against her back. "I'd like to say I can't wait to get off this island, but waking up with you in my arms is something I could get used to."

His husky tone filled her ear. The coarse hair on his chest tickled her back, but she didn't mind. She loved the feel of Will next to her.

"I'm getting pretty spoiled, too." She snuggled deeper into his embrace. "I'm never going to want to leave."

"Maybe that's how I want you to be," he replied, nipping her shoulder.

"We can't stay here forever," she laughed.

"As long as you don't leave Alma, I'm okay with going back."

A sliver of reality crept back in. Catalina shifted so that she could roll over in his arms and face him.

"I don't plan on working as a maid forever," she informed him, staring into his eyes. "And after what you told me about your father, I think it's best if I don't work there anymore. I can't work for a man who completely altered my future. I stayed with James because I adore him and I moved on to Patrick because I needed the job, but now that I know the full truth, I can't stay there."

Will propped himself up on his elbow and peered down at her. "I understand, but stay in Alma. Stay with me."

"And do what?" she asked, already knowing this conversation was going to divide them. "I have goals, Will. Goals that I can't ignore simply because we're… I don't even know what this is between us right now."

"Do you need a label?" he asked.

Part of her wanted to call this something. Maybe then she could justify her feelings for a man who'd let her go so easily before.

She had no idea what she was going to do once she got back to Alma. Working for Patrick was not going to happen. She'd put up with his arrogance for too long. Thankfully she'd only worked for him a short time because up until recently, James had been the one occupying the Playa del Onda home. Catalina had had a hard enough time working for Patrick knowing what she did about her mother, but now knowing he'd manipulated his son and crushed their relationship, Catalina couldn't go back there. Never again.

So where did that leave her? She didn't think she was quite ready to head out with her designs and start pursuing her goal. She had a few more things she'd like to complete before she made that leap.

"What's going through your mind?" Will asked, studying her face.

"You know the sewing set you got me?"

Will nodded.

"You have no idea how much that touched me." Catalina raked her hand through his blond hair and trailed her fingertips down his jaw, his neck. "I've been sewing in my spare time. Making things for myself, for my mother. It's been such a great escape and when I saw what you'd gotten me, I..."

Catalina shook her head and fell back against the bed. She stared up at the ceiling and wished she could find the right words to tell him how much she appreciated the gift.

"So you're saying it was a step up from the flowers?" he joked.

Shifting her gaze to him, her heart tightened at his playful smile. "I may have cried," she confessed. "That was the sweetest gift ever."

Will settled over her, his hands resting on either side of her head. "It was meant more as a joke," he said with a teasing smile. "And maybe I wanted to remind you of what we did in the utility room."

Cat smacked his chest. "As if I could've forgotten. That's all I could think about and you know it."

He gave her a quick kiss before he eased back. "It's all I could think of, too, if that helps."

Catalina wrapped her arms around his neck, threading her fingers through his hair. "What are we going to do when we get back?"

"We're going to take this one day at a time because I'm not screwing this up again."

"We can't seem to function in normal life."

Will's forehead rested against hers as he let out a sigh. "Trust me, Cat. I've fought too hard to get you back. I'm going to fight just as hard to keep you."

Catalina prayed that was true, because all too soon she was going to have to reveal the final secret between them if she wanted a future with this man.

Cat lay on the deck sunbathing in that skimpy bikini, which was positively driving him out of his mind. Right now he didn't give a damn that the radio was beyond repair or that their phones weren't getting a signal. For two days they'd made love, stayed in bed and talked, spending nearly every single moment together.

Perhaps that's why he was in such agony. He knew exactly what that lush body felt like against his own. He knew how amazingly they fit together with no barriers between them.

Will couldn't recall the last time he'd taken this much time away from work. Surprisingly he wasn't getting twitchy. He'd set his plan into motion a couple months ago for Rowling Energy and it shouldn't be too much longer before everything he'd ever wanted clicked into place like a perfectly, methodically plotted puzzle.

Will folded his arms behind his head and relaxed on the seat opposite Cat. But just as he closed his eyes, the soft hum of an engine had him jumping to his feet.

"Do you hear that?" he asked, glancing toward the horizon.

Cat sat up, her hand shielding her eyes as she glanced in the same direction. "Oh, there's another boat."

Will knew that boat and he knew who would be on board. Good thing his brother hadn't left to go back to training for football yet because that meant he could come to their rescue. Which was what he was doing right now.

"Looks like our fairy tale is over," Catalina muttered.

He glanced her way. "It's not over," he corrected. "It's just beginning."

As James's yacht closed the distance between them, Will slid his shoes back on. "Stay here. I'll wave James to the other side of the dock where the damage isn't as bad. And I'll carry you on board once we're secure."

Cat rolled her eyes and reached for her wrap draped across the back of the white sofa. "I can walk, Will. My ankle is sore, but it's much better than it was."

Will wasn't going to argue. He'd win in the end regardless.

As soon as James was near enough, Will hopped up onto the dock and made his way toward the other end. By the time James came to a stop, Bella was at his side, a worried look etched across her face.

"Coast guard has arrived," James said, coming up behind his wife.

"I figured you'd come along sooner or later," Will replied.

James took in the damage to the dock and the yacht. "Damn, you've got a mess. That must've been one hell of a storm. It rained and there was some thunder and wind in Alma, but no damage."

"Let me go get our things," Will told his brother. "I need to carry Cat, too. She's hurt."

"Oh no," Bella cried. "What happened?"

"I fell."

Will turned to see Cat leaning over the side of the yacht. "You're supposed to be sitting down," he called back.

"I'm fine. I will need some help off this thing, but I can walk if I go slow."

Will shook his head. "I'll carry her," he told his brother. "Give me a few minutes to get our personal stuff gathered."

Once they transferred everything Will and Cat needed to his brother's yacht and Will carried a disgruntled Cat on board, they were ready to head out. The trip back to Alma was filled with questions from Bella and James. Their worry was touching and Will actually found himself loving this newfound bond he and his brother shared. This is what he'd been missing for years. This is what their grief had torn apart after their mother had died. But now they were slowly making their way back to each other.

"I wasn't quite sure which island you went to," James said as they drew nearer to Alma's coastline. "I went to two last night and had to start again today when I couldn't find you."

"Did you tell anyone what was going on?" Will asked.

"No." James maneuvered the boat and pulled back on the throttle. "Bella and I are the only ones who know where you were."

Will was relieved nobody else knew. He didn't want to share Cat or their relationship with anyone just yet. He wanted to bask in their privacy for a bit longer.

"Dammit," James muttered as they neared what was supposed to be a private dock where Alma's rich and famous kept their boats. "The damn press is here."

"What for?" Cat asked, her eyes widening.

"There were a few reporters here when I left earlier,"

James stated as he steered the yacht in. "They were speculating because Will's yacht had been missing for a few days and they knew a storm had come through. They asked me where you were and I ignored them."

Will groaned. So much for that privacy he'd been clinging to. "Don't they have anything better to cover? Like the fact Juan Carlos is going to be crowned king in a few weeks? Do they seriously have to focus on me?"

Cat's eyes remained fixed on the throng of reporters and cameras turning in their direction.

Will crouched down before her seat and smoothed her hair back from her face. "Ignore them. No matter what they say, do not make a comment. They'll forget about this by tomorrow and we can move on."

Her eyes sought his and she offered him a smile. "Ignore them. That I can do."

Will stood back up and offered her his hand. "I'm going to at least put my arm around you so you can put some of your weight on me. Anyone looking will just think I'm helping you."

"I'll carry her bag," Bella offered. "I'll go first. Maybe they'll focus on James and me. I can always just start discussing my upcoming fund-raiser for my foundation next weekend. I'm okay with yanking the reporters' chains, too."

Will couldn't help but laugh at Bella's spunk. She was the perfect match for his brother.

As they made their way down the dock, Will kept his arm secured around Cat's waist. James and Bella took the lead, holding hands as they wedged through the sea of nosy people.

The reporters seemed to all start shouting at once.

"Where have you been for three days?"

"Was your yacht damaged by the storm?"

"Were you stranded somewhere?"

"Who is with you, Will?"

The questions kept coming as Will tried to shield Cat from the press. The whispers and murmurs infuriated him. Seriously? Wasn't there other newsworthy stuff happening in Alma right now? Dammit, this was one major drawback to being a wealthy, well-known businessman. And if he thought for a second he could have any privacy with Cat now that they were back, he was living in a fantasy.

When he heard someone say the word "staff" he clenched his jaw. He wouldn't respond. That's what they wanted: some type of reaction. He heard his father's name and for reasons unbeknownst to Will, the gossipmongers were starting to piece things together rather quickly. Where the hell would they have seen Cat? On occasion his father would allow a few press members to attend certain parties thrown by the Rowlings if there was a charity involved. Cat had been James's maid, too, though.

Will groaned as he kept his sights on his brother's back as the foursome pushed through to the waiting car in the distance. They couldn't get there fast enough for Will.

"Is your mistress a member of your family's staff, Mr. Rowling?"

The rude question had Cat stiffening at his side. "Keep going," he murmured. "Almost there."

"Wasn't she working for your brother?"

"Is she on Patrick's staff?"

"How long have you been seeing your father's maid?"

"Weren't you just engaged to your brother's wife?"

"What does your father think about you and his maid?"

Will snapped. "This isn't like that. You're all making a mistake."

Catalina's gasp had him jerking his gaze toward her. "Dammit," he muttered beneath his breath. "You know that's not what I mean."

Those damn words echoed from the last time he'd said them to her. And this time they were just as damaging when taken out of context.

Easing back from his side, Cat kept her eyes on his. "I'm not sure, Will. Because only moments ago you said ignore them and you said we'd take this one day at a time. We've only been back in Alma five minutes and you're already referring to me as a mistake."

Will raked a hand through his hair. From the corner of his eye he spotted James and Bella standing close. For once the reporters weren't saying a word. They waited, no doubt hoping to really get something juicy for their headlines.

"Marry me."

Okay, he hadn't meant to blurt that out there, but now that the words hovered between them, he wasn't sorry. Maybe Cat would see just how serious he was about them.

"Marry you?" she asked, her brows drawn in. "You're not serious."

He stepped forward and took her hand. "We are not a mistake, Cat. You know we're perfect together. Why wouldn't you?"

Cat stared back at him, and then shook her head and let out a soft laugh. "This is ridiculous. You don't mean this proposal so why would you do this to me? Why would you ask that in front of all these people? To prove them wrong? Because you got caught with the maid and you're trying to glamorize it?"

"Dammit, Cat, this has nothing to do with anyone else. We can talk later, in private."

He didn't want to hash this out here in front of the press. And he sure as hell didn't want to sound as if he was backpedaling because he'd chosen the worst possible time to blurt out a proposal.

Crossing her arms over her chest, she tipped her chin up just a notch, but enough for him to know she was good and pissed. "Would you have proposed to me if all of these people hadn't been around? Later tonight when we were alone, would you have asked me to marry you?"

Will gritted his teeth, clenched his fists at his side and honestly had no reply. He had absolutely no idea what to say. He didn't want to have such an intimate talk in front of the whole country, because that's exactly what was happening. The press would no doubt splash this all over the headlines.

"That's what I thought." Cat's soft tone was full of hurt. "I'd say it's officially over between us."

When she turned, she winced, but just as Will reached to help her, Bella stepped forward and slowly ushered Cat to the car. James moved in next to Will and ordered the press away. Will didn't hear much, didn't comprehend what was going on because in the span of just a few minutes, he'd gone from deliriously happy and planning his future, to seeing that future walk away from him after he'd hurt her, called her a mistake, once again.

This time, he knew there would be no winning her back.

Sixteen

"What the hell is this?"

Will turned away from his office view to face his father, who stood on the other side of his desk with a folder in his hand. Will had been waiting for this moment. But he hadn't expected to feel this enormous pit of emptiness inside.

"I see you received the notice regarding your shares in Rowling Energy." Will folded his arms across his chest and leveled his father's gaze. "Your votes in the company are no longer valid. I held an emergency meeting with the other stockholders and we came to the decision."

Patrick's face reddened. "How dare you. What kind of son did I raise that he would turn around and treat his father like this?"

"You raised the son who fought for what he wanted." Will's blood pressure soared as he thought of all he'd lost and all he was still fighting for. "You raised a son who watched his father put business first, above family, and to hell with the rest of the world. I'm taking Rowling Energy into new territory and I need sole control. I'm done being jerked around by you."

Patrick rested his palms on the desk and leaned in. "No, you'd rather be jerked around by my maid. You two made quite a scene yesterday—it made headlines. You're becoming an embarrassment and tarnishing the Rowling name."

Will laughed. "What I do in my personal life is not your concern. You poked your nose in years ago when you threatened to dismiss Catalina if I didn't dump her. I won't be manipulated ever again and you will leave Cat alone. If I even think you've tried to—"

"Knock off the threats," his father shouted as he pushed off the desk. "Your little maid quit on me and has really left me in a bind. If you were smart, you'd stay away from her. You two get cozy and she quits. I don't believe in coincidences. Those Iberra women are nothing but gold diggers."

Will stood up straighter, dropped his arms to his sides. "What did you say?"

Patrick waved a hand in the air, shaking his head. "Forget it."

"No. You said 'those Iberra women.' What did you mean?"

Will knew Cat's mother had worked for Patrick years ago. Maria had been around when James and Will had been young, when their mother was still alive.

"What did Maria do that you would call her a gold digger?" Will asked when his father remained silent.

Still, Patrick said nothing.

Realization dawned on Will. "No. Tell me you didn't have an affair with Maria."

"Every man has a moment of weakness," Patrick stated simply. "I expect this past weekend was yours."

Rage boiled to the surface. Will clenched his fists. "You slept with Cat's mother while my mother was still alive? Did Mum know about the affair?"

The thought of his sweet, caring mother being betrayed tore through Will's heart. Part of him prayed she never knew the ugly acts his father had committed.

"She found out the day she died." Patrick let out a sigh, his eyes darting to the ground. "We were arguing about it when she left that night."

For once the great Patrick Rowling looked defeated. Which was nothing less than he deserved. Will's heart was absolutely crushed. He reached out, gripped the back of his desk chair and tried to think rationally here. Finding out your father had an affair with the mother of a woman you had fallen for was shocking enough. But to add to the intensity, his mother had died as a result of the affair.

Dread settled deep in Will's his gut. Did Cat know of this affair? Surely not. Surely she would have told him or at least hinted at the knowledge. Would this crush her, too?

"Get out," Will said in a low, powerful tone as he kept his eyes on the blotter on his desk. "Get the hell out of my office and be glad my freezing your voting rights in this company is all I'm doing to you."

Patrick didn't move. Will brought his gaze up and glared at the man he'd once trusted.

"You have one minute to be out of this building or I'll call security."

"I never thought you'd turn on me," his father replied.

"I turned on you four years ago when you threatened the woman I love."

Will hadn't meant to declare his love for Cat, but it felt good to finally let the words out. And now more than ever he wasn't giving up. He was going to move heaven and earth to win her back because he did love her. He'd always loved her if he was honest with himself. And he wanted a life with her now more than ever.

Bella was having a fund-raiser this coming weekend and Will knew he was going to need reinforcements. He wasn't letting Cat go. Not this time. Never again.

"I figured you'd be at work today." James sank down onto the chaise longue on his patio as Maisey played in her sandbox. "You look like hell, man."

Will shoved his hands in his pockets and glanced toward the ocean. "I feel like hell. Thanks for pointing it out."

"You still haven't talked to Catalina?"

Maisey squealed, threw her toy shovel and started burying her legs beneath the sand. Will watched his niece and wondered if there could ever be a family for Cat and him. She wanted a family and the more he thought of a life with her, the more he wanted the same thing.

"No, I haven't seen her." Will shifted his focus to his brother and took a seat on the edge of a chair opposite him. "Bella's fund-raiser is going to be at the Playa del Onda house this weekend, right?"

"Yes. Dad will be out of town and that house is perfect for entertaining. Why?"

"I want you to ask Cat to help with the staff there." Will held up a hand before his brother could cut him off. "I have my reasons, but I need your help in order to make this work."

James shook his head and stared down at his daughter for a minute before he looked back at Will. "This could blow up in your face."

Will nodded. "It's a risk I'm willing to take."

"What's in it for me?" James asked with a smirk.

Will laughed. Without even thinking twice, he unfastened the watch on his wrist and held it up. "This."

James's eyes widened. "I was joking."

"I'm not." Will reached out and placed the watch on the arm of his brother's chair. "You deserve it back. This has nothing to do with you helping me with Cat. The watch is rightfully yours."

James picked it up and gripped it in his hand. "We've really come a long way," he muttered.

Will had one more piece of business to take care of and he was not looking forward to this discussion at all. There was no way James knew of the affair or he definitely would've said something. Will really hated to crush his brother with the news, but James deserved to know.

"I need to tell you something." Will glanced at Maisey. "Is your nanny here or is Bella busy?"

James sat up in his seat, slid his watch on and swung his legs around to the deck. "Bella was answering emails, but she can watch Maisey. Is everything okay?"

Will shook his head. "Not really."

Worry and concern crossed James's face as he nodded. After taking Maisey inside, he returned moments later, closing the patio doors behind him.

"This must really be something if it has you this upset." James sat back down on the edge of his chair. "What's going on?"

Will took in a deep breath, blew it out and raked a hand through his hair. "This is harder than I thought," he said on a sigh. "Do you remember the night Mum died? Dad woke us and said she'd been in an accident?"

James nodded. "I heard them arguing earlier that evening. I was heading downstairs to get some water and heard them fighting so I went back upstairs."

Will straightened. "You heard them arguing?"

James nodded. "Dad raised his voice, and then Mum was crying and Dad was saying something else but in a lower tone. I didn't hear what all he said."

Will closed his eyes and wished like hell he could go back and…what? What could he have done differently? He'd been a kid. Even if James had gone downstairs and interrupted the fight, most likely their mother still would've walked out to get away from their father.

"What is it?" James prodded. "What aren't you telling me?"

Will opened his eyes and focused on his brother. "Dad had an affair. They were arguing about that."

"What?" James muttered a curse. "Has that man ever valued his family at all?"

"There's more." Will hesitated a moment, swallowed and pushed forward. "The affair was with Maria. Cat's mum."

Will started to wonder if James had heard him, but suddenly his brother jumped to his feet and let out a chain of curses that even had Will wincing. James kicked the leg of the chair, propped his hands on his hips and dropped his head between his shoulders.

"If I'd have gone downstairs that night…" he muttered.

"Mum still would've left," Will said softly. "We can't go back in time and you're not to blame. Our dad is the one whose selfish needs stole our mother. He crushed her. She would've done anything for him and he threw it all away."

James turned. "Does Cat know this?"

Shaking his head, Will came to his feet. "I doubt it. She's never said a word to me."

"Do you think once she knows the truth she'll take you back?"

Yeah, the odds were more than stacked against him, but he refused to back down. Nobody would steal his life again. And Cat was his entire life.

"I don't even know what to say about this," James said, staring out to the ocean. "I never had much respect for Dad, but right now I hate that man."

"I've made his life hell." Will was actually pleased with the timing. "As CEO of Rowling Energy, I've frozen his shares. He can no longer vote on any company matters that come before the board."

James smiled. "If this action were directed to an enemy, dear old Dad would be proud of your business tactics."

"Yeah," Will agreed, returning the grin. "He's not too proud right now, though. But I have more pressing matters to tend to."

James reached out, patted Will on the back. "I'll do what I can where Cat is concerned. I know what this is like to be so torn over a woman."

Torn wasn't even the word.

"I never thought either of us would fall this hard." Will pulled in a deep breath. "Now we need Bella to convince Cat to work the party. I can take it from there. I just need you guys to get her there."

Seventeen

If Catalina didn't adore Bella and her valiant efforts to raise money for the Alma Wildlife Conservation Society which she'd recently founded, Catalina wouldn't have stepped foot back into this house.

But Patrick was out of town and Bella and James had caught Catalina at a weak moment, offering her an insane amount of money to help set up for the event.

In the past week since she'd last seen Will, she'd not heard one word from him. Apparently she wasn't worth fighting for after all. Not that she would have forgiven him, but a girl likes to at least know she's worth something other than a few amazing sexual encounters.

Catalina hurried through the house, hoping to get everything set up perfectly before the first guests arrived.

Okay, fine. There was only one person on the guest list she was trying like hell to avoid.

She'd spent this past week furiously working on her

final designs. She didn't have the amount of money saved up that she wanted before she left Alma, but it would just have to be enough. Alma had nothing left to offer her. Not anymore.

Catalina took a final walkthrough, adjusting one more floral arrangement on the foyer table before she was satisfied with everything. She'd already double-checked with the kitchen to make sure the food was ready and would be served according to the set schedule. She'd also told Bella she would be back around midnight to clean up. There was just no way she could stay during the party. That had been her only condition for working tonight, and thankfully Bella had agreed.

Catalina checked her watch. Only thirty minutes until guests were due to arrive. Time to head out. She'd opted to park near the side entrance off the utility room. Just as she turned into the room to grab her purse and keys, she ran straight into a very hard, very familiar chest.

Closing her eyes, she tried like hell not to breathe in, but Will's masculine aroma enveloped her just as his strong arms came around to steady her.

"Running away?" he whispered in her ear.

Knowing she'd never get out without talking, Catalina shored up all of her courage and lifted her gaze to his. "I'm not the one who usually runs."

Keeping his aqua eyes on her, Will reached around, slammed the door and flicked the lock. "Neither of us is getting out of here until we talk."

"I don't need you to hold onto me," she told him, refusing to glance away. No way was he keeping the upper hand here just because her heart was in her throat.

"I want to make sure you'll stay put."

He dropped his hands but didn't step back. The

warmth from his body had hers responding. She wished she didn't fall so easily into the memories of their love-making, wished she didn't get swept away by such in-triguing eyes. Even through their rocky moments, Catalina couldn't deny that all the good trumped the bad…at least in her heart.

"I'll stay." She stepped back until she was flat against the door. "If I don't listen now, I know you'll show up at my apartment. Might as well get this over with."

Why couldn't he be haggard or have dark circles be-neath his eyes? Had he not been losing sleep over the fact he'd been a jerk? Why did he have to be so damn sexy all the time and why couldn't she turn off her hor-mones around this man who constantly hurt her?

"There's so much I want to say," he muttered as he ran a hand over his freshly shaven jaw. "I don't know where to start."

Catalina tapped her watch. "Better hurry. The party starts soon."

"I don't give a damn about that party. I already gave Bella a check for the foundation."

"Of course you did," she muttered. "What do you want from me, Will?"

He stepped forward until her body was firmly trapped between his and the door. Placing a hand on either side of her head, he replied, "Everything."

Oh, mercy. She wasn't going to be able to keep up this courage much longer if he kept looking at her like that, if he touched her or used those charming words.

"You can't have everything." She licked her lips and stared up at him. "You can't treat everything like a busi-ness deal, only giving of yourself when it's convenient for you or makes you look good in the public eye."

Will smoothed her hair away from her face and she

simply couldn't take it anymore. She placed her hands on his chest and shoved him back, slipping past him to get some breathing room before she lost her mind and clung to him.

"I'm actually glad you cornered me," she went on, whirling around to face him. "I didn't want to run into you tonight, but we both need closure. I don't want to leave Alma with such awkwardness between us."

"Leave Alma," he repeated. "You're not leaving Alma."

Catalina laughed. "You know you can't control everyone, right? I am leaving. In two weeks, actually. My mother and I have tickets and we're heading to Milan."

"What's in Milan?"

Catalina tucked her hair behind her ears and crossed her arms. "My new life. I've been working for nearly four years and I'm finally ready to take my clothing designs and see what I can do in the world. I may not get far, but I'm going to try."

Will's brows drew in as he listened. Catalina actually liked the fact that she'd caught him off guard. He'd been knocking the air out of her lungs for a good while now and it was only appropriate she return the favor.

"I know you're angry with me for blurting out the proposal in front of such an audience, but you have to listen to me now."

"I'll listen, but you're wasting your time if you're trying to convince me of anything. We're not meant to be, Will. We've tried, and we weren't successful either time. I don't want to keep fighting a losing battle."

"I've never lost a battle in my life," he informed her as he took a step closer. "I don't intend to lose this one."

"You already lost," she whispered. "On the island we were so happy and for that time I really thought we could come back here and build on that. But once again, I was naïve where you were concerned. As soon as we stepped foot back in Alma, you turned into that take-charge man who didn't want to look like a fool in front of the cameras. You were embarrassed to be seen with the maid, and then when you realized just how much of a jerk you were being, you opted to propose? Did you honestly think I'd accept that?"

Will was close enough to touch, but he kept his hands propped on his hips. "I reacted without thinking. Dammit, Cat we'd just had the best few days together and I was scared, all right? Everything about us terrifies me to the point I can't think straight. I've never wanted anything or anyone the way I want you and I've never been this afraid of losing what I love forever."

Catalina gasped. He didn't just say... No, he didn't love her. He was using those pretty words to control her, to trick her into...

What? What was his end game here?

"You don't love me, Will." Oh, how she wished he did, but that was still the naïve side of her dreaming. "You love power."

"I won't deny power is important to me. But that also means I can use that power to channel some pretty damn intense emotions." He leaned in, close enough for her to feel his breath on her face, yet he still didn't touch her. "And I love you more than any business deal, more than any merger or sale. I love you, Catalina."

She didn't want to hear this. He'd used her full name so she knew he was serious, or as serious as he could be.

"I don't want this," she murmured, trying to look away, but trapped by the piercing gaze. "I have plans, Will, and I can't hinge my entire life around a man who may or may not put me above his career."

And even if she could give in and let him have her heart, she carried this secret inside of her that would surely drive another sizeable wedge between them.

"Listen to me." He eased back, but reached out and placed his hands on either side of her face. "Hear every single word I'm about to tell you. For the past four years I've fought to get you back. At first I'll admit it was because my father wanted something else for my life and I was being spiteful, but the longer you and I were apart, the more I realized there was an empty ache inside of me that couldn't be filled. I poured myself into work, knowing the day would come when I'd take over Rowling Energy. Even through all of that, I was plotting to get you back."

He stared at her, his thumb stroking back and forth along the length of her jawline as if he was putting her into some type of trance.

"Just the thought of you with another man was crushing, but I knew if I didn't fight for you, for us, then you'd settle down and I'd lose you forever. I've always put you first, Cat. Always. Even when we weren't together, I was working my way back to you."

When she started to glance away, he tipped her head up, forcing her to keep her eyes on his. "You think I was working this long to win you back just to have sex with you? I want the intimacy, I want the verbal sparring matches we get into, I want to help you pick up those little seashells along the beach and I want to wake up with you beside me every day for the rest of my life. Rowling Energy and all I have there mean nothing in the grand scheme of things. I want the money and the power, but I want you more than any of that."

Catalina chewed on her bottom lip, trying to force her chin to stop quivering. She was on the verge of losing it and once the dam burst on her tears, she might never regain control.

"Before you decide, I don't want anything coming between us again," he went on. "I need to tell you something that is quite shocking and I just discovered myself."

Catalina reached up, gripped his wrists and eased his hands away from her face. She kept hold of him, but remained still. "What is it?"

"There's no easy way to tell you this without just saying it."

Fear pumped through her as her heart kicked up the pace. What on earth was he going to reveal? Whatever it was, it was a big deal. And once he told her his shocking news, she had a bombshell of her own to drop because she also couldn't move forward, with or without him, and still keep this secret.

"I found out that my father and your mother had an affair."

When Catalina stared at him for a moment, his eyes widened and he stepped back. She said nothing, but the look on his face told her all she needed to know.

"You already knew?" he asked in a whisper. "Didn't you?"

Cat nodded. Will's heart tightened. How had she known? How could she keep something so important from him?

"You've known awhile," he said, keeping his eyes on her unsurprised face. "How long?"

Cat blinked back the moisture that had gathered in her dark eyes. "Four years."

Rubbing the back of his neck, Will glanced down at

the floor. He couldn't look at her. Couldn't believe she'd keep such a monumental secret from him.

"I didn't know when we were together," she told him. "My mom told me after we broke up. I was so upset and she kept telling me how the Rowling men... Never mind. It's not important."

Everything about this was important, yet the affair really had nothing to do with how he felt for Cat. The sins of their parents didn't have to trickle down to them and ruin their happiness.

"I still can't believe you didn't say anything."

Cat turned, walked to the door and stared out into the backyard. Will took in her narrow shoulders, the exposed nape of her neck. She wasn't wearing her typical black shirt and pants. Right now she had on a pair of flat sandals, a floral skirt and some type of fitted shirt that sat right at the edge of her shoulders. She looked amazing and she was just out of his reach, physically and emotionally.

"I wanted to tell you on the island," she said, keeping her back to him. "I tried once, but we got sidetracked. That's an excuse. I should've made you listen, but we were so happy and there was no such thing as reality during those few days. I just wanted to stay in that euphoric moment."

He couldn't fault her for that because he'd felt the exact same way.

"There's just so much against us, Will." She turned back around and the lone tear on her cheek gutted him. "Sometimes people can love each other and still not be together. Sometimes love isn't enough and people just need to go their own way."

Will heard what she was saying, but how could he not hone in on the one main point to her farewell speech?

"You love me?" He couldn't help but smile as he crossed to her. "Say it, Cat. I want to hear the words."

She shook her head. "It doesn't mean anything."

"Say it." His hands settled around her waist as he pulled her flush against him. "Now."

"I love you, Will, but—"

He crushed his lips to hers. Nothing else mattered after those life-altering words. Nothing she could say would erase the fact that she loved him and he loved her, and he'd be damn it if he would ever let her walk away.

Her body melted against his as her fingers curled around his biceps. Will lifted his mouth from hers, barely.

"Don't leave, Cat," he murmured against her lips. "Don't leave Alma. Don't leave me."

"I can't give up who I am, Will." She closed her eyes and sighed. "No matter how much I love you, I can't give up everything I've worked for and I wouldn't expect you to give up your work for me. We have different goals in different directions."

The fear of losing her, the reality that if he didn't lay it all on the line, then she would be out of his life for good hit him hard.

"I'm coming with you."

Cat's eyes flew open as Will tipped his head back to see her face better. "What?"

"I meant what I said. I won't give you up and you're more to me than any business. But I can work from anywhere and I can fly to Alma when I need to."

"You can't be serious." Panic flooded her face. "This is rushed. You can't expect me to just say okay and we'll be on our way to happily-ever-after. It's too fast."

Will laughed. "I've known you since you were a little girl. I dated you four years ago and last weekend you spent nearly three days in my bed. You said you love me and I love the hell out of you and you think this is too fast? If we move any slower we'll be in a nursing home by the time you wear my ring on your finger."

"I can't think." Once again she pushed him aside and moved past him. "I can't take all this in. I mean, your dad and my mom…all of the things that have kept us apart. And then you corner me in a laundry room of all places to tell me you want me forever."

"So we don't do things the traditional way." He came up behind her, gripped her shoulders and kissed the top of her head. "I'm done with being by the book and boring. I want adventure, I want to be on a deserted island with the only woman in the world who can make me angry, laugh and love the way you do. I want to take care of you, I want to wear out the words *I love you* and I want to have no regrets from here on out where we are concerned."

Cat eased back against him, her head on his shoulder. "I want to believe all of that is possible. I want to hold on to the hope that I can still fulfill my dreams and I can have you. But I won't give up myself, no matter how much I love you, Will."

Wrapping his arms around her waist, he leaned his cheek on her head. "I wouldn't ask you to give up anything. I just didn't want you leaving Alma without me. We can live wherever you want. I have a jet, I have a yacht…well, I'll have a new one soon. I can travel where I need to be for work and I can take you where you need to go in order to fulfill this goal of yours. I want to be with you every step of your journey."

"I want to do it on my own," she stated, sliding her hands over his.

"I wouldn't dream of interfering," he replied. "I'll

support you in any way you need. I'll be the silent financial backer or I'll be the man keeping your bed warm at night and staying out of the business entirely. The choice is yours."

Cat turned in his arms, laced her hands behind his neck and stared up at him. "Tell me this is real. Tell me you don't hate me for keeping the secret and that you will always make me first in your life."

"It's real." He kissed her forehead. "I could never hate you." He kissed her nose. "And you'll never question again whether you're first in my life."

He slid his mouth across hers, gliding his hands down her body to the hem of her shirt. Easing the hem up, he smoothed his palms up over her bare skin, pleased when she shivered beneath his touch.

"Are you seriously trying to seduce me in a laundry room all while your sister-in-law is throwing a party to raise money for her foundation a few feet away?"

Will laughed as his lips traveled down the column of her throat. "I'm not trying. I'm about to succeed."

Cat's body arched back as her fingers threaded through his hair. "I hope no partygoers take a stroll through the backyard and glance in the window of the door," she panted when his hands brushed the underside of her breasts.

"We already made headlines." He jerked the shirt up and over her head, flinging it to the side without a care. "Another one won't matter at this point."

"What will your brother think if you don't show at the party?"

Will shrugged. "James is pretty smart. I'd say he'll know exactly where I am."

Cat started working on the buttons of his shirt and

soon sent the shirt and his jacket to the floor. "We still don't have a solid plan for our future."

Hoisting her up, Will sat her on the counter and settled between her legs. "I know how the next several minutes are going to play out. Beyond that I don't care so long as you're with me."

Will kissed her once more and eased back. "But I already have the perfect wedding present for you."

Cat laughed as her arms draped over his shoulders. "And what's that?"

"A maid. You'll not lift a finger for me ever. I want you to concentrate on your design career and the babies we're going to have in the future."

When Cat's smile widened and she tightened her hold on him, Will knew the four years he'd worked on getting back to her were worth it. Everything he'd sacrificed with his father and personal life was worth this moment, knowing he was building a future with the only woman he'd ever loved.

* * * * *

THE LONE STAR CINDERELLA

MAUREEN CHILD

To Kate Carlisle and Jennifer Apodaca—great
friends and wonderful writers who helped keep
me sane during the writing of this book!

One

Dave Firestone was a man on a mission.

The future of his ranch was at stake and damned if he was going to let scandal or whispered rumors ruin what he'd spent years building. It had been months now since Alex Santiago had disappeared and Dave *still* felt a cloud of suspicion hanging around his head. Time to find out one way or the other what the law in town thought of the situation.

He climbed out of his 4x4, tugged the collar of his brown leather jacket up around his neck and squinted into the East Texas wind. October was rolling in cold, signaling what would be an even colder winter. Nothing he could do about that, but Dave had driven to the border of his ranch to get at least one part of his life straightened out.

A tall man wearing a worn, black leather coat and a tan, wide-brimmed hat was patching the barbed-wire fence that separated Dave's ranch, the Royal Round Up, from the neighboring ranch, the Battlelands. Behind the man in black, another man, Bill Hardesty, a Battle ranch hand, unloaded wire from a battered truck. Dave nodded a greeting to Bill, then focused his attention on Nathan Battle.

Nathan looked up as Dave approached. "Hey, Dave, how's it going?"

"Going fine," he said, because Dave Firestone never admitted to having a problem he couldn't solve. "I went by the main ranch house and Jake told me where I could find you. Didn't think I'd find the town sheriff out fixing fence line."

Nathan shrugged and glanced out over the surrounding land before shifting his gaze back to Dave. "I like getting out on the ranch. Gives me a chance to think. Clear my head. My brother does most of the heavy lifting on the Battlelands, but I'm a full partner and it feels good to get back to basics, you know?" Then he grinned. "Besides, Amanda's on a remodeling binge, getting ready for the baby. So we've got one of Sam Gordon's construction crews at the house all the time. Being out here..." he said, then sighed in pleasure. "Quiet."

From his spot on the truck, Bill snorted. "Enjoy it while it lasts, boss. Once that baby comes you can kiss 'quiet' goodbye forever."

Nathan chuckled, then said, "Just unload the wire, will ya?"

Dave ignored the byplay. He wished he'd found Nathan alone out here, but he was going to have his say whether Bill was listening in or not.

Things had changed a lot around Royal in the past few months, Dave thought. Nathan and Amanda were married and expecting a baby. Sam and Lila were expecting twins. And then there was the reason Dave had come to see Nathan on his day off.

The disappearance of Alex Santiago.

He wouldn't claim to have been friends with Alex, but he'd never wished the man harm, either. This vanishing act of his was weird enough to keep the people in town talking—and most of them were talking about how Dave and Alex had been business rivals and wondering if maybe Alex hadn't had some help in disappearing.

Dave had never been one to give a flying damn what people had to say about him. He ran his life and his business the way he saw fit, and if people didn't like it, screw them. But like he'd just been thinking, things had changed. Irritating to admit that gossip and the threat of scandal had chased him out here to talk to the town sheriff, but there it was.

"Yeah, I get that. My foreman's the best there is, but I like doing ranch work on my own, too. Always have," Dave said, snatching his hat off to stab his fingers through his hair. "And I hate to ruin your peace and quiet…"

Nathan hooked his pair of wire cutters into the tool belt at his waist and looked at Dave. "But?"

"But," Dave said, with the briefest of glances toward Bill, who wasn't even bothering to hide his interest in the conversation, "I need to know if you've got anything new on Alex's disappearance."

Scowling, Nathan admitted, "I've got nothing. It's like he dropped off the face of the earth. No action on his credit or debit cards, either. Haven't got a clue what happened to him and, to tell you the truth, it's making me nuts."

"I can imagine," Dave said and tipped the brim of his hat back a bit. "It's not doing much for me, either."

Nathan nodded grimly. "Yeah, I've heard the whispers."

"Great." Just what he wanted. The town sheriff listening to rumors about him.

"Relax." Nathan waved one hand at him and shook his head. "I know what the gossips in this town are like, Dave. Hell, they almost cost me Amanda." He paused for a second as if considering what might have been. Then he shook his head again and said, "If it helps any, you're officially *not* a suspect."

He hadn't really thought he was, but it was good to hear anyway. It didn't solve his problem, but knowing that Nathan believed in his innocence was one less thing to worry about. Dave knew how it must have looked to everyone in town. He was among the last people to have seen Alex before he went missing. And the argument they'd had on Main Street had been witnessed by at least a dozen people.

Plus, it was pretty much common knowledge around Royal that Alex had snapped up the investment property that Dave had had his eye on. So yeah, Dave had been furious. But he hadn't wanted anything to happen to Alex.

"Glad to hear you say that," Dave finally said. "In fact, it's what I came out here to ask you. Feels good knowing I'm not a suspect, I'll admit. But it doesn't change how people in this town are looking at me."

He'd been in Royal three years, and he would have thought people would know him by now. But apparently, one whisper of juicy gossip was all it took to have people looking at him with a jaundiced eye.

Nathan dropped one hand to the top of the fence post and said, "People talk, you can't stop it. God knows I've tried. And in a town the size of Royal, that's about all they've got to do to fill the time, you know? Doesn't mean anything."

"Not to you, maybe—and I'm grateful, don't get me wrong," Dave told him. "But I'm trying to land a contract with TexCat and—"

Nathan chuckled and stopped him. "No need to say more. Hell, Texas Cattle is legendary. Everyone in the state knows about Thomas Buckley and how he runs his company. The old man is such a straight arrow…" He broke off. "That's why the concern over the gossip."

"Yeah, if Buckley hears those rumors, I'll never get the contract with him to sell my beef." Scandal could sour the deal before it was made, and damned if Dave would let that happen.

TexCat was the biggest beef buyer in the country. But it was a family-run company and Buckley himself ran it along the narrowest lines possible. No scandal had ever touched his company, and he was determined to keep it that way. So if he got wind of rumors about Dave now, it would only make all of this more difficult.

"Ol' Buckley is so worried about what people think," Bill pointed out from his spot on the truck, "I hear he *sleeps* in a three-piece suit."

Dave frowned and Nathan shot Bill a look. "Is that wire unloaded?"

"Almost," Bill said and ducked his head as he went back to work.

"Sorry," Nathan said unnecessarily, then grinned. "Everybody's got something to say about everything around here. But you already know that, don't you?"

"You could say so," Dave muttered.

Still smiling, Nathan added, "Where Buckley's concerned, it's not just the rumors you've got to be worried about."

Dave frowned. "Yeah, I know."

Nathan's smile widened. "Buckley only deals with married family men. Last time I looked, you were single. I figure the rumors and whispering should be the least of your problems. How're you planning on coming up with a wife?"

Dave huffed out a disgusted breath. "Haven't figured that part out yet. We're just at the beginning of negotiations with TexCat. I've still got some time." He jammed his hat back on his head and hunched deeper into his jacket as a sharp, cold wind slapped at them. "I'll think of something."

Nathan nodded. "If not, TexCat isn't the only beef buyer in the world."

"No," Dave agreed. "But they're the best."

He wanted that contract. And what Dave Firestone wanted, he got. Period. He'd clawed and fought and earned his success the hard way. Not a chance in hell he'd stop before he was finished.

Mia Hughes opened the pantry door and stared inside at the nearly empty shelves as if expecting more food to suddenly appear. Naturally, that didn't happen. So, with a sigh, she grabbed another package of Top Ramen and headed for the stove.

"Honestly, if I have to eat noodles much longer…" She filled a pan with a cup of water, turned on the fire underneath and watched it, waiting for it to boil. She glanced at the package in her hand. "At least this one is beef flavor. Maybe if I close my eyes while I eat it I can pretend it's a burger."

Well, that image made her stomach growl. She slapped one hand to her belly as if to appease it somehow. It didn't work. She was on the ragged edge and had been for a few weeks now.

As Alex Santiago's housekeeper, she'd had access to the household account at the bank. But she'd been using that money to pay utility bills and the hundreds of other things that had come up since Alex had disappeared. She hadn't had any extra to waste on trivial things like her salary or *food*. So she'd made do with the staples that had been in the pantry and freezer. But the cupboards were practically bare now and only ice cubes were left in the freezer. And it wasn't as if she had money coming in. Even her intern position at Royal Junior High was ending soon. She couldn't go out and get a job, either. What if Alex called the house while she was gone?

"Of course," she reassured herself aloud, "the upside is you've lost five pounds in the past couple of weeks. Downside? I'm ready to chew on a table leg."

Her voice echoed in the cavernous kitchen. The room was spotless, but that was due more to the fact that it hadn't seen much action in the past few months than to Mia's cleaning abilities. Though she took her duties as housekeeper seriously and kept the palatial mansion sparkling throughout. Still, since Alex went missing a few months ago, there hadn't been much for Mia to do in the big house.

The water came to a boil and she stirred in the dried noodles and flavor packet before putting the lid on the pan again then moving it off the heat to steep. While she waited for her lunch, she wandered to the wide windows overlooking the stone patio and the backyard beyond.

From this vantage point, she could also see the rooflines of Alex's neighbors, though the homes in the luxurious subdivision known as Pine Valley weren't crowded together. Each home was different, custom designed and built by the owners, and each sat on a wide, wooded lot so there was plenty of privacy.

Right now though, Mia had too much privacy. She'd been alone in the house since Alex's disappearance. Alone with a phone that hadn't stopped ringing in weeks. Reporters hounded her anytime she left the house, so she rarely left anymore. Since Pine Valley was a gated community, only a few reporters had managed to sneak past the gate guard to annoy her. But she knew that wouldn't last. The longer Alex was gone, the more brazen reporters would become.

A wealthy man going missing was big news. Especially in a town the size of Royal.

She tapped her short, neat fingernails against the cold, smooth, black granite countertop. Mia's stomach did a slow turn and she swallowed hard. Alex had been good to her. He'd given her a job when she'd most needed one. He'd allowed her the space to continue her education and because of that, she was close to getting her counseling degree.

Not only did Mia really owe Alex, she liked him, too. He'd become a good friend as well as her employer, and Mia didn't have many friends. She stared blankly out the window and absently noted the treetops whipping in the cold October wind. She shivered involuntarily and turned her back on the view. She didn't want to think about winter coming and Alex still being gone. She hated not knowing if her friend was safe. Or hurt. But she had to keep positive and believe that Alex would come home.

She also couldn't help worrying about what she was going to do next. The bills had been paid, true. But her tuition was due soon and if Alex wasn't there to pay her…

When the phone rang, she jumped and instinctively reached for it before stopping herself and letting it go to the answering machine. Weeks ago, she'd decided to let the machine pick up so she could screen her calls, in an attempt to avoid reporters and the unceasing questions she couldn't answer.

Still, she was always hoping that somehow the caller might be Alex, telling her he was fine, and sorry he'd worried her and oh, that he was wiring more money into the household accounts. Not very realistic, but Mia's innate optimism was hard to discourage.

The machine kicked on and after the beep, a female voice asked, "Mia? You there? If you're listening, pick up."

Smiling, she snatched up the receiver. "Sophie, hi."

"Still dodging reporters?"

"Every day," she said and leaned back against the counter. Her gaze slid to the backyard again and the trees waving and dancing in the wind. "They don't give up."

"At least they can't get past the gate guard there to bother you in person."

"A few of them have managed, but one call to security and that's taken care of." Though she hated feeling as though she was living through a medieval siege. And she had to admit that living alone in this big house made her a little nervous at night. Yes, Royal was a safe place, and a gated community should have made her feel even more secure. But with Alex gone and the world wondering *why,* Mia was always worried that someone might come sneaking around the house at night, looking for clues or a story. But Mia didn't want her thoughts to go to the dark side. Alex was missing, yes. But she couldn't allow herself to think he was gone forever.

"My offer to come and stay with me for a while still holds, you know."

Sophie Beldon was a good friend. She was also Alex's

assistant, and since his disappearance, the two women had become even closer friends. Together, they'd done all they could to search for Alex, and still had come up empty. But they had another plan now. One that had Mia looking for more information on Dave Firestone, a business rival of Alex's. Of course, she hadn't actually *started* on that plan yet, since she had no idea how to go about it.

"Really, thank you. It's tempting, believe me," Mia confessed. But she couldn't very well move in with her friend and leave Alex's house unguarded. Not to mention that Mia hated the idea of mooching meals from Sophie. She didn't like asking people for anything. She was far too used to doing things herself and she didn't see that changing anytime soon. "It's really nice of you to offer, Sophie. But I really want to be here. In case Alex calls or comes back. Besides, I wouldn't feel right leaving his house vacant."

"Okay. I can understand all of that," Sophie said. "But if you change your mind, the offer stands. So how's everything else going? Is there anything I can do?"

"No, but thanks." Mia cringed a little, hating that her friend knew just how bad off Mia was. The two of them had gone out to lunch just a couple weeks ago and when she'd tried to pay the bill, as a thank-you to Sophie for being so nice, Mia's debit card had been denied. Her bank account hadn't had enough in it to pay for a simple *lunch*. Mortified, Mia had been forced to let Sophie pay for their meals.

She hated this. Hated worrying about money. Hated worrying about Alex. She just wanted her nice, safe, comfortable life back. Was that really so much to ask?

"We're friends, Mia." Sophie's voice was soft and low. "I know you need money. Why won't you let me help you out temporarily? It would just be a loan. When Alex comes home, you can pay me back."

Again, so very tempting. But she didn't know how or when she could pay her friend back, so she couldn't accept the loan. Mia Hughes paid her own way. Always. Heck, she didn't even have a credit card because she paid cash or she didn't buy.

"Sophie," she said on a sigh, "I *really* appreciate the offer. But we've been looking for Alex for months and it's like he vanished off the face of the earth. We don't know when he'll come back." *If ever,* her mind added, but she didn't say it aloud, not wanting to tempt whatever gods might be listening in on them. "I'm fine. Honest. The thing with my debit card was just a bank mistake." Okay, a small lie, but one she would cling to. She didn't want her friend worried about her and she simply could not accept a loan. Mia had been making her own way in the world since she was eighteen, and she wouldn't start looking for handouts now. No matter how hungry she was.

"You have the hardest head," Sophie murmured.

Mia smiled. "Thank you."

"Wasn't a compliment," her friend assured her on a laugh. "But okay. I'll let it go. For *now*."

"I appreciate it."

"That's not why I called, anyway," Sophie said.

Instantly, Mia's friend radar started humming. Sophie had only recently become engaged to Zach Lassiter, Alex's business partner. After a shaky start, the two were so happy together, Mia was afraid that something had gone wrong between them. "Are you and Zach okay?"

"We're fine. He's great. This isn't about us."

"Okay, then," Mia said as she carried the phone across the kitchen, lifted the lid on her lunch and sighed before setting the lid back in place. "What is it about?"

"Remember how we talked about you going out to gather more information on Dave Firestone?"

"Yeah," Mia said. "I don't have anything yet, though. I'm not exactly a private investigator." She'd tried internet searches, but so far all she had found were the sanitized information blurbs you found about *any* wealthy, successful man. And she wasn't sure where to dig up anything else.

"Well," Sophie told her, "I have something. I just got off the phone with Carrie Hardesty."

Mia frowned, trying to place the name. Before she could say she didn't know the woman, Sophie was continuing.

"Carrie's husband, Bill, is a ranch hand on the Battlelands."

"Uh-huh." She still didn't see what this had to do with her or Dave Firestone or why she might be interested. And now she was hungry enough that she was even anxious for her beef-flavored noodle lunch.

"So Bill called Carrie to tell her he'd be home early today because he and Nathan had finished work faster than they'd thought despite an interruption."

"Okay…" Mia had to smile. She still had no idea why this should interest her, but Sophie's voice had taken on that storytelling tone, so she didn't stop her.

"Bill told Carrie that Dave Firestone had shown up to talk to Nathan."

Mia stiffened. Dave had been one of the last people to see her employer before he disappeared. She'd heard the talk around town. She knew that people were wondering if Dave had had something to do with Alex going missing. But she also knew that gossip was the fuel that kept small towns going, so she didn't really put a lot of stock in it.

Still, though, Dave Firestone was wealthy, determined

and too gorgeous to be trusted. Plus, she and Sophie had decided to check the man out.

"What was he talking to Nathan about?"

"Apparently, he went there to find out if he was a suspect in Alex's disappearance."

Mia sucked in a gulp of air. "He did?"

"Yep," Sophie said, then added, "but Bill says Nathan assured Dave that he was officially *not* a suspect."

Disappointment curled in the pit of her stomach. Not that she wished Dave Firestone arrested or anything, but she wanted answers. Soon.

"It's not surprising," Mia said, chewing at her bottom lip. "Dave Firestone is an important man around here. There would have to be *serious* evidence against him for Nathan to keep him as a suspect."

"I know." Sophie sounded as dejected as Mia felt.

"Tell the truth, Soph," Mia said. "Do you really think Dave is involved in Alex's disappearance?"

"Probably not." Her friend sighed.

"Me, either," Mia agreed.

"But he's the only link we have, Mia. I think we should stick to our plan and you should find out anything you can about him. Even if Dave is innocent, he might still know something that he doesn't even know he knows, you know?"

Mia laughed a little. "Sadly, I understood that completely."

Sophie added, "And according to what Bill told Carrie, Nathan admitted that he doesn't have a clue what happened to Alex."

Her heart sank a little further at that news. Of course, she'd thought as much. Nathan Battle had been working this case for months and he'd kept her apprised of his lack of progress. The sheriff and Alex were good friends, so

Mia knew that Nathan was just as much personally involved in the search as he was professionally.

And none of that had helped them find Alex.

In the time Mia had worked for Alex Santiago, she'd
known him to be warm, generous and kind. But he also
had secrets. No one was allowed in his home office, for
example. He had only allowed Mia in to clean once a
month and then only if he was present. And when she
and Sophie had started comparing notes, Sophie had told
her about the secret phone calls Alex had been getting.

Since Alex had been gone, Mia had searched his home
office top to bottom and Sophie had gone through his
emails and phone records, but they hadn't discovered
a thing.

Which told her that either Alex had taken whatever
he'd been safeguarding with him—or whoever had taken
Alex had also gone through that office and taken what
they'd found.

There was that now familiar twist of worry inside.
Where was Alex? Was he hurt? Was he...

"He'll show up," Mia said, cutting short a disturbing
train of thought. "There's a reasonable explanation for all
of this and when Alex comes back, it will all make sense."

"You really believe that, don't you?"

"Absolutely." *Almost,* she added silently. But Mia had
spent so much of her life searching for the silver lining
in dark skies that it was instinctive now. She wouldn't
give up on Alex and, until he was home, she would do
whatever she could to help find him.

Even if it meant eating enough flavored noodles to
sink a battleship.

"Oops," Sophie said suddenly, "Zach's at the door.
He's taking me to lunch at the diner. I'll talk to you later,
okay?"

Mia said goodbye, wishing she were at the diner right now, too. What she wouldn't give for a hamburger, fries and a shake. Sighing, she let the wish go and dumped her noodles into a bowl. Grabbing a fork, she took a bite and tried to swallow her disappointment along with the noodles.

A knock sounded at the front door and Mia took it as a reprieve from her boring lunch. She set the bowl down on the counter and headed through the house. Whoever it was knocked again, faster and louder this time, and she frowned. Did another reporter get past the gate?

At the doorway, she glanced through the glass panes on one side of the heavy door and gaped at the man standing on the porch. Before she could think about it, she yanked the door open and faced Dave Firestone.

He wore black jeans, a dark red collared shirt, a battered brown bomber jacket and scarred boots. He held his hat in one fist, and his dark blond hair ruffled in the wind. His gray eyes locked onto her and Mia felt a jolt of something unexpected sizzle inside her.

"Mia," he said, his voice deep enough to rumble along her spine, "I think we should talk."

Two

"What're you doing here?"

Dave took a good long look at the woman standing there glaring at him. Her long, dark brown hair was, as usual, pulled back from her face and twisted into a messy knot at the back of her neck. She wore faded blue jeans and a long-sleeved, navy blue T-shirt. Her feet were bare and he was surprised to see her toes were painted fire-engine red. Mia Hughes had never seemed like the red nail polish type to him. She was more of a pastel woman, seemingly determined to fade into the background. Or so he'd thought.

Something inside him stirred whether he'd wanted it to or not. He lifted his gaze to hers and the strength of her even stare punched out at him. Her wide blue eyes were unenhanced, yet they still seemed to captivate him.

He didn't want to be captivated.

"I think we should talk. About Alex."

"How did you get in here? The gate guard should have called me."

"I asked him not to." He shrugged. "He knows me, so it wasn't a problem."

"Well, it should have been. He never should have let you in here without contacting me." She folded her arms across her chest.

Dave scowled. He wasn't used to being kept cooling his heels outside. But Mia Hughes was guarding Alex Santiago's front door like a trained pit bull. "I think it'd be better if we went inside to talk."

"First, tell me what this is about." She cocked her head and the toes of one foot began to tap impatiently.

"I'm not your enemy." He took a step closer and noticed that she didn't move back but held her ground. He could admire that even as she frustrated him.

He'd come here to compare notes. To see if she knew anything that might shed a light on Alex's disappearance. But damned if he was going to have this conversation on the porch.

"No," she conceded. "You're not." Her stance relaxed just a fraction. "And I was going to call you later anyway…"

"Is that right?" Surprised, he took another slow look at her and he noted that her eyes were gleaming with something he could only call interest. "About what?"

"About Alex, of course," she told him with a shake of her head.

"Well, it's good that I showed up today, isn't it? Because that's just what I want to talk to you about." He glanced over his shoulder at the empty, meticulously kept grounds before looking back at her. "I want to know if there's anything you know about Alex that you haven't told Nathan Battle."

"Of course there isn't," she said, clearly insulted. "Do you really think I haven't been helping the police? I've done everything I can think of to find Alex."

"That's not what I meant," he said, cutting her off before she could erupt into a full-on rant. Hell, Mia Hughes was usually so quiet he hardly noticed her. But apparently on her own turf she wasn't so reticent.

"It better not be," she countered, and those blue eyes of hers flashed dangerously.

"Look, you don't have to be so defensive. Alex and I weren't exactly friends…"

She laughed shortly.

He frowned and continued, "But that doesn't mean I wish him harm. Hell, right now I want to find him more than anybody in this town."

A second or two passed in tense silence before she sighed and her stance relaxed. "Okay, I can understand that."

"Thanks," he muttered. "So can I come in and talk to you about this now?"

"I guess—" She stopped, looked over his shoulder at the yard and said, "Don't!"

Instantly on alert, Dave whirled around and saw a young man, somewhere in his early twenties, aiming a digital camera at them and clicking away.

"Hey," Dave said, stepping off the porch toward the man.

The guy jumped backward, shaking his head and grinning. He held out a digital recorder and shouted, "Great pictures! Chester Devon from All The News blog. Care to comment?"

"The only comment I have is one you can't print, Chester," Dave told him as he stalked toward the reporter, who had somehow slipped past the Pine Valley gate guard. "And no pictures, either."

"Free country, man," Chester countered, still grinning. "I think my readers will be interested to see Santiago's housekeeper and a suspect in his disappearance looking so cozy…"

His readers, Dave thought. All ten of 'em. Still, if this guy posted pictures to his blog, they would eventually get around and make for more of the kind of scandal he was trying to avoid.

"Cozy? Oh, for—" Mia broke off, then spoke up again, louder. "I'm calling security."

Just what he needed, Dave thought grimly. Not only a reporter but security coming over, too. More food for the local gossips. He couldn't do anything about Mia's call to security, but maybe he could head the reporter off at the pass.

"I'll give you a thousand dollars for your camera."

"Are you serious?" the kid asked with a laugh. "No way, man."

Great. A budding reporter with morals. Or maybe Dave just hadn't hit the guy's price yet. "Five thousand."

Chester wavered.

Dave could see it in the kid's eyes. He was thinking that with five grand in his pocket he could buy a better camera, maybe get a job at a real newspaper.

"I don't know…" Chester ran one hand across the chin sprouting a few stray whiskers. "With this kind of shot, I could maybe get a job at a paper in Houston."

Dave understood the kid's dreams. He'd had a hell of a lot of them himself once. And he'd worked his ass off to make sure they all came true. Didn't mean he was going to be the rung on the ladder beneath Chester's feet, though.

"Haven't you heard, kid? Newspapers are dinosaurs."

"True…"

Dave had the kid now. This guy wasn't enough of a poker player to hide the avarice in his eyes. Everyone had his price, Dave reminded himself. All he had to do was find the right number and this guy would cave. "Call it ten thousand and I want your recorder, too."

"Seriously?" Chester's eyes lit up. "You got a deal, man."

The kid followed while Dave went to his car, grabbed a checkbook from the glove compartment and wrote out a check. He signed it, then held one hand out.

"Let's have 'em," Dave said. The kid laid his camera and the recorder on Dave's palm, then snatched the check. He stared at it for a couple seconds, a slow smile spreading on his face.

"This is seriously cool, man. With this, I can get out of Royal and move to Houston."

"Good." The farther away the better, as far as Dave was concerned. "You should get moving before security gets here and starts asking you uncomfortable questions."

The kid looked up and grinned. "I'm practically gone."

A second later, Chester was sprinting off across the yard, and then lost in the scrub oaks and pines defining the edge of Alex's lot. Probably scaled the fence to get in here, Dave thought and had to give the kid points. He approved of determination. He also approved of getting rid of the kid as easily as possible.

Ten thousand was nothing. He'd have paid twice that to keep Chester quiet. As that thought moved through his mind, Dave realized that his problem might not be completely solved. Just because Chester didn't have photographic proof didn't mean he'd be quiet about Dave's visit to Mia.

So it was time to put a different spin on this. His mind raced with possible solutions and almost instantly, he came up with a workable plan. And if he worked it right, this could actually solve all of his problems. He glanced toward the house, where Mia was again standing in the open front doorway.

A Pine Valley security car pulled up to the curb and a uniformed guard stepped out. Before he could speak, Dave pointed and called out, "He ran toward the ravine."

The security guard hopped back into his car and went in pursuit, but Dave knew that kid was going to evade the guard. He'd gotten *in* to the gated community without being caught, hadn't he?

"What's going on?" Mia stepped out onto the wide, brick porch. "How'd you get him to leave?"

"Made him an offer," Dave said as he walked toward her.

She blinked at him. "You paid him off?"

"I did." Dave took the porch steps and stood directly opposite her. "Bought his camera and recorder."

She looked up at him and he could see disdain in her eyes. "It's easy for you, isn't it? Just buy people if you have to."

"I didn't buy *him*," Dave corrected with a smile. "I bought his stuff."

"And his silence," she added.

"In theory," Dave agreed. "But there's nothing to stop him from spreading this around, despite his lack of evidence."

She wrapped her arms around her middle. "Then paying him off accomplished nothing?"

"It bought me some time," he said, mind still racing.

"Time for what?"

"That's something we should talk about." The more he considered his idea, the better he liked it.

When Alex had disappeared, Dave had hired an investigator. He'd seen the writing on the wall and had known that sooner or later, people would start suspecting *him*. As always, he'd figured it was better to be prepared. The investigator hadn't turned up much information on Alex, but Dave now knew enough about Mia to convince him he could get her to go along with his plan.

"But first," he said, meeting her eyes, "tell me. Do you think I should be a suspect?"

She looked at him for a long, silent minute. He knew she was thinking that over and it irritated him more than a little that it was taking her so long to make a judgment call. "Well?"

She slumped one shoulder against the doorjamb. "Probably not."

His mouth quirked. "A resounding testimonial."

"I don't know you well enough for that."

"Right. Well. That's something else we should talk about." He glanced over his shoulder at the empty yard and scanned the tree line looking for another sneaky reporter. He'd learned over the years that reporters were like ants at a picnic. First you saw one. Then two. Then the picnic was over.

"Can I come in?"

"All right." She stepped back, allowing him to pass by. Dave caught the faintest whiff of a light, floral scent that reminded him of summer.

Once in the house, Dave headed for the living room. He'd been here before, to meet with Alex. It was a nice house. Plush but tasteful. Cream-colored walls, bold, dark red-leather sofas and chairs and heavy dark tables. The windows looked out across the yard and were tinted, making it easy to see out but almost impossible to see in.

"What's this about?" Mia asked.

Dave turned to look at her. "I'll come right to the point. Alex being missing is hard on both of us."

"Is that right?" she asked. "How are you suffering?"

"Gossip." He tossed his hat onto the nearest couch, then shoved both hands into his jeans pockets. "The whispers and rumors about me might screw up a deal I'm working on."

"A deal?" Her eyes widened. "Alex is missing and you're worried about a deal?"

"Life goes on." He said it flatly. Cold and hard. He saw reaction glitter in her eyes and he could appreciate that. He admired loyalty. "I didn't have anything to do with Alex's disappearance and I don't think you did, either."

She laughed shortly. "Well, thanks very much. I didn't know I was a suspect."

"Why wouldn't you be? You're his housekeeper."

"You can't be serious."

"Why not?"

The look on her face was pure astonishment. And no, he wasn't serious. No one would ever suspect Mia Hughes of anything illegal. She was quiet, shy—or at least she had always seemed so until this morning—and she didn't exactly come off as a femme fatale. First, she was too skittish to be involved in any kind of plot. She'd blow the whole thing in minutes if it came down to it. And secondly, she was just too all-American-girl-next-door.

Shiny red toenails notwithstanding.

But throwing her off balance was just what Dave needed. Because he needed her. In fact, she was damn near perfect. The plan that had occurred to him while he was dealing with the would-be reporter actually depended on her. If she agreed—and she *would*—then he had a way to explain him being here—should the kid decide to go ahead and post to his blog anyway. And it might also appease Thomas Buckley and his narrow view of life. What Dave needed was a wife. Not a real wife, mind you. But something temporary. Something that would buy him the time he needed to clinch the deal he wanted. But the women he normally went out with would never convince Thomas Buckley they were the home-and-hearth type.

Mia Hughes, on the other hand, was just the woman for the job.

"I've got a proposition for you."

"And why should I listen?"

"Because it benefits both of us," he said simply. "And you're too smart to say no before you've heard me out."

Her lips pressed together and her eyes narrowed. "Flattery?"

"Truth."

She took a breath and blew it out again in a huff. "Okay, I'm listening."

He rubbed one hand across his face, then waved at the big red-leather sofa. "Have a seat."

Obviously still on guard, she walked to the couch and perched on the edge, clearly ready to bolt the moment he said the wrong thing. Well, Dave wasn't about to blow this. He had never once gone into a negotiation blind and today was no different. Didn't matter that he hadn't come here with this plan in mind. He was flexible enough that he could turn any situation around to his favor.

Dave stood in front of the couch, looking down at Mia. "I need a wife."

"*Excuse* me?" She started to rise but he waved her back down.

"Relax," he said. "I'm talking more of a fantasy wife than the real thing."

Fantasy? It was laughable, really. In what parallel universe would Mia Hughes be *anyone's,* let alone Dave Firestone's, fantasy? This was either some bizarre joke or he really was nuts.

"Relax?" Mia jumped to her feet, unable to sit still a moment longer. She and Sophie had wanted to check Dave out, which was the main reason Mia had allowed him into the house in the first place. But if she'd known what he was going to say she'd have left him on the porch and thrown the deadbolt to keep him out. "I really think you should go."

He shook his head and stood his ground. He was so tall that even with Mia on her feet, he was looking down at her.

"Not until you've heard me out."

"Oh, I think I've heard enough," Mia assured him. She tried to move past him to lead him to the door, but he laid one hand on her arm and stopped her.

She felt the burn of his hand on her skin and told herself to get over it. To pay no attention. But inside, her hormones were concentrating on that rush of heat. This was so not good. He was too tall. Too gorgeous. Too sure of himself.

He smiled as if he knew what she was thinking, feeling. Well, she'd wanted to know more about Dave Firestone. Now she knew just how formidable he was. And she was worried he was just a little crazy.

His hand fell from her arm and, despite her best intentions, Mia missed that blast of heat from his fingertips. Okay, maybe he wasn't nuts. But he was…distracting.

Then he was talking again. "I'm working on a deal with Texas Cattle—the best company in the state for beef buying—but the head of the company is a pretty conservative guy. He only deals with family men. Thinks they're more stable or something. Anyway, the upshot is, I need a temporary wife—or at the very least a fiancée. Just long enough for me to seal this deal. Once that's done, we'll 'break up' and it's over."

"You're crazy."

"Just determined," he assured her. "I know money's got to be tight with Alex gone."

She stiffened and lifted her chin.

"With him wherever the hell he is, you're not being paid and," he paused to let that sink in, then added, "the household account you have access to is almost dry."

Stunned, she whispered, "How do you know that?"

"Same way I know you've got school loans to pay off, tuition due in a month and that your debit card was declined at the diner last month."

Embarrassment roared to life inside her and she felt heat crawl up her cheeks to flood her face. Bad enough that her friend Sophie knew how little money she had. Having Dave Firestone know it was almost too much to take.

The question was, *how* did he know it?

"Are you spying on me?"

He laughed. "Hardly. I had an investigator looking for Alex and, since you're the man's housekeeper, you got checked out, too."

A wave of outrage crested over the embarrassment, smothering it completely. "You had no right."

"Whether I did or not, it's done," he said easily, as if

invading her privacy meant nothing to him. And, it probably didn't. "The point is, you need money. I need a wife."

"What?"

"I think you heard me."

"You can't be serious." This was, hands down, the most bizarre conversation she'd ever had. A *wife?* He wanted to *pay* her to marry him?

"I don't joke when I'm making a deal."

He stood there, tall and gorgeous and completely at ease, as if he owned the world—and from what she knew of him, he *did* own a good chunk of it. But his attitude was so confident, so…superior. As if he knew absolutely that she would agree. Well, he had a surprise coming.

"No deal," she said and instantly felt a sense of righteous satisfaction. Sure she was out of money and eating Top Ramen and daydreaming about hamburgers. But she wasn't so desperate that she was willing to sell herself to a man who already thought far too highly of himself. "I'm not interested in being your wife…real, temporary *or* fantasy."

"Sure you are," he said easily and gave her a half smile that tipped up one corner of his mouth and flashed a dimple at her. "You don't want to be interested but you are. Why wouldn't you be? Mia, this is a good deal for both of us."

She hated that he was right. She didn't want to be interested but she was. The whole situation was too strange. His offer was crazy. And yet…she looked around the empty living room. This place had been her first real home in too many years to count. She had cared for it and watched over it in Alex's absence. But the truth was, if he didn't come home soon, she didn't know what she would do.

The money was almost gone. Soon, she wouldn't be

able to pay the monthly bills. She had no idea what she'd do then.

People in town were already speculating about Alex's disappearance. This couldn't possibly help the situation.

"What about the local gossips?" She shook her head. "Don't you think they'll be a little suspicious of your sudden engagement plan?"

He frowned. "Hadn't considered that," he mumbled. "But it doesn't matter. In this town, the gossips love a good romantic story better than anything else. They'll glom on to our whirlwind romance and let go of suspicion."

He was probably right, she told herself. The main gossip chain in Royal was female and they were more interested in fairy-tale romantic stories than anything else. This might actually take the heat off them where Alex's disappearance was concerned.

Oh, God, she didn't know what to do.

"Think about it, Mia," he said and she could only imagine the snake in the Garden of Eden had sounded just as convincing. "This would solve both of our problems."

"I don't think so," she said, though her grumbling stomach disagreed. Still, she wasn't starving. She had a roof over her head and noodles in the pantry. And she had her pride, right?

Oh, God. Her pride was already shattered. Dave Firestone knew she was out of money. Knew how desperate she was. And he knew just what kind of temptation to use against her.

"You're considering it."

"I'm considering lots of things," she told him. "Like throwing you out, finishing my lunch and then maybe polishing the kitchen floor. Lots of options."

"So I see," he said, a slow, knowing smile curving his mouth. "Any idea which one you're going to go with?"

"I haven't decided yet," she said on a sigh.

"Let me make it easy for you, then." He moved in closer and Mia felt caught in the steady gaze of his eyes. "I'll pay you ten thousand dollars to pretend to be my fiancée until I get that deal with TexCat."

"Ten thousand—" She broke off, stunned at the offer. Just the thought of that much money made her head swim. She could pay the bills. Take care of Alex's house until he got back. She could make a payment on her tuition and finish her counseling degree.

She could buy *meat*.

"And," he said.

"There's more?"

"Yeah. Along with the ten thousand," he said, voice dropping to a low, seductive level, "I'll pay off your college loans. You could start your career out fresh. No debt."

Staggered, Mia actually swayed on her feet. That was a tremendous offer. If she didn't have to pay back school loans, she could build a life for herself much more quickly. Glaring at him, she said, "You're really evil, aren't you?"

He grinned, fast and wicked. "Just a master negotiator."

He was that, she told herself.

"Still want to polish the kitchen floor?"

She frowned at him. "Ten thousand dollars."

"That's right."

"And my loans paid off."

"You got it."

"How long would we have to pretend?"

He shrugged. "Shouldn't take more than a month."

Nodding, she tried to think clearly despite the racing, churning thoughts in her brain. "A month as your fiancée."

"Yeah."

Her eyes narrowed on him. "And what does this 'pretending' entail?"

It took a second for him to get what she meant and then he laughed shortly. "Trust me, your virtue is safe. When I want sex, I don't have to pay for it."

She could believe that. Heck, just standing next to him had her skin buzzing. He probably had women throwing themselves in his path all the time. Which made her wonder why he hadn't asked one of the no doubt *legions* of women littering his bed to be his pretend fiancée.

Maybe, she thought, none of them needed money as much as she did. Well, that was depressing.

Just to be sure of where she stood, Mia said, "Then we agree. No sex."

"Agreed."

She kept talking. "No touching of any kind. No kissing—"

"Hold on," he stopped her in midstream. "We have to convince this guy we're a real couple. So there *will* be touching. And kissing. And there will be you looking at me with adoration."

She laughed.

He frowned.

"Fine, fine," she said, waving a hand at him. "I'll be a good fiancée and the occasional touch or kiss—in public—is okay."

"Then we have a deal." He held out one hand to her and waited for her to take it. "You should come to the ranch for dinner tonight. We can work out the details there."

Nodding, Mia slid her hand into his and couldn't help feeling that just maybe she was swimming in waters *way* too deep for her.

Three

Dave pulled the collar of his dark brown leather jacket up higher on his neck and squinted as he climbed out of his 4x4. He took a deep breath, dragging the cold air into his lungs with a smile. Just being on his ranch settled him like nothing else could.

Land swept out to the horizon. He took a long look around, taking in the wooded area crowded with wild oaks. The stock watering pond shimmered a dark blue beneath the lowering sun and the grassland was dotted with Black Angus cattle. He tossed a glance at the dark, cloud-studded Texas sky. October was rolling in cold, signaling a rough winter to come.

But he was prepared. No matter what Mother Nature threw at him, Dave was ready. He had the ranch he'd always wanted, more money than he knew what to do with and the future was looking good—except for one small fly in his proverbial ointment. But, he reminded himself, he'd found a way to take care of that, too. Who would have guessed that Mia Hughes would be the solution to his problem?

One thing he'd learned over the years, though, was that sometimes answers came when you least expected them. And he was quick enough to take advantage of opportunities when they presented themselves.

He'd worked for years to get this ranch. He'd sacrificed, wheeled and dealed and risked more than he cared to remember. But he'd finally done it. He'd reclaimed the life that should have been his from the beginning. And he'd done it in style.

Damned if he'd be defeated now.

His ranch would be a success without TexCat and he knew it. But the bottom line was they were the best, and he wanted that contract to prove his ranch was the best. It was a milestone of sorts for Dave and he wouldn't rest until he'd reached it.

Walking away from his 4x4, he tugged his hat down lower over his eyes, stuffed his hands into his jacket pockets and headed for his ranch foreman, Mike Carter. Somewhere in his late fifties, Mike was tall and lean and the best ranch manager in Texas.

"Hey, boss," he said as Dave approached. "We found those ten yearling calves we were missing huddled together in Dove canyon."

With this much open land, cattle tended to wander, following the grass. And the young ones were always straying from the safety of the herd, going where they were easy prey for wolves and coyotes. It was inevitable to lose a few head to predators every year, but Dave was glad to hear they'd recovered the stock safely this time. "Good news. You got all of 'em?"

"All but one." Mike pulled his hat off and tipped his face into the wind. "Wolves got that one. Found the signs."

Nodding, Dave frowned. The one thing he did *not* have control over was nature. If wolves wanted to pick off a calf, there wasn't much he could do about it. Losing one was hard, but they'd saved nine, so he'd have to accept that and be grateful for it.

"Fine. But I don't want to lose anymore. Let's move the herd farther from the canyons, make it harder for the young ones to wander off."

Mike grinned. "Already done. Got a couple of the boys moving cattle to the west pasture."

"Good." Dave glanced around, his gaze sweeping across his land, and he knew he'd never tire of the view. Acres of good Texas earth stretched out for miles in all directions. There were rolling hills, meadows that ran so thick with sweet grass the herd couldn't manage to eat it all. There were wooded acres of oaks, a dozen stock ponds and a couple of lakes with the best damn trout in Texas. It was everything he'd planned for, and now Dave just needed to seal the ranch's success.

"I bought some first-calf heifers this morning," Dave said, remembering the phone call he'd made before setting out to talk to Nathan and Mia. "They'll be here by Friday and should start calving in the next couple of weeks."

"Good deal," Mike said. "We can always use new stock. But what about that new beef contract with Tex-Cat?"

Frowning, Dave said, "I'm working on it. Should know something soon. Meanwhile, start culling the herd, separating out the stays from the gos."

"We'll do it."

When Mike went back to work, Dave told himself he should do the same. Ranch work wasn't all done outside.

There were papers to go over, bills to pay, calls to make. Plus, he had a "fiancée" coming over for dinner and he'd better let his housekeeper, Delores, know.

He drove back to the main house, but rather than go inside, he walked to his favorite spot on the Royal Round Up ranch. He skirted the flagstone decking that ran the length of the sprawling ranch house, walked around the massive free-form pool and took the rough-hewn stairs to the rooftop, wraparound deck.

From that vantage point, he could see for miles. His gaze slid across the beautifully maintained grounds, the stocked trout lake that lay just beyond the pool and then to the massive guesthouse he'd had built two years before.

The guesthouse was an exact replica of the ranch house that had been his family's until he was ten years old. Until his father had lost the ranch and then took off, leaving Dave and his mother on their own. He'd built the damn guesthouse as a trophy. A way of reclaiming the past. And as a way of giving his mom a place to call her own. A place where she could take it easy for a change. But the hardheaded woman refused to leave her small apartment in Galveston. So the completely furnished, three bedroom, three bath guesthouse stood empty.

Until Dave could change his mom's mind. Which he would manage to do eventually. Hell, he'd gotten Mia Hughes to agree to his proposition, hadn't he?

The wind pushed at him as it raced across the open prairie, carrying the scent of grass and water and *land*. His land. He felt like a damn king when he stood up here surveying the stronghold he'd built.

He slapped both hands onto the thick, polished wood rail and leaned forward, letting his gaze move over the view. His hands tightened on the railing in front of him as he eased the jagged edges inside him by staring out at his property. Good Texas pastureland stretched to the horizon and it was all *his*. He'd come a hell of a long way in the past several years and there was more to do yet.

Landing that deal for his cattle was paramount for the rest of his plans. He wanted his ranch supplying the beef to the best restaurants and organic grocers in the state of Texas. And TexCat would help him accomplish that. Without that contract, Dave's plans would take a lot longer to come together. And if this bargain with Mia worked as he thought it would, the deal was as good as done.

Smiling to himself, he gave the railing a slap, took one last look at the vista rolling out into the distance and then took the stairs down. He'd head back to the main house and get some work done before it was time to meet with his fiancée.

Scowling, he realized it might take some time to get used to even *thinking* the word *fiancée*.

He ducked his head into the wind and muttered, "A hell of a thing to need a *wife* to make a deal."

Mia didn't know what to wear.

Was there a protocol for having dinner with a pretend fiancé who was *paying* you to pretend to love him so he could sell cattle? She laughed a little. It sounded bizarre even to her, and she was living it.

"Oh, God. I'm letting him *pay* me."

Her chin hit her chest and she took a long, deep breath to try to steady the nerves jumping in the pit of her stomach. It didn't help. Sighing, she flipped through the tops hanging in her closet and listened to the clatter of the hangers sliding on the wooden rod. She wasn't finding anything. It had been so long since she'd been on an actual *date*—she stopped short at that thought.

This wasn't a date. This was...

"I don't even know what this is," she muttered and grabbed a dark blue cable-knit sweater from the closet. Why she was worried about this was beyond her. What did it matter what she looked like? It wasn't as if she was trying to impress Dave Firestone, for heaven's sake.

"Exactly," she told herself. "This is business. Pure and simple. He didn't ask you to dinner because you swept him off his feet."

Mia laughed at the very idea. She was so not the type of woman to catch Dave's eye. No doubt he went for the shiny, polished women with nice hair, beautiful clothes and the IQ of a baked potato.

Potato.

"Oh, God, I hope he has potatoes at dinner." She sighed again. "And steak. I bet there's going to be steak. He's a rancher, right, so he's bound to like beef."

Her mouth watered and her stomach rumbled so loudly it took her mind off the nerves still bouncing around in the pit of her belly. Shaking her head, she carried the sweater out of the closet and tossed it onto the edge of her bed.

Since taking the job with Alex Santiago as his housekeeper, Mia had been living in the private suite of rooms off the kitchen of the big house. Living room, bedroom and bath, her quarters were lavishly furnished and completely impersonal but for the few personal touches she had scattered around the place.

Mia had been travelling light most of her life, so she didn't have a lot of *things*. There were a few photographs and a ratty stuffed bear she'd had since she was a child. But mostly, there were books. Textbooks, paperback thrillers and romances, biographies and sci-fi novels. Mia loved them all and hated to get rid of a book. She'd recently treated herself to an ebook reader, but as much as she loved the convenience, she preferred the feel of a book in her hands.

"And you're stalling," she told herself as she walked to the bathroom. Staring into the mirror, she looked into her own eyes and gave herself a stern talking-to. "You're the one who agreed to this, so you're going to suck it up and do what you have to do. It's only temporary. One month and you'll have enough money to pay the regular household bills and no school loans hanging over your head. Of course, if Alex isn't found by the end of the month, then you're right back where you started...." She stopped that thought as soon as it popped into her head. Alex would be found. And with the money from Dave she could pay pesky things like the water and gas and electric bills. Thank heaven Alex didn't have a mortgage on the place because she didn't know how she would have made the payment.

One month. She could do this. And get her life back on track.

Sounded good, she thought as she picked up the hair dryer and turned it on. She ran her fingers through her long, dark brown hair as the hot air pushed at it. Okay, she was nervous. But she could do this. How hard could it be to pretend to be crazy about Dave Firestone?

At that thought, she remembered the buzz of something...interesting she'd felt when he'd laid his hand on her arm. Thoughtful, she set the dryer down onto the pale cream granite counter and stared at her own image in the mirror. "Probably didn't mean anything," she assured her reflection. "I was probably just weak from hunger. Any man would have brought on the same reaction. It just happened to be Dave."

The woman in the mirror looked like she didn't believe her and Mia couldn't blame her. It had sounded lame to her, too.

Shaking her head, she walked back to the bedroom, grabbed a pair of dark wash jeans from her dresser drawer and tugged them on over a pair of pale pink bikinis. When she had them zipped and snapped, she pulled on a white silk tank top, then covered it with the dark blue sweater. She stepped into a pair of black half boots, then walked back to the bathroom.

Her hair was still damp, so instead of the tight knot she usually wore it in, Mia quickly did up a single, thick braid that hung to the middle of her back. She didn't bother with makeup. Why pretend to be something she wasn't? There was going to be enough pretending for her over the next few weeks. Might as well hold on to *some* form of reality.

With that thought in mind, she flipped off the light and walked through her apartment. She stopped long enough to snatch up her black leather shoulder bag, then she was out the door and into her car before she could talk herself out of the craziest thing she'd ever done in her life.

An hour later, she was so grateful she hadn't changed her mind about coming.

"Steak done the way you like it?" Dave asked from across the table.

"It was perfect," Mia answered, though the truth was, she had been so hungry, if they had trotted a cow through the living room, she might have gnawed on it raw. At the moment though, she was comfortably full of steak, a luscious baked potato swimming in butter and sour cream and the best fresh green beans she'd ever eaten.

She sighed and lifted her coffee cup for a sip.

Dave was watching her, and she noted one corner of his mouth quirk.

"What's so amusing?" she asked.

"You," he admitted. "I've never seen a woman enjoy a meal so much."

She flushed a little, then shrugged. No point in pretending she hadn't been hungry. He had already checked her out, so he probably knew just how many packages of Top Ramen were left in the pantry. "Maybe you should broaden your horizons a little. Date a woman who eats more than half a leaf of lettuce."

He grinned. "Might have a point."

Her eyes met his and in the soft light of the dining room, his gray eyes looked as deep and mysterious as fog on a cold winter night. He wore a black sweater, black jeans and his familiar, scarred boots and he looked, Mia thought, dangerously good.

"I like your house," she blurted when his steady stare was beginning to make her twitch.

"Thanks," he said and glanced around the dining room. Mia did the same, taking another long look at her surroundings. Sadly, between her still unsteady nerves and the fact that she'd been so seduced by the scent of the meal, she hadn't taken the time to really get a good look at the room.

One thing Mia had noticed was that every doorway in the house was arched. There was a lot of wood and a lot of stone throughout—definitely a man's house. Even the dining room was oversized, and somehow so...male. The table could easily seat twenty. Heavy oak, the table's thick edges were covered with intricately carved vines and flowers. Each chair boasted the same carvings and the seats were upholstered in dark red leather.

A black wrought iron chandelier provided the lighting, and framed paintings of the Texas landscape dotted the walls. Her gaze slid back to meet Dave's and she felt that jump of nerves again. Well, she was going to have to get over that.

"Come on," he said, pushing up from the table and holding out one hand to her. "I'll show you around. You'll have to know the place if you're going to be my fiancée."

"Okay…" She turned her head toward the closed door leading to the kitchen.

"What is it?" he asked.

Mia looked at him. "No dessert?"

Surprised, Dave laughed and this time it was real laughter, not the sardonic smirk or the condescending chuckle Mia was more familiar with. Amazing how real emotion could completely change Dave's features from gorgeous to heart-stopping.

Oh, Mia hadn't counted on this. Okay, yes, she'd felt that mild sizzle earlier today when Dave had touched her. But that could've been static electricity, too. In fact, she hadn't felt any interest in a man in so long, she'd begun to think she was immune.

Now was not a good time to find out she wasn't.

"Come on," Dave said again, "I'll take you on a tour, then we'll have dessert in the great room."

"All right," she said, and stood, putting her hand in his. She determinedly ignored the fresh sizzle she felt when his hand met hers. Instead, she focused on the promise of sugar in her near future.

He kept a firm grip on her hand as they walked from the dining room and Mia idly listened to the sounds of their boot heels on the tile floor. When she'd first moved in as Alex's housekeeper, she had been so impressed with the flawless beauty of his home. It was elegant and lovely in an understated way that she'd come to admire over the past couple years. But now, seeing Dave's house, she was bowled over by the sheer scope of the place.

It was lovely in a completely different way from Alex's home. This was rustic, and as she'd already thought, completely *male* in an unapologetic, straightforward manner. The floor tiles were beige and brown with splashes of cream to lighten the feel. The walls were a mix of stone and wood and textured, cream-colored plaster. Dark beams bracketed the high ceilings and arched windows boasted leaded glass. Every door was a curved slab of heavy, dark wood that made Mia think of centuries-old English estates.

"You've seen the dining room and the great room," Dave was saying as he led her down a long hallway. "This is the main living room." He kept walking, then paused to open another door. "My office."

She caught a quick glimpse before he was moving on again and saw more dark wood, a large desk and a stone fireplace that looked as wide as her living room at home.

"This is the game room." He stopped again, swung a door open and Mia saw a huge flat-screen TV hanging on the wall, a pool table, a couple of vintage video games and a well-stocked bar.

"You've got PAC-MAN."

"Yeah." He looked at her. "I'm surprised you know the game."

"I spent a lot of time in arcades as a kid," she said and let it go at that. No reason to tell him that while her father was earning a living playing poker in bars and casinos, she was left to her own devices and had become a champion at video games.

A flicker of admiration shone in his eyes. "We'll have to have a match sometime."

They passed through the foyer and Mia glanced at the

clear panes of glass arranged in a wide arch around the double front door. It was dark out, naturally, but there were solar lights lining the walkway to the circular driveway. When she'd arrived, she had noticed the number of outbuildings. There was a barn, a paddock and several smaller houses all at a distance from the main house. The Royal Round Up was a prosperous, working ranch that no doubt required dozens of employees.

The whole place was huge. Dave was even more wealthy than she had guessed him to be. Which explained how he could offer to pay off her school loans without so much as blinking. She had no idea how to live like this. Not even how to *pretend* to live like this. Yes, she worked for Alex and he was wealthy, too, but in his house, she was the housekeeper. She wasn't expected to act as though it was her own home. To act as though living like this was second nature to her. The more she saw, the more anxious Mia became. What had she gotten herself into?

"This hall takes you back around to the kitchen," Dave said, and she glanced where he pointed. More art on the walls. More miles of gleaming tiles. She would never be able to find her way around this house. Plus, she didn't even have the kind of wardrobe the fiancée of a wealthy man would wear. She didn't fit into this world and she knew it. How could she possibly pull this off and convince anyone? Maybe, she told herself, it would be best if she just backed out of this deal right now. It wouldn't be a complete waste; she *had* gotten a terrific steak dinner out of it.

An inner voice complained that without Dave, she'd be paying back college loans for the rest of her life. But surely that was the saner approach to take. Nodding, she braced herself to tell Dave that she simply couldn't do it.

She'd thank him and get out fast before she could change her mind.

Just then, he stopped in front of another door and threw it open. "This is the library."

If he continued speaking, she didn't hear him. All she could think was *books.* Acres of *books.* Floor to ceiling shelves lined with thousands of *books* ringed the cavernous room. There were couches, chairs, tables and reading lamps. There was a fireplace and giant windows overlooking the front lawn. With sunlight streaming through that glass, the room would be beautiful. The spines of the books lining the shelves must shine like rainbows, she thought, moving into the room and turning in a slow circle to take it all in.

"Finally found something to impress you, huh?"

"Hmm? What?" She glanced at him and smiled. A man who had a room like *this* couldn't possibly be a bad guy. Maybe she should rethink her earlier decision. "Oh. It's wonderful. Are you in here all the time?"

He leaned one shoulder against the doorjamb and shrugged. "Not as much as I'd like. Usually I'm in my office or out on the property."

But he loved the room, she could tell. And this one, beautiful library was enough to convince Mia that she might be able to handle this, after all. They at least had books in common.

"Oh, if I had this room, I'd never leave it."

"Not even for dessert?" he teased.

She gave him another smile. "Okay, maybe I'd have to leave once in a while, but," she added, looking around her again at the thousands of books, "I'd always come back."

"Steak, dessert, video games and books." Dave looked at her for a long minute. "You're an interesting woman, Mia."

Weird, he probably meant, she assured herself. But that was all right. She could live with that.

She met his gaze squarely. "Well, you're a surprise, too."

"Yeah? In what way?"

"I never would have thought *you* would have a room like this."

He gave her a sardonic smile. "I should probably be insulted."

She shook her head. "Not really. I guess it's just the impression you give off."

"Which is?"

"A man who only cares about the next deal."

"That's not far wrong."

"No," she said, "I've seen this room now. So I know there's more to you than that."

He frowned a little as if he didn't enjoy her delving into his psyche, no matter how shallowly she went.

"Maybe this room is just for show," he said.

"No, again," she said and leaned out to run the tips of her fingers along the richly detailed leather spines of the closest books. "That table alongside the chair by the fire has a book on it. With a bookmark at the midpoint."

He nodded thoughtfully. "Okay, good eye."

"You can't fool me now," she told him. "Any man who can appreciate a room like this is more than he appears to be."

"Don't count on that," he said softly. Then, shaking his head, he added, "You know, I always thought you were the shy, quiet type."

"I'm surprised you thought about me at all."

"Well, then, we're both surprised tonight," he said,

and stood back to allow her to pass him into the hallway. "Should be an interesting month."

"Or," she muttered as she slipped past him, her shoulder brushing across his chest, "a train wreck."

Four

"My bedroom and four guest rooms are upstairs," he said, and waited a moment before adding, "Shall we continue the tour?"

"Oh, I think I've seen enough," Mia assured him. Not only was she feeling uncomfortable about this whole thing, there was something else going on, as well. Some weird flashes of heat kept shooting through her and every time he touched her hand, she felt a buzz all the way down to her bones. No, seeing his bedroom probably wasn't a good idea.

"Your call," he said as he reached for her hand again. "But you should be familiar with the whole house. Be comfortable here. Learn your way around so you can convince anyone that you're used to being here."

"I don't know that I'm that good an actress."

Mia was really trying not to feel the heat between

them, but his hand over hers was strong and warm and hard to ignore.

He was talking again, his deep voice seeming to echo off the high ceilings. "Good actress or not, you're motivated to make this happen."

"True," she said, because why deny it? They both knew the only reason she was here with him right now was because he'd made her an offer impossible to refuse. Which, really, Mia told herself, she should always keep at the front of her mind.

Anytime she was tempted to think of Dave as charming or when he seemed to really like her…she had to remember that he was simply playing a role. Getting into the whole act of pretending to be crazy about her. That, and the fact that he was clearly a master manipulator.

"So does this house come with a map?"

"You'll get used to it," he said.

"Highly doubtful," Mia countered as he led her toward the great room.

"You haven't even seen the outside yet."

"Why such a big house?" she asked. "I mean, you live here alone." She looked around. The place was gorgeous but massive. "What's the point of having so much room for one man?"

He stopped walking and studied her for a long moment. "Did you ask Alex the same question about his place?"

She laughed. "This is easily twice as big as Alex's house."

He gave her a quick grin filled with satisfaction. "It is, isn't it?"

Were men *always* competing? she wondered idly. Were they always striving to keep one pace ahead of whoever they saw as their rival?

"So there is no point to this giant house."

"It was the best," he said simply. "I always get the best."

Until now, Mia thought, wondering again why he'd chosen *her* for this subterfuge. Of course, maybe he didn't know any other really desperate women. Another wave of depression swamped her but she pushed through it to keep her mind on what was happening.

"Still think you should see my bedroom," he said.

"I don't see why."

He glanced back at her and gave her a half smile. "Because you're my loving fiancée who would be completely at ease there."

"Right." Not at ease. Not even close. Her stomach started jumping again and lower portions of her body heated to a slow boil.

In a house this size, she told herself, you could have five or six kids running around and still find acres of room to have some space to yourself. When she was a child, she would have loved a house like this. Especially that library. She would have camped out in that room and been deliriously happy.

Of course, when she was a kid, she would have been ecstatic with any house to call her own. A place where she could belong, bring friends. A room of her own to do homework in or daydream. Instead, she'd moved from hotel to motel back and forth across the country as her father followed the next poker game.

Watching Dave, she had to wonder if he was actually happy here. Or if the house was more a *trophy.* A tangible sign of success.

When they walked into the massive great room, Mia paused a moment to look around. The fire had been lit in the hearth and the snap and hiss of flames devour-

ing wood whispered in the air. A few of the table lamps
had been turned on, and pools of golden light fell across
the furniture. Tan leather couches and chairs sprawled
alongside light oak tables. Wide windows at the front of
the house would, in daylight, afford an amazing view of
the yard. Now, though, night crouched on the other side
of the glass and the sea of blackness was broken only by
the soft glow of the solar lights placed along the walkway.

Dave took a seat on one of the couches and reached
for the white thermal coffeepot sitting on the low table
in front of him.

Mia's gaze fell to the plate of brownies and cupcakes
beside the coffeepot, and she walked over to take a seat
within reach of the dessert tray. She picked up a napkin
and a brownie and took a bite. Chocolate melted on her
tongue and she closed her eyes and sighed a little in appreciation. When she opened her eyes again, Mia found
Dave watching her. His gray eyes looked smokier than
ever and his lips were tight. Tension radiated from him.
"Is everything okay?"

Dave took a breath and blew it out again. He was suddenly rock hard and in pain. Who would have thought it?
Mia Hughes wasn't exactly the kind of woman he usually
went for. There was no cleavage displayed. No short skirt
to afford him a view of silky skin. No lipsticked mouth
to tempt him. Not even a damn seductive smile.

And yet when she'd taken a bite of that damned
brownie and made that soft groan of pleasure, his body
had lit up like a lightning strike.

"Yeah," he said shortly as he fought to get a grip.
"Fine." He poured them each a cup of coffee, then reached
for a manila envelope lying on the table. Back to business, he told himself. Keep focused.

He pulled out a single sheet of paper, glanced at it then handed it to her along with a pen.

"What's this?" She took the paper but kept her gaze on his.

"Our agreement in writing. We'll both sign it so there won't be any questions later."

"A contract?"

"Easier all the way around to have everything laid out in black-and-white." Dave wasn't the kind of man to leave anything to chance. If there was one thing he'd learned over the years, it was that most people couldn't be trusted.

He took a sip of coffee and watched her as she skimmed the document.

Dave knew what it said. He would pay her ten thousand dollars up-front. All school loans to be paid off at the end of the month or the closure of his deal with Tex-Cat, whichever came first. In return, she would feign love for him and do everything necessary to make sure this game worked.

She read it through and he saw her wince once or twice. He wondered what had brought on the reaction, then reminded himself that it didn't matter. They had a deal and he'd hold her to it.

"Questions?"

"One." She looked at him. "How do we explain to people in town that all of a sudden we're engaged? I mean, the whole point of this is to avoid gossip and scandal, right?"

He'd considered that, of course. Dave always thought through any proposition. "We'll say it's a whirlwind kind of thing. Unexpected. Passionate."

She laughed and he frowned. Not the reaction he'd expected. Outrage, maybe, or even embarrassment. But not outright laughter. "What's so funny?"

"You," she said as she shook her head and took another

bite of brownie. She sighed a little and his groin tightened even more. If she had more than the one brownie, he might explode.

"No one's going to believe that," Mia told him. "I'm so not the type of woman a man like you would go nuts for."

He studied her for a long minute and had to admit that she had a point. If he'd noticed her at all over the past couple of years, it was only as Alex's housekeeper. He'd never looked beyond her quiet demeanor or the plain way she dressed and fixed her hair. His mistake, he thought now, looking into blue eyes that were the color of a Texas summer sky. He'd never noticed her full lower lip, the dimple in her right cheek or her quick wit. Mainly because he'd never bothered.

He was bothering now, though, and he sort of wished he wasn't.

"Okay, you have a point."

"Thanks very much."

He ignored the sting in her words and said, "Mainly it's the clothes. You need to go shopping."

She laughed again and that dimple winked at him. "With what? If you think I'm going to spend my ten thousand dollars on dressy clothes I won't need when the month is over, you're crazy."

"Fine." He nodded sharply. He could see her side of this. He took the paper from her, made a quick note and initialed it. "We'll make it ten thousand for you, five thousand for shopping expenses—"

"Five—"

"And your school loans. Deal?"

"Of course not! I'm not letting you buy me clothes."

"It's an act, Mia," he told her, voice firm and unyielding. "I'm paying you to play a part. I'm only giving you the props you need to make it real."

She shook her head and he sensed her pulling away. She might be sitting right beside him, but mentally she was out on the road, driving home and putting all of this behind her. So he put a stop to it.

"We agreed on this deal. This is just another facet of it. Nothing's changed but your wardrobe." He looked her over again and said, "You should go into Houston. They'll have more to offer."

"Any suggestions on what you'd like me to wear?"

He heard the sarcasm and again, he ignored it. "Tailored clothes would be best, I think. Get a couple of cocktail dresses while you're at it."

She huffed out a breath and stared at the agreement in her hand. "I don't know."

"Sign it, Mia," he said, holding out a pen. "One month and your loans are paid off and you and I go our separate ways. You know you want to, so just do it and get it over with."

She nibbled at her lower lip long enough to have Dave want to squirm just to relieve the pressure in his jeans. He'd thought the coming month would be a breeze. Now he had to wonder if maybe he wasn't signing up for a month of misery.

Although, he thought, maybe not.

Yeah, he'd told her that sex wasn't part of their deal, and it wasn't. But that didn't mean it had to stay that way. They were going to be spending a lot of time together. Giving him plenty of opportunities to seduce her and get her into his bed.

Damn, the thought of *that* had him getting even harder. Odd that Mia Hughes was hitting him so hard. Probably because she wasn't even trying. Had made a point of saying she didn't want to have sex with him.

Nothing more intriguing than a challenge.

"I really hate doing this," she muttered, then signed her name on the dotted line.

They were both committed to this path now, and there was no turning back.

Mia had no idea where to shop for the kind of clothes she needed. She'd never had enough money to worry about it before and even if she had, she didn't think she'd be comfortable paying several hundred dollars for *one dress*. Jeans, T-shirts and sweatshirts were her usual wardrobe, along with sneakers and sandals. The thought of her joining, even briefly, the kind of society that only the rich experienced would have been laughable if it wasn't so terrifying.

She was so not a part of the world Dave Firestone belonged to. How was she supposed to fool anyone into thinking any different? Not only did she not have the clothes for the part, she didn't have the attitude. She needed help and, thankfully, she knew just the place to find it.

Which was why Mia had come here, to the Royal Diner.

In June, Amanda Altman—now Battle—had come home to Royal and taken over the day-to-day running of the family diner with her sister, Pam. It hadn't been easy for the Altman sisters to get over their past and build a bridge to the future, but they'd managed it. And it hadn't taken Amanda and Nathan Battle long to rekindle their romance. Now they were married and Amanda was pregnant and driving everyone in town crazy with her decorating and shopping plans.

Mia smiled just thinking about her friend. She and Amanda had connected almost immediately when they'd met, and over the past few months they'd become friends.

Since Mia didn't have many, she treasured the friends she did have.

Mia claimed one of the booths along the wide front windows that offered a view of Main Street. But instead of watching the people passing by, Mia looked around the familiar diner. It was old-fashioned, she supposed. When Amanda had come home she had upgraded a few things, though not enough to change the feel of the place.

The walls had been painted. Once a bright white, they were now a soft, cool green and dotted with framed photos of Royal through the years. The old chipped and scarred red counter was now a shining sweep of a deeper, richer red. The black-and-white-checked floors had been polished and the red vinyl booth seats had all been revamped. There were new chairs pulled up to the scattering of tables and sunshine streamed through the windows lining Main Street.

There was an old-style jukebox in the corner, though thankfully it was quiet at the moment. It was still morning, too late for breakfast and too early for the lunch crowd that would stream in by noon. At the moment, there were just a few customers, huddled over their coffees or chatting softly in small groups. The clink of silverware on plates was its own kind of music and settled the nerves that seemed to have taken up permanent residence in Mia's stomach.

This was all Dave's fault, she told herself. Waving money in front of a desperate woman was just…she frowned. Very, very smart. He'd known just how to reel her in. And now that she was in, she had to stop worrying over it. Too late to back out, Mia told herself, as she silently admitted that she probably wouldn't quit now even if she could. Just a few minutes ago, she had deposited the fifteen-thousand-dollar check from Dave that she had needed so badly. The deed was done. She could pay bills, buy groceries and find a way to hang on until Alex returned.

He *would* return, she assured herself. And now that she would be spending lots of time with Dave, maybe she would be able to discover information that would help locate Alex. Not that she believed Dave had had anything to do with Alex going missing. But he might know something and not even realize what he knew.

And… She was rationalizing her involvement in this crazy plan of his.

It was one month—and maybe not even that long, if he could land that contract for his cattle sooner. When the time was up she'd be free and clear to start her own future unencumbered by massive debt. A good thing. The heat she felt around Dave? A bad thing. That swirl of nerves erupted in the pit of her belly again and she had to fight them into submission. Not easy.

Somehow, she had to find a way to keep her hormones in check and remember that none of what would be happening between her and Dave was real.

She spotted Amanda and waved when her friend smiled in greeting. Pam was running the cash register, and beyond the pass-through into the kitchen, Mia spotted their chef putting a plate together.

Morning in Royal, Mia thought. There was comfort here. Familiarity. Things she'd longed for most of her life, she had found here. And she would do whatever she had to to keep them. Even entering a deal with a man who was dangerously attractive.

"Brought your usual iced tea." Amanda walked up to the booth and set a glass down in front of Mia.

"Thanks." Her usual. Wasn't that a gift, Mia thought,

to be so well-known in a place that she had a "usual" order.

"I'm so glad you came in this morning," Amanda said. "I've got a few pictures I want to show you."

"More baby room ideas?" Mia asked.

Amanda laughed and lovingly patted her slightly rounded belly. Mia caught the gesture and felt one sharp, swift tug of envy. Amanda had a man who loved her. While Mia, on the other hand, was going to pretend to be in love for a hefty paycheck.

"I know," Amanda said with a grimace. "I've become an HGTV zombie. I swear, Nathan's afraid to come home after work because he never knows what new project I'm going to hit him with."

"Nathan's nuts about you."

"Yeah," Amanda said with a private smile. "He really is. Which is why he didn't even flinch when I had Sam Gordon's crew break out the wall in the baby's room so they could add a connecting door to our room."

Amanda and Nathan lived on the Battlelands ranch in a house Nathan had had built a few years ago. It looked like a Victorian but it had all the modern conveniences.

"A connecting door makes perfect sense."

"It really does," Amanda agreed as she slid into the bench seat opposite Mia. "Of course, I'm also having Sam add on a balcony to our room, and Nathan was a little surprised to find gaping holes in *two* of our walls when he came home yesterday."

This is another reason why Mia had come to Amanda for help. Their lives were so different. Not only did Amanda have a home and a family to call her own, but she was a part of the very society that Mia would be pretending to belong to. The Battle family was every bit as wealthy as Dave Firestone and Amanda had found a way to not only fit in, but thrive.

Hopefully, she could help Mia do the same, however temporarily.

She took a quick drink of her tea and swallowed, pushing down the huge knot lodged in her throat. "I'd love to see the pictures of the baby's room," she said, looking up into Amanda's smiling face. "And I've got a favor to ask."

Instantly, Amanda's smile faltered and she reached out one hand across the table to lay it on Mia's arm. "A favor? Is everything okay?"

"Everything's fine, why?"

"Because you never ask for anything," Amanda pointed out. "I swear, if you were on fire, you wouldn't ask for water."

Mia blinked at the apt analogy. She hadn't realized that her friends knew her so well. But she'd learned long ago to stand on her own two feet. To not count on anyone or anything. And to never ask for help—because invariably people would see that as a sign of weakness.

Wow. Childhood issues, she told herself. Amazing how much she had held on to from when she was a girl. It was never easy to be objective about your own past and your life choices, but even Mia could see how her childhood had affected her as an adult. Heck, until the past few years, her past had kept her from even attempting to make friends. Thankfully, she'd at least been able to overcome that hurdle.

Smiling, she said, "I promise, Amanda. If I ever need water that badly, I'll *ask*."

"Deal." Amanda waved to her sister, indicating she was taking a short break. "Okay, now, before I run to the back and get my three-ring binder with all of my decorating pictures to show you…you first. Whatever you need, I'll do it."

"Without even knowing what's going on?"

Amanda shrugged. "We're friends."

A rush of warmth spilled through Mia at those two simple words. Having a friend to count on was such a gift, she didn't think she would ever take it for granted.

"Thank you. I really appreciate it."

"I know you do, sweetie. So what's going on, Mia?"

God, she hardly knew where to begin. Cupping her hands around the tall glass in front of her, Mia started talking. She started at the beginning and told Amanda all about the reporter and Dave and the offer he'd made and why she needed to go shopping. When she finally wound down, she took a long drink of her tea and waited for Amanda to tell her she was crazy.

Instead, her friend grinned. "That is so fabulous."

"You really think so?"

"Well, come on," Amanda said, lowering her voice. "Honey, I know you hate to admit it, but you really *do* need the money."

Instantly, Mia flushed, remembering how her debit card had been refused right here at the diner just a few weeks ago. Amanda was right. She *did* need the money. And she *did* hate to admit it.

"I know things will be better when Alex comes back…" Amanda paused and both of them were silent for a moment, thinking about their missing friend. "But for now, it's perfect. You each need something, and with this one little deal, you'll be setting up your future. How much better can it get? Plus," she added with a wide smile, *"shopping."*

Mia was still laughing when Abby Price entered the

diner and walked up to the booth smiling. "What's so funny?"

"Nothing," Amanda said with a wink for Mia. "What can I do for you, Abby?"

Abigail Price was taller than Mia, with long, wavy red hair and an air of elegance about her. She also had a ready smile, a loving husband and an adorable, adopted three-year-old daughter, Julia.

"Well," Abby was saying, "you know the day-care center at the TCC is almost ready to open for business."

The day care had been at the center of a contentious battle in town for months. The Texas Cattleman's Club had been around for generations and they were pretty much stuck in the mud when it came to changes. It had only been a couple of years since they'd allowed women to become members. And now those women were spearheading the move to provide a safe, comfortable place for children to stay when their parents needed to be somewhere else.

Most people in Royal were all for it, but there were a few who were still fighting it even though it was a done deal. Before Alex disappeared, he had told Mia all about the TCC meeting in which the decision had been made to go ahead with the facility. Naturally, it had been Beau Hacket and his cronies, like the Gordon brothers, who had argued against it. Mia thought if Beau and his bunch had their way, everyone would still be driving wagons hitched up to horses. The man hated change of any kind and didn't care who knew it.

But bullies hadn't been able to stop progress, and the day-care center was nearly ready to open.

"Since everyone in town is talking about nothing else these days," Amanda said, "yeah. I know."

"Well, I was thinking," Abby said, "that we should

have a launch party, so to speak. You know, sort of an open house, to let everyone come in to see what we've done."

"That's a great idea," Mia said. "I know I'd love to see it."

"Thanks!" Abby smiled at Mia, then turned back to Amanda. "But we'll need food and that's where the diner comes in. I know you and Pam do catering and I'm thinking small sandwiches, potato salad, some vegetable platters…"

"We can do that, absolutely," Amanda told her. "Do you want to go over the menu and what you'll need now?"

"Oh, no. I've got a million things to do," Abby told her with a quick glance at her watch. "But I'd love it if we could talk it all over tomorrow sometime."

"That's perfect. Pam and I will be here all day, so come whenever it's convenient for you."

Abby bent to give Amanda a quick hug. "Thanks. Now, I've really gotta run. See you, Mia!"

And she was gone.

"Abby's pretty much a force of nature, isn't she?"

Amanda agreed. "She's always in high gear, that's for sure. Now," she said, "let's get back to the fun stuff. *Shopping.*"

Mia laughed and took a sip of her tea. "I'm glad you think it sounds fun. I have no idea where to go or what to buy."

Amanda clapped her hands together, then scrubbed her palms. "I, on the other hand, know *just* where to go."

"Dave suggested Houston."

"Of course he did." Amanda waved that suggestion aside. "Men don't know anything. We don't have to go into the city. All we have to do is head down the street to Monica's shop."

"Monica?"

Amanda laughed a little. "Monica Burns. She's on the outskirts of town and she has this darling dress shop. Monica carries great stuff you won't find in department stores. Really different, really gorgeous."

"Why have I never heard of her before?"

Amanda cocked her head to one side. "Shop often, do you?"

Mia laughed. "Okay, no."

"Have to warn you, though," Amanda added, "she's pricey."

Pricey. Well, that's the kind of stuff she had to have and, thanks to Dave, she could afford it.

"Oh!" Amanda leaned over the table and lowered her voice. "You know what else we should do?"

"I'm almost afraid to ask. You look way too eager."

"That's because this is a brilliant idea," Amanda told her. "We should go to the day spa. Get the works."

"The spa?" Mia's voice defined the hesitation she felt over that plan. Saint Tropez was a local, upscale hair salon and day spa. Mia had never actually been inside— frankly, even if she could have afforded it, she would have been too intimidated to go in. She wasn't exactly the mani-pedi kind of girl, after all, and she hadn't gone for a haircut in years.

"You don't have to sound so horrified. I didn't suggest a trip to a torture chamber." Amanda shook her head and smiled.

"You might as well have," Mia admitted.

Her friend sat back and gave her a long look. "You said yourself you have to look the part of Dave's fiancée."

"Yes…"

"Well, sweetie," Amanda said gently, "that's going to take more than new clothes."

Mia laughed. How could she help it? "Thanks very much."

"Oh, I didn't mean it the way it sounded. I just... Okay, take your hair, for example."

She lifted one hand to the knot at the back of her neck. Her hair was neat and tidy. What else did she need, really? "What's wrong with my hair?"

"Nothing that a trim and some highlights and throwing away your rubber bands wouldn't fix."

Mia frowned thoughtfully. She kept her hair twisted and off her neck because it was easy. And, she silently admitted, because she was used to being...invisible. It was comfortable. Safe. No one noticed a woman who did everything she could to *avoid* being noticed.

But she'd been working for years to build a new life, hadn't she? Why else had she gone back to school? Worked as an intern at Royal Junior High? And if she was building a new life, did it make sense to hold on to the past? To cling to her old ways of doing things? To continue to hide when what she really wanted was to embrace the life she'd always dreamed of having?

She took a deep breath and asked, "How much do you think I should have trimmed?"

Amanda grinned. "Trust me."

Five

That afternoon at the Royal Round Up, the ranch hands were moving the herd to winter grass and Dave was happy to be on horseback joining them. Yeah, he could have stayed back at the main house and just issued orders, but running a ranch was in his blood. Nothing felt better to him than being on a horse, doing the work necessary to keep a ranch this size operating.

Every month of the year had different demands when you worked and lived off the land. In October, there was plenty to get accomplished while getting ready for winter.

Dave tugged his hat brim lower over his eyes and guided his horse after a steer wandering off on its own. He turned the animal back toward the herd, then mentally reviewed the list of chores still to be done.

After they had the cows, bulls and steers moved to their winter field, the six-month-old calves would be separated from their mothers and weaned. Then the vet would have to come out and vaccinate them before they were turned out to the pasture along with the rest of the herd. Dave knew that a lot of the ranchers in the area turned the calves into feedlots, where they spent their days caged up in small pens with hundreds of other animals. Nothing wrong with the system, Dave supposed, but he preferred keeping his cattle free-range even if it did mean more work for the ranch hands.

His gloved hands tugged at the reins and sent his horse off to the right, where one or two of the heifers were beginning to stray. A cloud of dust hovered over the moving herd and swirled around the cowboys moving in and out of the steers with calm deliberation.

"Hey, boss."

Dave looked over as Mike Carter rode up, then drew his horse alongside. "Herd looks good."

"It does," Mike agreed, squinting into the late afternoon sunlight. "I sent a couple of the guys ahead to set up the temporary weaning pens for the calves."

"Good. If we can finish separating the calves from the cows by tomorrow, I'll have the vet come out the day after to take care of their inoculations."

"That'll work," Mike told him. "We can get the identification ear tags on them at the same time and have the work done, I figure, by the end of the week." He grinned. "Just in time for the first-calf heifers to arrive."

Dave smiled, too. "Always something, isn't it?"

"If you're lucky," Mike agreed. "By the time the doc's finished inoculating the calves, the first year heifers should be here. He can check them over at the same time. Save himself another trip to the ranch."

"Good idea," Dave said, watching as a couple of the cowboys swooped around the edge of the herd, guiding them toward the winter grasses.

There hadn't been much rain this year and the grasses were sparse. He'd already cut back on the number of head of cattle they were running, in spite of the fact the stock ponds were still full and water wasn't really an issue for the herd. The point was, the grasses had dried out and without enough rain, they wouldn't be coming back.

Ranching was always a series of strategic maneuvers. Paring down the herd, moving calves and saving breeding stock. You had to plan for weather you had no way to predict and try to outthink Mother Nature from month to month. It wasn't easy, but it was all Dave had ever wanted.

Right now, his concern was the land. Making sure it stayed healthy. Dave was thinking they needed to thin the herd again. With the first-year heifers arriving, and their calves born come spring, the ranch would be carrying more beef than the land could support if they didn't act soon. Now was the time to make that beef sale.

"We've got to get that deal with TexCat, Mike." He shook his head as the dust cloud rose even higher as if to highlight exactly what Dave had been thinking. "The grass can't support too big a herd for long."

"You heard anything from Buckley?"

"Not in a few days," Dave told him, and felt a flash of irritation. He wasn't used to not being in charge on a deal. Now he was in the position of having to wait on someone else, and Dave didn't *do* waiting. When he wanted something, he went out and got it. Hell, he thought with an inner smile, he'd gotten a fiancée when he needed one, hadn't he?

"When are you meeting him next?"

Dave frowned. "I'll set something up with him in the next week or so. Want to give him time to have our operation checked out."

"Buckley's not an easy man to deal with, but he's fair,"

Mike said. "He'll figure out we've got the best beef in Texas soon enough."

Dave did have the best beef around, and everyone knew it. Hell, his cowhands did everything short of singing the steers to sleep at night. The herd was free-range Black Angus. Organic, too—no antibiotics, no feedlots. He'd put his heart and soul into building this ranch, and now he had a fiancée who would convince Buckley that Dave Firestone was a settled, trustworthy man. Everything was moving as it should.

So why was he still feeling…off balance?

It was Mia.

The woman kept slipping into his thoughts. Ever since their meeting the night before, he hadn't been able to keep her completely out of his mind. And he knew why. She hadn't been what he'd expected and Dave wasn't used to being surprised. When he made a move—in business or his personal life—he went in knowing exactly what would happen. Knowing ahead of time how his adversary would react.

Mia had thrown him. Without even trying, she'd aroused him. Intrigued him. And set him up for more surprises. Which he didn't want.

"So, is your mom coming out to stay over Christmas again?"

Dave came up out of his thoughts and shot a look at his foreman. Mike's expression was hard to read, as if he were trying to be deliberately casual.

"Yeah," Dave said. "She'll be here in November, like always. Stay through the first of the year."

Mike nodded. "Sounds good."

Frowning, Dave briefly wondered why his foreman was so interested in his mother's upcoming visit. Then he shrugged it off. Bigger things to think about.

"Looks like you've got company, boss."

Mike jerked his head off to the west, and when Dave looked in that direction he saw a man on horseback headed their way. Even at a distance, Dave recognized him.

Chance McDaniel. Chance owned a thriving guest ranch and hotel on the other side of Royal. He made millions by hosting city people who wanted to pretend to be cowboys for a week at a time. Then there was the four-star hotel on the property that was a popular spot for weddings, conferences and all kinds of gatherings.

But McDaniel's Acres was a working ranch as well as a dude ranch. Chance ran some beef and horses on his land, too. The two of them often shared the work at busy times of the year, lending out cowhands and doing whatever was needed. He was a good friend and like Dave, preferred, when possible, to be out riding a horse to doing just about anything else.

When he was close enough, Dave held up a hand in greeting. "What are you out doing?"

"Heard you were moving your beef to winter pasture," Chance said with a shrug. "Thought I'd ride over and lend a hand if you need it."

"Hell, yes, we can always use another cowboy," Dave said. "Appreciate it."

Chance grinned. "Beats being at McDaniel's Acres today. My guys are helping tourists try their hand at roping. Set up a plywood steer and they're taking turns using a lasso." Laughing, he added, "There's gonna be more than a few of them looking for aspirin tonight."

Laughing, Mike said, "It ain't easy being a cowboy." Then he nodded and moved off to join the other hands circling the slow-moving herd.

The two friends rode in silence for a few minutes until

Dave finally said, "You usually enjoy watching city guys try to ride and rope. So why are you really here?"

Chance glanced at him. "Thought I'd let you know that the state investigator's staying at my hotel."

"She is?" Dave felt like he'd just taken a hard punch to the gut. He'd heard about the FBI-trained investigator, of course. Nothing stayed secret for long in Royal, and it wasn't as if Bailey Collins was trying to keep a low profile, either.

She was working out of the Dallas office and had been looking for Alex for weeks. Dave had spoken to her once himself and he knew that she'd worked with Nathan to discover that Alex Santiago had a few secrets of his own. In fact, Santiago might not even be his real name. Questions brought more questions and there simply weren't any answers to be had. But knowing that Bailey Collins was staying at McDaniel's Acres told Dave that she wasn't going anywhere. Which meant that she wasn't finished looking into Alex's disappearance. Frowning to himself, Dave realized that though Nathan Battle might not consider him a suspect, Bailey might feel differently.

Dave looked at his friend, waiting. It didn't take long for Chance to continue.

"I'll say, the woman's gorgeous, really." He gave a fast smile. "If you can get past what she does for a living."

"Why's she staying on?" Dave asked it, but he knew damn well why the woman was still here. A wealthy man didn't just drop off the face of the earth and not leave a ripple.

There were people asking questions. Reporters hadn't let go of the story at all. If anything, they kept digging deeper. Asking more questions, raising suspicions. Naturally, the state would want its investigator to stay put and keep gathering information.

Hell, when Alex did finally turn back up, Dave wanted to punch him dead in the face for causing all this.

"She's talking to people," Chance was saying. "She's been all over my ranch already, chatting up the cowboys, looking for any piece of information she can turn up."

"Great."

"Yeah." Chance snorted. "She questioned me once and I think she's looking for another shot at me. So far, I've managed to avoid her."

"By coming over to help your friends ride herd?"

"Doesn't hurt," he admitted.

Dave didn't blame him. He was sick and tired of talking about Alex Santiago. Hell, he and Alex hadn't exactly been friends before the man took off or whatever. Yet, ever since he'd been gone, Alex had become a huge part of Dave's life. Gossip, innuendo and scandal kept hanging over him like a black cloud threatening a storm.

And Chance had had it just as bad for a while. He'd been dating Cara Windsor until Alex had moved in on him. Then Cara and Alex had become an item and Chance was left on the sidelines. Naturally the gossips in town had run with that, painting Chance as a pissed-off lover wanting revenge. Which was laughable. Chance had liked Cara, but not enough to make Alex disappear.

"Looks to me like she plans on talking to everyone who knows Alex." He glanced at Dave. "Which would surely include *you*. I'm thinking you're going to look real interesting to her seeing as how you and Alex were rivals, so to speak."

"Great." Snatching off his hat, Dave pushed one hand through his hair, then settled the hat into place again. "Nathan just officially cleared me of suspicion and now I've got someone else coming in to set the town gossips raging again."

"Yeah, and they'll be all over it."

Disgusted and frustrated, Dave muttered, "Gonna go over real big with Thomas Buckley, too."

"That pompous old goat? He hates everything."

"Yeah, but I can't afford to have him hating me at the moment."

"The contract for your beef?"

"Exactly."

Chance nodded grimly. "Maybe this woman Bailey will be discreet."

"Won't matter," Dave said. "Once folks in town realize she's looking at me, the gossip will start up and it will reach Buckley."

"You can get Nathan to vouch for you there," Chance pointed out. "How're you going to handle the whole have-to-be-a-family-man-to-sell-to-TexCat thing though?"

"That part I've got covered," Dave said, with just a touch of smug satisfaction in his voice. Quickly, he outlined his plan and his agreement with Mia.

Chance gave a long, low whistle. "You're clever, I give you that. But Alex's housekeeper?" He shook his head slowly. "To some—including Bailey—that might look like you're trying to buy her silence."

"What?" Dave hadn't looked at it like that at all. Now that Chance had brought it up, though, it made a horrible kind of sense.

"Hey," Chance said, "not to me! I know you didn't do anything to Alex. I'm just saying that suddenly turning up engaged to the housekeeper of a man who's disappeared might start even more tongues wagging."

He was right and Dave knew it. But the plan was set and damned if he'd back out now.

"They're gonna wag no matter what I do," Dave told

him. "At least this way, they're all talking about what I *want* them to talk about. The engagement."

"It ain't easy living in a small town, is it?"

"Not by a long shot," Dave agreed. "Still, you want to give it up and move to Houston or Dallas?"

Chance grinned. "Hell, no. Where would I ride my horse in the city? Besides, when you're *not* the center of gossip, it can be downright entertaining."

"Yeah," Dave countered, "but when the gossip's about *you,* it's a damn sight less fun."

"True."

Dave frowned. "Think I'll be spending as much time as I can out here with the cattle." He couldn't see a woman from the city hopping a horse to chase him down for an interview.

"Can't say it's a bad idea," Chance admitted. "Let's face it, Dave. You and I were the top suspects when Alex took off, and they haven't found anyone else to take our places, have they?"

"No," Dave said thoughtfully.

Nodding, Chance continued. "Y'know, when Alex *does* get back, he's got a lot to answer for."

"Damn straight, he does." Dave kneed his horse into a hard run and Chance was right behind him. A couple hours of hard work should be enough to clear their heads for a while.

Amanda didn't waste time once she'd made up her mind. Before Mia even knew what was happening, she and Amanda were at Saint Tropez being pampered.

Just walking into the day spa, you could feel tension slide from your body on a sigh. There was soft, ethereal music piped in from discreetly hidden speakers high on the pale pastel walls. There were fresh flowers scenting the air and frosty pitchers of lemon water sitting on silver trays alongside crystal goblets. The colors in the place were designed to soothe tattered nerves. Soft blue, sea-foam green and varying shades of cream covered every surface. Chairs were plush and overstuffed, lamps were dim and the aestheticians were warm and welcoming.

Since Mia had never done anything like this before, she was completely out of her element and grateful to have Amanda as her guide to the world of "girlie."

She should probably feel guilty for spending this kind of money, Mia told herself. But somehow, she just couldn't seem to drum up the guilt. She was way too busy feeling...relaxed. For the first time in months, her mind was blissfully blank and her body was free of tension.

"You're sighing," Amanda said.

Mia did it again, then smiled. "I'm lucky I'm not just a puddle of goo on the floor. You know, I've never had a massage before and—"

"You poor, deprived girl," Amanda interrupted.

"I know, right?" Mia looked over at her friend with a smile. "It was amazing. Every muscle in my body is taking a nap."

"Oh, mine, too. Of course, since I've been pregnant, I can take a nap anywhere." She laughed a little. "Na-than swears I fell asleep standing up in the kitchen the other night."

Mia smiled to herself as Amanda continued talking about Nathan and the coming baby and their plans for the future. She was happy for her friend. Really. Amanda and Nathan had had to get past a lot of old hurts and mis-trust to find their happiness now. But at least silently, Mia could admit to feeling more than a twinge of envy.

After growing up as a wanderer, she'd finally found the place that was home. But she was still looking for the family she wanted to be a part of so badly. For the love that had eluded her all of her life.

"Mia?" Amanda's voice cut into her thoughts. "You okay?"

"What?" She jolted in her chair. "Sure. Why?"

"Because Natalie's asked you three times if you like the shade of nail polish on your fingers and toes."

"Oh!" She winced, looked at the woman sitting at her feet and said, "I'm sorry. I zoned out."

"Happens all the time here, believe me," the woman said with a knowing smile. "So, the dark rose works for you?"

Mia checked out her fingers and toes, wiggled them for effect and said, "Yes, thanks, it's great."

Another first, she thought. Mia had never treated herself to a mani-pedi before. But she wouldn't confess that to Amanda.

"Good. Now I'll get you some wine while you dry and then we'll escort you into the salon for your color and trim."

She winced at the thought of facing a haircut and highlights. A small thread of fear slid through the relaxation that held her in its grip. Before she could think about it too much, though, Natalie was back, handing Mia a glass of white wine. She'd also brought a glass of ice-cold lemon water for Amanda.

"Wine," Amanda said wistfully as she looked at her own goblet of water. "I miss wine. And caffeine."

"Yes, but when nine months are up, you'll have a baby in exchange for your sacrifice. That seems fair."

"It does," she agreed. "Though I've already told Nathan to bring a bottle of chardonnay to the hospital. I'm going to want a glass or three right after delivery."

An hour or so later, Mia was sitting in a salon chair

staring into the mirror at a stranger. She smiled and the reflected woman smiled back.

Okay, there had been some nerves when Tiffany had come at Mia's head with a pair of shears. But the panic had dissolved when she'd realized that the beautiful Tiffany was only trimming and shaping Mia's long-ignored hair. But before she could admire herself, Tiffany had mixed up some color and affixed it to Mia's head with small sheets of aluminum foil.

While she sat under a hot dryer, wondering what she'd gotten herself into, Amanda had been right there, chatting and laughing with the other women in the salon. Even though Mia wasn't part of the conversation, she felt as though she were.

There was that tantalizing sense of belonging that she'd yearned for most of her life. This was her home. She had friends. She had purpose. And now…she had a fiancé. Who, she told herself as Tiffany blew her hair dry, was going to be very surprised the next time she saw him.

"You're being really quiet," Amanda said.

"Just thinking."

"About?"

"About today, mostly," Mia said with a half smile. "This was a great idea, Amanda."

"Wasn't it?" A short, delighted laugh spilled from her as she walked up behind Mia's chair and met her gaze in the mirror. "Honestly, sometimes I'm just brilliant. Of course, I'll seriously owe Pam for taking diner duty herself until our extra waitress comes in. But it was worth it."

"It was." Mia swiveled around in her chair and stood up. "I feel more relaxed than I ever have."

"Well, you look great, too." Amanda did a slow circle around Mia. "I love what she did with your hair. It's still long and it's so thick I could hate you for it…"

Mia laughed and gave her head a shake, watching in the mirror how the long, layered waves swirled out, then shifted right back into place. It was amazing. She hadn't even known her hair could *do* this.

"...and the layers. I love the highlights, too. It's still dark brown, but there's warmth mixed in there now, too."

Mia lifted one hand to slide her fingers through her hair. "It feels softer, too."

"Mia?"

A voice spoke up from the side and both women turned to look at the speaker. Piper Kindred was standing in the open doorway. "Is that you, Mia?"

"It is," she said and grinned like a fool. How fun it was to see the surprise on her friend's face and to imagine how much greater Dave's shock was going to be. "Amanda talked me into a spa day."

"And doesn't she look fabulous?" Amanda said. "Well, except for the faded jeans and the long-sleeved T-shirt. Shopping is next on our list."

Piper's curly red hair was drawn back into her usual ponytail. She wore dark blue jeans and an oversized black sweatshirt covering up a curvy figure. Her green eyes were shining and her lips were curved in a wide smile.

"Good luck with that, Mia. Amanda's always loved shopping, but I don't envy you at all."

"Exactly how I feel about it," Mia admitted.

Amanda shook her head at both of them. "And you call yourselves women. Where's your gender pride?"

"Women do more than shop," Piper pointed out with a chuckle. "Like say...work as paramedics?"

"Yes, yes," Amanda retorted with a grin. "We all know you're a paramedic and that's wonderful. But there's no reason you can't be female while you do it."

Piper winked at Mia. "I'm always female, Amanda. I'm actually here for a haircut and a pedicure."

Amanda waved one hand in front of her face. "Hold me up, Mia. I think I might faint."

Mia laughed, delighted with the banter between the two old friends.

"Very funny," Piper drawled, then turned her gaze back to Mia. "Seriously, though, you look terrific."

"Thanks," Mia said. "The terror was well worth it, I think."

"Since she just got engaged to Dave Firestone," Amanda was saying despite Mia's look of stunned shock, "I thought it was time she knocked his socks off."

"Really?" Piper's eyes widened. "Well, congratulations. Kind of sudden, isn't it?"

"Yes," Mia said, throwing a quick frown at Amanda. "We were sort of swept off our feet."

"And now she's almost set to do even more sweeping," Amanda interrupted. "When Dave gets a look at her, it's going to blow him away."

"Hmm…" Piper glanced into the mirror at her own reflection. "Maybe I could use a makeover myself."

"Any particular reason why?" Mia asked.

Piper shrugged and shook her head. "It's just, the work I do, the men I work with all look at me like 'one of the guys.' I think even Ryan Grant—my best friend, mind you—forgets I'm a woman most of the time."

Mia could understand that. She'd been ignored or overlooked for most of her life. At least Piper had her co-workers' respect. She wasn't invisible. But now, after experiencing the past few hours, Mia knew what the Saint Tropez salon and day spa could do for Piper.

"We could fix that," Amanda said in a tempting, singsongy voice. "Just let me know when you're ready and we'll have you buffed and polished and I would *love* to get you out of those sweatshirts you wear."

Piper laughed and stepped behind Mia as if to use her as a shield. "Down girl," she said, still laughing. "You've already got your 'project,' so stay away."

"Fine, fine," Amanda said. "But you'll be sorry. Mia is going to be the talk of the town when I'm finished with her. You just wait and see."

"Oh, man…" Mia murmured, as nerves rose up inside her again. *The talk of the town?* She didn't know if she'd be able to handle that.

"Yep," Piper whispered. "You're toast now. Once Amanda gets going, nobody can slow her down. Good luck!"

Amanda took Mia's hand and dragged her from the room, already talking about what they would be buying at Monica's. Mia threw one last look back at Piper and was not reassured to see the other woman laughing.

Six

Mia sipped her glass of sauvignon blanc and willed the wine to soothe the nerves jittering in the pit of her stomach. Apparently, though, it was going to take a lot more than a sip or two.

She had a seat at the bar in the lounge at Claire's restaurant. The bar was as elegant as the restaurant itself. Small, round tables, candles flickering in the center of each of them. The polished mahogany bar shone under the soft glow of overhead lighting. Smooth jazz sighed from speakers tucked against the ceiling, and a long mirror backed the bar itself, reflecting the patrons seated in the room. Some, like Mia, were waiting to meet their parties and have dinner. Some were there for a quiet drink with friends.

She gave her own reflection a wry smile and still hardly recognized herself. In the deep scarlet, long-sleeved silk blouse and black slacks, she was out of her

comfort zone and into foreign territory. It wasn't just the
new clothes or the hair, or even the makeup she'd taken
the trouble to apply, though. It was the whole situation.
The subterfuge. The lies that would dominate her life for
the next month.

And, she was forced to admit, if only to herself, that
being around Dave constantly wasn't going to be easy,
either. He was too gorgeous. Too sure of himself and far
too touchable.

In just a couple of days, her life had been turned upside down. Now, instead of being curled up in her suite
at Alex's house, watching TV, she was here, wearing silk,
drinking wine and fighting the urge to bolt.

Being in the bar wasn't helping the situation any, either. She felt out of place, alone on her barstool. She'd
never been comfortable in places like this, despite the
elegance. Mia had spent too much of her childhood in
the back rooms or kitchens of bars and restaurants and
casinos. The clink of glasses, the murmured conversations and the smell of alcohol awakened a memory, and
for just a moment or two, she was ten years old again.

*The back room of the bar was small and so well lit
Mia didn't need the pocket flashlight she always carried
so she could read wherever she happened to be. Tonight,
she sat in a corner, a glass of root beer at her side, and
tried to concentrate on the magical world of Narnia.*

*But the poker game going on across the room from
her made it really hard. Men argued and grumbled and
the laughter from the women sounded sharp and brittle.*

*She looked around the group of men and caught her
father's eye. He winked at her and Mia smiled. This was
just one more poker game in a never-ending chain of
them. This bar was in St. Louis, but winter was coming
and her father had promised they were headed West after*

he got a stake from tonight's game. Vegas, he'd said. With maybe a side trip to California and Disneyland.

Mia smiled to herself and shifted her gaze back to her library book. Her father always made wonderful promises. But she had learned when she was just a little kid that she couldn't always count on them.

"How you doing, Princess?"

She looked up from her book into her father's big blue eyes. She had his eyes, he always told her. And her beautiful mother's nose and mouth. Every night before bed, her father showed her pictures of the mother she couldn't remember. The pretty woman had died when Mia was still a baby. It was sad, but she still had her daddy and that was enough.

"I'm fine, Daddy."

"Hungry?"

"Nope, I'm just reading."

"Just like your mom," he said and kissed her forehead. "Always have your pretty nose in a book." He smiled and smoothed one hand over her hair. "One of these days, sweet girl, we're gonna hit the jackpot. We'll buy us a house with a library just like the Beast's in that cartoon movie you love. You'll have your own room you can decorate any way you want and you can go to school."

That was her favorite dream. She couldn't even imagine going to sleep and waking up in the same room every day. A house to call her own. On a nice street, maybe with trees and a swing in the backyard. And she could have a puppy, too. And the puppy would love her so much it would sleep in her bed with her. And she could go to school and have friends and every day when she came home on the bus her dog and her father would be waiting for her, so happy to be together again.

But it wasn't going to happen. Her daddy was a pro-

fessional gambler and she already knew that they had to go where the games were.

So they did.

"Hey, Jack," someone called out. "You playin' or what?"

"Right there," her father answered, then leaned in and kissed the tip of Mia's nose. Whispering, he said, "Another hour or so, Princess, and we'll head back to the hotel. Tomorrow morning, we'll get on the road early and head for Vegas. You good with that?"

"Yes, Daddy." Her father never left her alone in a motel room. Too afraid of losing her, he always said. But the truth was, Mia wouldn't have stayed even if she could have. She wanted to be where her father was. They were a team and he was all she had. They might not have a puppy or a house, but that was okay because wherever Jack Hughes was, that was home.

"That's my little good-luck charm," he said and kissed her again. "Another hour, tops."

She would have waited for him forever.

Dave grabbed the cell phone when it rang and said, "Hello?"

"Dave, did you buy me a new car?"

He smiled at the familiar voice and the note of outrage in it. "Who is this?"

"Very funny," his mother retorted. "Now explain the new Lexus that was just delivered."

"What's to explain?" he asked as he checked for traffic then loped across the street. He was headed for Claire's to meet Mia for dinner. He hadn't wanted to bother scouring the parking lot for a space, so he'd parked on the street and walked over. "You needed a new car, now you've got one."

"My old car was fine," his mother said with a sigh of exasperation.

"Key word there being *old*," Dave told her. Then he stopped outside the restaurant, leaned against the edge of the building and let his gaze sweep the small town while his mother talked in his ear. After a long day on the ranch, he was tired and hungry and eager to get his deal with Mia started.

He'd already stopped at McKay's jewelers for a ring. Which, he knew, thanks to Erma McKay, owner and one of the top links on the Royal gossip food chain, would be all over town before he got to the restaurant. Dave smiled to himself as he remembered Erma's nose practically twitching as she'd sniffed out his story of a whirlwind romance and a surprise engagement.

He glanced up and down Main Street. It was dusk, so streetlights were blinking to life. Cars were pulled into the parking slots that lined the street in front of the shops. A kid raced down the sidewalk on his skateboard, wheels growling in his wake.

The jeweler's box in his jacket pocket felt as if it was burning through the fabric. He had never considered getting married. Or if he had, it was in a "someday maybe" sort of context. Now, even knowing the engagement was a farce and all his own idea, he felt a proverbial noose tightening around his neck. Dave hadn't exactly grown up with the best example of a working marriage, so why in hell would he be interested in tying himself down to risk the same sort of misery?

"David, this has to stop. You can't keep buying me things," his mother said flatly, and that caught his attention.

"Why not?"

"Oh, for heaven's sake, enjoy your money. Go buy something fun for yourself."

He had, he thought. He'd bought himself a fiancée, but not being an idiot, he didn't say that out loud. "Mom…"

"I'm serious, David. If you want to give me something, make it grandchildren."

Dave shook his head as a woman with two kids, one of them howling as if he was being tortured, went past. Kids? No, thank you. "Cars are easier. Just enjoy the Lexus, Mom."

"How can I when I know you're spending your money on *me?*"

"I'm doing it for myself," he said, knowing just how to get gifts past his too-proud-for-her-own-good mom. "I worry about you and if you're in a safe, new car, that's at least one thing I don't have to worry about."

She sighed on the other end of the phone and Dave knew he'd won this round. His mother had worked her ass off taking care of him and seeing that he got all of the opportunities she could manage. And if he had his way, she'd be treated like a damn queen now. Even if he had to fight her to make it happen.

"I don't know where you got that hard head of yours," she said in a huff. "But I'm out of time to argue with you. I'm meeting Cora for dinner, so I've got to run."

"Me, too. I've got a dinner date."

"Ooh." His mother's radar instantly went on alert. "Who is she?"

Dave grinned. "Have a good time, Mom."

"Fine, fine." Exasperation coloring her voice, she said, "You're an evil son to not tell me about this woman, but you have fun, too."

Still smiling, he hung up, stepped into Claire's and headed directly to the bar, knowing that Mia would be there waiting for him, since he was late. That thought wiped the smile from his face. Dave didn't do late. He was always on time, always in control, and the fact that that control had started slipping the minute he got involved with Mia hadn't escaped him.

He scanned the bar quickly, thoroughly, and didn't see her. Had she stood him up? Changed her mind about the whole thing? Well, damned if he'd let her back out now, he told himself. They had a plan and they were going to stick to it, even if she...

He caught a woman's gaze in the wide bar mirror and his breath left him in a rush. It was her. Mia. And she looked...amazing.

Mia was, quite unexpectedly, Dave told himself, the most beautiful woman he'd ever seen. How could this stylish, sophisticated brunette sitting alone at the bar possibly be Mia? Where was the tidy bun at the back of her neck? The unadorned eyes and the naked lips? Admiration mingled with desire inside him and frothed into a dangerous mix. He took a moment to catch his breath, and to enjoy the view. Her legs looked impossibly long in her sleek black slacks and he found himself wishing she'd worn a damn dress so he could get a good look at those legs.

He had to wonder if that glance they'd shared in the mirror had displayed the hunger in his eyes. Damn, he hadn't had a rush of pure, unadulterated lust like this in— Hell, he couldn't even remember the last time he'd *wanted* anyone this badly.

If he hadn't already decided to seduce her into his bed, seeing her tonight would have made the decision for him. He was hard and eager and ready to say screw dinner and just whisk her back to the ranch. Unfortunately, he thought, she was going to take some convincing. Still, there was nothing he liked better than a challenge.

"Mia?"

She blinked, and her eyes lost that faraway look and focused on him in the mirror. Her lips curved and his groin tightened.

Damn, it felt like a fist to his chest. Amazing what a woman could do to a man with a single look and a knowing smile. Were her eyes always that big? he wondered. Were they really so deep it seemed he could dive into their depths and drown?

"Dave?" Her voice shook him. It was deep, filled with concern. "Are you okay?"

Get a grip. "Yeah. Fine. Just…" His gaze swept her up and down. "Stunned. You look beautiful, Mia."

She actually flushed, and until that moment, Dave would have bet cold hard cash there wasn't a woman alive who could still do that.

Something fisted in his chest and breath was hard to find. He had to regain the upper hand here. Fast.

"Hope you didn't wait long." Not an apology, he assured himself. Just a statement.

"No." She gave him a curious look, as if she was wondering why his voice had suddenly shifted to cool and businesslike.

Well, hell, if she knew how he'd had to fight for that dispassionate tone, she'd have all the power here, wouldn't she?

"Are you ready for dinner?"

"Yes, but they haven't called our table yet and—"

"My table's ready when I am," he told her.

Both of her perfectly arched eyebrows lifted on her forehead. "Well, I hope you use your power for good instead of evil."

He laughed shortly. He hadn't expected to actually *enjoy* Mia's company. She was just full of surprises. So, to continue her comic book theme, he said, "With great power comes great responsibility."

She gave him a wide smile as a reward and lust roared up inside him, hotter than before. Shaking his head, he told her, "Leave your drink. We'll have champagne at the table."

"Champagne?" she asked as she took his hand and slid off the bar stool. "Are we celebrating?"

"Shouldn't we be?" he asked, catching her soft, floral scent as she moved closer. "We're engaged, right?"

"Yes," she said after a moment or two, "I guess we are."

Her fingers curled around his and Dave felt heat slide through him so fast it was like a sudden fever.

But fevers burned themselves out fast; he'd do well to remember that.

He led her through the bar to the restaurant, where the hostess recognized him instantly and picked up two menus. "Welcome back, Mr. Firestone. If you and your guest will follow me…"

The young woman headed into the interior of Claire's, where the lights were dim and the pristine, white linen tablecloths shone like snow in the darkness. Candles flickered madly, sending shadows dancing across the walls. Couples and larger groups sat at the tables and booths, their low-pitched voices no more than white noise. The same smooth jazz from the bar sighed into this room as well and gave the whole place a sense of intimacy.

Dave had brought a few dates here before, but mainly he used Claire's as a place to talk business. The waitstaff was attentive but not cloying, so you had plenty of time to talk without being interrupted constantly.

Tonight, though, was a different kind of business.

And damn if he'd risk his future because his rock-hard body was screaming at him.

With his hand at Mia's back, he steered her through the maze of tables and chairs. The cool silk of her shirt and the heat of her body mingled together to twist his guts into a knot that tightened with every breath.

The hostess showed them to Dave's usual table, a secluded booth at the back of the restaurant, and once they were seated she moved off, leaving them alone. Mia picked up her menu immediately and Dave smiled. It was actually nice to be out with a woman who liked to eat. Most of the women he spent time with never ate more than a salad and, even with the dressing on the side, they seldom finished their meal. A little irritating to pay for food that ended up being tossed.

She looked at him over the top edge of her menu. "I've never been here before. It's lovely."

"Yeah," he said, glancing around. "I suppose it is."

He'd become so accustomed to Claire's that he hadn't bothered to even notice his surroundings in longer than he could remember. Now, seeing it through Mia's eyes, he saw that it was more than a handy meeting spot. It was refined, yet casual enough to be comfortable.

In the candlelight, Mia's skin looked like fine porcelain, her eyes reflected the dancing flame in the center of the table and her hair fell in long, soft waves over her shoulders. The top two buttons on her silk blouse were undone, giving him a peek at smooth skin that only made him want to see more.

Sure, he'd been attracted before, but this Mia was at a whole new level. She'd surprised him, and that wasn't easy to do. He wondered what she was thinking as she stared back at him and realized that it was the first time he'd even cared what a woman was thinking. She was hitting him on so many different levels, it was almost impossible to keep up.

To get his mind off what his body was clamoring for, he said, "When I walked in tonight, you looked a million miles away."

"What?" she frowned. "Oh." Shrugging a bit, she said, "I was just remembering."

Curiosity pinged inside him. "Remembering what?"

"My father," she said simply.

He hadn't expected that, either. Her voice was soft, filled with fond affection that he couldn't identify with. He laid the menu down since he didn't need to read it anyway. Dave knew what he was going to order. Same thing he always got. Steak. Potatoes.

Instead, he focused on Mia. Her eyes drew him in and he tried to figure out what exactly she'd done differently. Makeup, sure. Eyeliner and a soft brown shadow on her lids. But it was the emotion in her eyes that grabbed at him. "Where is he now?"

"He died about ten years ago."

"Sorry," he said and meant it because he could see what the man's loss meant to her.

"What about you? Is your father still alive?"

He stiffened. See? He told himself. This was why he rarely took notice of someone else's life. It inevitably turned around on him. "No idea."

"What do you mean?"

"He walked out on my mom and me when I was ten. Never saw him again."

Her eyes instantly went soft. "Oh, Dave, I'm sorry."

He didn't want sympathy. Didn't need it. He'd long ago left behind the boy who'd missed his father. Dave had done just fine without the man who'd walked out on his responsibility. His *family*.

"I don't know what to say," Mia murmured.

"Nothing to say," Dave assured her, and wished the waiter would bring the champagne he'd ordered ahead of time. "Long time ago. He left. We lost our ranch and my mother became a cook for the family who bought the place."

His voice was clipped, cool, giving away nothing of the still-hot bubble of rage that these memories brought to him. Even after all these years, Dave could feel the helplessness that had gripped him as a boy.

Watching his mother work herself to the bone as an employee in what used to be her home. Hearing her cry at night and knowing there was nothing he could do. Hating his father for walking away, and yet at the same time, praying every night that he would come back.

But he didn't. And Dave had grown up quickly. He'd made a vow to become so rich no one would ever be able to take away what was his again. He would take care of his mom and make sure she never had to work for someone else.

And he'd done it.

Made good on his promise to himself. Made himself into a man others envied. And he wouldn't stop now.

Mia was still staring at him, and he could see hesitation in her eyes. As if she was arguing with herself internally about whether to offer sympathy or congratulations on what he'd become. He'd save her the question.

"The past doesn't matter."

"You really believe that?" she asked.

"I do. All that counts is now and the future you build."

"But it's the past that made us who we are."

"You're right. But you can't change the past, so why think about it?" he asked.

"To learn from it? To remember the good things?"

Their waiter showed up at their table, ending their conversation as he carried a silver ice bucket with a chilled bottle of champagne inside. They were silent as the waiter popped the cork and poured a small amount into a wineglass for Dave to try. When he approved it, both glasses were filled and the waiter took their orders.

Dave smiled to himself as Mia ordered the same thing he had. Steak and a baked potato.

"Still hungry?" he asked, before she could return to the conversation about the past. He was done looking backward.

She shrugged. "No point in pretending not to have an appetite. This isn't exactly a date, is it?"

He laughed a little. "So women only pretend to not be hungry when they go out?"

"Sure," she said. "I bet every skinny woman in the world goes home after a date and dives into her fridge when no one's looking."

"Speaking from experience?"

"Not really," she admitted with a shrug. "It's been a *long* time since I was on a date."

"I don't get that." She was gorgeous, funny and smart enough to know a good deal when it was presented to her. Why wouldn't men be interested?

She picked up her champagne and sipped at it. A slow smile curved her mouth when she swallowed and a twist of need tightened Dave's guts. Damn, she was a dangerous female.

"I haven't had time for dating, really," she was saying. "Getting my degree has taken up all my time, and then there's taking care of Alex's house to be able to pay for school. Not to mention the interning at Royal Junior High. So, dating? Not really a priority."

"I can understand that," he said, impressed with her work ethic and determination to carve out her life on her terms. "You have a goal, you do what you need to do to make it happen. I did the same thing."

"How do you mean?"

The restaurant was quiet, just the hum of low-pitched conversations and the background music that drifted in and out of notice. The candlelight created an air of intimacy, so Dave could have believed that he and Mia were the only two people in the room. Maybe that was why he'd told her what he'd never discussed with anyone else before.

He took a sip of champagne and thought how different his life was now than it had been just ten years before. Back then, it was cheap beer and big plans. He started talking, his voice hardly more than a hush.

"I worked my way through college, like you." His fingers, curled around the stem of the wineglass, tightened slightly as memories rushed through his mind. He never looked back, so when he did, it jolted him. "Took whatever job I could. Paid for school, and saved whatever else I could. In my geology class, I met a guy, Tobin Myer."

"Interesting name," Mia said.

"Interesting guy," Dave countered. "He didn't have many friends. Spent most of his free time exploring, doing tests on vacant land."

"What kind of tests?"

He chuckled and relaxed into the telling. He wasn't sure why talking to Mia was so damn easy and didn't think he should delve too deeply into that. "Y'know, even now, I couldn't tell you. Tobin could, of course. He could talk for hours about mineral deposits, shale, oil traces… the man was born with dirt in his blood, I swear."

"You liked him."

Dave glanced at her. "Yeah. I did. We were both loners. I didn't have time for friends and parties. Tobin was too far out there for anyone else to give a damn about him so… Different reasons, but we were both still alone. Maybe that's why we connected. Anyway…" Enough of the psychological B.S. "Tobin found a piece of land that had him excited. Said the signs of mineral deposits were through the roof. But he needed a backer. Someone with enough money to buy the land and be his partner in developing it."

"You."

He nodded. "Me." Hell, even he found it hard to believe that he'd taken the risk, spent the money it had taken so long to put together. "I took my savings and invested it in Tobin and that parcel of land."

"I'm guessing," she said, lifting her wineglass, "that since we're sitting here drinking this lovely champagne and you're paying me an extraordinary amount of money for a few weeks' time, Tobin was right."

"Oh, he was better than right," Dave told her. "That piece of land was worth a fortune."

"So you sold it?"

"No, we leased it to a huge oil and gas company outside of Dallas," he said. "They wanted to buy, of course, but instead we kept the title, and in exchange they paid us a boatload upfront and a hefty royalty every quarter."

"Your idea?"

"Absolutely." He grinned, remembering his first big deal. He'd stood his ground with the big company, kept Tobin from having a stroke due to anxiety and he'd pulled it off. "Tobin would have taken their first offer, he was so excited to be right about the land."

Dave could still feel the rush of satisfaction that had filled him when he and Tobin had made the deal. They'd each received a small fortune on signing and the royalty checks over the years had only gotten bigger. That was what had given him the means to buy his ranch and build his house, and was the seed money for everything that had come to him since.

"Do you still see Tobin?"

He looked at her. "Yeah, I do. He's based out of Dallas now, but spends most of his time in his jet, checking out land all over the country. Still following that love of dirt."

"And you're still partners."

"Ever hear of MyerStone Development?"

"Actually, yes. They're in the business section of the paper a lot and—" She stopped and smiled. "You and Tobin."

"Me and Tobin," he said, and lifted his glass in a salute to his partner.

"So the past can be nice to look back on."

He caught her eye and nodded. "Touché."

They ordered their meal, and throughout dinner, they talked of everyday things. What was new in Royal. The fact that there was no news about Alex, and then, finally, just how they would convince Thomas Buckley that they were a couple.

The longer he was with her, the more Dave figured he had the answer to a lot of problems. Over cake and coffee, he made his move.

"I think you should move into the ranch with me."

Seven

Mia froze with the last forkful of cake halfway to her lips. "What?"

She looked like a deer caught in headlights. Good. He preferred her off balance. This would all work much better if he could keep Mia dancing in place just to keep up with him.

"Finish your cake," he urged. "You know you want to."

She popped the piece of double-chocolate lava cake into her mouth and chewed frantically. While she was quiet, Dave went on.

"Think about it for a minute. We're engaged. We'll be meeting with Buckley out at the ranch anyway. It'll be handier with you there."

She swallowed, waved her fork at him and argued, "But you told me that Buckley is really conservative. He probably wouldn't approve of us, well, living together."

"We're engaged."

She took a breath, blew it out and reluctantly set her fork down.

"Which reminds me," Dave said, reaching into his pocket for the jeweler's box.

When she saw the dark red velvet, her eyes went wide and she dropped both hands into her lap. "What did you do?"

"Mia, no one's going to believe that a man like me proposed without a ring."

Her eyes met his and he could see nerves shining back at him. Again, good. If her mind was whirring in high gear, she wouldn't be thinking clearly about much of anything.

"I don't know…"

"We're already in this. The ring is just a symbol of our bargain."

"A symbol." She took another long, deep breath, then grabbed her fork again and scraped it across the dessert plate, catching every last drop of the chocolate sauce. She licked the fork clean and had zero idea what watching her tongue move across the tines was doing to Dave.

"It's just a piece of jewelry," he said and flipped the box lid open.

She gasped and he smiled. Eyes wide, she stared at the ring and slapped one hand to her chest as if to hold her heart in place. "You can't be serious."

Pleasure filled him. Her expressions were so easy to read that he could see that she both wanted the ring and wanted to run. When she reached out a hesitant finger to touch the five-carat diamond, he knew he had her.

Her fingertip slid across the wide surface of the diamond, then dropped to follow the smaller, channel-set diamonds that surrounded it. After a long minute or two, she lifted her gaze to his.

"It's gigantic."

"It sends a message."

"Yeah. 'Here I am, robber! Take me!'"

"In Royal?" He laughed, shook his head and plucked the ring from the box. Sliding it onto her ring finger before she could pull her hand back, he said, "What it will say to everyone here is, Mia belongs to Dave."

"Belongs."

She whispered the word, but he heard it. And just for a second, that imaginary noose tightened. He ignored the feeling and focused on the plan.

Her gaze fixed on the ring for a long moment before meeting his eyes again. "I'll wear the ring—"

"Good."

"But as for moving in with you—"

"It makes the most sense."

"But I have to take care of Alex's house."

"Alex isn't there," he reminded her quietly.

"I know but—"

"And the longer he's gone, the more intrusive the reporters are going to get," he went on. "Right now, most of them are being stopped at the gate. But a few have gotten through to harass you."

"True."

"More will come. Especially once word about us gets out. They'll start speculating about us getting together. Why not be at my place? No reporter will be able to reach you there, and you can check on Alex's house whenever you want."

"I don't like leaving Alex's house," she admitted. "What if he calls? What if he needs help?"

Frowning, Dave paused and thought about it before saying, "We'll have the phone company forward calls to my place. Good enough?"

She was thinking about it. He could see her working through internal arguments, trying to decide what she should do. But he'd have his way in this.

Having her at the ranch would cement their "engagement" for everyone in town and Thomas Buckley. More than that, having her in his house would speed up the seduction—which he was really interested in. Just sitting across the table from her was making him crazy.

Every time she chewed at her lip or took a deep breath, Dave felt a slam to his center. Mia Hughes was going to be his. On his terms. Soon.

"Mia, you're living alone in that big empty house, and there's no reason for it," he reminded her. "For the next few weeks, move in with me. Take a break."

She laughed. "A break?"

"Yeah. No house to clean, no worries."

"*You'll* worry me," she admitted.

"Me? I'm harmless."

She laughed again, and he liked the sound of it. "You are many things," she said, "but harmless isn't one of them."

"Not afraid of me, are you?"

"Said the big bad wolf," she murmured, then shook her head. "No. I'm not afraid of you, Dave. I'm just…"

"…going to agree."

"Do you always get your way?"

"Always," he said.

She looked at the ring, then him and finally said, "Then I guess you win again. Okay. I'll move in."

"That wasn't so hard, was it?"

"You have no idea."

"Here," Dave said, sliding his untouched chocolate cake across the table toward her. "You look like you could use this."

She picked up her fork and dug in. "Thanks."

* * *

After a week at the Royal Round Up Ranch, Mia was no more at ease than she had been the day she'd arrived. If anything, her nerves were stretched a little tighter. Royal had been buzzing about their engagement for days. Whenever she went into town, she was stopped a half dozen times on Main Street with people wanting to talk about her "romantic, whirlwind engagement." Which only made her feel like a cheat. And if there's one thing her father had taught her, it was that "cheating is the coward's way."

She hated lying. Hated playing a part. And really hated thinking about what everyone in town would be saying when her engagement ended.

But that was a worry for further down the road. Right now, even though it wasn't easy, she was grateful to be at the ranch because Dave had been right. The reporters were even more intrusive than before, though none of them could get to her here at the Royal Round Up.

She steered her old Volkswagen Bug through the gates of the ranch and waved at the guard Dave had posted there. No reporter could get past that guard, and if anyone tried to just hop a fence and cross the ranch, they'd get lost long before they made it to the main house.

Smiling to herself, Mia drove down the winding road toward the ranch house, her mind wandering as she traveled the now-familiar route.

It had been a weird week. Oh, she was used to his house now, had even learned her way around. And in spite of its size and innate elegance, it was a homey place. Warm and welcoming. Her bedroom, directly across from Dave's, was bigger than her entire suite of rooms at Alex's house. And she was getting very used to waking up to a spectacular view of Dave's ranch. The land stretched out forever, marked by stands of wild oaks and stock ponds. It was quiet, as it could only be in the country, and at night, the sky was velvet, covered by a blanket of stars so thick it took her breath away.

It wasn't her surroundings making her nervous.

It was Dave.

And it wasn't as if he'd gone out of his way to make her jumpy. On the contrary, he'd done nothing but be very nice. Thoughtful, even. They had dinner together every night and spent hours in the library she had loved from the moment she first saw it. He took her on rides around the ranch and introduced her to his mare, due to deliver her foal any day.

Every time she turned around, there he was. Gorgeous. Warm. Sexy. He was turning her inside out and she had the distinct feeling he was doing it on purpose. That he knew by his constant attention he was wearing down her resistance. Seducing her.

And damn if she wasn't enjoying it.

It was a bad idea, though. Mia knew that. This wasn't going to be her home. He wasn't going to be hers for any longer than it took to make the deal he wanted so badly. Nothing about their relationship was real. Except the wanting. And the desire that thrummed inside her all the time was as insistent as a heartbeat.

But if this was seduction, it was the long way around. He hadn't even tried to kiss her.

"Why not?" she muttered, then glared at herself in the rearview mirror.

When this whole deal had begun, she'd made a point of saying that sex wouldn't be a part of it, so why was she...disappointed that he was keeping to their bargain?

"Because you can't stop thinking about him, that's

why," she told herself and gritted her teeth as her car hit a bump on the gravel road.

That was the simple truth. She thought about him all the time. And the fact that he was so determined to keep his distance was driving her a little crazy.

"Which is just wrong and I know it," she said aloud. It wasn't as if she was a highly sexual woman, after all. She'd been with exactly two men in her life, and neither one of those occasions had been worthy of mention. There hadn't been fireworks. The angels hadn't sung.

So why was she so hot and bothered by the thought of Dave?

"Oh, for heaven's sake." The spectacular house rose up in front of her and she drove on, past the circular drive-way that curved around the house. Instead, she parked her car closer to the barn. Mia just couldn't bring herself to park her beater car in front of that gorgeous house. It would be like seeing a pimple on the face of the Mona Lisa.

She looked through the windshield and saw a couple of the ranch hands at the paddock, where Mike Carter was putting a young horse through its paces. Dave was there, too, arms hooked over the top rail of the fence and one booted foot propped on the lower rail. Over the past week or so, she'd discovered that the Dave who lived and worked at the ranch was a wildly different man than the cool, focused businessman she'd first known. It was as if he kept his soul here at the ranch and without it, he was a different man.

Unfortunately for her, she'd been attracted to the hard, distant businessman…but the rancher was unbelievably hard to resist.

Mia sighed, stepped out of the car then reached back in for her bags and the small blue glass vase that held three daisies and a red carnation. She looked at the bedraggled flowers and smiled. A grocery store special, they couldn't have cost more than five dollars and they meant more to her than two dozen roses would have.

"Mia!"

She turned at the sound of her name and saw Dave striding toward her. Late afternoon sun was behind him, and her breath caught in her chest as she watched him approach. His hat was pulled low on his forehead. He wore a blue work shirt, the sleeves pushed up to his elbows, and faded jeans that clung to his long legs and stacked on the tops of his scarred brown boots.

Dave Firestone was the kind of cowboy that would make any woman's heart beat just a little faster than normal. So she really couldn't be blamed for enjoying the view, right?

When he was close enough to reach out and touch her, he stopped, glanced at the flowers she held and smiled. "You want to tell me who's giving my girl flowers?"

His girl. Something warm curled in the pit of her stomach and she was forced to remind herself that he didn't mean it. Just part of the game they were playing. The ranch hands were close by and no doubt watching them, so he was playing to his audience.

"I told you today was the last day of my internship at Royal Junior High…"

"Not even the end of the semester, was it?"

"No. The school board makes fall internships short and then does follow-ups come spring. Gives us more time to devote to schoolwork."

"Okay…"

"Well, two of my kids bought me these," she said, glancing down at the flowers that meant so much to her.

"Nice kids," he said.

She looked up at him. "They really are. I'm going to miss them."

He moved in closer. Close enough that she caught the scent of his aftershave still clinging to his skin. Her heartbeat sped up in response.

"You'll see them all again in the spring. And then again after you get your degree and start working there full time."

Since she still had a few months of school left and there was no guarantee of a job when she was finished, Mia could only hope he was right.

"You were late getting home," he said. "I was worried. Thought maybe this…*car* of yours finally gave up the ghost."

She frowned at him. Okay, her old VW wasn't exactly a luxury ride, but it was loyal, she knew all of its quirks and as long as she added a quart of oil a week, it kept running. It fired right up every morning, and it got her where she needed to go and that was enough for her. Mia didn't have enough money to think about making a new-car payment every month. "Don't make fun of my baby."

He shook his head. "Nothing funny about this car. It should have been junked years ago."

As if he could hear her thoughts, he changed the subject. "Leave your bags here," he said and scooped everything but the flowers from her arms, then stacked them on the hood of the car. "There's something I want to show you."

Excitement shone in his eyes and that half smile of his that she loved so much was tipping up one corner of his mouth. He was irresistible. She set the vase of flowers down on the hood. "What is it?"

"You'll see." He caught her hand in his and headed for the barn.

Mia had to hurry her steps to keep up with his long-legged stride. The warmth of his hand against hers simmered in a slow heat that slid through her system to settle around her heart.

The men gathered at the paddock called hello to her as they passed and she smiled, enjoying the sensation of being part of ranch life—even if it only was temporary. With that sobering thought in mind, she followed Dave into the shadow-filled barn.

It smelled like hay and horses and she heard a shuffling sound from animals shifting position in their stalls. Dave led her to the far stall, then pulled her close to look over the edge of the door.

"Oh, my..." Mia's heart twisted in her chest. Dave's mare, Dancer, was nuzzling a brand-new foal, still shaky on its impossibly long, thin legs.

"Happened just a couple hours ago," Dave whispered, his breath warm against her ear. "Dancer came through like she'd done this a hundred times before."

"I'm so glad," Mia said, wrapping her arms around him for an instinctive hug. She knew how much the horse meant to him. He'd even been planning to have a vet attend the birth because he didn't want to take chances with the mare's life.

And that endeared him to her. He might pretend to be cold and shut off, but the truth was, he had a big heart. He was just careful whom he showed it to.

"Yeah," he answered, looking down into her eyes as his arms closed around her, drawing her even closer. "Me, too. I raised Dancer, so she means a lot to me."

"I know." She couldn't look away from his fog-gray eyes. She held her breath, afraid to speak, afraid to shatter this sudden shift into intimacy.

His gaze moved over her face like a caress. "It's weird,

but I was anxious for you to get home, so I could share this with you."

"Really?"

"Yeah." He lifted one hand to cup her cheek. "Wonder what that's about?"

"I don't know," she said, "but I'm glad."

"Me, too," he said, and bent his head to hers.

She was dazzled with the first brush of his lips against hers. Sighing, she leaned into him and he held her tighter, pressing her body along the length of his.

Mia was lost, spiraling away into the heat and desire burning inside her. She forgot all about where they were. The barn and the horses faded away. The voices from the cowboys outside silenced and it was just her and Dave, locked in a moment that filled her with pleasure despite a tiny, tiny touch of worry.

When he parted her lips with his tongue and the kiss deepened into something amazing, the worry dissolved under an onslaught of emotion so thick and rich that Mia's mind shut down completely. She leaned into him, her arms tightening around him, her tongue tangling with his in a wild dance of a passion she'd never felt before.

Their breath mingled, their bodies pressed together and Mia heard Dave groan as he claimed her again and again. His hands swept down to the hem of her shirt and slid underneath it. The touch of his hands against her bare back was magic and she suddenly wanted more. Needed more.

But he tore his mouth from hers and left her struggling to catch her breath, fighting to find her balance. She leaned her forehead against his chest and shivered. "Why did you stop?"

He chuckled and his voice sounded raw and strained when he answered, "Because we're in a damn barn, Mia.

With my ranch hands right outside that door. If we're gonna do this, then we're gonna do it right."

He paused, lifted her chin until he could look into her eyes and asked, "We *are* gonna do this, right?"

There was her out. Time to snap out of this sexual haze and remember what she was doing here. Who she was with. And why. He'd just handed her the chance she needed to reach for calm, cool logic and call off whatever it was that was happening between them. She should be grateful. Should be smart. Should tell him, "No, we're not."

"Absolutely," she said. "When?"

"I'm thinking *now.*"

"Oh, good idea." Mia was still trembling. Still shaking from needs awakened and screaming inside her. "Where?"

"Your room. Fifteen minutes."

"Right. Fifteen minutes." She took a breath and blew it out. "Why so long?"

He laughed and she did, too. This was ridiculous. She was acting crazy. She'd never done anything like this before. It was so out of character for her. And she liked it a lot.

"Because," he said, letting her go long enough to adjust his jeans, "I'm not going to be able to walk across that yard for at least ten minutes."

She flushed, then grinned. Wow. She'd never done that to a man before. Had him so hard he wasn't able to walk. It felt…great.

"Okay, then," she said, taking another breath, which only succeeded in fanning the flames licking at her insides. "I'll be waiting."

His gray eyes burned with an intensity that was new to her as he promised, "I'll get there as fast as I can."

Nodding, Mia scuttled out of the barn, waved to the guys in the paddock and hurried toward the house. She stopped at her car long enough to pick up her things, then she practically ran to the ranch house and the staircase that led to her bedroom.

Mia didn't have much time. She raced up the stairs, praying she wouldn't run into Dave's housekeeper as she went. She hit her bedroom at a dead run and pulled her clothes off as she hurried across the room to the attached bath. She hopped into the shower and thanked heaven she'd shaved her legs the day before. When she was finished, she dried off and slipped into the heavy, white robe hanging on the back of her door, tying the belt with shaking hands.

She was taking a step here. A big one. She hadn't meant for her relationship with Dave to go this far, but now that it had she wouldn't regret it. Instead, she was going to grab at the chance fate had handed her. For years, she'd been locked away in schools, libraries, tucked up in her suite of rooms at Alex's house. *Life* had been passing her by and she'd hardly noticed.

Mia took a deep breath and slapped one hand to her belly in a futile attempt to quell the butterflies swarming inside. She hadn't once, in the past few years, had so much as a date. She'd been too focused on her future to enjoy her present.

Well, today that stopped. Today, Mia Hughes was going to take the time to live a little. To be with a man who *wanted* her. Whatever happened tomorrow, she'd simply have to deal with it, because she wasn't going to back away.

Mia sat down on the edge of her four-poster bed and, to distract herself from the nerves of waiting, glanced around the room that had become so familiar over the past week. The whole house was golden oak and rough-hewn stone, and her room was no different. There was a deeply cushioned window seat below the arched bay windows that overlooked the backyard. The view was of rolling green grass, stands of live oaks and ponds for the Black Angus cattle that wandered the fields. A stone fireplace, cold now, stood against one wall, and on the opposite wall was a dresser beside a walk-in closet. It was perfect. Just like the rest of this house.

And right now, all it was lacking was Dave.

A knock on her door startled her out of her thoughts. She opened the door, looked up at Dave and knew that somehow this was meant to be. She wasn't going to question it. She was just going to *live*.

"You look like you're silently arguing with yourself," he said, his voice a low rumble of sound that seemed to reverberate in the big room.

"Nope," she said, shaking her head. "No arguing."

"No second-guessing?"

"No."

"No changing your mind?"

"No."

"Thank God." He stepped into the room and used one bare foot to kick the door shut behind him. "If you had changed your mind…"

"What?" she asked, excitement jolting to life inside her. "What would you have done?"

"Left," he admitted, then added, "and would have sat in my room, moaning in pain."

"That would have been a shame."

"Tell me about it," he said with a grin as he closed in on her. "You've been making me crazy, Mia."

"I have?" Oh, that was lovely to hear. She hadn't known she was capable of driving a man crazy.

"Oh, yeah." His gaze swept up and down her body and then met her eyes. "What's under the robe?"

"Me." She lifted her hands to the belt at her waist, but he stopped her.

"Let me."

She stood perfectly still while he untied the belt and pushed her robe open. The cool air in the room brushed her skin, raising goose bumps that were dissolved in the heat of Dave's touch.

His hands smoothed over her hips and up to cup her breasts. She swayed, but kept her eyes open, determined to see him, to experience every moment of this time with him.

He'd taken a shower, too, before coming to her. His dark blond hair was still damp. He wore a black T-shirt, jeans and he was barefoot. He looked sexier than she'd ever seen him and that was saying something.

He bent to kiss her and she moved into him, relishing the buzz of sensation as his mouth met hers. Once, twice and then he straightened up, looking down at her again. "Gotta have you, Mia."

"Yes, Dave." She reached up, wound her arms around his neck and whooshed out a surprised gasp when he scooped her up into his arms.

She laughed, delighted. It was all so romantic, she could hardly believe it was happening to her.

He took a step and stopped. "I surprised you," he said, grinning.

"You did."

"I like your smile."

She liked a lot about him. Staring into his eyes, Mia knew she should call a halt to this and knew just as well that she wouldn't. Sighing, she said, "Oh, this is really going to complicate things."

Dave shook his head. "Doesn't have to."

"Of course it does. Sex always complicates things."

"Complications aren't necessarily a bad thing."

"I hope you're right."

His grin widened briefly. "I'm always right."

He laid her down on the bed and she pushed herself up onto her elbows to watch as Dave stripped out of his clothes. In seconds, he was on the bed with her, gathering her up in his arms and rolling them across the mattress until she was breathless. Legs tangled, hands explored, mouths tasted, teased. Breath came fast and short and whispered moans and murmurs filled the room.

Mia arched into him when his mouth closed over her nipple. Lips, tongue and teeth worked her already sensitive skin until she was twisting and writhing beneath him, chasing the feeling that was growing inside her.

Mia had never felt like this. Never even come close. Dave was stroking her, dipping his fingers into her heat, touching her inside and out. And with every caress the fire engulfing her grew brighter, hotter. Her hips lifted into his hand, as she instinctively moved toward the release waiting for her.

"I've wanted to touch you like this for days," Dave murmured, then closed his mouth around one of her nipples.

"Oh…" She held his head to her breast and her eyes closed with the sheer bliss of the moment.

"I love the little sighs and moans you make," he said, lifting his head to look down into her eyes. "I love the way you feel. I love the scent of you."

Love. Love.

But not the Big L. A corner of her mind realized that

and made sure she didn't cling to any false hopes. He didn't *love* her. He loved what they were *doing.* And so did she. *Don't think,* she ordered her mind and deliberately turned off everything but the sensations cresting inside her.

Again and again, he stroked, delved, caressed and nibbled. Foreplay became forever-play. She wanted him inside her and he kept making her wait. He was pushing her so high, so fast, she could hardly breathe with the wanting.

No one had ever touched her like this. No one had ever made her *feel* so much. He kissed her, using his tongue to steal the last of her breath. Mia didn't care. At that moment, all she cared about was finally, finally reaching the climax he was promising her with every stroke of his fingers.

When he broke the kiss and she reached for him, he grinned. "Hold that thought."

Then he eased off the bed, grabbed up his jeans from the floor and reached into one of the pockets. He tossed a handful of condoms onto the bedside table, then opened one of the foil packets.

A buzz of expectation sped through Mia as she shot a glance at the condoms, then at Dave. "Planning a long night?"

"Good to be prepared," he countered, and sheathed himself before joining her on the bed. "Now that I've got you where I want you, I may not let you go again."

"Who says I'm going to let *you* go?" Mia teased.

He grinned at her again. "That's what I like to hear." He dropped a kiss at the base of her throat. "You're so warm."

"Getting warmer every second," she said.

Smiling, he parted her thighs and knelt between them,

pausing long enough to slide the tip of one finger along her folds, making her shiver.

She planted her feet on the bed and lifted her hips into his touch. Licking her lips, she murmured, "Please, Dave. No more waiting."

"No more waiting," he agreed and entered her in one long stroke.

Mia gasped, looked up into his eyes and sighed as she reveled in the sensation of him filling her. He was part of her. His body and hers locked together. She wrapped her arms around his neck and didn't take her gaze from his as he moved within her. Over and over again, he rocked his hips against hers, setting a rhythm that she eagerly matched. They moved as one, their bodies each straining toward a shattering climax.

Their sighs and groans filled the room like music. Sunlight speared through the windows and spotlighted them on the wide bed as they came together in a need that swamped everything else.

Mia held on to him as tension gripped her, coiling tighter and tighter. She moved with him, met him stroke for stroke. She slid her hands up and down his back and felt his muscles bunch.

This moment was all. Nothing beyond this room—this time—mattered.

She stared into his fog-gray eyes and watched her own reflection there as her body erupted. Mia called out his name and clung desperately to him as a shock wave thundered through her.

She was still trembling when Dave reached the same peak she had. And together, they slid down the other side into completion.

Eight

Dave was shaken, but damn if he'd admit it—even to himself.

Lying there on Mia's bed, with her curled up to his side, he stared at the ceiling and tried to understand just what the hell had happened.

He'd put her in this guest room on purpose. So she'd be close enough to make seduction that much easier. Problem was, *he* was the one who had been seduced. And that hadn't been part of the plan at all.

"That was so good," Mia murmured, her warm breath brushing across his chest.

"Yeah, it was." Better than good, he thought, frowning a little as his brain began to click again now that the burn in his body had eased some. He'd figured from the beginning that getting Mia naked would take care of the desire that pumped through him every time he was near her. Instead, his body was stirring already at the feel of her hand stroking slowly across his chest.

Until today, he hadn't had a woman in more than six months. Just hadn't had the time or the inclination. Now it made sense, he thought. He'd needed a woman *badly,* so it was no wonder he'd been so frantic to get his hands on Mia.

The question was, why had the sex been so off-the-charts great? His mind was sluggish but still trying to find a way to save his ass. He'd spent more time with Mia than he had with any of the other women in his life. He *knew* her—had seen her at Alex's house. Talked with her in town. It was a connection that he'd always avoided with women before now, so of course the sex would be more…personal. More… Hell. Just *more.*

"I wonder if Delores has any chocolate cake left?" she murmured.

Dave laughed and looked down at her. Here he was, thinking about taking another bite out of her and she had already moved on to chocolate. Humbling to know your woman was more interested in your housekeeper's home-baked desserts than she was in taking another ride.

Changing her mind about *that* was just the kind of challenge Dave liked best.

He went up on one elbow and looked down at her. "Chocolate cake's got nothing on what I'm about to give you."

"Really?" She lifted one hand to stroke her fingers along his chest.

Dave hissed in a breath. "Oh, yeah. When I'm done, you won't even remember what chocolate *is.*"

As he slid down along her body, he felt her shiver and heard her whisper, "I can't wait…"

* * *

A few days later, Dave sipped his coffee and looked out the diner's window at the town of Royal, going about its day. He was tired. Hadn't been getting much sleep lately. He smiled to himself. Hell, once he and Mia had gotten started, there'd been no stopping either of them.

After their first night together, Mia had moved her things into the master bedroom and, Dave had to say, he was liking having her there. Strange because until Mia, he had never spent the night with a woman. It had always been get some, get gone. Easy. Uncomplicated. No expectations. No strings.

There weren't supposed to be strings now, either. But sometimes, Dave could swear he felt silky threads wrapping themselves around him, and he wasn't sure how to slip out of the knot that would only get tighter. Mia had been right, he told himself.

Sex had complicated the situation.

But he couldn't regret it. Hell, he'd have to be crazy to do that.

In fact, the only thing he was regretting was the fact that he had to leave her alone for a few days. Tonight, Dave was riding out with some of the ranch hands to where the herd was being held. The vet had already been out to inoculate the yearling calves and check out the rest of the cattle. He'd already taken care of the new beef that had arrived; now it was time for his regular herd to be checked over. Rather than ride in and out to the ranch, Dave and his employees would be camping out.

So he'd come to Royal to ask Nathan Battle to keep an eye on the ranch while Dave was gone. Not that he was worried about reporters getting to Mia. He was leaving enough of the ranch hands behind to see to her safety. But it never hurt to have a backup plan.

The Royal Diner was, as always, a morning hub of activity. He heard Amanda and Pam laughing at something, and the buzz of conversation from the other customers rose and fell like waves. Sunlight slanted through the windows, and outside an impatient driver hit the car horn.

From the corner of his eye, he saw someone approach, and expecting it to be Nathan, Dave turned his head and smiled a welcome. That smile froze in place when a lovely woman slid into the booth seat opposite him.

"Good morning," she said, shaking her hair back from her face and holding one hand out to him. "Remember me? I'm Bailey Collins. I work for the state investigator's office."

Dave shook her hand and released her. "I remember. We've 'talked' before."

He studied her for a second or two. She had shoulder-length dark brown hair with reddish highlights. Her chocolate-colored eyes were locked with his as if daring him to look away. If she was waiting for him to cower, she had a long wait coming.

His good mood drained away as if it had never been. Dave had already talked to cops and private investigators about Alex's disappearance and nothing had changed. He still knew nothing. Couldn't help in their search. Didn't have a clue what had happened to the man and was fast coming to the point where he didn't care, either. Sure, if Dave had a choice in it, he'd like to see Alex come back safely. But more than that, he'd like to see people leaving *him* the hell alone.

"What do you want?" he asked, though he already knew the answer to that question.

She gave him a wide smile and shook her head. "Well, aren't you charming?"

"I didn't realize charm would make a difference with you."

"It wouldn't," she admitted with a shrug.

"There you go, then." He wasn't going to play a game. Pretend to be understanding about all of this when his patience was long since shot to hell. So she could say her piece and get out of his life.

"All right," she said, "we're on the same page. I'm here in Royal to do my job, not make friends. I realize we've already spoken and that you're probably tired of answering questions, but I promise you, this will go much easier for both of us if you cooperate."

"Heard that before," he muttered.

She gave him a smile. "Look, why don't you tell me everything you know about Alex Santiago's disappearance."

"I'm sure you've read all the reports. I've told you already what I know and I can tell you now I haven't remembered anything new," he said, reaching for patience and just managing to grab hold of the tail end of it. "I've discussed it all with Nathan. With the feds. With you."

"And now," she said simply, "with *me* again."

Amanda walked up to the table, carrying a coffeepot. She looked from Dave to Bailey and back again. "More coffee?"

"Sure, thanks," Dave said.

"Me, too. Thanks." Bailey pushed the extra cup toward Amanda.

Once the cups were filled, Amanda gave Dave's shoulder a pat in solidarity, then moved off again.

"You've got friends in town."

"Guess I do," he said, nodding. Funny, he'd never really thought about it before, but in the years that he'd been in Royal, he *had* made some good friends. He was grateful for them. Especially now.

Bailey doctored her perfectly good black coffee with cream and sugar, took a sip and said, "Why don't you tell me one more time what you know about Alex's disappearance."

"It won't take long," Dave assured her. He launched into the story he'd already told too many times to count, and when he was finished, Bailey just looked at him for a long minute or two. They probably taught that move in investigator school. How to Make Potential Suspects Squirm 101.

But Dave had played with the big boys for a lot of years. He'd made deals, negotiated contracts and the one thing he'd learned had been "he who speaks first loses power." So he kept his mouth shut and waited her out.

It didn't take much longer.

"All right, thank you. I appreciate your time," she said and scooted out of the booth.

"That's it?" he asked, hardly daring to believe she wasn't going to pepper him with even more questions.

"You were expecting rubber hoses?" Her smile was friendly, but her eyes were still too sharp for comfort. "Oh. Just one more thing. I hear you're engaged to Alex's housekeeper Mia Hughes."

Dave went stone still. "And?"

"Nothing." She shrugged a little too casually. "It was sudden though, wasn't it?"

"I suppose. Is there a problem?"

She paused for a moment as if considering her answer before finally saying, "No. Look, I happen to agree with Sheriff Battle. You're not a suspect. But I have to talk to everyone who knew Alex. I'm hoping that someone knows something they don't even realize they know."

Nodding, Dave said, "Okay, I get that."

"Good." She stood up and bumped into Nathan Battle as he walked up to the booth. "Sorry, Sheriff, didn't see you there."

"It's okay." Nathan glanced at Dave, then looked at Bailey. "Am I interrupting?"

"No," she said with a last glance at Dave. "We're done here. Again, thanks for your time, Mr. Firestone."

When she walked away, Nathan took her seat, signaled to his wife, Amanda, for a cup of coffee then asked, "So what was that about?"

"The usual." Dave watched Bailey leave the diner and shook his head ruefully. "That was me, being officially ruled out by everyone."

"About time," Nathan said, wrapping one arm around his wife's expanding waist when she brought him coffee.

"Damn straight," Dave agreed and lifted his own coffee for a long, satisfying drink.

The next day, Mia was feeling Dave's absence. He'd ridden out early that morning with Mike Carter and several of the other ranch hands, and watching him ride off had torn at her. She hadn't even noticed over the past two weeks just how much she'd come to depend on having him around. They'd had a nice little routine going.

He worked outside and she studied in the library, preparing for her final exams. Yes, she still had time, but Mia wasn't taking chances with her future. They still managed to spend time with each other every day. They shared lunch, sometimes taking a picnic out to the lakeside. She helped him with the ranch ledgers and he'd showed her how to ride a horse. And one spectacular weekend, he'd arranged for his company plane to fly them to San Antonio. They'd had dinner on the River Walk and then went dancing. It had been the most romantic time in her life and it had ended all too soon. There had been warmth and laughter and an ease between them that she'd never felt with anyone else.

And now he was gone. Without him, the house felt bigger and far less warm. She could still smell him in the room they shared and caught herself listening for the sound of his boot heels on the floors.

But he would be gone at least two days, so Mia was just going to have to deal with it. Actually, being without him would be good practice for when this month with him was over. When she moved back to her suite of rooms at Alex's house, she wouldn't be seeing Dave again. Wouldn't go to sleep in his arms or wake up to his kisses every morning. Her heart ached at the thought of that and she realized just how deeply she'd allowed herself to fall in the past couple of weeks.

Oh, Mia knew that she had been ripe for the kind of acceptance and belonging she'd found at the Royal Round Up. The ranch hands were wonderful. Delores, Dave's housekeeper, had practically adopted her. And the big house felt like home.

She'd hungered for *home* for so long, it was no wonder Mia had embraced what she'd found here. But it was so much more than that. She didn't want to think about it. Didn't want to even consider it. But the sad, hard truth was that she was falling in love with Dave. Oh, she knew that road led only to misery, but she didn't know what she could do about it now. And maybe she wouldn't change it even if she could. Yes, there would be pain coming her way, but the only way to avoid that pain was to not feel the way Dave made her feel. And she wouldn't give that up for anything.

Strange how everything, your whole world, could change so quickly. Just a few weeks ago, she'd been half convinced that Dave wasn't to be trusted. That he might have had something to do with Alex's disappearance.

Now she knew that the only thing he was guilty of was making her love him.

"Oh, this is not good," she muttered, closing the book on her lap.

She was curled up in a wide, leather chair in the library. There was a fire burning in the hearth and outside, gray clouds scuttled across the sky while a cold October wind rattled the trees and buffeted the windows.

The room was cozy and comforting but without Dave, it was empty.

She glanced at the sofa where they usually sat, wrapped up together, talking, laughing, *kissing.* A sigh slipped from her as she thought about how little time she had left with Dave. He'd set up a meeting with the owner of TexCat for next week. Once he got the cattle deal he wanted, their time together would be over. And oh, how she would miss being here. Miss *him.*

When the phone beside her rang, Mia grabbed it, grateful for a reprieve from her own thoughts. "Hello?"

A woman's voice, quick and friendly. "Hello, may I speak to Dave?"

"No, he's out with the herd for a few days," Mia said, wondering who the woman was and why she wanted to speak to Dave. But in the next second she told herself that she had no right to wonder. She and Dave weren't a *real* couple, after all. But playing her role, she added, "I'm Mia, Dave's fiancée. Can I take a message?"

"His *fiancée?*" the woman repeated, her voice hitching a bit higher. "Isn't that *wonderful!* No, there's no message, thank you. I'll catch him another day. And, oh, congratulations!"

"Thank you," Mia said, but the woman had already

hung up. Okay, she thought, setting the receiver back into its cradle, that was odd. But since the mystery woman seemed more excited than angry to hear Dave was engaged, Mia felt better about her. Sure, she didn't have the right to feel jealous, but that didn't stop the sharp sting of it.

Jealous. She had to get past that, because once their time together was over, Dave would be dating other women. Women who would come here, to this house. Be with him in his bed. Stare into those fog-gray eyes as his body claimed theirs.

And after a while, she thought dismally, Dave probably wouldn't even remember her.

By the time Dave got back to the house two days later, he was dusty, tired and damned crabby. Of course, he knew the reason for his bad mood.

It was Mia.

Or rather, the *lack* of Mia.

Spending those long nights out on the ranch used to be something he looked forward to. Getting away from the house, from the business side of things and getting back to the heart of ranching. Working the cattle, sleeping under the stars with nothing but a few cowboys and the crackle of a campfire for company. It kept him connected to his land and to the men who worked for him.

Now, thoughts of Mia, hunger for Mia, had ruined the whole damn experience for him. What the hell did that make him? What had happened when he wasn't looking? She was slipping under his skin. Getting to him in ways that he hadn't thought possible. Her laugh. Her scent. The feel of her long, supple fingers sliding over his body.

Everything about the woman was more than he'd expected. Who would have thought that a shy, quiet housekeeper would be so multilayered? So easy to talk to? Hell, she even liked playing video games and had damn near kicked his ass at one of his favorites.

She was only in his life temporarily. Their bargain was a business deal, that was all. Didn't matter if he had a good time with her. Didn't matter that he wanted her more than his next breath. When the deal was over, they'd go their separate ways. That was the point of a signed contract, he reminded himself. Rules were laid out, plain and simple, so there were no mistakes and no recriminations. If he wanted to keep the relationship with Mia going after the terms of the contract had played out—then that left him open to all sorts of trouble. He'd learned long ago that the only way to have a woman in his life was to keep it simple. Hence, the rules. Without them... Even wanting Mia as he did, he didn't think he could continue to see her when this was over. It would get...complicated.

Promises made were too easily broken. He wouldn't set himself up for that kind of misery. Better to have the "rules" laid out in black and white.

Yeah, the deal had become a little more than he had planned. After all, he'd expected that one night of sex with Mia would ease the craving for her. Instead, it had only grown until she was all he could think about. So yeah, a flaw or two in the plan.

But he'd find a way to get his equilibrium back. And when he did, he'd discover a way to keep Mia at a distance even while he was inside her.

Nodding, he told himself to get right on that.

But not tonight.

Tonight, he wanted a shower, and then Mia.

He opened the front door and stepped into the golden lamplight of home. Then he tore his hat off and tossed it onto a nearby chair. "Mia! I'm home!"

His gaze scanned the foyer, the wide, curving staircase and the hallway beyond. Where the hell was she? Then he heard it. Quick, light footsteps. He grinned, turned in anticipation and felt the air *whoosh* from his lungs in surprise.

A short, trim woman with chin-length blond hair and fog-gray eyes threw herself at him with a delighted grin. Dave wrapped his arms around her, returned her bear hug and said, "Mom? What're you doing here?"

Behind his mother, at a slower pace, came Mia. Her gaze met his and he read the worry in her usually sparkling blue eyes. But before he could figure out what was going on, his mother started talking. And once Alice Firestone got going, there was no stopping her.

"I can't believe you didn't tell me about Mia," she was saying, and reached up to pat his cheek just a little harder than necessary. "You should have told me. I'd have come sooner."

He finally found his voice. "Sooner than what? How long have you been here, Mom?"

Alice patted her son's chest as she stepped back and beamed at first him, then Mia. "I called to talk to you and when Mia answered and told me the good news, I came right away!"

"She arrived later the same day you left," Mia said, flashing him a silent "don't say anything" signal with her eyes.

"Naturally, I had to rush out here and meet my new almost daughter," Alice was saying. "So I called Tobin and he sent his plane for me. I was here in just a couple of hours."

Tobin. Damn. Dave hadn't thought about explaining the situation to either his partner or his mother and now he was paying the price. His mom had been after him for so long to get married and give her grandchildren that she wasn't going to take it well when she found out the engagement wasn't real. Perfect. And God knew whom Tobin was telling the news to. Dave shot a look at Mia and could see that her thoughts were running along the same lines.

"Oh, and Tobin said to tell you that he and his wife are so excited for you. They're planning a trip here to meet Mia as soon as they get back from North Dakota."

Great, he thought. More explanations to come. That's perfect.

"David, Mia and I have had so much fun these past two days," his mother said. "She's just a delight! Did you know that she'd like to have four children? Oh," she said, waving a hand in the air, "of course you know. The two of you probably have names all picked out."

Four children? He fired a look at Mia and she shrugged helplessly, turning both palms up. Marriage. Kids. Hell, this was getting out of control fast.

"Just so you know, I'm okay with whatever names you choose. I'll just be so pleased to have grandchildren!" Alice gave him a wide smile. "This is so exciting, David."

Before he could speak, Alice turned to Mia. "You know, sweetie, I've been so worried about him. I hated to think of him living his life alone. And then there was the guilt of course, for not exactly providing a good example of a happy marriage—"

"Hardly your fault, Mom," Dave interrupted. Damned if he'd let her feel guilty because Dave's no-good father had walked out on them.

"That's nice of you to say, honey, but a parent worries about their child *always*." She reached up and brushed his hair off his forehead. "It doesn't matter if that child is an adult, the worry doesn't stop. Neither does the love. But you two will find that out for yourselves soon."

That noose he'd once felt locking around his throat was back again, tightening incrementally until Dave felt his breathing being choked off. Another glance at Mia and he read her expression easily. Misery and guilt. Well, hell, he knew how she felt, didn't he?

Damn, all he'd wanted was a shower and some hot, steamy sex with Mia. Now his brain was cluttered with his mother and imaginary children clambering all over his house. Talk about a mood killer.

Mia looked as if she wanted to crawl into a hole, and Dave understood. He should clear this up now, and he knew it. No point in waiting, because if he didn't cut his mother off at the pass, so to speak, she'd have a judge out at the ranch that weekend, performing a ceremony.

As if she read his thoughts, his mother said, "Mia and I were talking wedding plans, of course, *so* exciting. Mia insists you wouldn't want a large wedding...." She paused and watched him for confirmation.

"Yeah. I mean no, I don't."

"She knows you so well already," Alice said, eyes bright. "Isn't that lovely? So, we think it would be best if you hold the wedding right here on the ranch. There's plenty of room," she continued before he could say a word. "And Delores is full of wonderful ideas for a buffet menu. Mia and I can go shopping for her wedding dress—" She broke off and looked at Mia sheepishly.

"I'm sorry, honey. I'm just including myself, but of course if you don't want me to go with you..."

"It would be great, Alice," Mia said, her voice thick with emotion. "I'd love your opinion."

"Isn't that wonderful?" Alice turned back to Dave and gave him another hard hug before slapping one hand to her chest, overcome with emotion. "I always wanted a daughter, you know, and Mia and I already get along famously!"

Dave hugged his mom and regretted that he was going to have to burst her bubble. But that bubble would only get bigger and the hurt deeper, if he waited.

"Mom…" He looked over his mother's head to Mia who was shaking her head wildly and waving her hands. Narrowing her eyes, she glared at him and mouthed the word, *don't*.

Why the hell not? He scowled at her and she frowned right back, shaking her head again, even more firmly this time.

Fine, fine, he wouldn't say anything until he and Mia had had a chance to talk. Talking hadn't been on his agenda for tonight, but it looked like that was going to change.

Damn, he was too tired for all of this. He hugged his mother and let her go.

"Mom, I'm glad you're here, but after nearly three days on the range, I really need a shower."

His mother stepped back and sniffed delicately through her wrinkled nose. "I didn't want to say anything."

Wryly, he said, "Thanks."

Then his gaze shifted to Mia again and his mother noticed.

"Oh, you two must have a lot to 'talk' about." A smile flitted across her mouth. "Why don't you and Mia go on upstairs and I'll just head over to the guesthouse."

Dave was nodding. He was glad to see his mother, sure. But at the moment, he had other ideas on how to spend his time. At least he *had*, until this latest wrench had been tossed into his carefully laid-out strategy. Now he had the distinct feeling that Mia would want to talk before they did anything else.

When he just kept staring at Mia, his mother chuckled. "Okay, then, I'm going. You two enjoy your reunion and I'll see you both in the morning, all right?"

"That'd be good, Mom, thanks," Dave said, still staring at the woman who haunted his every thought. She chewed at her bottom lip and the action tugged at something inside him. Hell, maybe talking could wait after all.

He hardly noticed when his mother left until the front door closed behind her. In the silence, he and Mia stared at each other for a long minute. Then she rushed at him and he opened his arms to her.

Holding on to her tightly, Dave buried his face in the curve of her neck and lifted her clean off the floor. Mia wrapped her legs around his waist, then pulled back and looked at him. "I really missed you."

Danger signs fluttered to life inside him, but it was way too late to pay attention to them. "Yeah," he admitted. "Me, too. And *damn* you smell good."

She gave him a smile and shook her hair back from her face. "I'm sorry you got blindsided by your mom, but I didn't know how to tell you she was here. I tried reaching you by cell, but…"

"It's okay," he said. "Not much coverage at the far corners of the ranch. Gotta get a satellite phone. I'm guessing her showing up out of the blue was a bigger surprise for you than for me anyway."

"You could say that." Her arms were linked around his neck, her ankles crossed at the small of his back. "She's so great, Dave. You're really lucky to have her."

"Yeah, but this is kind of a mess."

"More than you know," she said and unwound her legs from his waist to drop to the floor. Her eyes were shadowed and he knew she was feeling badly about deceiving his mother. Well, hell, so was he.

"She brought me a present."

Warily, he asked, "What?"

"I'll show you," she said on a sigh. "It's upstairs in your room."

"Just where I wanted to go, anyway." He dropped one arm around her shoulder and, pulling her in close to his side, headed for the staircase.

He didn't want to think about the fact that being with Mia made him feel...complete. Didn't want to acknowledge that the cold, hard spots inside him had been eased into warmth just by seeing her.

Because once he acknowledged any of that, there would be no going back.

Nine

Dave's room held more oversized furniture, just like the rest of the house. The bed was massive. A light oak four-poster was positioned against one wall. A flat-screen TV hung on the wall opposite and a bank of windows, drapes open to the night, took up another wall. There were scatter rugs in dark colors spread across the gleaming wood floor, a fireplace crackling with heat and two comfy chairs pulled up in front of the carefully laid blaze.

When Mia had first moved her things into this room, she'd felt a little awkward, out of place. Now it was cozy, filled with amazing memories of nights spent in Dave's arms and the promise of more to come.

He stood in the middle of the room and stripped out of his shirt. Tossing her a quick look, he said, "I'm going to jump into the shower, then we'll talk."

"Okay." Was it cowardly to prefer to put off the conversation she knew they had to have? If it was, she was fine with it. A few more minutes to gather her thoughts couldn't be a bad idea.

She heard the water when he turned it on and instantly pictured him in the shower. His long, rangy body covered in soap suds, hot water streaming across the hard planes and lines of the muscles carved into his skin by years of physical work. She pictured him tipping his head back under the rain showerhead, letting the water stream through his hair and down his back.

Swallowing hard, Mia edged off the bed. She didn't want to think. She just *wanted.* Dave had been gone for days and she'd missed him. Missed his touch. His taste. His scent. She'd missed what he could do to her body and she knew that conversation could wait.

She didn't want to waste a moment of her time with Dave. She loved him and all too soon, she'd be living without him. That thought made her heart ache as she walked across the room. So she put it aside for now. There would be plenty of time later for sorrow, for misery. Right now, there was only love.

She slipped out of her clothes as she crossed the bedroom and was naked by the time she walked into the adjoining bath. It looked like a spa in here. As big as her own living room at Alex's place, the bath was done in shades of green and cream tiles. There was a giant Jacuzzi tub sitting below an arched window that offered a wide view of the front of the ranch. A double vanity stretched the length of one wall, and on the opposite side of the room was a shower that could comfortably hold six people. There was no door, and because the area was so huge, no water from either the overhead rain nozzle or the five side sprays could reach the floor.

Dave had his back to her as he washed his hair and for just a minute, Mia simply enjoyed the view. He had the best butt in the world. And the rest of him was just as good.

Quietly, she slipped into the shower behind him and the hot water sluiced across her skin as she wrapped her arms around his waist and pressed her breasts against his back.

He groaned, turned around and cupped her face in his palms. "This kind of surprise I could use every day," he whispered and dipped his head to kiss her, hard and long and deep.

Her mind fuzzed out, but her body leaped to life. Every inch of her skin was buzzing. Her insides lit up like a fireworks factory on fire and the sensation of the water coursing over them only added to the sexual heat stirring between them.

"I decided I'd rather not talk right away," she said when he came up for air.

"My kind of girl," he murmured, smiling into her eyes.

Mia wished it was true. Wished that what they had was more than a signed contract and a promise to lie to an entire town. She wished that what they felt when they came together would be enough to *keep* them together when the month was over, but she couldn't fool herself. Couldn't hang on to false hope. Couldn't set herself up for more pain than was already headed her way.

So, instead, she told her suddenly active mind to go to sleep. She didn't need to think. She only needed to *feel*. For now, that would have to be enough.

Still smiling, Dave used the soap dispenser on the wall of the shower and pumped some of the clear green gel into the palm of his hand. Then, scrubbing his palms together, he worked up a lather before cupping her breasts and smoothing the luxurious soap over her skin.

Mia sighed and swayed unsteadily. His thumbs worked

her nipples into hard peaks and a burning ache set up shop between her legs. She moved into him, and ran her hands up and down his back and over his butt. She grazed him lightly with her fingernails and heard him hiss in a ragged breath. She smiled, knowing that he was as wildly needy as she was.

"God, you feel good," he told her, bending to kiss the curve of her neck and trail his lips and teeth back up the column of her throat to her mouth. "Taste good, too."

She shivered as he turned her until her back was against the smooth, gleaming tiles.

"Bet you taste good all over," he whispered and slid down the length of her body, taking his time about it, kissing her, stroking her until Mia was a quivering mass of sensation, pinned to the wall.

"Dave…"

The hot water rose up in steam all around them, blossoming like fog in the big bathroom. Mia opened her eyes and looked down to where he knelt in front of her and she swallowed past the knot of need and anticipation clogging her throat.

Dave nudged her thighs apart with his fingertips, and still meeting her gaze, rubbed the core of her with the pad of his thumb. Electrical jolts shattered her and she gasped in response, instinctively widening her stance for him, silently inviting more of his attentions. Again and again, he stroked her until Mia was whimpering with need.

She reached for him blindly, threaded her fingers through his hair and said, "Dave, please. I can't…"

"Yeah, you can," he murmured, then leaned in and took her with his mouth. Lips, tongue, teeth all worked her already sensitized flesh. He licked and tasted and nibbled until Mia's nerve endings were strung so tightly she thought she might simply explode into millions of tiny, needy pieces.

She braced one hand on the shower wall and with the other, she cupped the back of Dave's head, holding him to her. Her hips rocked in the rhythm he set and her breath came in short, hard gasps. Tipping her head back against the shower wall, she opened her eyes, stared into the steamy fog and felt lost. As if she'd been swallowed by sensation. There was no up. No down. There was only Dave and what he was doing to her.

"Dave… Oh…my…" Every word was a victory. Every breath a triumph.

When he pushed her closer and closer to the edge of completion, Mia looked down at him, wanting to see it all. Wanting to have this picture in her mind. So when she remembered this time with him she'd have something specific to torture herself with.

Then his tongue did a slow swirl over one particular spot and the moment ended with Mia shouting his name as her body splintered all around him.

She couldn't stand, so Dave lowered her to the long, wide seat carved into the wall of the shower itself. Then he turned, adjusted a few of the shower jets, aiming them directly at the bench where Mia lay sensually sprawled.

"We're not done, you know," he said.

She fixed her eyes on him and gave him a slow satisfied smile. "I'm so happy to hear that."

Damn, this was some kind of woman, he told himself as he leaned over her, bracing his hands on either side of her head. She was beautiful and sexy and always ready for him. She was a match for him in a lot of ways, and if he were a man looking for a permanent woman, Mia Hughes would be the one he'd chase down and hog-tie.

But he didn't do permanent because there was no such thing. People made promises to each other all the damn time and broke them just as often. He wouldn't be part of that. Wouldn't make a promise only to let it shatter. Wouldn't walk out on his responsibilities. And the one way to make sure that didn't happen was to avoid making those "forever" kind of promises in the first damn place.

That's why he insisted on contracts for even the most minor deals. Harder to break a signed promise.

So he would have Mia as often as he could. He would give her all he had.

For the time they had together.

Then it would end.

She reached up and pushed his wet hair back from his face. Frowning slightly, she asked, "What're you thinking? You look so...sad, all of a sudden."

"It's nothing," he lied, and lowered his head to hers for a kiss. "Nothing."

She didn't look convinced, but he'd change her mind about that. His body was hard and hot and so damn eager he had to force himself out of the shower long enough to cross to the top drawer in the vanity. He yanked out a condom, tore the package open then worked the sheath down over his straining erection.

When he turned back to the shower, he saw that she was waiting, gaze fixed on him, and it wasn't worry he saw in her eyes now, it was need. Fresh. Raw. Powerful. He'd never been with a woman so in tune with his own desires. Mia was more than a match for him in so many damn ways he couldn't even count them all. But at the moment, it was their identical cravings that pulled at him.

He went back to her, and as the shower jets pummeled at their bodies, he levered himself over her and pushed himself into her depths.

Like every time with Mia, that first slide into her heat was a welcome into heaven. He felt surrounded by her, his body cradled within hers. She wrapped her arms around his neck, pulled his face down for a kiss, and he let himself drown in her. The heat of her. The sexual draw between them was overpowering, all consuming. And yet it wasn't just sex that simmered between them.

It was the connection he still feared and couldn't trust.

He moved inside her, pushing them both toward the climax he knew would crush him. Dave felt her shiver. Felt the first of the tremulous quakes racking her body and when she surrendered to them, he went with her. Giving himself up to what he had only found with Mia. The completion. The rush of pleasure, excitement and peace that existed only when he was in her arms.

A half hour later, they were dried off and in his bedroom. As she took a pair of jeans from a dresser drawer and tugged them on, he asked, "Sure you wouldn't rather just wrap up in robes? Be easier than getting out of all these clothes again later."

She whipped her hair back from her face and gave him a wicked smile that set his insides on fire. "A few clothes won't slow you down. Think of it as a challenge. Plus, I'm not cooking naked and I'm hungry."

He laughed. "Of course you are."

"Besides," she said as she tugged a long-sleeved, dark red sweater on over her head, "we still have to talk."

"Right." He grabbed a pair of his own jeans and pulled them on. He didn't bother with underwear, since his plan was to get her naked again as soon as he'd fed her. "Can't forget the talk. So. Before we head to the kitchen, you want to show me what my mom brought for you?"

She pointed. "It's in that box by the fire."

He spotted it on the table between the two armchairs. Barefoot and shirtless, he walked over and pulled the lid off. Beneath a layer of tissue paper was a white, lacy baby dress slightly yellowed from age. "What the—"

"It was your christening gown."

"Gown?" He turned around and stared at her, horrified. "I wore a dress?"

Mia laughed shortly and shook her head. "*That's* what's bothering you about this?"

"Hell, yes. Boys don't wear dresses."

"Not a dress. A gown."

"Same damn thing if you ask me." He dropped the offending item back into the box and set the lid in place again. "Why would she bring it to—" He broke off, tipped his head back and stared at the ceiling. "Oh, crap."

"Exactly." Mia sat on the edge of the bed, her bare feet dangling inches above the floor. "She brought it to me so we could use it for our baby's christening."

Mia wants four children. He could hear the glee in his mother's voice still. Four kids. And here's the dress they get to wear, poor things. Kids weren't in his plans, Dave reminded himself sternly even while a weird feeling crept over him. His mind provided an image to match that weird feeling and suddenly he had the mental picture of Mia, pregnant with his child. Even through the wave of terror the image projected, he could admit to himself that she looked lovely pregnant.

But there weren't going to be any babies.

He gave the closed box another glare and rubbed at the ache in the center of his chest. "This has gotten out of hand."

"I know."

Fixing his gaze on hers, he said, "You should have let me tell her the truth."

"I couldn't. She was so happy, Dave. So excited. So pleased for you and happy for *us*." Shaking her head, Mia sighed. "Alice has spent the past two days telling me all about you, showing me pictures of you as a child. She's…" Mia shrugged helplessly again. "I just couldn't tell her. And I couldn't let you, either."

"Mia, she's got to know." He wasn't looking forward to breaking that news, but he knew it had to be done.

Her voice was soft, but there was steel in her words when she said, "Please don't make me a liar to your mother."

"What? You're not a liar."

"Of course I am," she argued miserably. "While she was going on and on about how happy she was to have me for a daughter all I did was sit there, *basking* in it. She thinks we're really engaged and I *let* her think it. That makes me a liar and I can't stand the thought of her knowing."

"Mia…" He headed across the room to her, drawn to the slump of her shoulders and the distress in her voice.

She scooted off the bed and wrapped her arms around her middle in a classic self-protection stance. "I just don't want her to think badly of me, okay?" Looking up at him, she tried to explain. "I never had a mother, you know? I mean, she died when I was a baby and I always wondered what it would have been like if she had lived." She was talking faster now, as if words were gathering in the back of her throat waiting for their chance to be spoken. "How different would our lives have been? Having a mom teach you to cook. Going shopping for prom dresses. All the little things that I missed. I can't help but wonder what it would have been like to experience it all."

She took a deep breath and blew it out again. "I know how dumb that all sounds, but I swear, Dave, when Alice was talking to me and being so nice, I just…couldn't give that up by announcing that what you and I have is just role-playing. I couldn't do it."

He laid both hands on her shoulders and stared down into her eyes. "I get it," he said. "And trust me when I say I know how hard it is to get a word in edgewise when Alice Firestone is on a roll. She's like this gentle, sweet-natured steamroller. There's just no stopping her, so in your defense, she probably wouldn't have given you a chance to confess even if you'd wanted to."

Mia smiled up at him. "Steamroller, huh? She's a sweetie and you're lucky to have her."

"I know it," he said, "but she's flattened me a few times, too."

"Did you deserve it?"

"Probably," he admitted.

"Like I deserve it now," she muttered. Shaking her head, Mia shoved both hands through her hair, then let her hands drop to her sides. "But I'm asking you not to say anything to her, Dave. She's so nice and she loves you so much and she's so excited…. I'm a terrible person."

He chuckled and was rewarded with a frosty glare. "No, you're not. You're the exact opposite because you're worried about my mom's feelings in this."

"Yeah. I don't want her to think I'm a liar." Her head hit his chest. "Just don't tell her, all right? The month is almost up. You've got the meeting with TexCat arranged for next week. So just wait. When the deal is done, we'll break up as planned, and then she'll never have to know the real reason behind any of this. And she won't hate me." She tipped her head back to look up at him. "I really don't want her to hate me, Dave."

In that moment, he would have given her anything, promised her whatever she wanted. Her blue eyes were drenched with emotion and the subtle sheen of tears she refused to let fall. She hadn't asked him for a thing since this whole bargain had started, so this request seemed reasonable. Besides, he was in no hurry to tell his mother her dreams of grandchildren weren't going to happen.

"Okay," he said, wrapping his arms around her. "We won't say anything until we have to."

She snaked her arms around his waist and held on. "Thanks."

"Sure." He kissed the top of her head. "Still hungry?"

"Am I breathing?"

Dave laughed, released her and gave her bottom a swift swat.

"Hey!" She grinned at him. "What was that for?"

"I just couldn't resist that cute little butt of yours, I guess."

"Maybe you could not resist me again after we eat?"

He grabbed a shirt, yanked it on and snatched her hand, tugging her out and down the hall to the stairs. "This is going to be the fastest meal in history."

Her laughter bubbled out around them and just for a second, Dave didn't worry about how happy Mia made him.

Mia reheated the stew Delores had made earlier and Dave managed to throw together some garlic bread. It was...*cozy,* being alone with her in the huge kitchen. Just the two of them, with the night outside the wide bay windows and lamplight casting a soft glow over the room. That ache in his chest was back, but Dave ignored it.

After they'd eaten, Mia put together a plate filled with cake and cookies for Dave to take to his mother in the guesthouse.

"She's probably getting ready for bed," he argued,

since he'd rather take Mia back to their bedroom than take a walk.

"She's not ninety, Dave," Mia said with a laugh. "And she left before she got any of the cake."

Mia was polishing off a slice of Delores's famous mocha fudge cake as Dave picked up the plate with a resigned sigh. "I'll be right back."

Mia smiled at him and licked her fork lovingly. "Take your time...."

He watched her tongue make short work of the frosting on that fork and could only mutter, "Five minutes, tops."

Outside, it was cold, but Texas cold—so his bare feet on the flagstones didn't bother him a bit. He glanced around the ranch yard as he walked silently through the darkness. Dave noted lights on in the houses set aside for the ranch hands and frowned when he noticed the foreman's house was dark. Well, hell, on the ride home, all Mike had talked about was taking a shower and going to bed. Guess he meant it.

Shaking his head, Dave skirted the pool, walked past the line of Adirondack chairs and headed for the guesthouse. He'd built the damn place especially for his mother—he'd wanted her to live here, but to have her own space, too. Still, it had never been more than a way station for his mother, who refused to "be a wet blanket on her son's party." This time, though, he told himself, maybe he could get her to stay.

Once Mia was gone, the ranch was going to be... lonely. He frowned as that thought registered. Alone wasn't lonely, he insisted, but that argument was ringing false, even with him. He couldn't even imagine sleeping in his own bed without Mia beside him. Which told him that this whole situation was taking a turn he hadn't expected.

Dave was still frowning when he gave a perfunctory knock to his mother's door, then opened it. He stopped dead on the threshold and was pretty sure he'd been struck blind.

Mike Carter, wearing only a pair of white boxers, was *kissing* Dave's *mother*. Worse, she was kissing him back. And since when did mothers wear short nightgowns with spaghetti straps?

"What the hell?"

The couple broke apart at his shout and Mike whirled around to face Dave while at the same time shoving Alice behind him, standing in front of her like a human shield. "Dave—"

"What's going on here?" he demanded, then held up a hand. "Don't answer that!" He knew exactly what was going on and really didn't need any more details.

Dave set the covered plate down on the nearest table and took a step toward Mike. His friend. His foreman. The man he trusted more than anyone else in his life besides Tobin. "Mom, leave."

"I will not."

"Alice—" Mike said.

"Don't you start, either," Alice said and jumped out from behind Mike to face her furious son. "I will not run and hide as if I were a teenager being reprimanded by her parents. David Trahern Firestone, you just remember who the parent is here and who's the child."

"I'm no child," he ground out, hardly glancing at his mother. "And I want to know what the hell Mike is doing here like…*that.*"

Alice bristled again. "You watch your tone, David, do you understand?"

"No!" he shouted, throwing both hands into the air. "I *don't* understand. In fact, I think I'm having a stroke!"

"Oh, for heaven's sake!" Alice folded her arms across her chest and tapped the bare toes of one foot against the floor.

He couldn't think. Couldn't rationalize what he'd just seen, and then he heard himself babble, "What? How? When?"

"Dave, if we could talk…" Mike said, reaching for his jeans and pulling them on.

Fury was crouched at the base of his throat and betrayal was tightly wrapped around it like a fist. He could hardly talk, but he managed to say, "The only thing I'm saying to you is, you're fired."

His mother walked right up and slapped him. Dave just looked at her. She hadn't laid a hand on him since the year he was fifteen and took a ranch truck out for a joyride. "What was that for?"

"For being a boob," Alice told him, frowning. "You can't fire the man I love because you're embarrassed."

"I'm embarrassed?" He wasn't dealing with hearing his mother say she loved a man. That was just too much for any son to have to take.

"Alice—"

Dave and his mother both said, "Butt out, Mike."

"Yes, you're embarrassed," she continued, looking at him now with less anger and more understanding. "Do you think I don't know the signs? You intruded here and now there's no way out but anger."

"Intruded." Okay, maybe he had, but in his defense, he hadn't expected to find his mother with— Don't go there.

"Honey," she said, "I'm a grown woman, and now that you yourself have found someone to love, I'm sure you can understand—"

Hysterical deafness set in. It was the only answer. Dave saw his mother's mouth moving, but he couldn't hear her over the roaring in his own ears. Mike and his mother? How long had that been going on? And what was he supposed to do about it? What *could* he do about it? Scrubbing both hands over his face, he took a breath and muttered, "Mom, stop. I beg you."

"Huh." She sniffed and picked up the plate of cake and cookies. "Oh, these look wonderful. Thank Mia for me since I'm sure you didn't think of this."

How had he come out to be the bad guy here? Dave gave up trying to talk to his mother and instead focused on Mike, who was watching him with a steady stare. The older man's chin was high, his shoulders squared as if he were expecting a firing squad. Well, hell. Now Dave felt like an idiot.

They were all adults here and he had barged in without thinking. And he had to admit, if his mom was going to fall for a man, at least she'd picked a good one. Still, there were a few things that had to be said.

"I want to talk to you," he muttered and turned to go outside.

"I think—" Alice said.

"Alice, honey, it'll be all right." Mike kissed her forehead and walked outside.

Dave sighed as his mother warned, "If you fire him, I will personally make you sorry, David."

He blew out a breath, stepped into the cool night and stopped opposite his foreman. Mike still looked pugnacious, as if he were ready for anything. So just because, Dave punched him.

One swing and his fist slammed into the other man's jaw. Mike's head snapped back and his eyes flashed with fury. But he didn't lift a finger to defend himself.

"I figure you had that one coming, seeing as it's your mother and all. But hit me again and I'll hit back."

"How long has this been going on?" Dave demanded.

"I've been in love with your mother for years," Mike admitted on a sigh. "She wanted to tell you but I wouldn't let her."

"Are you using her?"

Mike glared at him. "I might just hit you anyway. I love her. And now that you've got Mia in your life, I figure you can understand how that feels. If you can't, I'll leave the ranch. You won't have to fire me. But know this. I won't give Alice up."

Everybody figured now that he had Mia he could understand love. Well, they were wrong. He didn't understand it, didn't trust it and didn't see that changing any time soon. Need was different. It was clean. Uncomplicated.

Dave's mind was racing. Everything was changing around him so fast he could hardly keep up. His world used to be so neat and tidy. He'd had complete control over his universe and he couldn't figure out where it had all gone wrong.

"Oh, relax," Dave told his old friend. "You're not fired and I'm not hitting you again— Unless," he added quickly, "you make her cry. Then all bets are off."

"Agreed," Mike said.

"Sorry I barged in," Dave said. "*Really* sorry. There are just some things sons shouldn't see."

Mike snorted a laugh. "Guess that's so. If it makes you feel better, I've about convinced Alice to move into the guesthouse permanently."

"Yeah?" He smiled, then frowned and jabbed a finger at his foreman. "If you're thinking you're living there with her—not unless you're married."

Mike grinned. "My pleasure. Now...I've got a reunion of my own to get back to."

Dave watched him go and shuddered. "No, some things a son should never even know about."

Back at the house, Mia watched as Dave stalked around the perimeter of the lamp-lit kitchen, talking more to himself than to her.

"I don't get it," he muttered. "Love? How the hell could she be in love? She loved my father and that didn't stop him from abandoning us."

"Mike's a good guy," she argued.

"Yeah," he agreed, never slowing his pace. "But that doesn't guarantee anything, either."

"There are no guarantees," Mia pointed out, turning in her seat to keep her gaze locked on him. He was shaking his head, muttering, and that frown carved into his features looked as if it was there to stay.

"That's the whole point," he told her. "Without a guarantee, why take the risk? Love is just a word. It doesn't *mean* anything."

"It means everything," she said softly and felt a hitch in her chest when he stopped pacing to stare at her.

She couldn't tell what he was thinking, and maybe that was just as well, she thought.

"No," he said quietly, "what you and I have is more. Desire is straightforward. Uncomplicated. It doesn't screw with your life and you don't get flattened when it ends."

Mia heard every word and felt them like a direct slap to the heart. He believed everything he was saying. She knew that. And she realized finally and at last that he would never allow himself to love her. Never risk his heart.

Which meant that though she was still here and with him, what they had was already over.

Ten

Thomas Buckley was an ass.

The owner of TexCat was short, balding and very well fed. His cheeks were red, his blue eyes were sharp and his ideas were straight out of the 1950s.

"A family man is a man to be trusted," Buckley was saying, smiling benevolently from behind his wide, ostentatious desk. "I always say if a man can't make a commitment to a woman, then he can't keep his word on a deal."

Dave had already sat through more than an hour of listening to the older man pontificate about morality and family values. It felt like a week. He could only imagine what Mia or his mother would say about Buckley's take on women being "the gentle sex, God bless 'em" and how they "don't understand men's business, but they keep our homes and raise our children and that's enough."

Seriously, Buckley was dancing on Dave's last nerve.

When he finally wound down, Dave asked, "So, we have a deal?"

"I've had my man go and check out your herd and he tells me it's some of the best beef he's seen in years." Buckley threaded his fingers together and laid them across his corpulent belly as he leaned back in his desk chair.

"Not surprised," Dave said quickly. "My ranch is completely organic. No feedlots, either. The land is managed so that the herd has free range and we don't take on more cattle than we can comfortably support."

Buckley nodded. "That was in the report, as well. And you say you're engaged to be married?"

Briefly, he gritted his teeth. "Yes. Mia's studying to be a school psychologist."

"Well, that'll be fine I'm sure, until your first child is born. Then she'll want to stay home."

If he gritted his teeth for much longer, Dave thought, he'd leave this office with nothing more than a mouth full of powder. "Plenty of time to think about that."

"You're right, you're right." Buckley sat up straight, held out his right hand and when Dave shook it, the older man smiled. "We've got a deal. Let's get the paperwork signed."

An hour later, Dave was back in Royal, glad to be back from Midland and the TexCat offices. He'd done it. His ranch's reputation was set now that he had that all-important deal. His plans for the future were looking good and the bargain he'd struck with Mia was now completed.

All that was left was to tell her the good news and end their faux engagement. Odd how that thought didn't fill him with pleasure. So instead of heading back to his own place, Dave drove into town to see Nathan Battle. He needed a friend to talk to.

"I don't see the problem." Nathan poured two cups of coffee and handed one to Dave. Carrying his own coffee, Nathan walked around his desk and propped his booted feet up on one corner.

The Royal jailhouse was small, but it boasted up-to-date equipment and a casual feel. Nathan had one deputy, and between the two men, the small town's citizens were taken care of.

"The problem is," Dave said, after a sip of the strong, hot coffee, "I don't need a fiancée anymore, but I don't want to end this with Mia, either."

"Ah." Nathan nodded sagely. "So, basically, you're screwed?"

"To sum it up, yeah."

"You don't have to end things, you know," Nathan mused.

Dave fired a hard look at his friend. "I've considered that..."

"And?"

"Don't know." He stood up, set his coffee on the edge of the desk and started pacing. The wood floors held plenty of scuff marks from generations of boots stomping across them, and the wide front window overlooked Main Street. Dave shoved his hands into his back pockets, stopped at the window and stared, not seeing the town beyond the glass.

His mind raced with more questions than answers. For the first time in years, Dave was unsure what move to make. All he knew was that he didn't want to lose Mia. Not yet, anyway.

Of course, he didn't plan to *keep* her in his life. They'd

made a deal after all. Signed a contract. Their engagement would end and they'd each go back to their own lives.

But he wasn't ready for that.

"Stop thinking about what you should do and tell me what you *want* to do," Nathan suggested.

Dave glanced at him over his shoulder. "What I want is to go home and see Mia."

"So do that and forget about the rest for now."

"Just like that?"

"What's the hurry? You said yourself the deal you made with Mia goes to the end of the month."

"Or until I get the contract, whichever comes first."

"There's no saying you can't renegotiate, though, right?"

"True." Great sex must have clogged his brain. Otherwise he would have thought of this solution himself. There was no reason he and Mia couldn't strike a new deal. They were good together. Maybe this was worth looking into.

"Give yourself some time to figure out what you want to do. The TCC's big Halloween party is in a few days. At least wait until after that."

He thought about it and realized that Nathan was right about something at least. Renegotiation could work. He wasn't ready to give Mia up.

"Dave, you don't have to have every answer to every question at all times."

He laughed and shoved one hand through his hair. "You know, until now, I always have."

"Things change," Nathan said with a shrug. "Trust me, no one knows that better than I do."

"Things are changing too damn much lately," Dave muttered.

Nathan chuckled. "Yeah, I heard about your mom and Mike Carter."

"Don't remind me," Dave said. It had been almost a week since the night he'd blundered into the middle of his mother's—whatever. He was almost used to the fact that his mom was in love. He wasn't used to Mike Carter living in the guesthouse with her.

Alice was happy like Dave hadn't seen since he was a kid, before his father left them. He was glad for his mom, but he couldn't understand how she could have faith again. Trust again, after how Dave's father had let her down. Abandoned them.

How did she let go of the past and risk taking another chance on love? Shaking his head, Dave told himself that Thomas Buckley had it all wrong.

Women were much stronger than men.

"Congratulations," Mia said and hoped she sounded more sincere than she felt.

"Thanks." Dave poured them each a glass of wine and handed one to her. They took their usual spots on the sofa in the library as he told her about the deal with TexCat.

She listened and tried to look happy for him, but inside she was a mess. Her heart felt twisted into a knot and breathing was so difficult, she didn't even sip at her wine, half-afraid she'd choke to death. That was it. It was done. She and Dave were over. The signed contract with TexCat signaled the end of their bargain.

Now she could move back to Alex's place and get on with her life. The only problem? She wasn't sure she *had* a life without Dave.

"I'd like you to stay," he said suddenly, grabbing her attention.

Mia's heart clenched. Her gaze locked on his. "What?"

He took her wine and set both glasses on the polished wood table in front of them before turning back to her. Dropping both hands on her shoulders, he pulled her in close, looked into her eyes and said, "I'd like you to stay—"

Hope roared to life inside her.

"—until the end of the month," he finished.

And hope drained away again, leaving her feeling surprisingly empty. He didn't want her forever. She'd been fooling herself thinking that maybe because *she* loved, that he did, too. Well, here was the eye-opener, the back-to-reality talk she'd been dreading for weeks.

"Why?"

"Why not?" he countered and gave her shoulders a squeeze.

Amazing, even though the heat of his hands was sliding through the fabric of her shirt to seep into her body, she still felt cold.

"Look, Mia," he said softly, "we've had a good time, right?"

A good time. She sighed. "Yes."

"So why let it end before either of us is ready?"

Because if she stayed much longer, she didn't know how she would leave at all. And she had to leave, she told herself firmly. She couldn't stay with a man who didn't love her. It would kill her by inches.

Shaking her head, she said, "I don't think that's a good idea."

"Why the hell not?"

She smiled. He really had a hard time when people didn't fall in with his plans. "Because we both have lives we have to get back to. I take my final exams soon and then I'll have to get busy looking for a job—"

"Royal School District is going to hire you," he said, brushing that concern aside.

"Maybe," she said. "But there's no guarantee. So I'll

have to apply to school districts in Midland and Houston, too."

He scowled at her. "You didn't tell me."

No, she hadn't. Because she hadn't wanted to think about it herself. The thought of moving away from Royal made her heartsick. She hated the thought of leaving before Alex came back and she was really hoping that Royal would hire her. And if they didn't, maybe she'd end up looking for a job here in town until everything was back to normal. Leaving without having the mystery of Alex's disappearance settled seemed impossible.

Besides, she didn't want to move from Royal, the only home she'd ever known. If she did, that would mean she wouldn't even be able to catch the occasional glimpse of Dave around town. Maybe that would be better, but at the moment, she didn't think so.

"The point is," she said, trying not to think about moving, "our time together's over."

He was still frowning when he said, "At least stay through the TCC Halloween party. That's only a few days away."

"Why?" she asked, suddenly so tired she wanted to go lay down with a pillow over her head.

"Because I'm asking you to," he whispered.

He never asked, she told herself silently. He ordered. Or growled. Or dictated. But he was asking her, and as she looked into his fog-gray eyes, she knew she wasn't ready to leave. Not yet. "I'll stay."

Three days later, Mia stepped out of the ranch house in time to see her VW being towed away. She took an instinctive step or two to chase after it, even knowing there was no way she could catch it.

She glanced around the ranch yard, hoping to find

someone to tell her she'd just had a hallucination. Instead, she saw Dave, standing beside a brand-new, shiny, luxury SUV.

For the past several days, he'd been...different. Ever since their talk in the library the night he'd gotten the deal with TexCat, things had changed between them. Oh, they were still together every night, but even their lovemaking had a different feel to it. Like a prolonged goodbye that was tearing Mia apart, piece by piece.

Now, as he watched her, she saw the same expression on his face that had been there the past few days. Not cold, exactly. But more...distant than she was used to. It was as if every time he saw her, he was letting go. She felt as though there were a giant clock inside her ticking off the minutes, and when that clock hit zero, there would be nothing left between her and Dave.

So instead of enjoying their last week together, they were each of them holding back, protecting themselves and their hearts. If she had any sense, she'd leave. But she just couldn't. Even though being here was painful, being away from Dave would be worse.

He walked toward her, every step long and determined. His features looked carved from granite and his gray eyes gave nothing away.

When he was close enough, she asked, "Who took my car? And *why?*"

"That's not a car," he countered. "It's a disaster waiting to happen. Just yesterday you got stuck on the side of the road coming home from Alex's."

"I just needed some gas." Fine, she probably needed a new gas gauge, too.

"No, you needed a new car and now you've got one." He pointed at the silver beauty.

"You did *not* buy me a car," she whispered.

"Yeah, I did. Deal with it." His voice was clipped, his eyes fierce, as if he was preparing for battle.

Well, he was going to get one. Dave Firestone was used to rolling over people to get his own way, but she wouldn't go down without a fight. Even though there was a part of her insisting that she just shut up and accept that pretty, brand-new, worry-free car.

"This wasn't part of our deal," she argued, silencing her internal voice.

"Yeah, well, I renegotiated it on my own." He grabbed her shoulders and yanked her in close. "You told me you've applied for jobs in Midland and Houston. You think I'm going to worry about you off somewhere alone in that crappy car? Not gonna happen." Shaking his head, he let her go and turned for the barn.

"This isn't over!" she called after him, even though she knew it was. Her car was gone. She shifted her gaze to the new beast shining in the sunlight.

Mia moved closer and did a slow walk around the simply gorgeous luxury SUV. She opened the driver's side door and looked inside. The interior was navy blue leather and the smell… She took a deep breath and sighed it out. Mia had never in her life owned a *new* car. All of her cars had been new to her, but considerably aged by the time she'd gotten hold of them.

She reached out one hand and smoothed her palm over the baby-soft leather seat, and for one long second, she experienced pure avarice. What would it be like, she wondered, to drive a car and not have to worry about the engine falling out? To not have to carry a case of oil with you everywhere you went? To turn the key and have the engine fire right up without the help of prayers and desperate pleas?

Frowning, Mia forced herself to step back and close the

door. Her hand might have lingered on the door handle, but who could blame her? It was beautiful. And extravagant and she absolutely couldn't keep it. She and Dave had a deal. A signed contract. And a new car wasn't part of it.

"Isn't that lovely?" Alice came up behind her and Mia turned to smile a welcome.

"It is."

"Yet you don't look happy with it."

"It's great, Alice," Mia told her with a sigh. "But I can't keep it."

"Why ever not?"

"It's complicated," Mia said, hoping the other woman would accept that and let it go.

"Mia, I know David can be impulsive. Heck, he bought me a new car just a few weeks ago and didn't bother to tell me about it beforehand."

"But you're his mom."

"And you're his fiancée." She laid one hand on Mia's forearm. "Did he surprise you with this? Are you angry that he didn't talk to you about it? Is it that you don't like the color?"

Mia laughed. Imagine saying no to a new car because you didn't like the color. "No, the color's just right. And I like surprises…"

"Then why shouldn't he buy you a car?"

"Because we're not getting married," she blurted. Oh, God. The words had just jumped from her mouth before she had a chance to stop them. She slapped one hand to her mouth, but it was too late. The truth was out and now Alice would hate her and Dave would be furious that she'd told his mother.

"I know."

"What?"

Alice smiled, put her arm around Mia's shoulder and

gave her a squeeze. "Honey, I know my son better than anyone. He doesn't go from 'never getting married' to 'I'm engaged' overnight. I knew something was up, I just didn't know what."

"Alice, I'm so sorry..." This wasn't fair. She was so nice. So understanding. So...mom-like. "I didn't want to lie to you, but I didn't want you to hate me and I asked Dave not to tell you, so it's not even all his fault. It's just so complicated."

Alice gave her another hug. "Good stories always are," she said and started walking toward the house. "Now, why don't we get some tea and some of Delores's cookies and you can tell me everything."

Too late to do anything else, Mia nodded, and allowed herself to be mothered for the very first time.

Over two pots of tea and enough cookies to make even Mia a little sick, she told Alice the whole story. When she finally wound down, she was spent. Tears still dampened her cheeks, but her breathing was easier than it had been since she'd started living a lie.

"You love my son, don't you?"

"Yes," Mia said, "but it doesn't matter."

"It's all that matters." Alice poured more tea for each of them and said, "David loves you, too."

Mia had to laugh. He wanted her, she knew that. Heck, they couldn't be in the same room together for more than five minutes without leaping at each other. But desire wasn't love and want wasn't need.

"You're wrong."

Alice shook her head. "There's a shiny new SUV parked out front that says different."

"The car?"

"It's more than a car, honey." Alice sat up, reached out

and took Mia's hands in hers. "Remember, a few weeks ago, David had a new car delivered to my house."

"Yes, but you're his mother."

"And he loves me. Worries about me driving a car he doesn't think is safe."

"He hates my car," Mia murmured.

"So he replaced it with a much safer one. And if he didn't love you, why would your safety matter to him?"

"I don't know...." She'd like to believe that. But how could she?

"It's David's way, Mia," Alice was saying. "Ever since he was a child, he's had trouble with the word *love*. But that doesn't mean he doesn't *feel* it."

A tiny kernel of hope settled in the pit of her stomach, but Mia couldn't put too much faith in it. Because if she did and Alice was wrong, her heart would be crushed beyond repair.

Loud music pumped out of speakers. Orange and black streamers and balloons hung from the ceiling, drifting with the movements of the crowd. Dry ice near the punchbowl sent clouds of vapor into the air. Vampires danced with angels, zombies loitered near the buffet table and a princess stole a kiss from a troll.

All in all, the TCC costume party was a rousing success. The club wasn't just celebrating Halloween this year, but also the opening of the new day-care center. So much fuss had been made about the center over the past few months, it was a wonder anything had gotten done.

But Mia had already taken a tour of the new day-care center and she was impressed with the place. Glancing into the large, well-appointed room, she saw lots of tiny tables and chairs for the kids. Bookshelves were stocked with row after row of wonderful stories. There were cribs for infants and on one side of the room small easels were set up, ready for little artists to paint their masterpieces.

"Isn't it wonderful?" A woman's voice spoke up from right beside her and Mia jumped. She hadn't noticed anyone approach.

The woman was a few inches shorter than Mia, with jaw-length blond hair and brown eyes that were sparkling with excitement.

"I'm sorry," she said. "I didn't mean to sneak up on you. But I saw you looking in at the day care and couldn't resist coming over." She held out one hand. "I'm Kiley Roberts, and I'll be running the center."

"Mia Hughes. It's nice to meet you." Mia shook her hand and said, "I was just thinking how impressive it is that the center has come together so nicely despite all the battles."

"Oh, I know." Kiley sighed a little. "I'm glad it's all settled and over. My little girl, Emmie, can't wait to start coming here."

"How old is she?"

"Two," Kiley said, "and she's the light of my life." She paused, spotted someone walking into the center and said, "Excuse me, I should go direct another tour."

Mia nodded as the woman moved off, practically dancing with excitement for the opening of the center. She envied Kiley Roberts, Mia realized. Kiley had a plan. A future stretched out ahead of her, and she had a child. A family.

Smiling wistfully, Mia turned away from the center, walked over to the open doorway into the main room and looked out over the gathered crowd. She spotted Dave across the room at the bar, standing beside Nathan Battle. The two men laughed at something and Mia's heart twisted in her chest. Dave looked wonderful as an Old

West outlaw. Dressed almost entirely in black, he looked dangerous and sexy. A lethal combination, as Mia knew only too well.

As if he could feel her gaze on him, he turned, met her eyes and gave her the half smile that never failed to tug at her heart. God, how she would miss him.

He left Nathan, made his way over to her through the crowd and when he stopped directly in front of her, he said, "Did I mention that you make the most beautiful saloon girl I've ever seen?"

Her costume deliberately went along with his. Her dark blue satin dress was trimmed with black lace at the bodice and the hem of her full skirt. She wore fishnet stockings, black pumps and her upswept hair had blue feathers tucked into the mass.

"I think you might have said something along those lines," she said.

"It's worth repeating." He took her hand and led her toward the dance floor. "Dance with me, Mia."

She couldn't have resisted him even if she'd wanted to.

He pulled her into the circle of his arms and began to sway in time with the music. All around her, the citizens of Royal were celebrating. There was laughter and shouts and conversations pitched at a level to be heard over the music.

Mia laid her head on his chest and followed his lead around the dance floor. It was magical and sad and special all at once. She'd have loved for the music to spin on for years, keeping them here, locked together. But she knew that couldn't happen; all too soon, the night would end and, like Cinderella, her magic would be over.

"Marry me, Mia," he whispered.

And the whole world stopped.

Eleven

"What?"

Dave grinned. He'd caught her off guard. Good. Just how he wanted her. If she was off balance, she wouldn't be so eager to argue with him. He'd never met a more hardheaded woman.

"Marry me." Hell, even he couldn't believe he was serious. But the thought of losing Mia was driving him nuts.

She went limp in his arms and he took that as a good sign. The noise level inside the club was near deafening and to make his case he'd need to get where he could talk to her loud enough to be heard.

"You want to get married?"

"Absolutely," he told her, bending his head so he wouldn't have to shout and so that no one else could hear him. "I've thought it all out and it's the best solution to the situation."

The past few days had been crazed, him knowing that

she would be leaving and not having a way to keep her there, short of tying her to his bed—which didn't sound like a bad plan to him at all.

But since that would be a temporary solution, he'd come up with something better. A marriage based not on love but logic.

She shook her head as if to clear it, then looked into his eyes and asked, "You love me?"

Something fisted tight around his heart, but Dave ignored it. This wasn't about something as ephemeral as *feelings*. This was about— Hell.

"Who said anything about love?" He frowned a little and danced them over to a corner of the floor where they would be more alone. When they were far enough away from the crowd, he backed her into a corner and stared down at her. "I'm not talking about love. I'm talking about a contract."

"A what? You mean a prenup?"

"No." He smiled at her. "I mean a contract where we promise each other we'll stay together. No divorce. No leaving. And we both sign it."

"You're kidding, right?" She blinked up at him and he had the distinct impression he was losing her.

He couldn't lose her. That was the one thing he'd figured out over the past few days. The thought of her moving to Midland or Houston was enough to drive a spike through his heart. So, yeah, he could admit that he cared for her. A lot. But he wouldn't offer a promise that was too easily broken. Love was too iffy. Too…dangerous.

"A signed contract is better than some lame promise to love and cherish. It's a legal document," he insisted. "One you can count on."

"Dave…a contract isn't a guarantee against failure."

All around them, Royal was in party mode. The music continued to pump into the room and wild laughter and shouts rose up behind them. Dave had come here convinced that he'd found a way to keep Mia with him. Now, though, here in this darkened corner in the middle of a celebration, Dave felt as though he were losing a war.

"No, it's not. But it's a start. Running your life on emotion is asking for trouble," he told her flatly. "I know because I've seen it up close and personal. I want you with me, Mia. But I can't promise love."

She reached up, cupped his cheek in the palm of her hand and said, "And that's the only thing I want from you."

Her hand dropped from his face, but he caught it in his and dragged it back up, holding her there, feeling the heat of her even as he saw a chill creep into her eyes. He had to keep trying, though, because he'd never once given up on something he wanted.

"We're good together, Mia," he said and saw a flash of hurt dart across her eyes. "You know it. We've been happy this past month."

"Yes, we have," she said, pulling her hand free of his. "But it's not enough for me. Not anymore."

"Why *not?*"

"Because I love you, Dave." She took a deep breath, blew it out again and gave him a sad smile. "I didn't mean to, it just happened."

A quick flash of something bright and amazing shot through Dave in a split second before his brain kicked into gear and rejected the emotion. He'd learned long ago that "love" was just a word. He stiffened. Looking down into her face, he read the truth in her eyes and took an emotional step back. "Love wasn't part of the agreement."

"No," she said sadly, "it wasn't."

He glanced over her head at the crowd in the room behind them, away from her eyes, giving himself a chance to take a mental breath. To get a grip. It didn't help much. "I'm not interested in love, Mia. I told you that from the beginning."

"Yeah, you did." Mia shook her head so hard, one of the feathers in her hair came free and floated to the floor. "I should have listened. But I love you anyway."

He scraped one hand across the back of his neck, then looked into those eyes of hers again. "Stop saying that," he muttered darkly. "People say that damn word so easily."

"I don't," she told him flatly. "I've never said 'I love you' to a man before. Ever."

He gritted his teeth. "Love wasn't part of our deal."

"And the deal is all-important?" she asked. "Rules? Contracts?"

"Without them, you've got nothing," he countered, his voice harsh and deep. "Love is a setup for the letdown, that's all. Throw that word out and you're supposed to forget common sense. You're supposed to believe—" he broke off and caught himself before saying "—you believe promises and one by one they're broken."

"What're you talking about?"

"Love," he snapped and wondered when this whole thing had gone to hell. "My mother believed. My father said he loved her. Us." He laughed shortly and heard the sharp, ragged edges of it. "Didn't stop him from leaving. Walking away, leaving Mom to survive however she could. We lost our home. We lost everything. I became the man of the house when he took off. I was eleven.

I stopped being a kid and watched my mother's world crumble around her. Because we believed in *love*."

"Dave…" She reached out to him but he stepped back. "That's awful and I'm so sorry…"

"Didn't ask for your pity."

"Sympathy, not pity," she corrected. "And your mom is in love again. Do you think Mike will break her heart?"

"He better damn well not."

Shaking her head, Mia said, "He won't. He's a good man and he loves her. Your mom is willing to take a chance again, so why can't you?"

God, it was hot in there. He felt like he couldn't breathe. He'd spilled his guts and she was picking them up and handing them to him. And Dave didn't have a damn answer for her. He didn't understand how his mother could trust again. Believe again. He only knew that he couldn't. He wanted Mia. Cared for her more than anyone he'd ever known. But if he used the word "love," he'd lose control.

"I won't give you promises, Mia," he told her, gathering the threads of his control. "I'll give you a contract. My word. In writing."

"Without the promise, the contract means nothing, Dave. Don't you see that?"

"Why are you doing this?" he demanded, reaching for her, grabbing hold of her shoulders and dragging her close. "We had a deal. You weren't supposed to bring emotions into this."

She laughed a little, but it was a broken sound. "Pesky humans, you just can't trust them to keep their hearts out of things."

"Damn it, Mia, I don't want to lose you. We can still have something good together."

"No. But we could have had something *great*."

"You're wrong."

"Looks like I was wrong about a lot of things," she whispered. Slowly, she pulled the huge diamond ring from her finger and held it out to him. He stiffened, gritted his teeth against the unfamiliar swell of helplessness filling him and took the ring from her, closing his fingers over the cold, hard stone.

She walked past him then, without another word. He wanted to reach for her, pull her into his arms and never let go. But he knew it wouldn't do any good. She was already gone.

He'd lost.

Amanda and Nathan gave Mia a ride to Alex's house. Thankfully, her friends didn't ask any questions. The gate guard at Pine Valley let Mia into the house and when she was alone in what had once been her home, she gave in to the tears strangling her.

All the silly, foolish hope she'd been hanging on to for weeks dissolved in that flood of sorrow. By the following morning, Mia was still miserable, and looked every inch of it.

She forced herself to get up and on with her life, because even though her heart hurt and her eyes were still red and swollen from crying, she had to keep moving. If she surrendered to her misery, she'd never leave Alex's house again.

A glance out the front window let her know that Dave had had her new car delivered. Had he brought it himself and left without seeing her? Had he had one of the ranch hands deliver it instead so he wouldn't have to risk seeing her? Did it matter?

She looked at the shiny new car in the driveway and Alice's words came back to her. *He gave you a car because he loves you.* Mia would like to believe that, but unless he actually said the words, she couldn't.

Her purse and clothes were all in the SUV, carefully packed in her suitcases. She carted everything inside and once she'd unpacked, she realized that she had better go grocery shopping. Delores wasn't around to spoil her anymore. She was on her own again and she better get used to it.

In town, she stopped in at the diner to thank Amanda for the ride home and found the whole coffee shop buzzing. People seemed angry, confused, as they gathered in groups to talk. Mia took a seat at the counter and when Amanda poured her a cup of coffee, she asked, "What's going on?"

"You haven't heard yet? The whole town's talking about it. I got the story from Nathan, of course, and I just could hardly believe it." Amanda bit her lip, shook her head and said, "It's the day-care center at the TCC."

Mia had a bad feeling about this. "What happened?"

"Someone broke in last night and vandalized it."

This wasn't the first time someone had tampered with the day-care center, Mia knew. But this sounded far worse than before.

"Oh, no! But it was so beautiful. And ready to open." She hated thinking about the loving care that had been brought to that space only to be destroyed.

"They broke all the tables and chairs and spray painted the walls with some really ugly graffiti." Amanda set the coffeepot down and placed both hands protectively on her rounded belly. "They even went in and destroyed Kiley's office. Ruined her computer, broke the printer. It's just a mess. The whole place."

"But who would've done such a terrible thing?"

Amanda looked around the diner, her gaze flicking across all of the familiar faces there before coming back to meet Mia's eyes. "To tell you the truth, I don't have a clue."

Mia winced. "Beau Hacket?"

Amanda nodded. "I'm sure he and his friends, like the Gordon brothers or Paul Windsor, are right at the top of the list. I know lots of people in town were against this, but I just can't picture someone I've known my whole life being so vicious."

"They'll still open the day care though, won't they?" Mia asked, hating to think that the wonderful place would never welcome children.

"You bet they will," Amanda told her. "Those of us who support the center are going to make sure of it." She took a breath and said, "Anyway, how're you doing this morning?"

"Not good," Mia admitted.

"Yeah. I, um, noticed you're not wearing your ring...."

She looked at her own naked finger, then dropped her left hand into her lap. "No, I gave it back to Dave last night."

"Aw, sweetie, I'm sorry."

"Thanks," Mia said with a tight grimace she hoped would pass as a smile. "Me, too."

"You need sugar. Cinnamon roll. On the house."

Mia didn't think she could eat anything, since for the first time in forever, food held no appeal. But she appreciated the gesture. "Thanks, Amanda."

Her friend patted Mia's hand and gave her a supportive smile. "It'll get better, sweetie."

"It has to," Mia said. Because she was so far down, there was nowhere to go but up.

The next couple of days were hard.

Dave worked himself into exhaustion all day and then lay awake all night. He couldn't stop his brain from racing. Couldn't stop the leapfrogging of thought to thought to thought.

There was Alex Santiago—still missing and no one had a clue where to look for him next. There was the destruction of the day-care center at the TCC. As far as he knew, there were no clues to the perpetrators there, either. He hadn't had a chance to talk to Nathan, so he knew nothing more than what was reported in the local paper, and judging by that, there were no suspects yet.

Then there was TexCat—and the deal for his beef that was at the heart of everything that had happened over the past month. He'd gotten that deal and had lost Mia. He'd secured his ranch's future—his organic beef would now have the stamp of excellence recognized all over Texas. With that contract in hand, he could grow his herd and expand his contacts. It was all good. But his personal future looked pretty damn grim.

His room still smelled of her. Her scent clung to her pillow, and when he reached across the cool sheets in the middle of the night blindly searching for her, he came up empty.

Hell, he couldn't even take a shower anymore without remembering the two of them on that wide bench seat. How Mia had looked with water streaming down her beautiful body. How she'd clutched at him and called his name. How she'd made him feel…whole.

Delores made his favorite foods, hoping to cheer him up, but how the hell could he choke down that mocha fudge cake when all he could think about was how much Mia had loved it?

Mike worked the ranch alongside Dave, but the foreman was so damn happy with Dave's mother he was hard to be around. And as for Alice Firestone, the woman was bound and determined to make sure that her son knew he was the instigator of his own misery.

"You've been many things in your lifetime, David," she said now over a glass of wine. "But I've never known you to be a coward."

His head snapped up and he looked at her through narrowed eyes. He was too tired for this. Tired down to his bones. He'd spent the day on his horse, riding over the acreage that meant so much to him. Losing himself in the land because that was all he had left. Now it was night again and he wasn't looking forward to trying to sleep in that big, empty bed upstairs.

She waved away his furious look. "Don't think you worry me with that lord-of-the-range glare. You can't fool me. I know you're hurting."

"You're wrong," he said flatly, and tossed his glass of sixty-year-old scotch down his throat as if it were foul-tasting medicine. The burn through his system was the only warmth he'd felt in days.

He wondered idly where the hell Mike was. Once the foreman arrived, they could sit down to dinner and this interrogation of his mother's would end.

"I'm not wrong, and that's what's bothering you," she said. Like a pit bull with a bone, his mother never let go once she'd clamped onto something. "You and I both know you miss Mia."

He poured more scotch. "I never said I didn't."

"Never said you did, either, but we'll let that go for the moment." Alice took a sip of her wine, set the glass down on a side table and crossed the wide great room to her son's side.

Heat from the fire in the hearth reached out to them and the crackle and hiss as flames devoured wood were the only sounds for a moment or two. Dave poured himself another drink, thinking he was going to need it.

Alice had been at him for two days, demanding that he do the right thing for himself—and for Mia. But he'd tried to do the right thing and Mia had shot him down. He'd offered her marriage and had that offer tossed back into his face.

Of course, his mind taunted him, you didn't offer her what she *needed* to hear....

Scowling down at his scotch, he tossed that one back, too. But when he reached for the bottle to pour another, his mother's hand on his arm stopped him. "David, that's not the answer."

"Not looking for an answer, Mom."

"You should be," she told him. "But since you won't, I'll just give it to you."

He groaned and shook his head. "Could you just leave this alone, Mom?"

"No."

"Didn't think so."

"Your problem is, you love Mia and you're afraid to admit it."

"I'm not afraid," he said tightly, though a part of him wondered if she wasn't right.

"Of course you are," she told him, taking one of his hands into hers and squeezing it. "When your father left us, you closed in on yourself."

He frowned. Yeah, he knew that, but for some reason, he'd always thought he'd been successful at hiding it from his mom. He should have known better.

"I saw it happening, but I didn't know how to fix it," she said softly.

He didn't want her feeling guilty about any of this. She'd done her best by him when his own damn father hadn't cared enough to stick it out and try. "Mom—"

"No, listen to me, David." She turned her face up to his and met his gaze squarely. "You were protecting yourself. A little boy who was so hurt he didn't know what to do with himself. But, David, you can't stay locked away your whole life."

"I'm not," he insisted, though his argument sounded hollow even to himself.

"Your father made mistakes. But he wasn't afraid to say the words *I love you*."

"No," Dave said wryly. "He just was too much of a coward to stay and see to his family."

"Maybe it was cowardly, maybe it was something else. We'll never know," Alice said, her voice nearly lost in the crackle of the fire. "But if you let what he did inform the decisions you make now, don't you understand that you're cheating yourself?"

"Hey," Mike called from the doorway. "Sorry I'm late."

Alice gave her son's hand one last pat, then turned to greet her fiancé. The older man bent his head for a kiss and Dave watched as his mother threw her arms around Mike for a big hug.

He smiled to himself, grateful now that the first shock of seeing his mother with a man was over, that she'd found happiness again. That she'd found love.

And maybe she was right to call him a damn coward. Hadn't his mother suffered more than he had? Losing her husband, her home, her livelihood? She'd become a single mother overnight and Dave had never once heard her complain or even bad-mouth his father.

Instead, she'd gone on. Built a life for herself and her son. She hadn't wasted time worrying over a past that was dead and gone.

How could he do less?

"Dave?" Mike asked from across the room. "You okay?"

He looked at his foreman. "Yeah. I think I am. Or anyway," he added as his mind started clicking, "I think I will be."

The following night when the doorbell rang, Mia left the email she'd just received and went to answer it. She grabbed the bowl of Halloween candy, ready to greet yet another group of kids shouting, "Trick or treat!" With a smile she didn't feel plastered to her face, she opened the door and looked into familiar, fog-gray eyes.

"Dave? What're you doing here?" She looked past him and saw ghosts and vampires and one tiny Chewbacca running up to the house across the street. "How did you get past the gate guard? I told him not to let you in."

He frowned. "Explains why it took fifty bucks instead of twenty this time."

"Oh, for—" Of course he'd bribed the gate guard. Why wouldn't he? Dave Firestone did whatever he had to do to get what he wanted. She grabbed the edge of the door and tried to shut it, but he was too fast for her.

He slapped one hand to the heavy oak panel and said, "Let me in, Mia. Please."

Surprised that he even knew that word, she could only nod and step back.

"What do you want, Dave?"

He snatched his hat off and tossed it to the couch behind him. "That's gonna take some time."

God, he looked so good. Lamplight played over his features and pooled around the two of them as if locking them into a golden bubble of light. It had been three days since she'd seen him and it felt like forever. Mia's every instinct screamed at her to throw herself at him. To lose herself in the heat of him. To kiss him again and feel the electrical charge sizzle between them.

Heck, she'd been so lonely, there was part of her ready to tell him she'd accept his stupid contract. That she didn't need him to love her. All she needed was *him*. But if she did that, gave in to her own urges, then she would be cheating them both out of what they could have had.

"Trick or treat!"

Mia jolted and clutched the bowl of candy to her chest. "I'm sorry. Kids."

She forced herself to smile as she turned to the ballerina and the soldier standing on her front porch.

"Don't you guys look great?" she said, holding the bowl out to them. She felt Dave standing right behind her and it made her so nervous she had to grip the bowl to keep from dropping it. "Take two each."

"Thank you!" they answered, then ran off the porch and down the steps to their parents, who were waiting on the sidewalk.

Mia waved the family off, fought down the pang of realization that she would never have children with the man she loved then closed the door and turned to face the man who held her heart even though she couldn't have him. Steeling herself against whatever might be coming, she said, "Okay, Dave, what is it?"

"I want you to marry me."

"I can't believe you came all the way over here to offer me the same empty proposal." Regret and disappointment twisted together in the pit of her stomach. She shook her head and said, "I'm not interested in a contract, Dave. I already told you that."

"I didn't say anything about a contract."

Then what did he mean? And why was he here? That blasted bit of hope that was still lying buried in the bottom of her heart began to warm. Mia looked up at him and waited.

Dave stared into her deep blue eyes and started talking. Words rushed from him in a torrent. Didn't seem to matter that he'd been practicing a perfectly good speech all the way over here. Because it was gone and all he was left with was what was in his heart. He hoped to hell it would be enough.

"Mia, these past few days without you…" He scraped both hands through his hair, then let them drop to his sides again. "I know now what it feels like to walk around with a gaping hole in your chest where your heart used to be."

He reached for her, but she stepped back and he couldn't blame her. He hadn't given her a reason yet to come *to* him. But he was finally ready. Talking to his mother had helped. But the bottom line was that over the past few empty, lonely days, he'd finally realized that life without Mia wasn't worth living. He loved her. Whether he admitted it or not, he loved her. So why shouldn't she know it?

Reaching into his shirt pocket, he pulled out a ring box.

She shook her head and said, "I'm not taking that ring back, Dave."

"And I wouldn't expect you to." He grimaced tightly. "That other ring was big and gaudy and bought for all the wrong reasons. I was making a statement. Showing off. For this proposal, for the *real* proposal, I needed a ring that meant something." He opened the jeweler's box and showed her the new ring he'd purchased just that afternoon.

It was smaller than the other one. Three carats instead of five. The setting was different, too. No more modern, coldly elegant cut. This ring reminded him of Mia. Warm. Traditional. Steady.

She gasped when she looked at it and one hand crept up to the base of her throat as she lifted her gaze to his. "It's beautiful."

"The minute I saw it, I knew it was yours."

"Dave—"

"Do you remember," he asked, cutting her off neatly, "when I gave you that other ring, I said that it would tell everyone that Mia belongs to Dave?"

She chewed at her bottom lip, swiped at a stray tear trailing from her eye and nodded, clearly unable to speak.

"Well, this one's different," he told her quietly. "This one says Dave's heart belongs to Mia."

Her hand covered her mouth now and tears were

streaming down her cheeks. Every tear tore at him and Dave made a mental vow to never make her cry again.

"I don't know what to say." Her voice was choked, raw with emotion.

"Nothing yet," he said, stepping in closer, pleased when she didn't move back and away from him. "I'm not near finished talking."

She snorted a short laugh. "Always in charge..."

He gave her a half smile. "Always. Well, until tonight."

"Trick or treat!"

Dave laughed. Most important moment of his life being interrupted by groups of kids out for candy.

"Oh, God, I can't answer the door crying, I'll scare the kids." She swiped at her face, but Dave just picked up the candy bowl, opened the door and took care of things. When he stepped back inside, he set the bowl down and turned back to her.

"I've got a few more things to say and I'd like to get 'em said before the next crew of trolls and princesses shows up."

She laughed a little and nodded. "Go ahead."

"I've done some thinking and I finally realized that a contract is just as easy for some people to break as a promise is." He frowned to himself and took a breath before saying, "I was so busy getting everything on the dotted line, it didn't occur to me that if someone wants to lie or cheat...or leave, a contract won't stop 'em."

"No, it wouldn't," Mia whispered.

"But a promise made by someone who keeps their promises is as good as gold, right?"

She nodded. "Absolutely."

"Well, I keep my promises. And I want to make you one right now, Mia," Dave said, choosing every word carefully now because the next few minutes would decide his future and he for damn sure wanted to get it right. "I promise that I will always love you—"

Mia gasped, clapped a hand to her heart and started crying again. Made a man weak in the knees to see a strong woman cry—especially if he knew he was the cause. "Don't cry anymore, Mia, you're killing me."

"Dave…"

"I'm not afraid to say it now," he told her, reaching out to wipe away her tears with a gentle swipe of his thumbs. "I always thought if I never said the words, then I wasn't risking anything. But by not saying them, I was losing everything." He smiled at her. "And you know I don't like to lose."

"I know."

"So I'm promising you a lifetime of being loved. I want to marry you, Mia. I want our kids to wear that christening gown my mom gave you," he said, then paused and winced. "But not the boys, okay?"

She laughed and nodded. "Okay. We'll find manly outfits for our sons."

He grinned. "That's a deal. *Our sons and daughters.* Sounds good, doesn't it?"

"It sounds wonderful, Dave," she said, stepping up close to him. "It sounds perfect."

"Then marry me, Mia. Wear my ring. Tell the whole world that you hold my heart."

"Oh, Dave, of course I'll marry you." She watched as he plucked the ring from its velvet liner and slid it on her finger. He kissed it as if to seal it into place, then looked into her eyes.

"And you'll come home with me."

"As soon as I'm out of candy."

He grinned. "Tell me you love me."

"I love you so much," she said.

"Promise me forever," Dave whispered.

"I promise I will love you forever, Dave Firestone," she said, her heart in her eyes.

"That's all I'll ever need." He kissed her then, sealing their promises to each other.

As her arms came around him and he pulled her in close, Dave felt his world come back into balance. With Mia, with love, he had the world.

Then the doorbell rang and laughing, they handed out candy together.

* * * * *

BRIDE BY
ROYAL DECREE

CAITLIN CREWS

To anyone, like me, who dreamed they were
really a princess...

CHAPTER ONE

THERE WERE FEW things Maggy Strafford liked less than scrubbing the coffee shop floor—or really any floor, for that matter. Dental surgery. The stomach flu. Any and all memories of her unfortunate childhood in foster care. Still, there she was on her hands and knees, dutifully attacking an unidentifiable sticky patch on the hardwood floors of The Coffee Queen in the tiny, tourist-rich hamlet of Deanville, Vermont, just down the road from one of the state's most famous resorts. Because it was her job as the most recently hired barista on this, the first night the owners had trusted her enough to close up shop.

And for once in the bumpy carnival ride that had been her life since she'd been found by the side of the road as a feral child with no memory of where she'd come from, Maggy was determined to keep her job. Even if it involved scrubbing unidentified sticky things off the floor of a coffee shop in almost the middle of nowhere, Vermont.

She scowled when the bell on the door rang, announcing the arrival of one more coffee-obsessed tourist who couldn't, apparently, read the closed sign she'd flipped over on the glass. Or spare a glance inside to see all the chairs flipped up on the tables, clearly indicating the shop was closed for business. Or notice Maggy herself, there on her hands and knees on the floor, obviously not manning the espresso machine.

"We're closed," she called out as a blast of chilly winter air rushed in, swirling around her and making her wish she hadn't stripped off her thick sweater to do the end of day wipe down. She did not say, *which you can see right there on the door, assuming you can read*, because that kind of knee-jerk, snotty response was the Old Maggy. New Maggy was kinder and gentler. And had thus been steadily and gainfully employed for the past five months.

With that in mind, she summoned a smile as she tossed her sponge back into her bucket with enough force to make the brown water slosh alarmingly. She hated smiling on command. She wasn't exactly made for customer service and never had been, as her spotty employment record attested. But New Maggy knew better than to share her real feelings with anyone, especially not the customers, and who cared how rich and correspondingly annoying they were. Her real and inevitably prickly feelings were her personal business and best kept hidden away if she wanted to keep her current, surprisingly okay, situation. Which she did. So she aimed all her teeth at the door when she looked up.

And her half-assed smile toppled straight off her face.

Two heavily muscled and stern-faced men in dark suits that strained over their physiques strode inside, muttering into earpieces in a language that was definitely not English. They paid Maggy no mind whatsoever as she gaped up at them, moving swiftly past her where she knelt on the floor with a certain brisk efficiency that made her stomach flip over. In warning and a little bit of panic. She knew she needed to jump up and deal with them somehow, which her ingrained fight-or-flight monitor suggested meant running the hell away rather than confronting either one of them.

She braced herself to do just that.

But then another man walked in, flanked by two more muscle-bound goons with earpieces and cold, grim eyes. And giant, ugly handguns on their hips. *Guns.* The obvious security detail peeled off, each one taking a position at one of the front windows, all dark suits, hard gazes, and grim, bulging arms.

The man in the center took another step or two inside the coffee shop and then simply stood there, gazing down at Maggy as if he'd anointed himself the new messiah.

Maggy was no particular fan of arrogant men. Or men at all, if she was honest, given the less than stellar examples she'd encountered over the years, particularly in the foster care system. But she found her usual defense mechanisms—those being her smart mouth and her willingness to wield it first and ask questions later—seemed to have fled her completely.

Because the man standing there above her as if there was a sound track playing the "Hallelujah Chorus" as he did so was...something else.

He stood as if it was commonplace for him to find all sorts of people on their knees before him. As if, in fact, he was faintly bored that there was one more person at his feet. She should have loathed him on sight.

Instead, Maggy's heart slammed against her ribs—and didn't stop. She told herself he was nothing special.

Just another man, and an evidently pompous one at that. Obviously, ridiculously, eye-rollingly wealthy like so many of the people who descended on this little après ski town in the winters. They were a dime a dozen here, leaping in and out of their gleaming four-wheel-drive monstrosities and blinding people with their lazy, too-white smiles. They draped themselves over all the best tables in the town's restaurants, jacked up the prices in all the village's boutiques with their willingness to purchase T-shirts for upwards of a hundred dollars, and cluttered up the coffee shops with their paragraph-long orders of joyless fake drinks.

This guy is nothing special at all, Maggy assured herself, still gazing up at him as if this was a church and she'd taken to her knees to do a few decades of a very specific sort of rich man rosary on a dark winter evening. *This guy is interchangeable with all the rest out there.*

But that was a lie.

He was extraordinary.

Something seemed to *hum* from him, some intense power or perhaps that sheer *certainty* that seemed stamped into his very bones. It was more than simple arrogance. It was more than the tanned faces, white teeth, and high-end vehicles idling by the curb that the others in this town assumed made them demigods. It made it hard to look away from him, as if he claimed all the light in the shop—in the town, in the whole of New England—for himself. And he wasn't exactly hard to look at, she was forced to concede. He wore dark trousers and boots that Maggy could tell at a glance cost more than the fancy SUVs the usual tony ski bums drove. He wore one of those expensively flattering winter coats that exuded upper-class elegance and deep masculinity at once. He was tall, and not just because she was still kneeling. He had wide shoulders and the kind of rangy, offhandedly athletic physique that suggested he spent a lot of very hard, very physical time catering to his own strength and agility—a notion that made her stomach flip again, and this time, definitely not in warning.

But it was his face that was the real problem.

He was not a blandly attractive, run of the mill rich guy, like all the rest packed into Deanville at this time of year in their designer ski togs and indistinguishable store-bought tans. Not this man. His face was too relentlessly and uncompromisingly masculine. Too harshly male. He had a nose like an old coin and a hard, stern, unsmiling mouth that made a shocking, impossible heat uncurl, low and insistent, deep in Maggy's belly. If she was honest, lower than that. His gaze was the color of a hard rain and much too shrewd besides. It seemed to kick up some kind of electricity as he aimed it at her, as arrogant and aloof as it was ruthless.

And he stood there with that gray gaze trained on her as if he was used to nothing less than adoration from all he surveyed. As if he expected nothing less from Maggy.

"Who the hell are you?" she demanded. It felt like self-preservation. In that moment, she didn't care if she was fired for her tone. She didn't care if that meant she got behind on the rent of her shabby little room again. She didn't care what happened, as long as the raw, fierce *thing* that swept over her didn't take her down with it.

"That is perfect, of course," the man said, in a dry tone that made it clear that it was no such thing. "Crude and disrespectful at once. My ancestors turn in their graves as we speak." His voice was rich and deeply cultured, his English spiced by the hint of something else entirely. Maggy loathed the part of her that wanted to know what that *something else* was. Needed to know it, even. The man only gazed down at her, a faint frown marring the granite perfection of his dark, arrogant brow. "Why are you blonde?"

Maggy blinked. Then, worse, lifted a hand to the hair she'd dyed blonde three days ago because she'd decided blonde made her look more approachable than her natural dark chestnut color.

Then she went a little cold as his implication settled deep in her gut.

"Why are you watching me?" she demanded. Not in any sort of approachable manner, because there was friendly and then there was freaked out, and she was already a little too close to the latter. "Are you a stalker?"

There was a slight noise from the goons behind her at the counter, as if they'd reacted to that, but the man before her merely moved one of his index fingers. That was all. He was wearing the sort of buttery soft leather gloves she'd be afraid to touch with her rough hands and he merely lifted one finger. And that was that. Instant silence.

"You do not know who I am."

It wasn't a question. If anything, it seemed like an indictment.

"You do realize," Maggy said slowly, sitting back on her heels and wondering if she could use her bucket and sponge as some kind of weapon if things got serious here, "that anyone who asks that question is basically outing themselves as a giant, irredeemable douche."

His brow rose as if he had never heard the term. But there was no question, as his gray eyes glittered, that he recognized it as the insult it was.

Maggy had the strangest notion he was unused to insults altogether. And perhaps astonished that she dared change that. It meant he was even more of an untouchable rich guy than she'd already imagined—but she couldn't figure out why recognizing that made her a little breathless.

"I beg your pardon." His voice was dark. It rolled through her, making that breathless feeling worse and her chest feel tight besides. "A *douche*? Is that what you called me?"

She tipped her chin up in that way a battalion of counselors and former employers had told her was aggressive, and pretended not to notice the emphasis he put on that last word.

"The coffee shop is closed," she said flatly. "Please gather your goon squad and go and in future? Maybe take a moment or two to consider the fact that marching around with a pack of armed men with potential steroid problems isn't necessary when you're after a cup of coffee."

The man did nothing for a moment but gaze down at her, his dark eyes assessing in a way that washed over her and left strange goose bumps in their wake. Then he thrust his hands into the pockets of his trousers, widening his stance, in a manner that should have looked more casual. But didn't.

"Tell me," he said in that same commanding voice that seemed to resonate deep inside of her. "Do you have a small birthmark behind your left ear? Shaped like a lopsided heart?"

Maggy felt cold. As frigid as the winter air that had rushed inside when they'd arrived.

"No," she said. Though she did. And it took every bit of self-possession she had not to reach up and run her fingers over it.

He only studied her, his austere mouth flat. "You are lying."

"And you're creeping me out," she retorted. She clambered up and onto her feet then, aware again of an instant reaction from the goons—and, again, the way the man in the center stopped them with the faintest wave of one finger. "What is this? What do you want? I'm guessing it's not a Mexi-mocha soy latte with an extra shot."

"Is your name Magdalena, by any chance?"

Maggy understood then that this man already knew the answers to the questions he was asking. And it hit her like a kick to the belly that he was asking at all. It made the hardwood floors seem to creak and slide beneath her feet.

"No," she lied again. She couldn't have said why she was halfway to panicked, only that she was. "My name is Maggy. It's not short for anything." She pulled her phone from the back pocket of her jeans and clenched it tight in her hand. Maybe she even brandished it at him a little. "And if you don't leave right now, I'm calling the police."

The man didn't smile. His mouth looked as if perhaps he never had. Still, there was a silver gleam to those hard rain eyes of his, and her breath got tangled somewhere in her throat.

"That will be an exercise in frustration for you, I am afraid," he said as if he wasn't the least bit threatened by the notion of the police. Almost as if he welcomed it instead. "If you wish to contact the local authorities, I will not stop you. But it would be remiss of me if I did not warn you that doing so will not achieve the results you imagine."

Maggy couldn't have said why she believed him. But she did. It was something about the way he stood there, as if he was used to being mistaken for a very well-dressed and granite-hewn statue, and was about as soft himself.

"Then how about you just leave?" she asked, aware that her lips felt numb and that her stomach felt…weird, the way it kept flipping and knotting and then twisting some more. And meanwhile that place behind her ear where her birthmark sat seemed to be much too hot. As if it was lit on fire. But she didn't dare touch it. Not in front of this man. "I want you to leave."

But this man in all his haughty, brooding ruthlessness wasn't listening to her. She'd stood up and he was clearly intrigued by that. He let those shrewd gray eyes travel all over her, and the worst part was that she had the childish urge to cover herself while he did it. When really, what did she care if some weird guy stared at her? She didn't wear skinny jeans and tight thermal long-sleeved T-shirts that fit her like a second skin to admire her own figure.

Yet somehow, she got the impression he wasn't staring at her ass like all the other rich guys had when she'd worked down the street in one of the village's bars and they'd been after a little bit of local flavor in between ski runs and highly public divorces.

"It is uncanny," the man said, his voice lower now

and something like gruff. "You could be her twin, save the brazenly appalling hair."

"I don't have a twin," Maggy snapped, and she could hear that there was too much *stuff* in her voice then. The way there always was anytime some stranger claimed she looked *just like* their niece or friend or cousin. When she'd been a kid, she'd gotten her hopes up every time. But she was a lot older and whole lot wiser now and she recognized these moments for what they were—throw-away comments from people who had no idea what it was like to have been thrown away themselves. "I don't have anyone, as a matter of fact. I was found by the side of the road when I was eight and I can't remember a single thing from before then. The end."

"Ah, but that only proves my theory," the man said, something hard, like satisfaction, gleaming like silver in those eyes of his.

He pulled off his leather gloves as if it was part of an ancient ceremony. Maggy couldn't have said how he managed it, to somehow exude all of that brooding masculinity and yet be standing there doing nothing but *removing a pair of gloves*. He wasn't sacking the walls of a city or performing some athletic feat, no matter how it echoed around inside of her. When he was done—and when she was busy asking herself what on earth was wrong with her that she should find a man's strong, bare hands *illicit*—he pulled out a smartphone from his pocket, much larger and clearly more high-tech than the one she'd gotten recently when she'd felt so flush after her first month of regular paychecks here. Her fingers clenched hard on hers, as if she was embarrassed by her own phone, and she shoved it in her back pocket again. He swiped his screen a few times and then offered it to her, his face impassive. Though through it all, his gray eyes gleamed.

Maggy stared at his shiny, top-of-the-line smartphone as if it was a wasp's nest, buzzing a warning straight at her.

"I don't want to look at that," she told him. Because he was overwhelming and he didn't make sense and he was *too much*. And she was being smart not to let him reel her into anything, the way she'd always had to be smart, because it was that or be a victim. But that didn't explain the sudden, hollow sensation deep inside her. "I want you to go. Now."

"Look at the picture, please."

He didn't sound as if he was really asking. He didn't sound as if he ever *asked*, come to that. And she noticed he didn't promise that he would leave her alone if she looked as ordered, either.

So Maggy had no idea why she reached out and took the damned smartphone from him, making absolutely certain not to touch him. Or why the faint glint of approval in his stern gray gaze...did something to her. She swallowed hard and looked down at the smartphone in her hand, still warm from its close contact with his skin. Which should absolutely not have made her fight back a shudder.

Maggy focused on the screen in her hand. And then froze.

It was a picture of a woman.

She was standing somewhere beautiful, all gleaming lights and old stone, and she was looking back over one bared shoulder with a wide smile. Her dark chestnut hair was swept back into some kind of complicated bun and she was wearing the sort of dress real people never wore, long and sleek and seemingly threaded through with diamonds to match the bright strands draped around her neck.

If Maggy didn't know better, she'd have said it was a picture of her.

"What is this?" she whispered, aware as she did that her heart was pounding at her. That her stomach knotted so hard it hurt. That her head ached, hard and strange at her temples. "Who *is* this?"

The man before her didn't move a muscle. He didn't lift one of his powerful fingers. He didn't do anything, and yet there was something about the way he watched her then that took over the whole world.

"That is Serena Santa Domini." His voice was cool, and yet she was sure there was something like satisfaction in his voice, threaded in deep, like stone. "Better known as Her Majesty, the queen of Santa Domini, who died twenty years ago in a car crash in Montenegro." His gray eyes flashed with something Maggy didn't understand, dark and sure, but it hit her like a wallop all the same. "I believe she was your mother."

Reza Argos, more widely known and always publicly addressed as His Royal Majesty, King and Supreme Ruler of the Constantines, was not a sentimental man.

That had been his father's downfall. It would not be his.

But either way, there was no doubt that he was a king. That meant there was no room for the maudlin trap of sentiment, especially in a country like the Constantines that prided itself on its *correctness* with, it was true, a certain intensity that suggested a number of unpleasant undercurrents. Like all the whispers about his father's longtime mistress, for example, that no one dared mention directly—especially not after the way his father had died. Not that anyone said *suicide*, either. It was too messy. It hinted too strongly at the darkness beneath the Constantines, and no one wanted that.

It was all unpleasant history. Reza focused on the present. His trains ran on time. His people paid their taxes and his military zealously maintained his borders. He and his government operated transparently, without unnecessary drama, and in the greatest interests of his people to the best of his ability. He did not succumb to the blackmail of a calculating mistress and he certainly did not risk the whole country because of it. He was nothing like his father. More than that, the Constantines were *nothing* like their closest neighbor, the besieged Santa Domini, with its civil and economic crises these last thirty years.

Unsentimental attention to detail on the part of its rulers was how such a small country had maintained its prosperity, independence, and neutrality for hundreds upon hundreds of years. Europe might rage and fall and rise again around them, but the Constantines stood, a firm guard against encroaching darkness and Santa Dominian refugee crises alike, and no matter how grim and worrying it had all been these last three decades.

His father's descent into cringe-inducing protestations of *what the heart demanded*—followed by what might well have become a constitutional crisis had it not been stopped before the blackmail had truly ripped apart the kingdom—did not count. Since very few people knew how bad it had all gotten outside the royal family and the most highly ranked ministers.

Reza had held his tiny alpine country together since

his ascension to the throne at the tender age of twenty-three following what had been widely reported as his father's sudden heart attack, as the latest in a long line of monarchs from the House of Argos. The Constantines was a small country made up of two pristine valleys high in the European Alps. The valleys were connected by a vast, crystal blue lake, bristled with picturesque villages and plump, comfortable banking concerns, and were bordered on all sides by crisp snowcapped mountains and luxury ski resorts.

The Constantinian people liked the kingdom as it was. Untouched. A legacy of a bygone era, yet with all the comforts of the present day. That their longtime ally and closest neighbor, Santa Domini, had suffered a violent military coup when Reza was a child, had lost its exiled king and most of its royal family when he was eighteen, and had strewn out refugees seeking escape from the harsh military government all this time made Constantinians…upset.

Reza did not particularly care for the fact that his reign was often characterized as "rocky," purely because he'd had to spend so much of it handling his neighbor's messes and making up for his father's adulterous yearnings, the blackmail that had nearly brought the kingdom to war, and the suicide he'd had no choice but to conceal from the public lest all the rest of it come out, too. He'd handled that necessary lie. He'd handled his furious, spiteful mother. He'd even handled his father's awful mistress. It was unfortunate that no one outside his inner circle knew how much he'd handled. But things were looking up. Next door in Santa Domini, the usurper, General Estes, was dead. The rightful Santa

Dominian king's restoration to the throne had changed his country and calmed the whole region.

If this woman in front of him was the lost, long presumed dead Princess Magdalena as he suspected she was, that changed everything else.

Because Reza had been betrothed to the Santa Domini princess since the day of her birth. And while he prided himself on his ability to live without the mawkish sentiment that had brought down his father and led him straight into an unscrupulous woman's hands, he suspected that what his people truly wanted was a convenient royal fairy tale with all the trappings. A grand royal wedding to remind them of their happy fantasies about what life in the Constantines was meant to be was just the ticket. It would generate revenue and interest. It would furthermore lead to the high approval ratings and general satisfaction Reza's grandfather had enjoyed throughout his long reign. Contented subjects, after all, rarely plotted out revolutions.

He opted not to share the happy news with his prospective bride just then.

The woman before him shook slightly as she stared at the picture on his mobile. He'd expected joyful noises, at the very least, as he'd imagined anyone standing in a second-rate resort town undertaking menial labor might make upon learning she was, in all likelihood, meant for greater things than her current dire straits. Or a celebration of some kind, particularly given the circumstances under which he'd found her. On her hands and knees, scrubbing the floor like the lowest servant. Her hair like brittle straw around her bony shoulders, making her look even more pale and skinny than she already was.

Wearing the sort of fabrics that looked as if they might set themselves alight if they rubbed together.

Her mouth as foul and crude as the rest of her.

This, then, was his long-lost queen. The fairy-tale creature he would use to beguile his people and secure his throne, all rough, red hands and that sulky, impertinent mouth. He supposed he would have to make the best of it.

And if there was some part of him that was pleased that he could not possibly be in any danger from this creature—that she was about as likely to beguile him as was the exuberant potted plant in the corner—well. He kept that to himself.

She raised her gaze to his again, her eyes a deep, rich caramel that he found he couldn't read as he wished. He watched the curious way she set her frail shoulders and lifted her stubborn chin. As if she wished to hold him off physically. As if she thought she'd have a chance at it if she tried.

On some level, Reza was deeply appalled she might ever have had reason to lift a finger to protect herself. He was almost entirely certain that she was the lost princess of Santa Domini. *His* princess. A blood test would merely confirm what was obvious to the naked eye, as the family resemblance was astonishing. And the lost princess of Santa Domini, the future mother of the kings of the Constantines, was not a scrubbing woman. She was not this...hardscrabble washerwoman persona she'd concocted over the past two decades.

He told himself that he should find it in him to be sympathetic. If he was correct in his assumption about what had happened, she'd been granted a strange mercy indeed—but that made it no less merciful.

"I don't have a mother," she told him, without the faintest shred of deference. Or any hint of manners. And Reza admired her spirit, he supposed, even if he deeply disapproved of its application. "And if I did, she certainly wasn't the queen of anything, unless maybe you mean welfare."

Reza ignored that, already trying to work out how he could possibly take this…fake blonde sow's ear and create the appropriately dignified purse, one worthy of being displayed to the world at his side.

She had the bones of the princess she clearly was. That was obvious at a glance. If he ignored the tragic clothes, the questionable hair, and the decidedly un-refined way she held herself, he could see the stamp of the Santa Dominis all over her. It was those high cheekbones, for a start. The sweet oval of her face and that impossibly lush mouth that was both deeply aristo-cratic and somehow carnal at once. She was an uncivi-lized, hungry sort of skinny, a far cry from the preferred whippet-thin and toned physique of the many highborn aristocratic women of Reza's acquaintance, but she was evidently proud of the curves she had. He could imagine no other reason she would have gone to such trouble to wear her cheap clothing two sizes too small.

What Reza could not understand—what curled through him like smoke and horrified him even as it sent heat rushing through him—was how, when he had no worries at all that she could access his heart no mat-ter who she was, he could possibly want her in any way. This…renovation project that stood before him.

And yet.

It had slammed into him the moment he'd walked into the shop and it had appalled him unto the depths of his soul. It still did. He was the king of the Constantines. His tastes were beyond refined, by definition and inclination alike. His mistresses were women of impeccable breeding, impressive education, and all of them were universally lauded for their exquisite beauty, as was only to be expected. Reza did not dabble in shallow pools. He swam deep or not at all.

The woman he'd intended to make his queen, until he'd seen this creature before him now in a photograph ten days ago, was appropriate for him in every possible way. The right background. Unimpeachable bloodlines dating back centuries. An excellent education at all the best schools. A thoughtful, spotless, and blameless career in an appropriate charity following her graduation. Never, ever, so much as a breath of tabloid interest in her or her close friends or anything she did. Not ever.

The honorable Louisa had been the culmination of a decade of hard searching for the perfect queen. He hadn't imagined he'd ever find her until he had. Reza still couldn't entirely believe that he was here, across an ocean from his kingdom and his people and the woman he'd intended to wed, hunting down a crass, ill-dressed creature who had already insulted him in about seventeen different ways. It offended him on every level.

As did the fact that every time she lifted that belligerent chin of hers or opened her mouth to say something indelicate if not outright rude, the most appalling need washed through him and made him…restless.

His Louisa had been crafted as if from a list of his desired specifications for his potential queen, and yet he had never, ever felt anything for her beyond the sort of appreciation for her lovely figure he might also feel for, say, a pretty bit of shrubbery or an elegant table setting. Reza was the king of the Constantines. The state of his garden and the magnificence of his decor reflected on him. On his rule. On his country. So, too, would his choice of bride.

His feelings, appropriately, were that all of these things should be beyond excellence. And that sort of distant admiration was the only feeling he intended to have for his queen, as was appropriate. Unlike his father's disastrous affair of the heart.

"Perhaps you failed to understand me." He waited for the princess's unusual eyes to meet his and gritted his teeth against his body's unseemly reaction to her. It would be one thing if she were dressed like her mother had been in that picture. If she looked like the princess she obviously was instead of a castoff from *Les Misérables*. What was the matter with him? "Ten days ago my aide returned from a brief location scouting expedition in the area."

"A location scouting expedition." She echoed his own words in much the same way she'd said the word *douche* earlier, and he liked it about as much now as he had then. "Is that fancy talk for *a trip*?"

Reza could not recall the last time any person had managed to get under his skin. Much less a woman. In his experience, women tended to fling themselves into his path with great enthusiasm, if impeccable manners befitting his status, and if they found themselves on their knees, it was for entirely different reasons. He opted not to share that with her. Just as he opted not to share that he'd been planning an engagement trip to ask Louisa to become his queen in appropriately photogenic surroundings. He had not been at all interested in America for this purpose, but his enterprising aide had made a case for the enduring appeal of the New England countryside in winter and the smallish hills they called mountains here.

"I saw you in the background of these pictures." He eyed her brash, blond hair, looking even less attractive in the overhead lights the more she tipped her head back to glare unbecomingly at him. In the pictures her hair had swirled around her shoulders, feminine and enticing, the dark chestnut color suiting her far more. It had also made it abundantly clear whose child she was. "The resemblance to Queen Serena was uncanny. It took only a phone call or two to determine that your name matched that of the lost princess and that your mysterious past dovetailed with the time of the accident. Perfectly. It seems too great a coincidence."

Again, her chin tilted up, and there was no reason at all Reza should feel that as if her hands were on his sex. He was appalled that he did. Until tonight, his desires had always remained firmly under his control. Passion had been his father's weakness. It would not be his.

"I don't have a mysterious past," she told him. Her caramel-colored eyes glittered. "The world is filled with bad parents and disposable kids. I'm just one more."

"You are nothing of the kind."

She folded her arms over her chest in a show of belligerence that made him blink.

"I'll return to my original question," she said. Not politely. "Who the hell are you and why do you care if some barista in a photograph looks like an old, dead queen?"

Reza drew himself up to his full height. He looked down at her with all the authority and consequence that had been pounded into every inch of him, all his life, even when his own father had failed to live up to the crown he now wore himself.

"I am Leopoldo Maximillian Otto, King of the Constantines," he informed her. "But you may call me by my private family nickname, Reza."

She let out a sharp, hard sound that was not quite a laugh and thrust his mobile back at him. "I don't want to call you anything."

"That will be awkward, then."

Reza took possession of his mobile, studying the way she deliberately kept her fingers from so much as brushing his, as if he was poisonous. When he was a king, not a snake. How this creature dared to treat him—*him*—with such disrespect baffled him, but did nothing to assuage that damnable need that still worked inside him. She confounded him, and he didn't like it.

But that didn't change the facts. Much less what would be gained by presenting his people with the lost Santa Domini princess as his bride.

He met her gaze then. And held it. "Because one way or another, you are to be my wife."

CHAPTER TWO

"I GET IT," Maggy said after a moment. The word *wife* seemed to pound through her like an instant hangover, making her head feel too big and her belly a bit iffy, and if there were other, stranger reactions to him moving around inside her…she pretended she didn't notice. "Someone must have put you up to this. Is this some new reality show? *The Cinderella Games*?"

Reza—as the other six hundred names he'd rattled off, to say nothing of the title he'd claimed, were apparently not fit for daily use—blinked in obvious affront.

"Allow me to assure you that I have not, nor will I ever, participate in a *show* of any kind." He managed to bite out his words as if they offended him. As if the very taste of them in his mouth was an assault. Then he adjusted the cuffs of his coat in short jerks of indignant punctuation. "I am a king, not a circus animal."

Maggy found that despite never having seen a king in all her life, and having entertained about as many thoughts about the behavior of monarchs as she did about that of unicorns and/or dragons, she had no trouble whatsoever believing this man of stone and consequence was one.

"I'll make a note that you're not a sad, dancing elephant." Somehow, she kept from rolling her eyes in the back of her head. "Good to know."

"I suggest you look it up," he said, very much as if she hadn't spoken. Maybe for him, she really hadn't. It was entirely possible that a king simply wasn't aware that anyone else spoke at all. He nodded toward her hip, and the phone she'd stashed in her back pocket. "Pull up an image of the king of the Constantines on your mobile. See what appears. I think you'll find that he resembles me rather closely."

And Maggy opted not to explore why the certainty in his voice shivered through her, kicking up a commotion in its wake.

"It doesn't matter what comes up," she told him, careful to keep that shivering thing out of her voice. "I don't care if you're the king of the world. I still need to clean this floor and lock up the shop, and that means you and all your muscly clowns need to go." When he only stared at her in cool outrage, she might have smirked a little. Just a little. "You're the one who mentioned a circus. I'm only adding to the visual."

"What an extraordinary reaction." His gray eyes were fathomless, yet still kicked up entirely too many tornadoes inside of her. And his voice did strange things to her, too. It seemed to echo around inside of her. As if *he* was inside of her—something she was better off not imagining, thank you. "I have told you that it is highly probable you are a member of one of Europe's grand, historic royal families. That you are very likely a princess and will one day become a queen. My queen, no less. And your concern is the floor of a coffee shop?"

"My concern is the lunatic in the coffee shop with me, actually," she managed to say, fighting to keep her voice even. Because she knew, somehow, that if she allowed herself to feel the reaction swelling inside of her, it might take her right back down to her knees. And not by choice this time. "I want you to go."

He studied her for what seemed like a very long time. So long she had to rail at herself to keep from fidgeting. From showing him any weakness whatsoever—or any hint that she was taking him seriously when she wasn't. She couldn't. Princesses? Queens? That was nothing but little girl dreams and wishful thinking.

If there was one thing Maggy knew entirely too much about, it was reality. Cold, hard, grim, and often heartbreaking reality. There was no point whining about it, as she knew very well. It was what it was.

"Very well," he said after what seemed like a thousand years, and was that...*disappointment* that washed through her? Had she wanted him to keep pushing? She couldn't have. Of course she couldn't have. "If you feel you must continue with these unpleasant tasks of yours, then by all means." This time he waved a hand, and it was even more peremptory and obnoxious than his previous partially raised finger. It made her blood feel so hot and so *bright* in her veins that she flushed with it. With temper. And she was certain he saw it. "Don't for one moment allow your bright future to interfere with your menial present circumstances."

Maggy had wanted to hit quite a few people in her time. That was what happened when a girl found herself on her own and entirely alone in the world at eighteen, when the foster care system had spit her out. She'd found herself surrounded by bad people and worse situations in places where violence was the only reasonable response to pretty much anything. Still, she'd scraped by and she'd survived—because what was the alternative?

But she wanted to hit this man more. She even did the math as she eyed him there in front of her. His four goons would likely object to any manhandling of their charge, but she was closer to him than they were. She was sure she could land a satisfying punch before they flattened her. She was equally sure it would be worth the tackle.

She didn't know how she kept her hands to herself.

"I appreciate your permission to do my job." Maggy was not, in fact, anything remotely like appreciative. "Here's a newsflash. Even if you are a king, you aren't *my* king."

She watched, fascinated despite herself, as a muscle worked in his granite-hewn jaw, indicating the impossible. That this man of stone and regal airs was having his own set of reactions to her.

To *her*.

There was absolutely no reason she should feel that as some kind of victory when she didn't *want* to win this. Whatever this was.

"You will dine with me tonight," he told her, in the manner of one who was used to issuing proclamations and, more, having them instantly obeyed.

Maggy let out a short, hard laugh. "Um, no. I won't be doing that. Tonight or ever."

Reza only gazed back at her, and she told herself she was imagining that little suggestion of heat in his stern gaze. That she was a crazy woman for imagining it. That he was a *king*, for God's sake. That she shouldn't care either way, because it was her own, personal law that she didn't do complications of any kind.

And there was no pretending a man who pranced around calling himself a king in a coffee shop wasn't one giant complication, no matter how harshly compelling that fierce face of his was.

"Then I am happy to remain where I am," he told her after another long, tense moment.

"Until what?" She shook her head, then shoved a chunk of her hair back behind her ear. "You convince me that this insane story is true? I already know it isn't. Princesses don't go missing and end up in foster care no matter how many little girls wish they did. You're wasting your time."

"You cannot possibly know that until you take a blood test."

"Oh, a blood test? Is that all?" Maggy bared her teeth at him. "You can expect *that* to happen over my dead body."

He smiled then. And it was devastating. It…did things to his face. Made it something far closer to beautiful than any man so hard and uncompromising should ever look. It should have been impossible. It was certainly unfair. Maggy's mouth went dry. Parts of her body she'd stopped paying any attention to outside of their sheer biological functions prickled to uncomfortable awareness.

Oh, no, she thought.

"Let me tell you how this will go," Reza said softly, as if he knew exactly what was happening to her. As if he was pleased it was. "You will give me a blood sample. You will sit and eat a decent dinner with me tonight not only because I wish to get to know you, but because you look as if you haven't eaten well in some time. If ever. The blood test will confirm what I already know, which is that you are Her Royal Highness Magdalena of Santa Domini. At which point, you will leave this menial existence that is beneath you in more ways than it is possible to number and is an insult to the blood in your veins. And then, among other things, you will assume your rightful position in your brother's court and in the line of ascension to his throne."

She'd opened her mouth to protest his snide reference to her menial life, not to mention his idea that she was some wayward waif who'd never eaten a meal, but got caught on that last bit.

Maggy's heart seemed to twist in her chest. "My brother?"

And she knew she gave herself away with that. There was no chance this overwhelming man didn't hear the breathiness in her voice. The longing for that life so many people took for granted. A life with family. With *people* who were as much hers as she was theirs, whatever that looked like. The kind of life she'd never had— and had taught herself a long time ago to stop wishing for.

"Yes," Reza said. His harshly regal head canted to one side, though he kept his gaze on hers. "Your brother. He is the king of Santa Domini. Previous to his coronation, he was rather well-known as one of the world's greatest and most scandalous playboys. If you have been in the vicinity of a tabloid newspaper over the past twenty years, you will have seen a great deal of him, I'd imagine. Too much of him, I would wager."

Her hands felt numb. With some distant part of her brain, it occurred to her to think that was a strange reaction. That pins and needles should stab at her fingers as if her arms had fallen asleep when they hadn't.

When, despite what was happening here, she was very much awake.

"Cairo," Maggy whispered. Because even she knew that name. Everybody knew that name. She'd seen his pictures all over every magazine in existence for as long as she could remember, because there was nothing else to do while standing in line in sad discount supermarkets stocking up on cheap staples but look at pretty people doing marvelous things in exotic places. "Cairo Santa Domini."

Reza inclined his head. "The one and only. He is your brother. As someone who saw him in person not long ago and is now looking at you, I must tell you that there is absolutely no doubt that you are his blood relative."

Maggy shook her head. She took a step back and only stopped because she had nowhere to go, with his henchmen looming back near the counter. "No."

She didn't know what she was denying. Which part of this madness. Only that it was crucial to her sanity—to everything that had kept her upright and grimly moving forward all her life no matter what got thrown at her—that she keep doing so.

But his dark gaze was much too knowing on hers. She was sure he could see far too much. And the fact he could—that he seemed to have no problem whatsoever seeing straight through her when no one else had ever come close—shook through her like a winter storm, treacherous and dark.

"This will not go away, Princess," he told her, very matter-of-factly. And he didn't shift that gaze of his from hers. "Nor will I. And you can be certain that if I recognized you, so, too, will someone else."

"I think you're overestimating the amount of time

people in your world spend looking closely at people in mine."

Again, a curve of those stern lips, and she wasn't equipped to deal with that. She couldn't process it. She could only feel the way it flushed over her, like another kick of temper when she knew full well it wasn't that. She might not have felt anything like it in recent memory, but she knew it wasn't anything close to *temper*.

"You're decades too late," she threw at him. She didn't know where it came from. Or, worse, she knew exactly where it came from. That dark little hollow place she carried around inside of her that nothing ever filled. And she couldn't seem to stop herself once she'd started. "Everyone dreams they're secretly a princess when they're ten. Especially in foster care. But I'm over that now. This is my life. I made it, I'm happy with it, and I'm staying in it."

"Come to dinner with me anyway," he ordered her, and there was something about the way he said things as if they were laws instead of requests that, oddly, made her want to obey him. She had to lock her knees to keep from moving toward him. She, who was famous for her attitude problems and inability to follow the orders of people who were *paying* her to listen to them. What was *that*? "You can consider it a date."

Maggy assumed he was joking. Because he had to be joking, of course. No one asked her for dates, even roundabout ones like this one. She had *stay the hell away from me* stamped all over her face, she was pretty sure.

And the few times anyone had actually mustered up all their courage and asked that scrappy Strafford girl on a date, it had not been a king.

Not that she'd independently verified this man was who he said he was.

"I would rather die than go on a date with you," she told him, which was melodramatic and also, in that moment, the absolute truth.

Again that slow, coolly astonished blink of his, as if he required extra time to process what she'd said to him—and not, she was quite sure, because he didn't understand her.

"How much money can you possibly make in this place?" he asked.

"That's rude. And it's none of your business. Just like everything else about me is none of your business. You don't get to know everything about another person simply because you demand it or send your little minions to dig it up."

"By minions, am I to assume you mean my staff?"

"If you want to know things about someone, you ask. You wait to see if they answer. If they don't, it could be because they don't want to answer you because your question is obnoxious. Or because they think you're a random creepy guy who showed up with his personal collection of armed men after closing time to say a whole lot of crazy things, suggesting you might be delusional. Or that you won't go away no matter what you are. Or in my case, all of the above."

That muscle in his jaw clenched tight. "Consider dinner with me an employment opportunity." When she only stared back at him, that muscle clenched tighter. "An interview for a position, if you will."

"A position as what? Your next little piece on the side? While I'm sure competition for that downward spiral is intense, I'll pass. I prefer my lovers, you know, *sane*."

She knew she'd gone too far then. Reza went very, very still. His gray eyes seemed to burn through her. Her pulse took off at a gallop and she had to order herself to keep breathing.

"Be very careful, Magdalena," he advised her, his voice low and stern and still, it wound its way through her like a wicked heat. "I have so far tolerated your impudence because it is clear you cannot help yourself, given your circumstances. But you begin to stray too far into the sort of insults that cannot and will not be tolerated. Do you understand me?"

Maggy understood that he was far more intimidating than he should have been, and she was fairly hard to cow. She told herself it didn't matter. That she was as numb as she wished she really was, head to toe, except for that wildness deep in her core that she wanted to deny was there.

She rolled her eyes. "You don't have to worry about tolerating me. And I really don't care if you do or don't. What you do have to do is go."

He let out a breath, but she knew, somehow, he wasn't any less furious.

"I have already told you the only way that will happen and I am not in the habit of repeating myself. Nor am I renowned for going back on my word. Two things you would do well to keep in mind."

And Maggy thought, to her horror, that she might explode. And worse, do it right in front of him. Something was rolling inside of her, heavy and gathering steam, and she was terrified that she might break down in front of this granite wall of a man and humiliate herself. *Ruin* herself.

She didn't know him. She didn't *want* to know him. But she knew, beyond a shadow of a doubt, that she couldn't show any weakness in front of him or it would kill her.

"Fine," she gritted out at him, because when there were no more defensive plays to make, offense was the only way to go. She'd learned that the hard way, too, like everything else. "I'll have dinner with you. But only if you leave right now."

And then she wished she could snatch the words back the moment she'd said them.

Reza didn't smile or gloat. He didn't let that stark, hard mouth of his soften at all. And yet there was that silver gleam in his gaze that kicked at her anyway and was worse, somehow, than the gloating of a lesser man. Or it hit her harder, anyway.

He merely inclined his head. Then he named the fanciest resort within a hundred-mile radius, waiting until she nodded.

"Yes," she bit out, letting her sharpness take over her tone because it was much, much better than what she was afraid hid beneath it. "I know where it is."

"I will expect you in one hour," he told her.

Expect away, idiot, she thought darkly.

But she made herself smile. "Sure thing."

"And if you do not appear," Reza said quietly, because apparently he really could read her like a very simple book, "I will come and find you. I know where you live. I know where you work. I know the car you drive, if, indeed, that deathtrap can rightly be called a car at all. I have an entire security force at my beck and call, and as the sovereign of another nation, even one who is flying under the radar as I am here, I am granted vast diplomatic immunity to do as I please. I would suggest you consider these things carefully before you imagine you can plot your way out of this."

And he turned on his heel before she could come up with a response to that. Which was good, because she didn't have one. His men leapt to serve him, flanking him and opening the door for him, then swept him back out into the night.

The cold air rushed in again. The door slapped shut behind him, the echo of the bell still in the air.

Maggy was breathing too hard. Too loud. And she couldn't seem to operate her limbs.

So she made herself move. She sank back down to her knees and she scrubbed that damned sticky area like her life depended on it. And only when she was finished, only when she'd mopped the rest of the floor and dealt with her bucket in the utility room in the back, did she pull out her own phone again.

She looked at it for a long moment. Maybe too long.

Then she pretended she was doing something, anything else as she opened up her browser and typed in *king of the Constantines…*

And there he was. Splashed all over the internet. On the covers of reputed newspapers and all over their inside pages. In image after image. She saw articles about his childhood. His education at Cambridge. His coronation following his father's sudden heart attack and the war he'd wrenched his country back from in the months that followed. That same harsh face. That same arrogant brow. That same imperial hand waving here, there, everywhere as he gave orders and addresses and spoke of this law and that moral imperative and the role of the monarchy in the modern world.

It was him. Reza was exactly who he'd said he was.

Which meant that there was a very high probability that she was, too.

And this time, when Maggy went back down on her knees on the floor, it wasn't because she was in a hurry to get back to cleaning it.

It was because for the first time in her entire life, when she'd learned how to be tougher than tough no matter what, her knees failed to hold her.

CHAPTER THREE

BY THE TIME Maggy walked into the gaspingly precious and markedly high-class resort and spa, set in all its grand timber and soaring glass splendor some miles outside of Deanville at the foot of the local mountains, she'd done a great deal more research.

She'd gone home after locking up the coffee shop and she'd crouched there on her single bed in her narrow little room with her phone to her face, taking an internet crash course on the life and times of the Santa Domini royal family. And everything she'd discovered had made her...a little bit dizzy.

Could this be real? Could she have a history after all these years of being nothing but a blank slate? Would she finally discover how and why she'd been left by the side of that road twenty years ago? Was it possible that the answer really, truly was something like one of the many silly and fanciful stories she'd made up when she was a girl to explain it away?

She'd spent a lot of time and energy back then trying to explain to herself how and why she'd ended up the way she had. The possibility that she'd been a kidnapped princess had featured heavily in the rotation of the tales she'd told herself when she'd still had a little foolish hope left. After all, it was a much better story than the more likely one—that whatever adults had been responsible for her had abandoned her because they couldn't care for her or didn't want that kind of commitment any longer. For whatever depressing reasons adults would have to make such decisions. A few came to mind as more likely than finding out she was a misplaced princess. Substance abuse, for example. Mental illness. Poverty. She could take her pick and they all ended the same way: a sad eight-year-old girl on the side of a road with no memory of how she'd gotten there.

But that wasn't the sort of story Maggy had wanted to tell herself back then. Princesses won hands down every time.

"Don't get your hopes up," she'd snapped at herself, there in her rented room in an old, converted Victorian that had likely seen its better days when Vermont was still more or less one big farm.

She'd scrolled through pictures of the queen, the king. She'd taken great care not to think the word *parents*. Or the other, more personal words that indicated the kind of close relationships she'd never had with anyone. *Mother. Father.* And she'd sucked up her courage and taken a long, close look at the princess who had supposedly died in that car accident twenty years ago. She'd stared at that little girl's face, not sure what she saw when she looked at it. Or what, if anything, she *should* see. There was no sense of recognition. There was… nothing inside of her. No spark, no reaction. There was simply the picture of a little girl lost years ago.

And then she'd studied the many, many pictures of and corresponding articles about Cairo Santa Domini. He was once the most scandal-prone royal in all of Europe. Now he was the beloved king of the country he'd taken back from the military everyone seemed to assume had not only wrested control of his kingdom thirty years ago, but ten years after that had engineered that car accident in Montenegro to take out the exiled king. And in so doing, had killed everyone in the Santa Domini royal family save King Cairo himself, who had been in boarding school in the United States at the time.

He was potentially her only living family member.

It was possible, after all this time and a life lived entirely on her own in every conceivable way, that she *actually had* a living family member.

Maggy had felt as if she might be sick.

She'd thought a lot about simply getting into her junky old car and driving absolutely anywhere Reza—who it seemed really was the king he'd claimed he was no matter how little she wanted that to be true—was not.

But in the end, she hadn't done it. She'd thrown on the only dress she owned that was even slightly nice and she hadn't gone to too much trouble with the rest because he'd made his feelings about her appearance pretty clear. And then she'd driven herself over to the upscale resort instead of out west toward California. And yes, she had to sit in her car in the frigid parking lot until her hands stopped shaking, but that was between her and her steering wheel and the close, hard dark all around.

Maggy prided herself on the toughness she'd earned every day of the past twenty years, having had no one to depend on but herself. Ever. That meant that no matter how she felt—in this case, about as far from *tough* as it was possible to get without actually dissolving into a sea of tears, which she never allowed herself and certainly not in public places—she'd pulled herself together and climbed out of that car, her shaking hands be damned. She'd wanted answers to questions she'd stopped asking years ago. It was a little bit surprising *how very much* she wanted them, so long after she'd decided wondering about such things only made her weak. And how, with only the slightest provocation—if that was what she could call the appearance of an actual king in The Coffee Queen on Main Street—all those same old questions flooded her.

Making her realize she'd never really gotten over wondering who she was or where she'd come from the way she'd assured herself she had. She'd simply stuffed her urge to ask those things way down deep inside, where none of that could leak out into her daily life any longer. The way it had when she'd been much younger and much, much angrier about her lot in life.

When she started across the chilly, icy parking lot, well salted to make certain the wealthy people who could afford to stay here didn't slip, break their heads open, and then fail to pay their astronomical bills, she was caught for a moment in the dark grip of the cold night. It seemed to tumble down around her and she took as deep a breath as she could stand of the sharp winter air, tipping her head back so she could see all the far-off stars gleaming there above her.

Always watching. Always quiet, always calm. No matter what darkness was engulfing her, the stars shone through.

By the time Maggy made it to the front door of the resort, that great, raw thing inside of her that felt like the sort of sob that she'd rather die than let free had subsided a bit. Just a bit. But it was enough to keep her hands from shaking.

A hotel employee with a clipboard and a walkie-talkie waited for her in the slick, self-consciously rustic lobby of the hotel, a serene smile on her face, as if she and Maggy had already met a thousand times before. Maggy was certain they had not.

"If you'll follow me, Ms. Strafford," the woman said warmly. Maybe too warmly, Maggy thought, when greeting a complete stranger. "I'll take you where you need to go. Mr. Argos—" and there was specific emphasis on that name "—is waiting."

On any other night Maggy would have asked a few follow-up questions. Demanded to know how this woman knew who she was at a glance, for a start. But something told her she didn't want to know the answer to that question. That it would involve the word *appalling* again. And while Maggy felt her self-esteem was strong enough to withstand the snotty comments of an uninvited king in her coffee shop, there was no point testing that theory here, in the sort of five-star hotel broke girls like herself normally gave a wide berth.

Instead, she let the woman lead her back outside and into a waiting hotel shuttle, clearly set aside for her use. She didn't ask any questions then, either. She only settled into the seat she was offered in the otherwise empty vehicle and stared out the window, trying to keep her eyes on the stars as the shuttle wound its way out into the depths of the property, deep into the woods and halfway up the mountain. It stopped there. Maggy glanced out to see a guardhouse and gates, and heard many short bursts of noise on multiple walkie-talkies before the shuttle started to move again.

"It's only a few moments more," the woman from the hotel told her, still smiling so happily.

Maggy practiced smiling like a normal person. It was a skill she'd never mastered, given how little cause she'd had to go around smiling at random people. Or at all. In her experience, anyone who wanted her to *act friendly* and who wasn't paying her to do so was best avoided altogether. It felt awkward and wrong, as if she was *doing something* to her cheeks. She was relieved when the woman looked back to the shuttle driver instead.

Gradually, Maggy realized they were on a long driveway. It climbed farther up the steep incline in a corridor of evergreens and ghostly birch trees, then stopped beneath a towering palace of a house done in more timber and even more dramatic glass. It sprawled over the mountainside as if it had been placed there by divine intervention instead of the resort's developers.

She wasn't the least bit surprised that this was where Reza was staying.

And when she walked inside the soaring entry hall that must have commanded views over most of New England in the sunlight, she was equally unsurprised to find a battalion of servants waiting for her as if she'd strolled into Buckingham Palace.

Not that she'd ever been anywhere near Buckingham Palace. But she'd seen as many pictures of the British palace in the supermarket tabloids over the years as she had of Cairo Santa Domini and his exploits.

After her coat was taken and she'd been greeted approximately nine hundred times by uniformed staff members who pledged to attend to her every need, whatever those might be, Maggy was led off into the house. Each room she walked through was more impressive than the last. Here a library of floor-to-ceiling books and dark leather armchairs pulled close to a crackling fire. There what appeared to be a games room, with a pool table and a chess table and stout cupboards likely filled with every board game imaginable, if she'd had to guess. A large living area, ripe with comfortable couches and deep, thick rugs set out before the glass windows and an outside deck with views over the valley. A closer, more intimate den, with wide armchairs and enveloping sofas and the sort of wall of closed wood cupboards she figured hid television equipment.

Only when she'd walked for what seemed like miles was she finally delivered into a final room. This one was as magnificent as the rest. It featured cozy log walls and architecturally significant windows. There was a stone fireplace and a small seating area arranged around it, and in the center of that area stood a small table set for two.

Maggy stared at that intimate little setup for so long, her heart doing strange things in the back of her throat, she forgot to look around at the rest of the room.

"Do not tell me you have never seen a dinner table before."

His voice was dark and perhaps slightly amused. She jerked her head away from the table and the fire and there he was, standing near a small, personal bar, where he'd clearly just poured himself a drink.

Reza Argos. His Royal Majesty, the king of the Constantines.

Her heart went wild. She felt her pulse rocket through her, making her strangely aware of her temples, her neck. Her wrists. Her sex. Her hands felt numb again, and twice as shaky, and she couldn't tell if it was the

insane circumstances or if it was just him. His gaze
was gray and steady on her, and that made it worse.
That made it…dangerous in ways she was afraid to
consider too closely.

It had been one thing when she'd thought he was a
crazy person, there in the coffee shop. It had been easy
to keep her wits about her. But now she knew who he
was. And that seemed to make everything feel…pre-
carious.

"They buried that princess," she blurted out.

Because if she waited, she was afraid she wouldn't
dare ask. She was afraid of too many things, suddenly,
and they all had to do with his harshly fierce face and
those elegant hands. And the truth was that she *wanted
things*—and that, more than anything else, made her
chest feel tight and jittery. Maggy hadn't made it this
far by wanting things she couldn't have. She'd learned
better. And yet here she was anyway.

"With her parents," she continued when Reza only
gazed back at her, his gray eyes glittering as if he was
trying to read her. "I can't possibly be a person whose
body was recovered from an accident site, legally identified, and then very publicly laid to rest. No one can,
but especially not some random foster care kid on the
other side of the world."

"A very good evening to you, too." His dark voice
was reproving. And something else that moved in her,
deep and low.

Maggy told herself she could not possibly have cared
less what *moved in her*. And that she shouldn't feel it—
or anything—anyway.

"Oh, I'm sorry," she said. Or really *seethed*. "Did
you think I was here for my health? You told me a huge,

ridiculous fairy tale of a story earlier. If it's the lie it seems to be, I'm out of here."

Reza swirled the amber liquid in his crystal tumbler and eyed her over the top of it.

"*A* body was found, yes," he said, his tone cool. "It was said to be the princess's, but then, the entire royal family was identified by members of the very military who had ousted them. There is no telling who lies in those graves. But until now, aside from a few conspiracy theorists in dark corners of the internet, no one had any reason to doubt it was exactly who General Estes's government said it was."

"So in this conspiracy theory, the king and queen are alive, too?" Maggy did nothing to keep that scoffing note out of her voice. "And, what—are currently wandering around aimlessly, disguised as homeless people in Topeka?"

His regal brow rose in affronted astonishment. Or whatever the kingly version of that was, and what pricked at Maggy was that she felt that, too. Everywhere, as if his expression was specially calibrated to work inside her like a flush of heat. She shoved that weirdness aside.

"Topeka?" he echoed. As if she'd said *chlamydia*.

"It's a city. In Kansas."

Reza blinked. Very slowly. She understood that it was deliberate. It was how he indicated his displeasure. That, too, made her feel entirely too warm.

"And Kansas is one of your states, is it not?"

She practiced her smile. "Do you need me to give you a geography lesson?"

He didn't quite sigh. He seemed to grow taller and stormier at the same time, and somehow more formidable. He was wearing a dark suit that was unlike any suit she'd ever seen a man wear in her life. Calling it a *suit* seemed like an insult. It was molded to his tall, solid form, *doing things* to his broad shoulders and making it impossible to look away from all his lean, hard muscles and the planes of his well-cut chest.

"I understand that I must treat you as I would any stray, wild creature I happened upon," he said, almost musingly, his voice calm and light, though his hard gaze gleamed silver. "Your instinct is to bite first. It is no doubt how you survived this ordeal unscathed."

His gaze swept over her, from the top of her head where she'd clipped back her hair in what even she knew was a sad attempt at the sort of hairstyles she'd seen the queen wearing in those pictures to her shoes, which were the black stiletto heels she'd been required to wear during her brief tenure as a cocktail waitress last year. His gaze rose again, taking in every detail of her stretchy little black dress and making her feel as if she was stripped naked, before he found her gaze again.

"Relatively unscathed, that is," he amended.

And that was a different kind of heat then. The scorching reaction to the way he looked at her and then the slap of the insult. Maggy hated both versions. She had to order herself not to clench her fists. Not because she didn't want to hit him; she did. But because she didn't want him to have the slightest idea how much he got to her.

She had no idea how or why she knew that would be the death of her. Only that it would. And that she had to do whatever she could to avoid it.

"Two things," she managed to say, keeping the various rioting factions inside of her at bay and her voice as chilly as the winter night pressing against the windows. "First, I'm not a raccoon. It might surprise you to learn that I don't really like being compared to one. And second, is an insult called something different when it comes out of the mouth of a king?"

His mouth pressed into a hard line, and he set his glass down on the bar with a sharp *click*. He crossed the room in an easy step or two, which wasn't an improvement because then he was *right there*. Too solid. Too tall. And much too close.

He gazed down at her, his gray eyes like a storm, and she couldn't understand that. Why *he* seemed as if this was hard for *him* when it had so little to do with him. He was a messenger, nothing more. He wasn't the one who'd been discarded.

You don't know that you are, either, she snapped at herself.

But then everything stopped. Inside her. Out in the world. Everywhere.

Because he reached out his hand and he touched her. *He touched her.*

He fit his hand to her cheek gently. Very gently. As touches went, it was innocuous. Maggy had fended off far more intimate grabs at her person as a matter of course when she'd worked in that cocktail bar.

But this was Reza.

And everything changed.

His palm was hot. Hard. It molded to her jaw while his fingers brushed into her hair, then ran over that spot behind her ear where her birthmark lay. As if he knew exactly where it was. As if he knew exactly who she was. And something burst open inside of her. She'd never felt anything like it. It exploded wide-open, then rolled through her, sensation rocketing from her cheek to her limbs. She felt herself shake. Worse, she knew he could feel it.

She told herself to jerk away from him. But she didn't. She couldn't.

Her eyes were too wide. His were too gray.

"It is called an insult either way," he said quietly, and she thought she heard an echo of that impossible explosion in his dark voice. She was sure of it when he dropped his hand and adjusted the cuff of his jacket and the crisp white shirt beneath it. "But most people, of course, would pretend it was a bit of flattery instead, simply because it came from me."

What Maggy wanted to pretend was that her heart wasn't racing. That the lopsided heart behind her ear didn't seem to burn like a brand because he'd touched it. That she didn't feel trembling and silly and ridiculously vulnerable. That there wasn't that ominous prickling behind her eyes, and that deep in her core, she wasn't melting and much too soft.

But she couldn't quite get there. She took a deep breath instead.

"It must be nice to be king," Maggy said after a moment, and the funny thing was that there was no edge in her voice then. As if she'd forgotten to try to play the angles here. As if his touch had smoothed them all away, making her feel safe when she knew she wasn't. "I bet no one tells *you* that you need to modify your tone and attitude or you'll be out of a job."

His lips quirked. "Certainly not. No one would dare."

And suddenly, Maggy didn't care if she looked weak. She needed to put space between them. She needed to keep his hands away from her, because she didn't know what she might do with her own. She stepped back and she didn't care how silver that gleam in his eyes was.

"Come," he said then, and she didn't like that. The way his voice was so rich and warm, as if it was as much a part of the fire that crackled in the stone fireplace as it was of him.

Get a grip, she ordered herself.

He ushered her to one of the seats at that intimate table before the fire then, and everything got awkward as he held her seat. Or maybe she was the awkward thing here, while she could still feel his hand against her skin like a new tattoo, a red-hot pulse of sensation. She didn't let herself look at him. She sat down and was *aware* of him all around her, looming and compelling, as he pushed her closer to the table. It was such an odd, old-world sort of gesture, she thought as he took the seat opposite her. There was no reason at all she should feel so…fluttery.

She was absurdly glad that there was now a table between them.

As if responding to some secret signal, a breath after Reza sat down the doors to the room opened and their dinner was wheeled in by more uniformed servants. As they bustled about the table, a different man appeared at her side. This one wore a dark suit and a diffident smile, and held what looked like medical supplies in his hands.

"If I could take a quick sample, Ms. Strafford," he murmured, but his gaze was on the king.

Maggy's eyes flew to Reza's. Too much silver and too much hard gray beneath it. Yet Reza only gazed back at her, his mouth an unsmiling line.

"Do you want to know?" he asked quietly. "I think

you already suspect the truth. I know I do. But this is how we know for certain."

That question echoed inside of her like a drum, loud and low and long.

Did she want to know? He'd offered her this lovely little fairy-tale explanation for her life earlier this evening. A mere handful of hours ago. But she'd risen to meet it, armed with twenty years of her own secret fairy tales to choose from, rattling around inside of her and making all of this feel a whole lot more fraught with peril and meaning than it should.

Do you want to know?

Maggy told herself—sternly—that she wanted to confirm the fact that she was not Magdalena Santa Domini. That the only reason she was here was to prove him wrong, and it had nothing at all to do with that scraped-raw hollow deep inside her, that unleashed sob she refused to let out. That it had nothing to do with a lost little girl, tossed aside like so much trash, who had waited her whole life to belong somewhere.

That she was not a fairy-tale princess. That she'd gotten over imagining otherwise a long time ago. That there was nothing wrong with reality and who cared that once upon a time she'd wet her pillows every night with too many tears for too many fantastical stories that never came true.

She told herself she'd exorcised that little girl a long time ago. And that this, right here, was a way to make sure she never came back—because that little girl was dangerous. She didn't know any better than to *want* with abandon.

Maggy refused to meet Reza's gaze then. She ignored the little voice inside of her that warned her not to do this, no matter what might come of it. And then she held out her arm and let the smooth-faced man draw a vial of her blood, as quickly and efficiently as the other servants tended to the plating and presentation of the food.

That was it, then, she thought as the man gathered up his supplies, bowed slightly to the king, and took his leave. The answer was coming at her whether she liked it or not. Like a train.

"When will we know?" she asked. Despite her best attempt to keep from saying anything.

"Shortly." Reza's gaze was still on her, she could feel it. She kept hers on the edge of her heavy silver fork. More precisely, *one of* her heavy silver forks. "I've assembled a makeshift laboratory in the solarium."

That didn't surprise her at all. "Of course you have."

Maggy stared down at her plate as a first course was set there before her, not sure what it was and also not at all sure she could eat anything anyway. She told herself that was what happened when she had a needle stuck in her body three seconds before dinner, but she was fooling no one with that, least of all herself. She felt…outside herself. Turned inside out. Exposed in a way that didn't make sense, when this man had no more idea who she really was than she ever had.

The feeling only got worse when the staff retreated, leaving them alone in a bright little room that seemed to shrink tight around them.

"It is a country paté," Reza murmured, sounding remote and polite. As if he was commenting on the weather. "Locally sourced, I imagine."

Maggy blinked at her plate, then at him. And knew before she opened her mouth that she shouldn't. That there were too many vast, unwieldy things rocking around inside of her and making her...not quite herself. But that didn't stop her.

"I don't understand the point of this. You said you wanted to get to know me, which we both know isn't true. You don't want to know *me*. You have some fantasy about a lost princess. And I didn't agree to eat—" she wrinkled up her nose "—whatever this is."

"Your palate is likely far more refined, I am sure."

"My palate is basically Cheetos and beer," she retorted, which wasn't exactly true. She also enjoyed ramen. "Does that dilute royal blood? If so, I'm afraid you're not going to get the answer you want."

She had the impression he was clenching his teeth again, though she couldn't actually see it. Only that same muscle in his freshly shaved jaw, calling attention to the harsh perfection of his decidedly regal face.

But when he spoke, his voice was smooth. Calm. "I notice that you seem to have accepted both that I am the king I claimed I was and that you, too, might indeed be Magdalena Santa Domini."

Maggy wouldn't have called the feelings sloshing around inside of her just then *acceptance*. She shrugged, hoping to mask them a little.

"You're either the king of the Constantines or a very good impersonator," she told him offhandedly. "And I'm not sure an impersonator would go to the trouble or expense of renting out this ridiculous place for the sole purpose of conning a broke coffee shop barista." She considered that a moment. "I can't see any reason why anyone would bother conning me."

Again, she saw that mix of affront and astonishment all over his regal face.

"I am delighted that I have distinguished myself in

some way from those charming individuals who clamber about in places like Times Square, dressed up as some or other famous fictional character. For tips." He cut something on his plate, too precisely, as if *tips* was a filthy curse word. But then he looked at her instead of putting his food into his mouth, and she had the impression that edge in his voice made a far better knife than the one he held. In that hand of his she could still feel on her jaw. "The generations of monarchs who preceded me to the throne of the Constantines would no doubt be pleased that a son of the House of Argos has not been mistaken for a street corner hustler with a traveling act."

Maggy felt as if she was sitting on an earthquake, not a chair with a high, solid back. As if the more she pretended the whole planet wasn't shaking there, directly underneath her, the more it actually tore through her, shifting whole continents and ripping up the ground.

"I don't want to talk about country paté or my clothes or wild animals," she managed to say, her voice as edgy as his had been, if somewhat less precise. "You said a lot of things in the coffee shop today."

"I did."

"What happens…"

"Eyes on me, if you please. Not your plate."

Her gaze rose and met his of its own accord. As if she had nothing to do with it—because if left to her own devices, Maggy knew she would have ignored that order. Especially when she was lost in all that intent gray, focused on her as if nothing else existed.

And she couldn't believe she was going to ask the question. She couldn't believe that after all this time she was going to take so little care of herself when it most mattered—when she most needed to protect what little was left of her that could still be hurt. But she couldn't seem to keep herself from it.

"What happens if the blood test says what you think it will?" she asked, because she couldn't seem to help it.

And once again, she could see intense satisfaction all over him. It made him seem bigger. Harder. More dangerous than she thought a king ought to seem, especially when he wasn't doing anything but sitting there on the other side of a few fresh flowers and a couple of dramatic candles.

"Once your identity is verified it becomes a question of how and when to announce yourself to the world."

"You mean to Cairo Santa Domini." She frowned at him when he didn't respond, though he kept that hard, intent gaze of his trained on her. "Surely you would tell him first. If it turns out he's actually..." She couldn't say the word. But then she worried not saying it was more telling, so she forced it out, ignoring how it felt in her mouth. "If he's family."

"Of course," Reza said after a moment, but she wasn't sure she believed him. "But there are one or two matters to attend to before placing you in the spotlight your brother seems to roll around with him wherever he goes. It is a very bright spotlight, I must tell you, the sort that brings all manner of things out from the shadows. It is a decidedly relentless glare."

Maggy couldn't bring herself to worry about spotlights, of all things. She thought Reza meant that figuratively, but who knew? He was a real, live king. Cairo Santa Domini was also a real, live king. For all she knew, real, live kings traveled with actual physical spotlights wherever they went, as part of their entourages.

She concentrated on the other part. "Matters? What matters?"

Reza leaned back in his chair and studied her for a moment. She was caught by the forearm he'd left on the table, strong and hard, a hint of the excessively masculine watch he wore peeking out from his cuff. It was outfitted with enough inset gadgetry to man a space shuttle, she thought. Or, hell, operate a spotlight or two if he needed one.

"I do not wish to insult you, Magdelena."

"Maggy," she corrected him, but without the heat she should have summoned, mostly because she... liked that version of her name in his mouth. *Any* version of her name, for that matter.

Idiot.

He appeared not to hear her anyway. "But the fact remains that you have spent the past twenty years in a situation that can only be called somewhat suboptimal."

"I can think of a whole lot of other things to call my 'situation.'" She let out a short laugh. "None of them polite."

He inclined his head in that way of his that made her want to scream. And also maybe reach her own hand out, across the table, and touch his.

Obviously, she did nothing of the kind. Because that was *insane*.

"You will be the subject of intense scrutiny." He tapped one of his long, tapered fingers against the tabletop, as if to a beat in his head only he could hear. "It will make the coverage of your brother all these years seem mild in comparison. You cannot underestimate the draw such a story will have."

Maggy tried out one of those smiles again. "Everybody likes a princess."

"But that is the issue, of course." His stern mouth curved slightly, and she had the strangest notion that he was trying to be kind. "Not everyone will, and not in the same way. Particularly not a long-lost princess who has suddenly emerged fully grown to claim her place in the world with all its attendant privileges. And those who do not care for a princess who rises from the dead will attack you however they can. They will dig into your life here. They will rip you to shreds in the papers. They will use any ammunition they can find to shame you."

"Why?"

His gaze was matter-of-fact. "Because they can. Because they are paparazzi scum who love nothing more than tearing things down however possible. Because it sells." He shrugged. "You can pick any reason you like, but the manipulation of public sentiment will be the same."

Maggy swallowed. "In case you're wondering, you're not really selling this."

She reached out for her water glass and was horrified to see her hand was shaking again. She dropped it back to her lap and only frowned when Reza poured her a glass of wine instead and set it before her. Wine, she thought, would not help this situation at all. It would blur everything and complicate it far too much.

And God knew she'd never manage to keep her hands to herself with a glass or two of wine in her.

The fact that notion made her feel something like seasick didn't make it any less true.

"Never fear," Reza said as he sat back in his seat.

"You have a secret weapon that will make all of this child's play."

This time her smile came a little more easily. "Do you mean my biting wit? Or maybe you mean my famous charm. Both known as weapons in their way, you're right."

His gray eyes gleamed silver in the candlelight. "I mean me."

CHAPTER FOUR

"You," MAGGY SAID, sounding as resoundingly un-impressed as ever, which might have dented Reza's confidence somewhat had he not been, for all intents and purposes, bulletproof. He was the king of the Constantines. He'd learned from his father's mistakes and the collapse and war Reza had narrowly avoided. His confidence was unassailable. "You are my secret weapon."

"No need to fall all over yourself to thank me," Reza said drily. "It is but one of my many royal duties to aid a lost princess in her time of need."

Her captivating eyes narrowed. "Let me guess. You run a royal princess rescue and travel the world, collecting princesses wherever you roam and then holding adoption events on Saturdays."

Reza found himself paying far too much attention to her impertinent mouth, and not only because of the astonishing things that came out of it. He ordered himself to raise his gaze to hers again.

"I have always been good with strays, Magdalena," he told her, his voice low, and he was sure he could see goose bumps prickle over the exposed skin at her neckline. He liked that far more than he should when she was such an unrefined little thing, scrappy and sharp. "It is always about letting them know two things."

"Wait. I know this one." Her gaze flashed with something too dark for simple temper. "Something about how you're a mighty king. And then something else about how, in case anyone missed it, you're a mighty, mighty king."

He had no idea why, instead of igniting his outrage the way it should have done and would have done with anyone else, her arch tone and the matching look on her face made him bite back a wholly unexpected surge of amusement instead. Reza didn't know whether he was baffled by her behavior—or at himself. Both, perhaps.

"One," he said, as if she hadn't spoken, because that was clearly the safer course, "that they are safe at last. And two, that it is far better to have me as an ally than an enemy."

"I bet that goes over really well with the average puppy," Maggy murmured, as disrespectfully as ever. "It must make potty training a breeze."

And it occurred to Reza then, as they sat there on opposite sides of the small table and Maggy's guarded caramel gaze was fixed to his as if she was expecting an attack at any moment, that he was unused to participating in interactions with women when he didn't already know the outcome.

Such things simply never happened, not even back when he'd been at Cambridge and had enjoyed the illusion of slightly more freedom while his father had run the country toward ruin. He'd still had guards who made sure no one ever got too close to him or approached him without permission, especially any women he might have wanted to meet. And even then, he'd been too conscious of the responsibilities that waited for him and his own father's *do as I say, not as I do* expectations of his behavior to risk something that could end up in tabloid photographs and appalling tell-alls.

As a sitting monarch—and the son of a father who had bent the rules because he'd allowed himself to get into a position where he could be blackmailed in the first place—Reza obviously could not date. He could not participate in anything remotely like a date, in fact. In the years before he'd been seriously looking for an appropriate queen, he'd had to find his women a different way entirely, as there could be no chance meetings for a man in his position. No happening upon a bar or whatever sort of place single people congregated. No accidental meetings of the friends of his friends, given that no one appeared in his presence without both permission and a thorough vetting. Reza's advisers presented him with thick dossiers detailing any woman deemed appropriate for his notice. He sifted through them when he was of a mood until he found any who appealed to him. When he did, arrangements would be made to meet privately, usually at dinners like this one or with a careful selection of very old friends who proved indisputably loyal and discreet.

But the women in question, vetted or not, had ample time to decline the invitation to meet with him before they ever set foot in any room where he might appear. Refusals were not common, of course. Still, they happened every now and again. Reza was a powerful and public figure forever bound to his country first. Some women didn't wish to put themselves into that kind of fishbowl, and how could he blame them?

The ones who did, the ones who met him in artfully

arranged places like this one far away from the eyes of the world, were always sure things. Give or take a bit of artful flirtation and the appropriate amount of flattery on his side and awe on theirs, if they sat down with him, they were his.

His lost princess, however, was nothing like a sure thing. She had thus far ignored every reference he'd made to the fact they had been betrothed years ago and, beyond that, made no secret of the fact she did not exactly respect him or even note his eminence. These things were remarkable enough. But more than that, Reza found the unusual sensation of being in some suspense about what might happen here made him... restless.

Maggy sat before him as if she wasn't the least bit intimidated by him—still. When she'd clearly discovered that he was exactly who he'd said he was. It pricked at something in him, that her disrespect hadn't eased in any way. The truth was, he'd expected her to have a full personality shift into the sort of overawed obsequiousness that usually marked his interactions with other people. Especially because she was the only living human who had ever insulted him to his face. He'd imagined this woman would be even more determined to smooth things over with him now that she knew his identity.

That she did not appear to care in the least what he thought of her seemed to stroke him, like hot hands all over his body.

Which was not acceptable. At all.

"What exactly do you want to do to me?" she asked, snapping him back to the dinner at hand.

And for a moment Reza was entirely a man. Not a king. Another sensation that was entirely new to him, and threw him into his father's territory. *I am as much a man as I am a king*, his father's voice echoed in his head. It should have appalled him. Yet he was focused much too intently on her lush mouth, not to mention all the things he'd like to do with that mouth—

Enough. This was neither the time nor the place. This wasn't who he was. He'd made certain of it.

But his body was not paying the slightest bit of attention to his cool, rational mind. It wanted her.

He wanted her.

Not as the queen he'd been promised since her birth, though he wanted that, too. But as a man.

Reza had absolutely no idea what to do with that. Of course, it was not his emotions. Not with a woman who still looked like a servant. Though the fact it was something far more earthy didn't exactly thrill him.

"Because I have to tell you," she was saying, utterly unaware of what was happening to him as far as he could discern, and thank God for that, "as amusing as it is to be compared to an entire zoo's worth of rescue animals, I'm going to go out on a limb and say that, probably, I don't want to do it. Whatever it is."

He was relieved—to an unseemly degree—when the doors opened again and his staff swept in, trading out one course for the next with brisk efficiency. He ordered himself under control, and for the first time in a life dedicated to his duty and the necessity of projecting a great calm whether he felt it or not, he wasn't sure he could manage it.

What the hell was happening to him? Was he genetically predisposed to repeat his father's great folly? He would not allow it. He could not.

Reza glanced up when the door did not close behind

the waitstaff, to see his own personal aide waiting there. Something pounded in him, hard and triumphant. Because this was a formality. He was sure of it.

"Do you have a result?" he asked his man.

He was aware of the way Maggy stiffened in her seat across from him. And more curious, the fact she didn't turn around to look toward the door. She kept her eyes on the plate before her and her hands in her lap. He was certain that if he looked more closely, she'd have balled them into fists. But he kept his gaze trained on the man at the door instead.

"It is a match, sire," the man said, as Reza had known he would since the moment he'd seen that picture of Maggy ten days ago.

He nodded his thanks and his dismissal at once. His blood seemed to roar through him, making him hard and focused and *needy* in a way he didn't quite understand. He was not a man who *needed*. *A good king does not need the things a man does*, his mother had always told him. The memory set Reza's teeth on edge. He was a king who had all that he needed, thank you. He'd never felt anything like this in his life.

But he kept his voice cool when he spoke, amazed that it, too, was far more difficult than it should have been.

"Congratulations, Princess." He waited for her to look at him, but she didn't. He studied the elegant line of her neck that no cheap black dress could obscure. There were centuries of good breeding right there in her still form. And she would be his queen. All of him—man and king alike, not that he'd ever found there to be much difference between the two before tonight—exulted. "You are, as expected and now beyond any shadow of doubt, Magdalena of Santa Domini."

Naturally, *this* woman did not swoon. Or carry on in any way. Or even seem to react to the news that must surely have been near enough to magic or a lottery win after so many years of hardship and toil. She took a breath that was slightly deeper than any she'd taken before, that was all. Then she raised her head.

There was no joy there on her lovely face. No gleam of victory or relief. Her caramel gaze was flat. Blank.

Reza found her fascinating. And that was the trouble. He had wanted women before, in appropriately discreet ways. He had enjoyed their company, but mostly that was because every woman he'd ever encountered— especially in private—had dedicated herself to entertaining him until the inevitable day he lost interest. He hardly knew what to make of this, that his lost betrothed was about as enamored of him as she was of the table they sat at, and made no attempt to hide it. And while all his previous mistresses seemed to blur together in his mind, this princess who called herself Maggy and sat there before him with badly colored blond hair and a dress that could most charitably be called beneath her station…was not blurry at all. If anything, she was the only thing in sharp, intense focus.

He only just repressed the urge to shake his head, as if to clear it.

"What if there's been a mistake?" she asked.

"There is no room for error," he told her. He found it was preferable to discuss concrete facts than it was to interrogate himself about the strange things happening inside of him tonight. "For various security reasons, samples of many royal families' blood are taken and stored. One never knows the circumstances under which one's identity or paternity might be called into question. A sample of yours was given to my family when our betrothal contracts were executed. Your blood tonight has matched it." He studied her proud, intent face. "There is no mistake."

He watched, drawn to her in a way he chose not to analyze just then, as she reached up and rubbed behind her ear with one finger. Touching that birthmark that marked her, the same way he had earlier.

Again, he expected a reaction. And again, he was disappointed.

Maggy only swallowed, as if against a constriction in her throat, but when she spoke her voice was smooth. "What happens now?"

Reza needed to get ahold of himself. If only because it was unacceptable to imagine any scenario in which the king of the Constantines was the *less* composed person in a room. In any room.

"First, you must look the part," he said, forcing himself to concentrate on the practicalities. Not this madness that was sweeping through him, rendering him a stranger to himself. When he had known exactly who he was and all the contours of the life he would lead from the day of his birth, and had never deviated from that knowledge in all his life. Especially when it came to matters of the flesh, after his father's terrible example.

Uncertainty did not suit him. It horrified him, in fact. Deeply.

Maggy's unreadable eyes were fixed on him. "You said I already look like the late queen. Problem solved."

He noticed she did not refer to Queen Serena as her mother, but he tucked that away. "I'm afraid it is not your bone structure that the paparazzi will focus on."

"Oh, wait." Her caramel gaze turned hostile then. But

not surprised. "What you're trying not to say is that I don't look like a princess. I probably look like a cheap townie who's had to work her ass off to get anything she has, no matter how crappy it looks to visiting royalty. Because guess what? That's who I am."

Reza did not quite sigh. "I cannot imagine any reason the phrase *cheap townie* would exit my lips," he told her. He eyed her mutinous expression. "And certainly not as a description of the woman I am contracted to marry."

"I don't know why not," she retorted. Once again sliding right past their betrothal. Reza found that fascinating, too. What he didn't know was if that was because he was interested in what she tried to ignore—or if his ego was a bit stung by the continuing proof that this woman was the only one alive who, apparently, wasn't transported into a froth of joy at the idea of marrying him. He had the lowering suspicion it was the latter, especially as Maggy kept going, her voice hard. "You weren't quite this shy or retiring back in the coffee shop. Hit me with it. I can take it." She lifted her hands, palms up, but didn't shift her gaze from his. "Tell me all the ways I'm defective. I dare you."

Reza was not used to direct challenges. Much less outright dares. And he was certainly not used to such displays from those who ought to have found his very presence nothing short of miraculous. Worth gratitude, at the very least—but he shoved that aside. That was most definitely his ego talking. The inbred arrogance he'd been born with. He was self-aware enough to recognize he had both in abundance. What he didn't recognize—and did not care for one bit—was this uncontrolled, dark thing he couldn't identify as it swelled in him. It was as if with her, he truly was nothing but a man.

From one breath to the next, he couldn't decide if that was unforgivable or intriguing.

Nonetheless, he took that dare.

"That false color in your hair does not suit you," he told her, keeping his tone even, because he was a king, not a common lout. He did not attack those weaker than him, or in need of his aid. And no matter the mouth on her, his lost princess was very much both. He needed to keep his heavier artillery to himself. "And only partly because it is inexpertly applied. But the rest is a cosmetic matter, easily handled. A question of more appropriate clothing. Garments made to flatter your particular figure rather than off some bargain rack somewhere. Some tutoring in deportment, so you might comport yourself in a manner more in line with your heritage. Perhaps even some time in a spa to tend to your general air of exhausted desperation."

"It must be some spa," Maggy replied darkly, "to combat twenty years of poverty and loneliness. Will a massage do the trick, do you think? Or will I need something a little more theatrical to get the stink out, like some of those hot stones?"

"You asked me to tell you these things and I thought you could take it. Did you not say so?"

"This is me taking it. I didn't promise I'd be mute." She pressed her lips together for a moment. "Anyway, I don't care about cosmetic things. This might be hard for you to comprehend, but for some people, primping is pretty far down the list."

"That is all very well for a coffee shop drone in the middle of nowhere." He lifted his shoulder, then dropped it. "But we are no longer speaking of that woman. We are speaking of a princess who will return from the dead and find herself in the center of intense public scrutiny."

"You mean me. Not a random, theoretical princess. Me." Maggy shook her head. "And let me tell you something about me, since you're so interested. You can't pretend the last twenty years didn't happen, no matter what a blood test says. *I* certainly can't."

"Do you wish to be ridiculed?" he asked her quietly. "Do you imagine you will enjoy snide tabloid articles about your inability to attend to your own grooming? You didn't care for it when I called you a wild animal. Will you like it when the tabloids screech that you are a feral creature more deserving of a wilderness habitat than a palace?"

She looked as if he'd thrust his fork into her jugular, and he didn't much care for the sensation.

"These are realities you must consider now. Who you are is essentially meaningless. It is who you let them see that matters." He waved a hand at her dress, obviously mass-produced, which hugged her figure in a way that would have rendered his own ruthlessly correct mother pale with horror. Reza found that the man in him appreciated the close embrace of all that cheap, stretchy black material more than he wished to admit. "You cannot simply throw on any old thing and step out in it."

"This is the only dress I own," she said, her tone a frozen thing. "I apologize if it offends you. Had I known that I'd be having dinner with a mighty king, I might have made a trip to the mall."

He placed it then. She almost sounded as if he'd hurt her feelings. He couldn't imagine how.

"I am not insulting you," he told her, frowning. "I am trying to prepare you for what will come. You will need to plan your appearances very carefully, as you will no longer be a private citizen. You will represent the crown."

"As its ungroomed, trailer trash face in a cheap black dress. The poor crown. What if I tarnish it?"

Something inside of him turned over, surprising him.

"Do you think you are the only one who finds these boundaries and necessities absurd?" he bit out at her, and the fact he was shocked by the flare of his own temper should have kept him from continuing. But it didn't. "Insulting, even? Let me assure you that you are not. But there are things that matter more than your feelings."

"So far," Maggy said softly, "it seems that everything matters more than my feelings."

"You can, of course, be the sort of royal beloved by the tabloids for different reasons," Reza said, his tone grim. "There are any number of blue-blooded tarts who fall in and out of Spanish clubs and make fools of themselves at so-called 'edgy' parties in Berlin. The brightest beaches in the Côte d'Azur have dark and desperate shadows where many an heiress loses her way, usually quite publicly. This is always a path that is open to you, if you wish it. You would hardly be the first princess to choose hard partying over hard work."

"Yes," she said, her words a bare whisper, though her caramel eyes were fixed to his and glittered hard with something much darker—something he felt like an echo deep inside of him, and he didn't like it at all. "My goal in life is to be an international whore. It seems like such an upgrade."

Heat seemed to rise in the air between them, electric and impossible. Reza did not want to imagine this woman as any kind of whore, international or otherwise. Or perhaps the truth was, now that she'd said it, he was having trouble thinking of anything else except how much he'd like to descend into a few depths with her. And what the hell did that make him?

"The choice is yours." He sounded darker than he should have. Grittier. "I, personally, prefer a more respectable approach, but then I have been the ruler of the Constantines since I was twenty-three. There was no time for me to make a name for myself in all the wrong ways."

Maggy folded her hands in her lap and Reza suspected it was to keep them from shaking. And if so, he wanted to know if it was anger or some other emotion that worked in her—like maybe some faint echo of the things he felt inside himself that were causing far too much of a commotion. She sat tall in her seat, and he wondered if she knew how very regal she looked while she did it. Or if it was something innate in her. As if her very bones had been calling out her true identity all this time, if only someone had thought to look in the back of beyond and on the wrong continent.

"But nothing you're telling me is about me, really," she said after one long moment dragged into another. She held his gaze and there was no pretending he didn't still see the challenge in her eyes. In the proud tilt of her chin. It was as novel as it was astounding. "You didn't come all this way with a lab in your back pocket because you were concerned about *me*. This entire thing is all about you."

"I beg your pardon?"

That particular tone of his usually ended conversations and led straight to abject apologies and groveling. Maggy didn't appear to hear it—much less heed it. She looked at him with challenge all over her face and not a single trace of anything like respect.

"You don't care what kind of princess I am. You care what kind of queen I might make you, in the unlikely event I actually ever marry you."

Reza paid no attention to that roaring thing in him that was eating him alive. He focused on her, making no attempt to hide the full force of his intent. His need. His royal will that had so far gone uncontested in every way that mattered.

She might be something different than what he was used to. He might find her far more fascinating than was wise or good. She might seem to speak to a part of him he hadn't known was there and didn't like at all— as it seemed a bit too close to the sort of nonsense that had made his father a weak, sentimental, and ultimately dangerous man behind the mask of the decent enough king he'd been before the end. But that didn't change the fact that he would get what he wanted.

He always did.

"You are Princess Magdalena of Santa Domini," he told her. "It is not your choice whether or not to marry me, I'm afraid. It is your destiny."

Maggy didn't feel like a princess. She felt turned inside out. It stood to reason she didn't feel like anybody's *destiny*, either.

Especially not his. No matter what that blood test had said.

"In my experience," she said in a low voice, somehow keeping that raw, scraped hollow thing inside of her at bay a little longer, "*destiny* is a word people use when they don't have a good reason for doing the thing they want to do, but they want permission to go ahead and do it anyway."

Reza pushed back from the table then, getting to his feet. Maggy didn't know why it surprised her—or maybe that wasn't the right word. It was more that when he moved, she *felt* it. It seemed to wrap tight around her and tug. There was a certain powerful smoothness to him. A different sort of danger. It made her belly fold in on itself and feel something like precarious.

She didn't want to keep sitting there like a target while he was moving around the room, so she got to her feet, too, hardly sparing a glance for the perfectly prepared roast that she hadn't so much as touched.

The king who'd told her she was a princess and, more than that, *his* moved from the seating area near the fire to the windows and stood there. She knew he couldn't really be gazing out at the mountains. It was too dark and she could see her own reflection from farther back in the room. He clasped his hands behind him in a way she found deeply royal even if she'd never given a moment's thought to what that might mean before.

Whatever a king was supposed to be, Reza looked the part. It only called more attention to the fact that she was about as far away from a princess as it was possible to get. She didn't need to consult her phone to understand that a stretchy dress from a low-market chain store was not what most European royals wore. Not even that endlessly trendy royal from England who was always on the front page of everything.

What she didn't understand was the way her stomach twisted at the thought she'd somehow…let Reza down. *You are pathological*, she snapped at herself.

"You were promised to me at your birth," he said after a long moment. Maggy had the distinct impression he'd been watching her through the glass. And she was surprised at the gruffness in his voice. That and how it washed over her, like a caress. Like his hand against her face once more. She tried to blink that away. "Our fathers were, if not friends precisely, fond of each other and, more than that, committed to peace and prosperity in both our kingdoms. Combining our countries in marriage pleased them both—and made a great deal of sense in other ways, as well." Beyond him, the dark valley spread out toward the next set of hills, twinkling with village lights like grounded stars. But somehow, Maggy couldn't quite find them soothing. "I always knew I was to marry you. This meant that any youthful, adolescent shenanigans would affect you directly. I therefore kept such things to a minimum, so as to cause neither your father nor mine any embarrassment. Whatever life I wanted to lead, I always knew that there had to be room in it for you."

Maggy thought of her own adolescence. Empty and often painful. She'd thought of no one but herself because she'd had no one but herself. It wasn't selfishness if it was pure survival, surely. Because no one else had cared if she lived or died.

She had no idea how to reconcile those barren years with what he was telling her. The idea that anyone had ever cared about her, even in the most abstract way, simply didn't make sense.

"You must have hated me." Her voice was low. "I

would have hated it if I had to live my life based on some stranger."

Even as she said that, she knew it was a lie. That was true now. But there was a time Maggy would have given anything to think something—*anything*—she did or said or was mattered to another living soul.

Reza shook his head. In the glass, Maggy could see herself and his outline, as if the harsh beauty of his face was too much for mere glass to handle.

"You were mine," he said gruffly, and she told herself she didn't notice the way that seared into her. Like electricity. Like some kind of truth. "And I was under no illusions about the life I was expected to lead. I was bred to rule a country, not cater to my own self-interest. I assumed I would be lucky enough to rule it with a queen raised in a similar fashion, who would want the same things I did."

"What is that, exactly?" she asked, and there was some of that electricity in her voice, making it tighter than it should have been. "Because I wanted a roof over my head. A safe place to sleep. What does a king want from life that he doesn't already have every time he snaps his fingers?"

"My people safe, first and foremost," he told her, with another one of those shrugs that made her long for things she couldn't quite name. It was something about the width of his shoulders, the bold, masculine line of his back. "But beyond that, I want what any man wants, if for different reasons. Peace, prosperity, and heirs."

All this time, the conversation had been abstract. To Maggy, anyway. A princess who was to marry and become a queen to a man who was so indisputably a king. All part and parcel of the silly fairy tale this man kept spinning. He might as well have been talking about dancing candelabras or singing crabs for all the impact royalty was likely have on Maggy's life. Even after the aide had come back with the blood test results, she hadn't actually absorbed it.

Yet somehow, *heirs* was the word that smacked into her. It made her realize that whatever else was happening, Reza wasn't kidding around. About any of this. And that this wasn't a fairy tale. This was happening. To her. Right now.

Heirs.

His heirs.

Her heart was beating much too fast and much too hard. She crossed her arms over her chest and tried to hold herself together. And no matter that the empty place deep inside of her was…changing. Growing. Shifting. An earthquake from the inside out, and it seemed to throb, low and insistent, in her core.

"I've watched a lot of television shows where people carry on about heirs," Maggy managed to say. "I never thought it was a real thing anyone actually did. Meaning, I've literally never heard anyone use that word to describe their kids."

He turned to look at her then, and that was…not better. His gray gaze was dark. It seemed to punch straight through her.

"I will not be leaving my heirs a few pieces of chipped china and furniture of unknown provenance," Reza said softly, and yet there was somehow even more power in his voice than before. "And one does not generally refer to the princes and princesses of the Constantines as *kids*. Moreover, the Constantines are what

I will leave them. The House of Argos has held the throne for centuries."

She swallowed and was sure he could hear it. That was how dry her throat was just then. "I'm not sure I'm following you."

"I suspect you are following me perfectly well," he countered, and there was something different in his gaze then. Something almost lazy.

Maggy ignored the flush that moved over her. In her.

"You came to claim me because you thought I was this princess."

"And behold my prescience. You are."

She frowned at him—or more precisely, at the way that gleam in his gaze made her feel a different kind of itchy. Inside and out.

"You found me," she said quietly. "But now what? You want to whisk me off to some palace and make a queen out of me?"

He inclined his head. "I do."

"And where you come from, it's perfectly reasonable to talk about the heirs you need when you talk about things like marriage. To total strangers."

"Mine is a hereditary monarchy, Princess," Reza said in that same low, stirring way. "As such, I only have two jobs. One is to preserve the kingdom. The second is to pass it down to a child of my blood, as my ancestors have done since time immemorial."

"Why haven't you already married?" She studied him as he stood there, straight and tall and arrogant, making it clear he was subjecting himself to her questions because he chose to do so. Not because he had to. Maggy had no idea how he managed to make that so clear. She only knew that something in her thrilled to it. To him. "You've had twenty years to produce heirs with some other appropriate person."

"None of them were quite so perfect for me as you."

What amazed her, Maggy could admit, was how very much she wanted to believe that was a personal comment. A compliment of some kind. Was that how low she'd sunk? That she'd take anything—even this sheer madness—as evidence she didn't have to be quite as alone as she'd always been?

"And by *perfect*, you mean the blood in my veins."

He inclined his head again, though this time, there was something about his hard, stern mouth that got to her. Her heart kicked at her again. Harder this time.

"The blood in your veins is a factor, yes. As is the fact a marriage with a Santa Domini links our kingdoms in precisely the way our fathers envisioned. They were right about the benefits then. I am no less right about those same benefits now. Had all gone as planned, we would have married the moment you came of age."

There was no reason at all that should wind through her the way it did, more of that electricity and something sweet and melting besides. It shouldn't steal her breath, imagining that other life that had been stolen from her. Absurd wealth, yes, but also—and more important, to her mind—family. And perhaps in that alternate reality Maggy might have married this man the way he seemed to think she would have. Which would likely mean she'd already have his children, something she found both impossible to imagine and all too easy to conjure up.

That Maggy would have so much family she would never have to be alone again, unless she chose it.

But that Maggy had been killed in a car accident

twenty years ago. The fact Maggy had actually survived the crash didn't change that. She felt herself shiver slightly. Very, very slightly, and she instantly tried to hide it. Still, she thought he saw it.

"So the only difference between me in this scenario and any other trophy wife is that you live in an actual castle, not just a big, tacky house," she managed to say through that same too-tight throat, but she knew she wasn't fighting him any longer.

When exactly were you fighting him? a cynical little voice asked, deep inside. *When you raced to get to this hotel? At his beck and call?*

"I think you will find Constantine Castle to be something of an upgrade from your present circumstances," Reza said quietly, his gaze intent on her. "And that there will be trophies to go around."

And Maggy wasn't a fool. She'd never had the opportunity to be a fool. She'd grown up too fast and much too hard. Like any woman, especially one with limited means, she'd had no choice but to make a study of men. She knew rich men. She knew they did as they liked and expected those they trampled over to thank them for the privilege.

She could only imagine that a king would be even worse.

There was no such thing as fairy tales. She knew that. She'd lived it.

But it seemed as if Reza was the closest she'd ever come. Maggy could imagine a thousand ways she'd come to regret what she was about to do, but at least that would all be new. She'd done *this*. Poor, scared, alone. She was tired of *this*.

If he said she was a princess, she'd become a princess. If he wanted a queen, she'd do that, too. Hell, heirs weren't an issue, either—if she ignored the *how* and concentrated on what came after that. A baby or two meant that no matter what happened with this man who watched her as if he was another one of the looming mountains outside and he could wait there forever, she could never be discarded again.

She could have everything she ever wanted. All those dreams she'd learned to despise in herself, thinking them a weakness. All those longings she'd tamped down and hidden away, refusing to give in to their lure in the harsh light of day. She could have all of it and a fairy tale, too.

All she had to do was dare to claim it.

"It sounds wonderful," she said, and she ignored the way her voice cracked. Maggy concentrated on the king before her with the hard rain eyes and the future she wanted, no matter the cost. "I can't wait to see it."

CHAPTER FIVE

Walking away from the only life she'd ever known should have been harder.

That was the thought that kept poking at Maggy. It lodged inside her, growing strange talons and digging into her with every breath. She'd always known who she was, or anyway, how she was defined in the community. The lost girl. The discarded girl. She'd been told who she was a thousand times, by well-meaning counselors and harried teachers and unimpressed employers alike. She'd always known exactly what her life entailed, whether she liked it or not. Surely learning that she was wrong about that, that everyone she'd ever known was wrong about that—about everything— should have been as much of a blow as a gift.

But in reality, it couldn't have been easier.

"We will leave in the morning," Reza told her that first night in his sprawling mountain lodge, a certain anticipation making his gray eyes gleam. Or maybe the anticipation was in her, not in him. She couldn't tell. "Do not worry about your possessions or the details of your life here. My people will handle it."

And Maggy had decided to surrender to this, hadn't she? She wanted the fairy tale, whatever it took. She didn't argue with him. She went and sat back down at the table. Then she thought, *what the hell*, and sampled the roast, assuming her appetite would catch up with her. She even took a sip or two of the wine, which was so different from any wine she'd ever tasted before that she couldn't quite believe both could be called by the same name.

"I don't think I can leave the country," she said at one point, glancing up to find Reza still over by the windows, watching her as if she baffled him. There was something else there, in that endlessly dark and gray gaze of his, but she didn't want to look too closely at that. Or the fact she could feel it like an echo inside of her all the same.

"Why not?" he asked, with a mildness she somehow didn't trust.

Maggy shrugged. "I never got a passport. International travel wasn't really on my list of goals these past few years. I've been more interested in other things. Like a steady job, a safe place to crash. You know."

She knew full well he didn't know. That was why she'd said it.

But of course, Reza was unconcerned with such petty things as reality.

"I took the liberty of having my government issue you a passport marking you as a citizen of the Constantines," he told her. "I trust you will find it sufficient to cross any and all borders."

Maggy had a lot of follow-up questions then. When had he had this passport made? What name was on the passport, for that matter? Why was he so certain and simultaneously unconcerned—about everything? But none of those questions mattered, in the long run. They had nothing to do with her goals here, which were fairy tales and her very own family, the end. She needed to keep her focus trained on the prize.

So she only aimed another smile at him, each one easier and smoother than the last. He returned to the table to join her and she kept right on eating, because the courses his staff kept bringing in were a far cry from the cups of noodles she prepared on her hot plate.

Maggy stuffed herself so full she thought she might burst. And she didn't think she'd mind if she did.

The next morning a fleet of sleek, gleaming black SUVs appeared outside the rickety old house where she'd lived these past few years. Maggy came down to meet them with the very few things she considered necessities in a backpack. In a sweatshirt that said STOWE across the front in a nod to a nearby ski resort, her favorite pair of battered jeans, and the boots that had always made her feel tougher than she really was. Blank-faced guards handed her into the SUV in the center of the little convoy. She climbed in and slid across buttery leather seats so soft she was afraid she'd destroy them somehow simply by touching them with her clumsy commoner denim.

But then she found herself inside an enclosed space with Reza, and that was far more alarming than any potential damage she might do to soft leather.

Her heart took up that low, wild beat again. Her blood surged through her in a way that seemed designed to do damage. She was shocked it didn't. And there was that melting, clenching thing, too, low in her belly, making it hard to sit still.

Reza sat next to her as if the spacious backseat was a throne. He took up too much of the available room—

or maybe it was that he seemed to claim all the air. He was wearing what she guessed was the royal version of casual. A button-down shirt that looked softer than the leather beneath her, crisp and white against his olive skin, and it amazed her on some distant level how that made her mouth water. He set down the papers he was scanning to look at her as she settled in the seat beside him.

His gaze was stern as it moved all over her, from her hair in a sloppy ponytail to the scuffed toes of her favorite boots.

Maggy stared back at him, her chin rising of its own accord, far more defiant than the moment called for. But she was seized with a desperate panic as the moment dragged out, even if she thought she'd rather die than let him see it.

Would he think better of this bizarre plan of his? In the cold light of the too-bright winter morning, would he take one look at her and realize that she could never be anything but the discarded piece of trash she'd always been? That there was nothing the least bit royal about her no matter what a blood test had said?

"Today is the last day you will walk around dressed like this in public," he told her, his voice a very calm, very clear command. "And I can only take it as my personal mission to convince you that it is better you do not dress like this in private, either."

"I'm American," she told him, because she preferred to combat nerves with her mouth whenever possible. "I like jeans."

"You are not American," he countered in that same cool way of his that made her whole body overheat. "You have never been American, despite appearances. You are one hundred percent Santa Dominian."

He rapped his knuckles against the window, making her flinch. But it was only his signal to his driver, she realized a moment later. He was giving his men an order, he wasn't having her thrown back into the life she'd decided to leave behind her.

The relief that washed over her then was so intense she was afraid it might flip over the SUV.

"Santa Domini means nothing to me," she murmured. She could only hope he hadn't seen her reaction, or if he had, she assured herself he wouldn't know what it meant. "It's as much a fairy tale to me as you are."

She shouldn't have said that. If she could have snatched the words back, she would have. Maggy glared down at her ratty old orange backpack and tried to pretend she couldn't feel his assessing gaze light up the side of her face, like an open flame.

But the truth was, she felt it everywhere. She felt *him* everywhere.

"I have no objection to jeans, per se," he said as the SUV started down the road, surprising her. "There is a time and place for them, of course. These are not the eighteen hundreds. What I object to is cheap fabric and unflattering, mass-produced cuts that do not flatter your form in any way."

She forgot she was trying to avoid looking at him and shifted to frown at him then. "But—"

Reza only held up a hand, in that way of his, as if he was holding an invisible scepter. "When I have outfitted you in a manner consistent with your actual station in life, if you truly wish to spend your time in the clothes you've brought with you, then we will revisit this conversation."

He didn't wait for her response. He returned to his

papers without sparing Maggy another glance. And it took her longer than it should have to really notice that he'd ended the conversation entirely on his terms, not on hers.

I think you can probably get used to that, she told herself as Deanville slid past her window. *That seems very king-like behavior.*

But the truth was, she couldn't bring herself to care about that as much as she should have. She was too focused on all the things she *wasn't* feeling about leaving the only home she'd ever known. Maggy knew every street, every hill, every tree on the way out of town. She'd been found on Route 132 in Strafford, which was how she'd gotten her surname, and she'd spent the longest stretch of time in a foster home in Deanville. These things—these places—should have left their marks on her. They must have. Yet she felt far more marked, and indelibly, by the man who sat beside her.

And when the convoy delivered them straight out onto the tarmac of a private airfield, not far from a sleek jet embossed with a very intricate and glossy coat of arms, Maggy stopped worrying about the separation anxiety she definitely wasn't feeling about leaving her old existence. Instead, she started panicking slightly about the fact she'd never been on a plane in her life.

"Are you well?" Reza asked as they stood on the tarmac, the sun making the cold bite of the winter air seem less harsh than it was. "You've gone unusually quiet."

"You don't know me well enough to know what's usual or unusual," Maggy pointed out.

His hard mouth almost quirked. "Answer the question, please."

She took her time looking at him. At his ruthless,

forbidding face that seemed to fill a thirst in her she hadn't known she had. Maggy had no idea what that meant. She wasn't sure she wanted to know. But she wasn't used to anyone paying such close attention to her.

Something she really didn't want to share with him.

"I'm terrific," she told him. "Never been better, in fact."

She expected him to throw something back at her, or glare in his kingly way. Reza did neither. His expression was too fierce and his mouth was that stern, unsmiling line. But then her breath caught in her throat, because he reached out and smoothed his hand over the length of her ponytail, not quite tugging it, and for a moment it was as if they were the only two people in all the world.

It made her heart flip over.

She was very much afraid that he could hear it.

One mad beat of her heart. Then another. And then Reza dropped his hand and touched her gently at the small of her back, indicating she should walk ahead of him toward the jet while his aides converged around him.

And it took her the whole way up the metal stairs and into the plane, waved in by smiling flight attendants, to catch her breath and get the wild drumming of her pulse under control.

Once on board, she had other things to think about, like the fact there was gold everywhere. Dark, gleaming wood. Thick, soft rugs at her feet. Especially when she was shown past what looked like a luxurious hotel living room into a fully outfitted bedroom suite. On a *plane*.

"Please don't hesitate to ring if you need anything, Your Highness," the flight attendant who'd escorted her said with a smile. "Anything at all."

And it wasn't until the uniformed man walked away that Maggy realized what had happened. That when the man had said *Your Highness*, he'd meant Maggy.

She had to close the door of her suite and sit on the wide, soft bed for a little while then. Until she found her breath again and got her head to stop spinning.

This is what you wanted, she told herself, trying to breathe in and out without hyperventilating. She ran her palms up and down her thighs, the feel of her same old jeans somehow even more disturbing. As if they could somehow snap her back to Deanville if she wasn't careful. Maggy promised herself she'd burn them at the first opportunity.

This is who you are now, she chanted to herself. *You need to figure out how to deal with it.*

But it took her a long while to pull herself together.

The flight was long and smooth. It was also one of the most pleasant experiences of Maggy's life. Every time she stepped outside her suite, there was a different selection of tempting foods laid out in the living room area. Sometimes Reza was out there on one of the sofas, but other times he was off in one of the other rooms in the jet. There was a guarded office, a conference room, bedrooms. An area featuring armchairs and tables where more guards sat, mixed in with a set of always busy-looking people that Maggy assumed were the king's top aides. Maybe his cabinet. None of them looked up when she walked past, stretching her legs, and yet she was sure she could feel their eyes on her back.

And when they finally landed, it was dark.

"Is this your kingdom?" she asked Reza when he escorted her off the plane. There was a strange, heavy salt scent to the air as they crossed another, smaller tarmac and climbed into one more waiting SUV. All the lights had halos around them and her head seemed to spin. She felt hollow straight through.

"Not quite," he replied, and she told herself it was her odd exhaustion that was making him sound like that. As deep and as dark as the night around them. "This island has been in my family for a very long time. It was a gift from an ancient Venetian doge for services rendered, or so the story goes. It will serve as a decent way station, I think."

Maggy felt muddled and thick from the long flight. She wanted to ask him what he meant by calling this a way station. She wanted to ask him if he'd take her to see the sea for the first time. It took her another beat to realize that the ocean itself was that scent in the air, like a rough magic threaded through the night. But she couldn't seem to make her body respond to any of the half-cooked thoughts whirling around and around in her head. She slumped against yet another soft leather seat back and didn't know where the SUV ended and the strange feelings inside of her began. And meanwhile, the world outside the window was nothing but dark in all directions. No towns, no cities. No lights. As if he'd carried her off the side of the world.

She didn't realize she'd fallen asleep until there were suddenly too many lights and a new sort of commotion woke her.

Maggy pushed herself to sitting position and it took her much too long to recognize that she'd fallen asleep with her head on Reza's wide shoulder. The scent in her nose now wasn't the sea. It was him. Faintly spiced, warm male. A far deeper and more treacherous magic and this one seemed to pool deep inside of her, making her core tighten, then ache. Her breath left her in a rush and her eyes flew to his—

To find him watching her in that way of his, his gray eyes dark. And that all too knowing silvery gleam in his gaze. As if he could tell that just then—one hand at his lean, hard side and the other on his muscled arm, the impression of his shoulder against her cheek—she wasn't thinking of him as a king at all.

Something rolled over her, intense and searing. She was suddenly aware of how terribly, inescapably *hot* she was. So hot she was surprised she wasn't glowing like those lights, with her own bright halo marking her as out of her depth and overheated as she felt.

"We have arrived at the villa," he told her quietly. It occurred to her to wonder how long he'd sat there, letting her sleep on him, before waking her. The idea that it might have been more than the moment or two it took to park wound tight inside of her, lit white-hot and bright. "Can you walk or shall I carry you?"

She couldn't tell if he was kidding. Not that he struck her as much of a kidder. The air between them seemed…taut. Charged. Maggy let go of him entirely and threw herself back across the seats, then told herself she didn't care if he could see her panic. As long as there was space between them. As long as she stopped touching him.

It made that unsmiling mouth of his soften slightly.

"I can walk," she said. Too quickly.

Her voice gave away too much. She could hear it. And more, she could see the way his eyes went dark, the gleam in them very silver and very, very male. It connected hard to something she hadn't known was there inside of her, making her core shiver, then melt.

Over and over again.

"As you wish, Princess," Reza murmured, laughter in his voice that she could see nowhere on his harsh face. "Welcome to the island."

And then he climbed out of the SUV, leaving her to sit there with only her too-loud breath for company. Wondering what might have happened if she'd said something else. If she hadn't let go.

If she'd moved toward him rather than away.

Reza stood out on the wide stone balcony that surrounded the master suite in the villa, paying no attention whatsoever to the frigid winter temperature as he let the crisp sea air wash all over him.

He needed to wash himself clean of this affliction.

Of this abominable *need* that was eating him alive from the inside out.

He didn't understand what was happening to him. Why the slightest, most innocuous touch from Maggy all but wrecked him. How was she managing it? How had she located the chinks in his armor when he'd had no idea it was armor in the first place? He'd thought this was simply who he was—unassailable in all ways—until now.

Was he more his father's son than he had ever imagined? Was it possible?

The cold night beat at him, but he didn't move inside.

This island had always been his family's retreat. Back when Reza was a boy, this was where his parents took him at least once a year so that the royal family could have some time away from the pressures of court and the endless scrutiny of the public. When he was older, he'd realized it was where his parents came to hash out their differences—meaning, his father's betrayals—in a place his father couldn't retreat. The one place his father's mistress wasn't available at a moment's notice, allowing his mother the chance to pretend the other woman didn't exist. Fittingly, this was where they'd taught him that he was never, ever to behave as if he was flesh and blood and a mortal like all the rest. Like them.

This was where he'd learned that there was no room in the king for any hint of the man.

It does not matter what you say, Reza, but what you do, his mother had told him again and again, that harsh look in her gaze not for him, he understood in retrospect, but aimed at him all the same. *Your subjects want to follow a king they can admire and support, not a flawed, weak little man whose clay feet trip him up whenever he tries to stand.*

His mother had been a remote parent and a distant queen. She'd believed her place was behind the king, silent and beautiful and ever supportive, and no matter the whispers about her husband's long-term dalliance or where his obsession with that woman had led him as the leader of a country. As far as Reza knew, she had never indicated in any kind of public setting that she even knew the other woman existed. *The people are interested in the king, never his consort*, she would tell her aides reprovingly when they'd broach the possibility of an interview or an article, perhaps talking about both of her husband's women. And then she'd proved that her devotion outstripped her rival's beyond a shadow of a doubt when she'd followed the king into the hereafter within three years of the death she'd known full well was no random heart attack. She had been a beacon of *correctness* unto the grave, and all the better if she'd been able to use it as a weapon. That was his mother. Ferocious in her pain unto the end.

Reza had not brought Maggy, his feral princess, here by accident.

But even now, even as he stood out in the cold and tried to lecture himself back into the closed-off, hermetically sealed state he had long preferred, Reza couldn't quite manage it. He couldn't stop thinking about Maggy.

The fact he was thinking of her as *Maggy* at all, instead of the more sophisticated, regal, and thus far more appropriate *Magdalena*, was part of the problem.

She'd shuffled out of her house dressed like a Halloween costume version of a young American woman, all attitude and that stubborn chin. But then, her wide caramel eyes had told him she was far more anxious than she appeared. She'd looked more vulnerable in that harsh morning light. Less hardened by the life she'd led than she had the night before.

He hadn't known how to identify the feeling that had worked in him then. He hadn't the slightest idea what it was. It had taken him the entire ride to the airport, reading and rereading the same three sentences on the same damned document, to understand what it was.

Helpless.

He was Reza Argos. He was the king of the Constantines. He was not and never had been and never would be anything like *helpless*. The very idea was laughable.

But then he'd proved that wasn't true at all when he'd touched her again, running his hand over that brash, blond hair that was nonetheless silky and smooth against his palm. He'd stood too close to her out on that tarmac. She'd smelled vaguely of vanilla and coconut, and even that had slammed through him like a caress against the hardest part of him. And that same feeling had washed through him again.

He couldn't help himself. He couldn't stop.

He had no idea what the hell he was doing or when he'd become a slave to his feelings like his father. He only knew he couldn't allow it.

Reza was no untouched, untried boy. Yet here he stood on the other side of the planet, the cold wind from the Adriatic Sea pummeling him, and all he could think about was the way she'd looked at him back on a tarmac in the middle of nowhere in Vermont. What was happening to him?

Why was he *letting* this happen to him, and with the most unlikely creature imaginable? Did he care so little for his own pride—the promises he'd made himself that he would never, ever succumb to weakness like his father?

And that was before she'd fallen asleep on his shoulder.

It was a ten-minute drive from the airfield on the southern tip of the island to the magnificent villa that stood at its highest point, commanding views over the sea in all directions. And Reza had sat there perfectly still, unwilling to dislodge the soft weight of her.

Unwilling or unable. He couldn't decide which. He'd been lost somewhere in the heat of her body against his. The faint press of her against him. The way her head seemed crafted especially to fit right there on his shoulder—

"Sire."

His aide's voice came from behind him, snapping him out of the memory of her body next to his, and Reza didn't turn. He worried at what might be on his face. What he might reveal without realizing it. What might very well be shining off of him like a beacon, betraying every last thing he'd become. Showing that he'd turned into the very thing he hated.

"Is our guest settled?" he asked. He didn't like the effort it took to sound as calm as he usually did.

"Yes, sire. In the queen's suite, as you wished." His aide cleared his throat. "And everything is arranged for the morning, in accordance with your orders."

Reza turned then, nodding his acknowledgment and then following his aide back into the villa. He closed the doors against the winter chill, then stood in the great expanse of the bedroom that he'd once believed was the size of the world. He'd been allowed in here so rarely as a child. It had been his father's private retreat. He'd hidden away in here from the family he'd supposedly come to the island to spend time with in the first place.

As a small boy, Reza had wanted nothing more than to come in here. Now he viewed it as a monument to a past he had best start paying better attention to before he repeated it.

He hardly noticed when his aide left him to his thoughts.

The fact that he'd located the lost Santa Domini princess should have made him happier. He understood this. He'd not only found her, he'd rescued her from a life that was so far beneath her it astounded him. And more, he'd brought her here to this island to teach her not only how to step back into the life she'd been stolen from, but how to operate as his queen.

After all this time, he'd found his queen. The girl he'd been betrothed to when he was all of ten years old. The woman who represented a whole future he'd lost when that car had crashed in Montenegro when he was eighteen.

He'd mourned her—and the loss of the life they'd been meant to build together—for longer than he cared to admit.

But the trouble was, he wanted her. *Want* had never entered into it before, because it was irrelevant. Because he was not his damned father. His kingdom was what mattered. The promises their families had made and the contracts they'd signed were all that had mattered. He'd come of age expecting a queen who would take after his own mother and fade into the background, perfectly pedigreed and unquestionably correct, once she'd done her duty and provided him with an heir.

The trouble with Maggy was that all he could think about was taking her to his bed, and duty had nothing to do with it.

Which meant that for the first time in as long as he could remember, he wasn't doing his.

"What if I'm not a good king?" he'd dared to ask his parents on one of their visits here in a mild autumn. He'd still been so young. He hadn't understood the fierce chill between his mother and father as they'd all walked together. It was all he'd known. They'd strolled down the beach while sweet winds blew in from Venice to the west and off the Gulf of Trieste to the north.

"You will be," his father had told him, with that regal certainty in his deep voice that had straightened Reza's spine. His father had still been so much taller than Reza then, and Reza had been more than a little in awe of him. "Argos men have held the kingdom forever. You will do the same."

He had smiled when he'd looked down at Reza then, an unusual show of the emotion he usually saved for his extramarital relationship, or so the pictures Reza had been forced to destroy after his death suggested.

The queen had not smiled. Her cold eyes had seemed to burn. "You will have no choice."

Reza had never forgotten that.

Because having no choice but to put the kingdom first meant everything else fell into line behind it. Life was simple, in its way, and his father's terrible example had helped make it so. Reza was not burdened with the personal travails that took down so many other men in his position. He had no vices, because they would harm him and thus the kingdom. He had never felt trapped by the security details forever surrounding him and cutting him off from the rest of the world, he'd felt safe. No one touched him. No one had influence over him. He belonged only to his people and the two alpine valleys that had been there in his blood at birth.

And he was at an extreme disadvantage tonight because of it, as he stood in the middle of his bedroom floor, lost in unhelpful images of his future queen. One after the next, as if he had no control at all.

Because the startling truth was that he didn't have the slightest idea what to do with temptation. It had never been a factor.

Reza only knew he had to keep himself from surrendering to this—to her—whatever the cost.

CHAPTER SIX

REZA HADN'T BEEN KIDDING when he'd mentioned a spa, Maggy discovered the next morning.

She'd woken up after a strange night packed tight with odd dreams to find herself in a luxurious, sprawling ancient villa that somehow fused marvelous old Italian touches with surprisingly modern updates, from a perfect bathroom suite to its heated floors. More accurately, she'd been woken up by a cheerful attendant, who'd hurried her out of bed and into a soft robe, pressed an exquisitely made latte into her hands, and then led her through the achingly beautiful villa while she was still sipping at it.

Maggy was far too bleary-eyed to object. She had the hectic impression of graceful rooms filled with dancing morning light, and then she was being led through a warm, glassed-in area where a pretty pool gleamed bright blue in the sun. The attendant led her to the far side of the circular pool, then into an already hot sauna.

"Should you need anything at all, Your Highness, you need only press this button," the attendant told her, collecting Maggy's empty latte mug as she left and closed the heavy door behind her.

Maggy wasn't any more used to hearing herself

called that. *Your Highness.* She had to bite back an involuntary giggle. But then again, what part of any of this was she used to? She knew what a sauna was, but she'd never been in one before. She blinked as she looked around the wooden room. It seemed like an outward manifestation of how she felt already—hot and airless and finding it harder to breathe by the second.

But if this was what royals did, then by God, she would do it. She would do anything. *You* are *royal*, she reminded herself. *Your blood proves it.* She sat on the warm wooden slats as soothing new age music piped in, and wondered if maybe she was still sleeping. If maybe she'd wake up to find herself back in her narrow bed in her tiny room back in Vermont, late for work as usual. She reached down and pinched herself, viciously. On her thigh, then on her belly, but nothing happened. It hurt and it left her with two dull red marks, but that was it. She stayed put in this hot, cedar cell. Sweating wildly.

Even so, she couldn't discount the high possibility that this was a dream anyway. She'd had dreams like this before, in shocking, tactile detail. The difference was, Maggy intended to enjoy every minute no matter what. She was resolved. She tipped her head back, figured out how to breathe long and slow when the air felt nearly solid around her, and she let the deep heat soak into her.

When the lights and heat inside the sauna turned themselves off sometime later, she emerged, sleepy-eyed and wrapped in her robe again, to find that a personal spa had been assembled for her in the great, glassed-in space on the warm stones to the side of the pool. Attendants flocked around her, buffing and waxing whatever parts of her they could reach. She was manicured and pedicured. Her brows were shaped and her hair was set with color and then cut without a single word from her. She was served a steady stream of plates filled with colorful, astonishingly good food every time she made any kind of eye contact with anyone. She was massaged from head to toe and rubbed down with creams and rinses and who even knew what else, until she felt as if she'd been pummeled into the shape of an entirely new woman.

And when it was all done, her attendants wrapped her in a fluffy towel that could have enveloped a family of four and then led her back through the villa.

She'd been too dead on her feet the night before and much too bleary this morning as she'd been hustled down to the sauna area to really look around. But after a day of more pampering than she'd had in her whole life, she found she could hardly keep herself from happily soaking in the place as she followed the smiling women surrounding her.

Reza had called this *the villa*. But to Maggy, it was a palace. Polished marble stretching in all directions. Rooms filled with precious things beyond description. Couches that looked like works of art all their own, set on rugs that likely were. Gleaming pieces of desperately fancy furniture that were nicer than her entire previous life.

Everywhere she looked there were arches and windows, allowing her to see that the sea was *just there*. It was capped with white and surging deep blue and mighty in all directions, visible from every angle. Every room showed her a new view of the water, making it seem as if the villa itself was floating on the waves. Inside, the ceilings were high and set with intricate panels that she was sure probably had some fancy name she'd never learned. There was art on every wall, and Maggy didn't have to know anything about it to know what she was looking at was priceless. One or two paintings she even thought she might recognize, which she was aware meant they had to be so ridiculously famous someone who'd never looked at a single piece of art in a museum or anywhere else would know them at a glance.

She was in such a completely different world it made her head spin.

This is definitely a dream, that cynical voice inside warned her. *I wouldn't get too comfortable if I were you.*

But she wanted to be comfortable here, and no matter if she woke up tomorrow in her tiny room in Vermont. She wanted to be the princess Reza thought she was, with a family and a history at last. So she did nothing but follow her attendants back through the meandering wing that led to the set of rooms she'd been delivered to the night before. She ignored that voice deep inside. If this wasn't going to last, she wanted to enjoy every last bit of it. The smooth stone floors. The beautiful colors of everything she saw, from old-looking tables to tapestries on the ancient walls, to fresh flowers in every vase on almost every surface though it was still winter outside.

She walked through her private sitting room with its fireplace, cozy sofas, and shelves full of heavy-looking books arranged amid small statues. There were windows that doubled as doors leading out toward the sea, and it made her heart feel light that she could see so far. There was a smudge on the horizon that she was pretty sure was Italy. Or possibly Croatia. And that was according to the map on the sleek, very European smartphone an aide had handed her at some point earlier today.

"For your convenience, Your Highness," the man had murmured.

The phone had exactly one number programmed into it under the name *Reza Constantines*. Maggy had stared at it. But she hadn't dialed it.

She followed her little entourage into the vast, sprawling bedroom, set with delicate furniture that struck her as feminine and very thick rugs tossed across the stone floor. She'd crashed across the wide, four-poster bed last night in an utter daze as much from the flight as from her nap *on Reza*, and then she'd stared up at the magenta canopy until she'd drifted off approximately four seconds later. But now the bed was made up again as if for a magazine shoot and there were clothes laid out across its foot.

"His Majesty wishes you to meet him in his private salon," one of the attendants told her. "At your earliest convenience."

"I assume that means at *his* earliest convenience," Maggy murmured. She'd meant to sound dry, but she was far too relaxed. It came out much softer than it should have.

The women around her laughed, and that was its own head trip. Maggy was prickly, everybody said so. She couldn't remember the last time a group of people had laughed around her, unless it was *at* her.

"He is the king," one of the women said quietly. "We all serve at his pleasure."

And Maggy felt as if she ought to object to that,

on principle if nothing else, but somehow she couldn't quite bring herself to do it. *Later*, she told herself. *You can worry about* the king's pleasure *later—or maybe you'll just wake up.*

The women surrounded her again, and after a day of it she let them without another thought. She sat on the vanity stool and realized after a few moments that they were deliberately keeping her from looking in the mirror. She didn't fight it. This was her dream and she was going to eke every drop of this princess routine out of it before she was drop-kicked back to the real world.

Because there was always the chance that wanting this to be real would make it so.

One woman carefully made up her face while another blew out her hair. It took them some time. When they were done, they handed her a pile of soft, impossibly silky things it took her long, confused moments to realize were a bra and panties. Just of a far higher quality than the ones she'd bought herself in cotton value packs.

Even her feet looked like someone else's, she thought as she stepped into the deliriously silky panties behind the towel two attendants held up for her once she shed her robe. Tipped in a rich red now, buffed and sanded smooth and soft, they weren't *her* feet. *Her* feet were usually hard across the heels and aching. The panties fit perfectly, as did the matching bra, and she told herself she wasn't thinking about who could possibly have estimated her measurements so well.

She kept telling herself that even as that same, familiar heat that was all about Reza and his hard, stern mouth rolled over her, then pooled deep in her belly again.

But there was no time for blushing. Her attendants hurried her into the dress that waited for her at the foot of her bed, a dove-gray thing that didn't look very interesting when they held it up, but felt like a whisper once they pulled it over her head. The shoes they slipped on her feet were the same, so high she expected them to pinch and hurt, but instead she felt as if she was wearing bedroom slippers once she stood in them.

It explained a great deal about the things she'd seen famous people wear in magazines. Who could possibly have imagined all those crazy, acrobatic clothes were *comfortable*? No wonder Reza had been so dismissive about her clothes. It all made a lot more sense now.

She felt them fasten something around her neck, cool and slippery against her skin. Someone slid a ring onto her index finger, and then they were bustling her back out of the room. She could see that the sun was setting outside the windows, sinking in an orange blaze toward the sea, but she was dazzled by the lights inside the villa, too. They were everywhere, buttery and bright, making the hallway seem as if it was merry of its own accord.

Or maybe that was just her.

Her attendants hurried her down the hall, and it took her longer than it should have to make the obvious connection that her suite was only the next door down from Reza's—it was just that the rooms in the villa were very large and the hallway connecting them quite long. And in fact, the door in the far wall of her bedchamber that hadn't opened when she'd tried it last night must lead directly into his rooms—a notion that made every nerve ending in her body shiver to instant awareness.

But there was no time to process any of it, because

she was being led directly into the king's dazzling suite. His private salon was the size of a hotel ballroom, she thought wildly, looking all around her. The light here was as bright and glorious as the rest of the villa. It bounced off of all the inlaid gold in the different seating areas arranged in little clusters around the big room— here an elegant couch, there an impossibly graceful quartet of chairs. Even the walls themselves were lined with gold, interspersed with a deep crimson. It looked exactly the way Maggy would have imagined a king's room should look, had she ever had cause to think about such things.

And in the center of all that regal brightness stood Reza, in yet another perfectly crafted dark suit that made him look like a storm of a man, his gray eyes fixed to her as if this was the first time he'd ever seen her.

As if, she thought wildly, he'd been waiting his whole life to see her.

Maggy felt that gaze of his like a shudder, a wicked, rolling thing down deep inside of her. A new, dangerous heat bloomed there, then spread, washing over her limbs and making her pulse go liquid.

She was vaguely aware that the attendants left them. She didn't dare move—or she couldn't. And Reza only stood there for what seemed to her to be a long, long time, that stern gaze on her in a way that made her feel as if all the dizzy light in the room was trapped inside of her. A part of her.

She was certain he could see it. That he knew.

"I don't know what they did," she heard herself tell him. She had no idea what she was saying. How could she tell when she didn't sound anything like herself? "They wouldn't let me look."

He said nothing. He merely held out his hand.

Maggy didn't know why she didn't so much as hesitate.

The dream, she told herself, though her dreams had never been *quite* this vivid. *This is all part of the dream*.

The fairy-tale dream she hadn't allowed herself to truly indulge in for years.

She moved across the floor and took the hand he offered her, and only then—when a different blaze of sheer fire poured into her and made her heart kick at her—did she think to question why she'd thrown herself into it like that. Into him. Only then, when it was too late.

But Reza only led her over to a huge mirror left propped up against the wall in the farthest corner of the great room, looking as if it had stood exactly like that for centuries. It likely had. It, too, was edged in a heavy gold frame, as solid and certain as the king himself.

He positioned her in front of the glass and stood behind her. Much too close to her. One hand holding hers and the other a faint pressure at her waist. More of that delirious fire raced through her at the contact, making her legs feel weak. Maggy knew she should push herself away from him. Get his hands off of her, for a start. She knew she should do *something*.

But she couldn't seem to do anything but stare.

"Look at you," Reza murmured, his voice a rough velvet much too close to her ear and the birthmark he'd known was there from the start. "They did exactly as I asked. They made you who you are. Magdalena Santa Domini."

The woman in the huge, gold mirror was…not

Maggy. Or if she was, it was a version of herself that Maggy could hardly get her head around. A dream version she never would have dared imagine on her own. Never.

She knew it was her and yet…it couldn't possibly be her.

A princess, a small voice inside her whispered, with something like awe. *You look like a princess.*

They'd dyed her hair back to her natural color, a dark and lustrous chestnut, and they'd swept it back from her face. Still, the light picked up deep golds and russets that seemed to make her eyes glow. And her eyebrows looked elegant, in place of her usual unremarkable brows. Her whole face was smooth and she thought she looked different, and not only because of the subtle makeup they'd put on her. It took her a moment to realize she looked rested. Or not exhausted, anyway.

She'd never seen her own face so bright before.

The dress looked like something out of one of those glossy magazines she'd always pretended to loathe. The gray color was soft and interesting at once, making Maggy's pale skin seem to glow. It was a modest dress, she supposed, but it didn't seem that way. There was something about *how* it fell from a sophisticated neckline all the way to her knees, with only a slight indentation just beneath her breasts, that suggested a kind of restrained and high-class sex appeal without actually showing anything. The shoes did much the same thing, somehow managing to look elegant in a way Maggy didn't know shoes could. There was a gleaming diamond necklace around her neck and a chunky ring on her index finger featuring a collection of precious gems in a variety of colors, all of which caught the light and sparkled.

But more than all that, *she* looked like someone else. Completely different from the Maggy she'd seen in her own mirror yesterday morning before she'd headed out to meet Reza's convoy. If she hadn't known the reflection she was looking at was hers, she'd have easily and happily believed that it was some long-lost princess. And she hardly dared think it, but she really did look like that picture of the queen he'd shown her.

The queen. *Her mother.*

But she didn't want to think about that yet. Not yet. She took a breath and realized in the next instant that Reza was still holding her fingers in his as he stood behind her, his other hand at her waist. And suddenly she could think of nothing else. Except the tempting notion that if she leaned back the tiniest bit she could nestle herself directly against the wall of his chest.

She would never, ever know how she managed to keep herself from doing it.

"This is how you look after one day," Reza told her, his voice near her ear making her shiver. He was the one who stepped away then, something she couldn't read making his eyes silver. She fought to repress yet another shiver as she watched him in the mirror. "We will stay here several weeks. By the end of this time, I expect you will be able to acquit yourself quite well in the glare of whatever spotlight you might encounter."

"Yes," she said, because she had to say something. And she couldn't let herself say any of those things that clawed at her from that raw place, deep inside. She didn't want to think them. She wanted this. She wanted every last part of this. "I'm sure I will."

But even after he turned and headed across the room, Maggy stayed where she was before that great, tipped glass, staring at herself. Because she wasn't herself anymore.

She was the fairy-tale princess he'd made her into, just as he'd said he would, in the course of a single day.

And Maggy had absolutely no desire to ever wake up.

It was worse now she looked the part.

And much, much worse that he'd let himself hold her like that.

Reza told himself this mad obsession was beneath him. That he was in no position to lose himself in a woman like his father had done before him, particularly not this one. If she was to be his queen—and she was, of course, as their fathers had planned so many years ago—then the formalities needed to be observed above all else. The only thing he could think of that was worse than losing his head over an inappropriate mistress was doing the same thing over the woman who would have to bear his children. Where would it end? What destruction would he wreak? He couldn't imagine it. Or allow it.

He spent his days tending to matters of the crown from his office in the villa, surrounding himself with his advisers and running his country from afar. And if he insisted on an investigation into that long-ago accident and the following of twenty-year-old leads to figure out how a Santa Dominian child in a car accident in Montenegro had made it across the Atlantic Ocean to the United States, so be it. The Princess Magdalena was to be his queen. What had happened to her would be public record and, more than that, incorporated into the lore of the monarchy itself.

He filled her days with the very serious business of turning an abandoned American foster child into one of Europe's most celebrated royals.

He had her fitted for an entire new wardrobe that suited her position. He had Milanese courtiers fly in with one of a kind pieces for her to try on and choose between as she pleased, with the help and advice of his personal tailors. He flew in special jewelers from Paris to outfit her appropriately, so she might have a few pieces to wear until she regained her access to the Santa Dominian crown jewels, to say nothing of the Constantinian collection she would be expected to wear after their wedding.

And while all the outward trappings that would cement her as his betrothed in all the right ways were being attended to by the most fashionable people in the world, he brought in diction coaches to soften and shape her language. He couldn't teach her the Italian and German every Constantinian spoke fluently in so short a time, but he could work a bit on her English. Less rural American and more European, so it would sound better to the average Constantinian ear.

He brought in a former prima ballerina to teach his queen how to walk, how to stand, how to shake hands, and how to curtsy with varying degrees of deference. He made her sit with a selection of his aides and learn the rudiments of the kind of diplomacy she'd be expected to know inside and out at all formal functions. He had yet another aide talk her through the tangled history of Santa Domini and the Constantines, so she would be less likely to trip into any old, festering wounds that still lingered there, as such things tended to do between all ancient European nations. He had her consult with his own public affairs officers, to teach her how to handle cameras and reporters and the unsavory realities of public life in a tabloid world. He even brought in his formidable former nanny, now pushing eighty, to teach Maggy the same excruciatingly correct set of manners she'd taught him back in the day, at the table and everywhere else a royal might venture.

"A banquet is a performance," he heard Madame Rosso pronounce in her usual ringing tones from the formal dining room one afternoon, just as she had when he'd been a boy. "Your appetite has nothing to do with it. Indeed, you must worry about sating yourself on your own time. A banquet is an event at which you are royalty first and a hungry person never. Do you understand?"

"I understand," Maggy said. Sweetly enough that Reza paused outside the room, whatever errand he'd been on forgotten.

She was so understanding when asked anything these days. She always agreed, nodded, curtsied. She modulated her tone and softened her accent. It was as if she'd been possessed by an alien, Reza thought darkly—and the fact he should have been rejoicing over how easily she was taking to what she'd called *Princess School* in a rare flash of her old self one evening made him that much more annoyed with himself.

The truth, and he was all too aware of it, was that he was something far more dangerous than simply *annoyed with himself.*

Reza couldn't quite believe that he found himself missing the sharp-tongued bottle blonde who had looked at him with such blatant disrespect in Vermont. He told himself that of course he didn't. Not really. It was just that Maggy was immersing herself in her studies of all things royal and, in so doing, becoming the princess she'd always been meant to be. The real Maggy would come out the other side, he was sure of it.

Why on earth would you want her to come out the other side *of decent behavior?* he asked himself then, deeply irritated with his own frailties where this woman was concerned.

But he had no answer for that. The more appropriate she became, the harder he found it to resist her. It was as if the veneer of the princess he'd always wanted stretched over that fearless creature he'd met in Vermont made this woman into his own, personal, walking and talking downfall. No matter how steadfastly he refused to go there.

Meanwhile, he suspected he was a little too insistent about the dinners they shared every night. He told himself that these formal meals were a way to assess her progress. That they were necessary, and perhaps that was true. But he knew full well that wasn't why he found himself anticipating the dinner hour all day.

He was betraying himself and everything he stood for and he couldn't seem to stop.

One night he found her in the grand hall an hour or so before the bell was due to ring to announce dinner. She was counting out loud as she practiced waltzing by herself, her lovely face screwed up into a frown as she stared at her feet and held her arms in a rigid box in the air before her.

It was one thing to want her. That was bad enough.

But this…*melting* sensation in the region of his chest was something far worse than simply unacceptable. It was a different sort of danger entirely, he knew it. And it got worse the more she transformed before him. Tonight it very nearly ached.

Reza ordered himself to move on. To retire to his rooms and dress for dinner the way he knew he should, and maintain the level of formality between them that was the only thing keeping his sanity in check, he sometimes thought.

Instead, he walked into the ballroom.

Maggy was too busy counting to see him approach. "One, two, three, four. One two three four. *Onetwothree*—"

She stopped the moment she saw him. She seemed to freeze into place where she stood, those caramel eyes of hers wide on him, her arms still in the air as if she danced with a ghost.

And he was many things, most of them deeply unsavory at present and entirely too much his father's son, but he was no liar. He knew exactly what that heat was in her gaze. He felt the same thing storm through him, tying him into a thousand intricate knots that felt like fire.

"What are you doing?" she asked. He could tell from that strange tone in her voice that he must look particularly intense.

He should have cared about that. It should have set off every alarm inside of him, that he should betray himself at all, much less so obviously. But if it did, he couldn't bring himself to care.

If this was how his downfall started, he couldn't seem to mind. Not tonight. Not when she had transformed herself into every last thing he'd always, always wanted.

"Allow me to assist you," he said, his voice dark and low.

Reza didn't wait for her to respond. He had crossed the room by then, so he simply took her in his arms, ignoring the heat that blazed between them.

Well. It was more like he marinated in that heat. Soaked in it. Dared it to try to drown him.

He wrapped his fingers around hers. He liked, too much, her grip on his opposite shoulder. He held her at the correct distance and thought he deserved a medal or ten for refraining from pulling her up hard against his body the way he wanted to do.

And then he started to dance, sweeping her along with him. The fact that there was no music did not signify. There was her breath. There was his heartbeat, hard and deep and needy. Nothing else mattered.

Reza let himself admire her as they moved. His princess. His queen. Tonight her hair was piled on the top of her head, that dark, rich color he preferred, and she was wearing a shift dress that made her look very young and very chic at once. She was still slender, though she'd lost that hungry look over the past weeks. There was nothing at all to distract from her beauty now. Not one single thing.

And he liked having her in his arms almost too much to bear.

"It's hard to reconcile the woman I met in that coffee shop with you now," he said, because he couldn't seem to help himself. He couldn't keep from poking at the very thing he shouldn't touch. "You are so alarmingly agreeable."

"I'm the exact same person," Maggy replied, but he thought her response was too quick. Too pat. And he didn't like that she kept her gaze trained on his chin, as if she was deliberately keeping her eyes from him. Hiding, right there in his arms. "It's just that instead of trying to remember to pay my rent on time, I now have to remember which fork to use."

There was no reason so smooth and rehearsed a response should have bothered him. Reza told himself it didn't. This was what he'd wanted, after all. Indeed, this was what she deserved. She was a royal princess. She *should* appear this way, without any cracks and wholly unobjectionable. His odd nostalgia for the creature she'd become to survive what had happened to her demeaned them both, surely.

He was disgusted with himself. Still, he spun her around the room again and again because he couldn't bring himself to let go. He couldn't make himself do it.

You are a king, said a voice from deep inside of him, sounding very much like his mother's crisp, faintly starchy tones, in those dark days following what they'd all known was his father's suicide to avoid the mess he'd made of his life, his country. *Do you rule or are you ruled?*

He stopped then, abruptly. Maggy's momentum kept her going and she almost fell against him. He almost let her, to serve his own hunger—but at the last moment he righted her.

"I will instruct your dance instructor to pay more attention to your footwork," he heard himself say, his voice like a winter chill. "You cannot trip over foreign dignitaries without causing international incidents."

Her chin rose and she tugged at her hand to get him to release it. He only held it tighter.

"Given that I didn't know how to dance at all until a week or so ago, I think I'm doing fine." Her voice was even, but he was sure he heard a hint of that old fire beneath it.

How sad that he thrilled to it. But he did.

"It is not what you think that matters, Princess." His voice was too low, too telling. But all he could seem to do was stare at the tender place in the hollow of her neck, watching the way her pulse jumped. Reza told himself it could mean anything. That he shouldn't take it as a matching fire, no matter that he could see the echo of it in her gaze. "It is what I think."

He let her go this time when she tugged at her hand again. Maggy stepped back, her chin tilted at that mutinous angle he'd missed far more than he should have, and then, her challenging gaze on his, she executed a crisp and perfect curtsy.

It was perhaps the most eloquent *up yours* gesture he'd ever seen. Certainly directed at him.

"Bravo," he said. He wanted to laugh. But that wasn't the thing that wound tight inside of him, pulling him taut and making him ache. "But I must warn you not to attempt a repeat in front of any other monarch you might encounter. Particularly with all of your attitude on display. You might find yourself beheaded for the insult, and no matter that such things were outlawed centuries ago."

"If that was an insult, I must have learned how to do it wrong," she said, but her caramel eyes gleamed with that same hot challenge when they met his. "My deepest apologies if I offended you, Your Majesty."

And that was the last straw. His title in her mouth, crisp and pointed, as if it was another insult, even as it licked over him like something else entirely.

Reza didn't mean to move. He didn't know he did, but somehow the distance between them was gone, and worse, he had his hands wrapped around the smooth, entrancing place where her upper arms became her shoulders.

He was touching her skin, and not merely her hand. *At last.*

"Reza…" she whispered.

He ignored her. Because he was too close to her, he was *touching* her, and that changed everything.

All these games he'd been playing these last weeks fell away.

There was only this. There was only her.

He thought she said his name again, but it was as if it came from somewhere far away. Lost in the storm that washed through him. His thumbs dragged over her soft skin, back and forth as if he couldn't help himself. He watched, fascinated, as a fresh set of goose bumps rose and then swept across her throat, giving her away. Telling him everything he needed to know.

"You cannot taunt me with your brand-new manners and then take it back with my name, Princess," he told her, bending his head toward hers. "You cannot imagine that will work."

Her hands were flat against his chest, but she didn't push against him. Her fingers seemed to curl in, as if she was trying to find purchase against his jacket. As if she wanted to hold on to him.

And her full, lush mouth was *right there* within reach.

Reza stopped pretending he had any control left. He stopped pretending he could resist her when that resistance had grown more and more scant with every passing day.

He stopped pretending, full stop.

He damned himself fully, and then he took her mouth with his.

CHAPTER SEVEN

His mouth was as hard as it looked. Uncompromising and stern as it moved on hers, taking her and tasting her, encouraging her to do the same.

And when she did, when she met him, his taste filled her. Hot and ruthless and entirely Reza.

It was glorious. It was better than glorious.

This is no dream, something inside her whispered. *This is the fairy-tale kiss to end all fairy-tale kisses, and it's real.*

But for once, Maggy didn't care either way. She just wanted more.

She gave herself over to his demanding mouth. His kiss was heat and light, pouring into her and through her, kicking up fires wherever it touched. Her heart cartwheeled in her chest. Her head spun around and around. Her breasts seemed to swell with all the hunger that stormed through her, her nipples pulled to tight points, and between her legs she was nothing but a soft, molten ache.

His hands gripped her upper arms, firm and sure, and lifted her closer to him. And there wasn't a single thought in Maggy's entire being except *yes. More.* More of Reza. More of that stern, hard mouth. More of this wild, stirring electric hunger that tore through her, making her greedy and half-mad. Making her entirely his, as if this right here was where she truly belonged.

She wanted more.

Maggy surged up on her toes and she dug her fingers into the stone wall of his chest, and that was when he angled his mouth for a deeper, better fit.

And the world exploded.

All the heat and fire of these past weeks, all the sensation and need and longing, burst through her. He claimed her mouth, again and again, merciless and almost too hot to bear, and she couldn't seem to get close enough.

Maggy wanted more. She wanted everything.

He made a low noise she didn't recognize, but still it rolled through her and made her even warmer, as if there was some deep, feminine part of her that understood him in ways the rest of her couldn't.

She had always kept a part of her separate, no matter what, but here, now, in his arms, she melted. He kissed her again and again, and she met him with everything she was and everything inside of her and all the wildfire and yearning she'd been pretending wasn't there and Maggy knew, somehow, that there was no going back from this.

A princess was one thing. She could play that part, apparently. She even liked it.

But he kissed her as if she was the woman she'd always wanted to become.

As if she was truly his.

Very much as if he heard that dangerous thought inside her head—as if she'd shouted it out into the empty ballroom—Reza wrenched his mouth from hers. So fast and so unexpected that for a head-spinning moment, Maggy thought maybe she really had said it out loud.

Which would have been a disaster. She knew that. Having feelings for Reza could only complicate everything. Even this. Maybe especially this.

Would any of this have happened if you didn't *have feelings for him already?* an arch voice inside her asked. She ignored it.

His breath sawed out between them as if he'd been running, or maybe that was hers—she couldn't tell. But he didn't let go. His hands were strong and elegant at once, and he kept them wrapped tight around her upper arms.

Maggy knew she should have felt trapped. But she didn't. She felt safer than she could remember ever feeling before, and it didn't matter that the look on his face was anything but sweet.

"This cannot happen," he gritted out.

He was still holding her to him. His face, so harsh and fierce and stern and beautiful, was close to hers. And Maggy was plastered up against him, her breasts pressed to his chest, so hard she could feel her own nipples like twin points of fire where they brushed against him.

She should have been upset, surely. She should certainly have disliked his tone. She should have been… something. But instead she couldn't think of a single place she'd rather be than right here in his arms, no matter how or why or what intense reaction he was having to it.

"I thought you intended to marry me," she whispered, from that same, strange place she hadn't known was there, feminine and wise. She'd never flirted in her life. Why put something out there if she didn't care enough to mean it? But here, now, she tilted her head back and arched into him, smiling when his breath caught. "How will you manage that if we don't do this?"

He set her back from him then, and that felt like a much greater loss than it should have, surely. It felt as if he'd kicked her. For a moment she swayed as if she might topple over, so badly did every part of her want to be close to him again. Closer. The distance between them felt like a slap.

But yeah, that voice inside her poked at her. *Good thing you don't have any* feelings *for him.*

His gray gaze was so dark it looked nearly black. "Our marriage will be based on civility and respect," he grated at her, and he didn't sound like the Reza she knew at all. There was no distance there. No regal *certainty*. Something inside her prickled to awareness. "Not this…relentless hunger."

Maggy tilted her head to one side, then folded her arms over her chest, and who cared if her deportment instructor had forbidden her to do that. Repeatedly.

"I hate to break this to you, Reza," she said quietly. She realized as she spoke that she had no idea where her sense of calm came from. As if her body knew, way down deep inside, that she was safer here than she'd ever been anywhere else. Here, with him. No matter what was making him look at her that way. "But heirs are not made out of civility and respect. That sounds more like a handshake, which, unless it's different for kings, won't quite get the job done."

"This is who I am." His voice was even more ragged, his gray eyes were more storm than rain, and Maggy stared. That was temper on his face, she was sure of it.

Dark and furious. And with something else beneath that she understood instinctively, though she couldn't name it. She felt it inside her, like a new heat. "There is absolutely no place in my life for this kind of distraction."

"By *this kind of distraction*, do you mean a wife? Or a queen?" She studied him. "Or are you talking about a kiss?"

And then she watched him change, right there before her. She watched him beat back the storm and close himself off, one breath to the next. It was as if he rolled himself up tight into an armored ball. She watched his expression clear, then go cold. His gaze lightened, his mouth firmed. He stood straighter, somehow, and that intense, ruthless power that seemed to blaze straight out from inside him filled the whole of the ballroom.

This was the king of the Constantines in all his glory. But Maggy had kissed the man. She wanted him back. She wanted the storm.

She wanted to dance in it.

"You have taken to your role admirably," he told her, back to that stern, stuffy tone that she knew she should hate. She knew it. But instead it pulled taut inside of her, fire and need. "I anticipate we will be ready to introduce you to the world sooner rather than later."

"Do kings not kiss?" she asked mildly, in a provoking sort of tone her former employers and battalions of counselors would have used to prove her attitude was eternally bad. "I didn't realize that was a breach of royal protocol."

He looked at her with that arrogant astonishment she remembered from the coffee shop. But something had changed—inside her. She could see that same expression. She remembered how she'd felt about it the first time—or how she'd told herself she felt. But now it was like a lit flame, burning her from the inside out.

"I beg your pardon?"

It might have been phrased as a question, even if he used that scaldingly remote and royally outraged tone. It wasn't one.

Maggy shrugged. Deliberately. "You seem so…" She waved a hand at him, not quite as dismissive as his, but certainly a contender. "Upset. I thought maybe there was some royal proclamation forbidding the kingly lips from touching another's."

That muscle in his jaw clenched tight. "There is not."

"Then it's me that's the issue." She eyed him. "Is that what you're trying to tell me? That you have a problem with trailer trash after all? Even after all these weeks of playing Henry Higgins, just for me?"

Reza seemed to expand, hard and harsh, to fill the room, though he didn't move. Maggy could *feel* him everywhere. Pressing against her. Temper and divine right like a fog that stole inside and clogged the whole of the chamber.

"I will see you at dinner at the appointed time," he told her, his voice so cold she was surprised icicles didn't form. "We will discuss the history of the Constantines and the Santa Dominian line of succession."

She managed, somehow, to keep her expression blank. "That sounds thrilling."

His jaw looked tight enough to shatter. "We will never mention this unfortunate episode again, so allow me to make this clear now. You are not *trailer trash*. You are the daughter of a revered and ancient bloodline. And for the record, I do not have problems with anyone or anything. I solve problems or am otherwise above the fray, as is appropriate for a man in my position."

"Is that why you're so grumpy after a little kiss?" Maggy smiled at him when he glared at her, and she'd gotten a whole lot better at smiling since she'd come here. She was almost good at it now. "Because you're so above it?"

She thought he meant to say something. That perfect mouth of his moved and his dark gray eyes flashed, but he didn't speak. He merely inclined his head in that coolly dismissive way of his. Then he turned on his heel with military precision and marched from the room.

Maggy stood where he left her. She made herself breathe, deep and long, to get the shakiness out. Her mouth felt slightly swollen, sweetly battered from his, and she indulged herself, there in the middle of a fairy-tale ballroom on a faraway island, by pressing her fingers against her own lips. As if she could conjure up his kiss again that easily.

The truth was, everything had changed tonight. She thought he knew it, too, or why else would he have reacted that way? All this time, she'd told herself that she was happy to go along with this because it got her out of her hard, cold, empty grind and allowed her to live the sort of storybook life she'd tried so hard to stop letting herself dream because it was too painful every time she woke up. Because doing this meant she belonged somewhere, and she could never be rejected from a place she claimed with her blood. She'd told herself that was all that mattered.

But she'd been lying to herself. It had been as much about Reza as it had been about her remarkably stubborn princess dreams and the reality of that blood test. Maybe more.

She'd agreed to marry *him*, not a fairy tale. She'd left everything she knew because he'd come and found her. *Him*. Not some random person. Not one of the tabloid reporters who dogged the steps of every royal in Europe. Not the brother she was still coming to terms with having in the first place.

And she'd thrown herself headfirst into this crash course in becoming something other than trailer trash, which Maggy knew she'd been all her life no matter what he said to the contrary. No one in the foster care system had cared too much about her *ancient bloodline*. She hadn't done all this because she was particularly fired up about being a queen. Or even because the clothes were exquisite and she'd discovered things about herself she'd never have known before and would never have found out—like the fact emeralds didn't suit her, she preferred Louboutins to Jimmy Choos, and had an abiding appreciation for a very particular bath salt her attendants told her was handmade in one specific boutique in Bali. That was all its own delight, to be sure.

But deep down, if she was brutally honest with herself, she'd been trying her hardest to make herself into the kind of woman Reza wanted.

Maybe it wasn't even that deep down.

Every night she sat at the table in the formal dining room and turned herself inside out trying to make that ruthless mouth of his soften, just a little bit. Every night she trotted out pertinent facts and used the right utensils to show she was learning her numerous lessons. She sat with elegant posture and made the sort of easy and yet sophisticated conversation she'd been told—repeatedly—set a woman who would be queen apart from the masses. Educated and yet wry, compelling and yet not overly opinionated.

"The formal dinner table is no place for strong opinions," Madame Rosso told her again and again.

"Because heaven forbid it put a man off his food," Maggy had muttered once, glaring mulishly at the empty plate before her, several hours into a crash course on formal manners.

The king's former nanny had fixed her with a frank stare, all the way down the impressive length of her nose, the force of it making the white hair piled on top of her head seem to wobble.

"This is about diplomacy," she'd said in her crisp, clear-eyed way. "You are a royal princess. You will not be dining with people rounded up off the streets who might be in any doubt about the issues of the day. It is likely, in fact, that you will be seated with those who decide those issues. And when policy is served in the middle of a meal, it can only cause indigestion. A meal is the time one behaves as if the world is already perfect, war and strife do not exist, and everyone near you is a close, personal friend."

"Because no one needs to hear the opinion of a princess." Maggy had wrinkled up her nose. "I get it."

"Because the point of a princess is that you are a symbol," Madame Rosso had returned, her tone faintly chiding. "You are an amiable and benevolent reminder of what is for many a bygone time. It is called being gracious, Your Highness. In public, it is your greatest weapon. In private, of course, one expects you will have no trouble whatsoever making your opinions known however you choose and to whomever you wish."

And Maggy discovered that, in fact, she *wanted* to be gracious. She wanted to be a symbol of something positive as opposed to the poster child for neglect. She wanted to make this new role of hers her own in every possible way.

But most of all, she wanted to be Reza's.

Maggy could finally admit it, with her mouth still tingling from his mercilessly beautiful kiss. She wanted to be *his*.

She'd assumed that inhabiting the role of perfect princess was the way to do it, because that was what he'd said he needed from her, or wanted for her. The perfect princess, then the perfect queen. And all that entailed—heirs and grace and whatever else. But that was before he'd kissed her. That was before she'd seen that storm in him and wanted nothing more than to bathe in it.

That was before he'd claimed her mouth with his and brought her alive. Wickedly, deliciously, beautifully *alive*. More alive than she'd ever been before in all her life.

Which meant, she realized as she stood there in that ballroom filled with need and longing and *Reza* long after he'd left it, she needed to come up with a different plan.

Two nights later, after a series of such excruciatingly stiff meals she was surprised she hadn't turned to stone in the middle of them, Maggy decided it was time she tested the waters. He'd called what happened between them *a relentless hunger*. She wanted to see just how hungry he really was.

Because it turned out she was ravenous.

After another long, stiff dinner packed with a bar-

rage of dry facts and the king's dark glower from across
the exquisitely set table, they moved into one of the
many salons that littered the villa. Reza chose a different one every night, but what happened in each was
always the same. They would sit and talk about things
even more innocuous than what had passed for dinner
table conversation.

"This is ridiculous," she'd said on one of the first
nights they'd done this, scowling at him. "I'm not going
to tell you what I did in the summers while I was growing up. Why would you want to know?"

"This is called a conversation," he'd replied, his expression like granite, though she'd been sure she'd seen
a hint of that silvery gleam in his gaze. Or maybe she'd
just wanted it there, more than was probably healthy.
"It is much like dancing. It is all about the appearance
of being light and airy, the better to put the person you
are speaking with at his ease."

"If the person I'm speaking with isn't at his ease
after nine hundred courses and too much dessert, I don't
think me sitting here making up pleasant lies about my
summertime activities is going to help."

"You are not required to lie."

"Oh, okay." She'd glared at him, but she'd remembered to fold her hands in her lap so at least she looked
like a lady while she did it. "I'd be happy to tell you
about the summer I worked in the convenience store
because I wanted to save up enough money to buy myself new shoes for school in the fall. My foster mother
stole it from under my bed and spent it all on booze. Or
wait, maybe the time the only job I could get was as a
waitress in a sleazy motel restaurant, but the manager
fired me because I wouldn't have sex with him. Or I

know, the summer I got a great job in a cute boutique on Main Street, but they let me go because I didn't have a car and it took me so long to walk there every morning that I was always a sweaty mess when I arrived. That just wasn't the trendy boutique look they were going for, you see."

"You've made your point." His voice had been silken reproval, all the way through. She'd ignored it.

"What did you do in your summers?" she'd asked him. "Polish the crown jewels? Behead a few peasants for a little giggle? Use your scepter as a machete as the mood took you?"

"My summers were devoted to charity work," he'd said, surprising her more than she wanted to admit. "A different charity every summer from the time I was ten. Usually in a different country and for a different cause, and all of them quite hands-on. Many sick children, I'm afraid, though I also spent some time digging ditches. I was not raised to be the vicious and selfish monarch you seem to imagine." His brows rose. "Beheadings and machetes and the crown jewels do not figure strongly under my rule, you might be surprised to learn."

"I thought that was the point of being king," she'd said, but the edge had gone from the conversation. She'd seen that silver gleam in his gaze, the one that made her feel warm all over.

"The point of the kind of light, easy conversation we have after dinner is twofold," he'd told her after a moment. She'd become fixated on his hands then. The way he held one of them in the air as he lounged in his chair, looking as if he sat on a high throne instead of in an armchair. "First, it is happy. Sparkling. It allows you to guide the room in whichever direction you choose.

And second, it is more intimate. Guests will have eaten, perhaps have had too much to drink. It is highly likely this is where deeper topics will be discussed—but that won't happen if we all sit about in silence."

She'd looked at him. "I'm a diversion, then?"

He hadn't quite smiled. "My mother once held a room filled with men on the brink of war spellbound as she waxed rhapsodic about the balls she'd attended as a young woman. It was silly talk, but she made them laugh. It allowed my father to have a much needed casual aside with a man known at that time as the Butcher of the Balkans, and after that, the drums of war beat a little more quietly." He'd swirled something amber in his glass for a moment before fixing her with that fathomless gray stare. "Never underestimate the importance of that diversion, Princess."

Tonight, they settled into Maggy's favorite salon after their meal, which she decided was a good omen. It was an old study that felt more like a cozy library than a chilly sitting room. There was an ancient globe on a stand that had all the wrong names on countries with borders that had shifted a long time since. Hardbound books with gold-edged pages lined the walls. The fire was bright and warm tonight, holding the stormy winter weather outside at bay.

Maggy liked the rain against all the windows. It made her think of that hunger Reza had talked about. It made her feel it everywhere, roaring inside of her. Making her feel far braver than perhaps she should.

Reza was talking about something so light and so far removed from what she was thinking that she didn't pretend to follow it. He'd given her a glass of something as sweet as it was alcoholic, but she'd only tasted it once before putting it aside. She was after something else entirely tonight.

It took her a long moment to realize that Reza had stopped speaking. That the room had gone silent. That there was no sound at all save the fire crackling and spitting against the grate, and outside, the winter storm rattling the windows. That Reza's gaze was on hers, all that dark gray unreadable. If not outright forbidding.

Trouble was, it didn't intimidate her. She liked him granite and imposing. She thought the truth was, she liked *him*. Full stop.

"I apologize." He was quite obviously not sorry. That was clear from his tone, not to mention that frigid, regal expression on his face. "Am I boring you?"

Maggy stood then, trying to remember how to be graceful the way she'd been taught. She ran her hands down the front of her gown, a sweet fall of dark blue silk that brushed the floor despite the high shoes she wore. And any nerves she might have had now that she was really doing this—and she was really, truly doing this, no matter what—were swept away by the way Reza tracked the movement. As if he couldn't quite help himself. As if he wanted it to be *his* hands on her like that.

That was what she wanted to find out. If he did. If he wanted her as much as she wanted him.

If that kiss had been a mistake—or if it was the new beginning between them that it had felt like to her.

"I want to thank you," she told him.

He was lounging in yet another armchair, the way he always did. How he managed to give the impression of slumping without actually doing so was a marvel, she thought. A bit of royal magic. He'd opened the jacket of yet another perfect suit—and Maggy knew enough now to understand that the word for the kind of hand-tooled clothing he preferred was *bespoke*. That he had many such suits, all made to his precise specifications and all, like this one, a love song to his hard, solid, sculpted body.

She wanted to know the words to that song. Then she wanted to sing it.

Reza said nothing, and that was almost more alarming than all the cutting things he could have said. He only watched her as she moved toward him, though she could feel the weight of it, as if his gray gaze really was the hard, pounding rain that washed over the windows behind him. He remained silent when she came to stand before him, just inside the V of his outthrust legs.

"You've given me everything," she told him.

And even though she'd planned this to be light and airy, the way everyone kept teaching her these royal games of intrigue over waltzes and dinners and after dinner drinks were meant to be, it didn't sound that way when she said it. It occurred to her, once the words were out, that it was no less than the raw and simple truth.

Oh, well, she thought. *No use pretending now.*

She made herself continue. "I want to give you something in return."

"You will give me your hand in marriage soon enough." His voice was too low and a bit too rough, but he was watching her with a certain alertness that made her blood seem to quicken inside her veins. It encouraged her even as it moved in her like a deep, sweet caress. And most importantly, he didn't order her to step away from him. Or to take her seat again. "That is more than sufficient."

"I can't possibly give you any kind of gift you don't already have," she told him. Her heart was pounding inside her chest. Her eyes felt glassy. "So I thought instead I would give you something I've never given anyone else. Ever."

Something in his gray gaze changed then, like a new storm washing out the old. That hard mouth of his moved. "Princess. That isn't necessary."

But she had no intention of heeding that warning she heard in his voice. She wanted this too much. She wanted *him* too much. And she'd spent a lifetime refusing to allow herself to want things she couldn't have.

She didn't want to do it any longer. It felt like defeat, and that was a part of her old life. This was her new start. *He* was her new life.

Maggy wanted to taste every bit of it, starting with him.

She gathered up all her courage and every last bit of that greedy, ravenous hunger that stormed through her now and, if she was being as honest with herself as possible, had since he'd walked through the coffee shop door and she'd thought he was *extraordinary*. She still did. That made it easy to sink down on her knees before him, until she was kneeling up between his legs.

"Maggy."

She liked her name on his lips, and no matter the tone he used—just this side of a command. She liked the arrested, *aware* look on his harsh face and, even more, the way it shivered all through her, as if that silver gleam was inside her, too.

She shifted forward so she could put her hands on his thighs, then run them up toward his lap, her goal obvious.

Maggy thought of the coffee shop again, and how she'd thought he'd seemed like a man who was used to having people on their knees before him. Had she wanted to do this even then? Her mouth watered at the thought.

Reza didn't move. If anything, he got *more* still, as if he really did turn to stone beneath her hands. But it was a hot, masculine sort of stone. It made her belly seem to twist into a complicated knot, then sink down between her legs. Maggy tipped her head back so she could keep her eyes on his. Too much gray and too much silver besides, and when that muscle clenched in his jaw, she felt it in her core, molten and greedy.

She slid her hands up farther, reveling in the feel of his strong, corded thighs beneath her palms. All his power. All that heat. She sensed more than saw the way his hands gripped the arms of his chair.

"Maggy."

The way he said her name was supposed to stop her. She understood that. But he didn't actually order her to stop.

So she didn't.

She paused for the faintest moment at the top of his thighs, where she could see his hard length against his fly—growing larger and more fascinating the longer she sat there and looked at it. She slid her hands up farther still, only grazing the front of his fly in passing as she reached for his belt.

He jolted as if he would reach to stop her—but he didn't.

The sound of his buckle seemed louder than it should. Ruder and more delicious with only the snap of the fire behind it. Maggy felt herself flush, but she couldn't stop now. She was too close. Her breath kept tangling in her throat and between her legs, she felt a matching rush of sensation.

Molten heat, soft and wild, and all for him.

She pulled his trousers open, her heart punching at her hard. So hard it made her stomach flip over and over. Her hands trembled slightly. She didn't know which was worse, the longing that made her knees feel soft and weak beneath her or the panic that he might stop her at any moment when she was this close. When she was finally so close.

She reached into the opening she'd made and pulled out the hardest part of him, wrapping her fingers around the thick, hard length. She swallowed, hard, and looked up at him as she indulged herself, moving her hand all the way down to his root, his silken smoothness against her palm making her whole body shake with need.

His face was set, that muscle in his jaw something like ferocious. He was so fierce, so harsh, he should have scared her—but he didn't. He never had. She understood that glitter in his gaze now, the way she had the other night when he'd kissed her. She felt it racing through her, making her feel clumsy and needy and maddened with this same hunger.

And she knew that whatever else happened, however stony he became, he wanted her exactly as much as she wanted him.

The knowledge felt like safety. Like freedom. Like both at once, wrapped up together and indistinguishable from one another.

Maggy wrapped her free hand around him, too. Then she tipped herself forward, kept her gaze on his as she opened her mouth, and sucked him in deep.

CHAPTER EIGHT

REZA DIDN'T KNOW how he didn't embarrass himself on the spot.

Maggy's hot, clever mouth closed over him, the world exploded into bright red need and a mad rush of pure lust, and he was nearly lost.

Nearly.

She took him deeper. She wrapped her fingers around the base of him and she tested his length against her tongue. She pulled back and lavished attention on the broad head before sucking him back in again.

She'd said she'd never done this before, and he was amazed at how...primitive that made him. How possessive.

He thought her inexpert attempt to please him with her sheer enthusiasm and that hot, wet mouth of hers might actually kill him.

But if this was how he was going to die, Reza thought it might be worth it. He kept his hands fisted hard on the arms of his chair. He let her play with him, her dark hair swirling around her bare shoulders and moving over his thighs like heat. He watched in dark fascination and that same red-hot greed as she took him deeper. Then deeper still.

He felt her everywhere.

And he had never wanted anyone or anything more.

He knew that should have alarmed him, that razor's edge of desire that was a bit too close to desperation. He knew what indulging in this, in her, made him. He knew he should push her off, reclaim his control, insist on all the cold, clear boundaries that had to stand between them or everything else would shatter—

But he couldn't do it.

He didn't *want* to do it.

Reza wanted her. *Her.* He wanted his princess, his queen, the woman who had been promised to him at her birth. The girl he'd lost before she'd had a chance to grow up into his woman. The future that had been wrenched away from him when he'd only just become a man. He wanted the queen he'd mourned throughout his twenties.

He wanted the real, live, insanely beautiful woman who knelt before him and *thanked him* with every blazingly slick slide of her smart, hot mouth along the hardest, neediest part of him. Again and again and again.

And he had already damned himself when he'd kissed her in that ballroom. Why not enjoy the flames?

All the lies Reza had told himself since he'd seen that photograph with his own lost princess bride in the background, all the walls he'd built since then and tried to keep solid, all the thousands of ways he'd pretended he could maintain his boundaries against this woman who had been born to be his, the power she wielded over him because she was his lost Magdalena and because she was his Maggy besides—it all simply crumbled around him.

And Reza found he didn't much care, because in the

wreckage there was still her, his princess, knelt there between his legs with her mouth against him, driving him straight toward that cliff.

"No," he bit out, aware of the harshness of his voice only once he heard himself, the echo of his furious, ungovernable hunger rough in the quiet of the room.

Maggy froze, pulling her mouth free of him while her hands were still wrapped tight around him. But even that was too much. Reza muttered out something in Italian, a curse or a prayer and he didn't know which, reaching down to pull her off of him before he lost his last little shred of control. He eased her up from between his legs even as he moved out of the chair, sliding down to the floor to kneel there with her.

Then he took her face—her exquisite, impossible face, intelligent and lovely and *his*—between his hands.

"Reza," she whispered, her hands moving to curl around his wrists. "I want—"

"*I* want," he corrected her gruffly. "And believe me, Princess, I intend to have what I want. Everything I want."

And then he took her mouth with his, and let that bright red desire for her wash over him. He couldn't taste her deeply enough. He couldn't hold her close enough. He angled his jaw, tangling his tongue with hers. He indulged that sharp greed inside of him, letting one hand move to fist in her thick hair while the other learned that delicious arch of her back, then settled on the sweet curve of her bottom.

It wasn't enough. Reza feasted on her mouth the way he'd wanted to forever, and even more since that kiss in the ballroom. She shivered as she kissed him back, rubbing her breasts against his chest as if she was as desperate as he was. As needy. As impatient.

And everything had changed tonight.

The brakes were off. The walls were down.

There were so many reasons he shouldn't do this—but chief among them was the fact that with Maggy in his arms, her mouth beneath his again, and her lush, lean body pressed against him, he couldn't think of a single one of them.

To hell with the king of the Constantines. Tonight he was nobody but Reza.

With Maggy that felt like a revelation instead of a disaster.

He lost himself in her taste. The scent of her skin, vanilla and coconut, as if she was a touch of the tropics in the middle of the winter storm outside. The sheer, dizzying perfection of her mouth against his and the way her taste inflamed him and wrecked him, over and over again.

Reza lost himself in sensation. In her. In the perfection that was his lost princess, finally found. Finally exactly where she'd been meant to be all along.

He let his hands move over her again, restlessly testing her curves and making her moan into his mouth. He trailed a line of fire and need down the length of her elegant neck, learning every inch of her and where a lick or a graze of his teeth made her shudder. He bent to taste the plump, smooth thrust of her breasts above the bodice of her dress and in the mad fire of that he took her down with him to the soft, thick rug.

And then she was beneath him, her caramel eyes shining and her mouth faintly damp from his. *Finally.* Reza remembered her down on her knees in that coffee shop, staring at him as if he was an unwelcome intrusion. He remembered her soft and asleep on his shoulder in the back of the SUV, so vulnerable and so trusting at once. He could still feel her mouth all over the length of him, while the taste of her rocketed through him and made him something like thirsty.

She was his. Here, now she was entirely his. *At last.*

Her gaze was wide. Dark with the same need that moved in him. Her hair was a dark cloud around her, gleaming in the firelight, and it took everything he had to hold himself there for a moment, up on his elbows above her. As if he needed to etch this moment into his memory forever. Maggy reached up and pushed his jacket off his shoulders and he let her do it, tossing it aside as soon as possible. And then he hissed out a breath when she went further, reaching up beneath the tail of his shirt to get her hands on his skin.

It was like fire. It was better than fire. Her hands were a torment and a blessing as one traced its way up his spine and the other moved lower to test his backside against her palm.

He needed to be closer to her. He needed…everything.

"I need to be inside you," he gritted out, and he was too far gone to care that he sounded wrecked. Like a stranger to himself. Like a man with no brakes, no control, nothing.

Like a man, not a king.

It should have stopped him dead. But Maggy was clinging to him, her mouth to his.

"I need that, too," she whispered. "I need you, Reza."

And everything shifted then. It got hotter. Wilder. Deeper red and far more intense.

Reza reached between them and pulled her filmy,

silken dress up and out of his way with rather more intent than finesse. He didn't care that he'd lost all his ease and grace and caution, not when her smooth, sculpted legs were bared to his gaze. He ran his hand up, growling his appreciation of her taut thigh and continuing until he reached the tiny little scrap of silk and lace between her legs.

He held himself above her, his gaze hard and greedy on hers, as he stroked his way beneath that little scrap and found her scalding heat at last.

She shivered beneath him as he tested her with one finger. Two. So hot and soft. He thought she might kill him and he couldn't think, just then, of a better way to go than wrapped up tight in all her molten heat.

"Maggy—" he began, but he didn't know what he meant to say. Maybe he'd simply needed her name on his lips.

"Please." Her voice was stark. Greedy. Her gaze was dark and glassy at once, and she was writhing beneath him, every part of her a sweet, scalding invitation. "Please, Reza."

"Use your hands," he ordered her, low and sure. "Guide me in, Princess. Take me deep."

He felt the way she jolted against him at his words. He saw the fire dance over her face, making her gaze a gleaming thing, over-bright and needy.

Then her hands were on him again, a torment and a glory. She wrapped her fingers around his aching length, raising her hips to him as she did as he'd commanded and guided him toward her entrance, using one hand to rake her panties to one side. Reza bent to take her mouth as she lifted herself up, impaling herself on him. He slid one hand around to hold her bottom where he wanted her, and then he thrust into her. Deeper and then deeper still, too hungry, too greedy, to wait the extra seconds it would take to undress either one of them any further.

And when he was buried to the hilt, they both froze, their eyes locked to each other. His whole length snug inside of her, deep and hard.

The whole world narrowed down to this. Here. The two of them.

His princess. His queen. At last.

"Please…" she whispered. Again. And he thought he'd never heard a prettier sound than his tough little princess begging him.

Reza began to move.

It was throwing himself into an inferno, again and again and again. It was a wild taking. A deep, greedy possession.

It was perfect. *She* was perfect.

She wrapped herself around him and Reza couldn't get close enough. Deep enough. He couldn't taste her enough. Her wicked mouth. Her sweetly elegant neck. Her gorgeous, ripe little breasts.

He wondered if anything would ever be enough when it came to this woman. Even this.

Right here, right now, he didn't care.

And then suddenly, it was too much. He felt his control go liquid, and it took everything he had to haul himself back from that edge even as he maintained his hard, deep pace.

He reached between them and found the very center of her need. He rubbed her there, keeping his strokes deep and hard.

"Come for me," he growled against her neck.

And she obeyed him. She clenched against him and she shuddered all around him, then cried out his name as she fell.

And Reza followed her straight over the side of the world.

Outside the villa, the winter storm raged on through the night.

But Maggy was far more interested in the one she was caught up in with Reza, inside, where it was dry but not quite safe. Not when there were so many things to discover about him. And so many things he could do to her.

She wanted to do every single one of them.

When she came back into herself, there on the floor of the study, she felt wrecked—but in a beautiful, glorious way. As if her skin could hardly hold all the things she felt inside.

Reza lifted himself above her, his face dark. Unreadable.

And for a moment it was hard to tell where the rain outside ended and he began.

Then he lifted his hand and brought it to her face, stroking down her jaw. As if she was precious to him. As if he cared—

Maggy knew that was foolish. That she was only going to hurt herself, thinking such things about a man like him, so ruthless and mighty above all else.

She thought he would say something then. She thought he would go out of his way to remind her that he was a king and she was beneath him the way everyone else he encountered was beneath him. That he held all the power here, one way or another.

But he didn't say a word.

After a long moment lost in his endless gray gaze, Reza pulled out of her and rolled away. She hardly had time to process the loss of his silken and steel length within her, his hard body against her, his heat all around her, because he was standing then. He rose from the floor to his feet in an unconscious show of all that forbidding grace that made him who he was. He hauled up his trousers and fastened them, then looked down at her where she still lay there, spread out on the thick rug on the floor of the salon.

Boneless.

Something moved over his face, too quick for her to read, and then he held out his hand.

It reminded her of the coffee shop, and Maggy didn't know how she felt about that. Only that it seemed to trigger something raw and unwieldy inside of her, swamping her where she lay. She sat up, trying to fight it off, tugging her dress back down to cover her legs.

And Reza merely waited there, his hand extended, as if he could do so all night.

The only reason you're hesitating to take his hand is that you're too eager and you don't want him to know it, she told herself caustically.

She decided that was stupid. She'd already proved her eagerness with her mouth. What was the point of pretending otherwise now? She'd already given herself away entirely. There was no going back.

Maggy held out her hand and let him lift her to her feet. Then he hauled her against him. He kept tugging until she was off balance, and then he simply bent at the knees and swept her up into his arms.

"Reza," she began, high against his chest with that

unsmiling mouth of his *right there* and his harshly com-pelling face *so close*—

He didn't so much as glance at her as he started to move.

"Hush," he murmured as he shouldered his way out of the study and started down the long hall toward their rooms. "Not tonight."

Maggy took that as gospel.

He carried her through the dimly lit villa, and Maggy did nothing but wrap one arm around his neck and let him take her where he liked. She had only passing impressions of rooms with lights on and flickering candles in the sconces along the ancient walls. She saw the door to her own room as they passed it, and let a breath out then, resting her head against his strong shoulder.

Inside his suite, Reza moved quickly through the private salon where he'd stood with her before that tilted mirror. He carried her down another hall that was more like a paneled foyer, past what looked like an office and another, even more private study. She lifted her head from his shoulder when he entered yet another room, then kicked the door closed behind him.

There was a vast stone fireplace on one wall, taking over the whole of that side of the room with a fire dancing cheerfully in its grate. It was the only light in the bedchamber. She saw a few chairs and a sofa arranged before it, but then he was lifting her up and placing her on a vast, supremely kingly bed. Four stout, carved columns rose in each corner, but there was no canopy here to relieve the male stamp of it. Only acres of mattress and soft linens in dark, brooding colors.

And Maggy didn't care about any of that. She cared about the man who stood at the side of the wide, high bed, his glittering gaze fixed on her while the firelight played all over him and made him look more like a myth than a man.

He didn't speak.

And that look on his face was so intent, so fierce, that Maggy followed suit.

Reza undressed her carefully. His hard hands smoothed over her ankles and unbuckled the delicate straps of her shoes, then tugged them off. He found the fastening to her gown at its side and pulled the zipper down, then lifted her to sweep the dress away. His gaze glittered hot when he looked at her then, in nothing but the tiny panties she'd held to one side before, but he didn't haul her to him. He only hooked his fingers in the lacy sides of the panties and slid them down, then off.

When she was naked, he looked at her for a long, long while. He raked his fingers through her hair, almost as if he was arranging it to suit himself. Then he let his hands wander, testing her collarbone with one finger. Then finding her nipples with his thumbs while he lifted her breasts into his hard palms.

He leaned in then, putting his lips over one nipple and sucking until it hardened against his tongue. By the time he made his lazy way to her other nipple, she was shivering again, that same fire lit again inside of her and burning bright.

Reza stepped back then, and Maggy pushed herself up to her knees so she could watch him as he rid himself of his clothes with a certain ferocity that made that knot low in her belly pulse. Then glow.

When he was naked, Maggy heard herself let out a reverent sort of sigh that she could no more keep inside than she could have stopped herself from getting on her knees earlier.

He was beautiful. He was made of hard planes and delectable ridges, all lean muscle and corded, male power.

Reza crawled onto the bed with her, one arm around her middle to shift her into the center of the mattress.

"Reza…" she tried again, because the wild, raw hollow inside of her was growing, pushing everything else aside, caught in the storm of sensation. His thighs were a rough delight against hers. She could feel him again, hard and insistent, against the soft skin of her belly. And he was settled on his elbows above her, his fingers deep in her hair.

"Quiet, Princess," he murmured. "This is a time for action, not words."

And then he took her mouth with his, showing her exactly what he meant.

He tasted her everywhere. He spread fire and need everywhere he went. He explored her body, inch by inch, tasting her and touching her, then flipping her over so he could do the same to her other side. His mouth moved down the length of her spine, torturously slow, and she felt his hard mouth curve against her skin when he made her shudder.

By the time he turned her over again she was making no attempt to hide her moans, her pleading. His face was dark as he came over her, his eyes nearly black with passion.

And when he slid into her, she burst apart, sensation shattering her into a thousand pieces.

"Beautiful," he murmured as she shook and shook, her fingers pressed deep into his back. "You are so beautiful, my Magdalena."

Then he began to move.

Slow. Lazy.

Unbearably hot.

He rode her, sweet and easy, through her shattering, then kept on going, tossing her from one peak straight into a brand-new fire.

He played with her mouth, her breasts. He acted as if he had all the time in the world. And when she started to lift her hips to meet him again, when that tension wound around and around inside of her and made her cling to him and arch into his thrusts, he let himself go.

Reza gathered her close and pounded into her, every drag of his hips throwing her closer and closer and closer still, until she broke again, flying apart into scraps of fire and need and something far greater than either.

And she held him tight as he followed her, shouting out her name.

It took a long, long time for him to stir, and when he did, his gaze came to hers in the flickering light. Maggy had to bite her lip to keep back the things that threatened to spill over then. The truths she hadn't wanted to face but could hardly avoid now, naked with him like this.

She didn't know what he saw on her face. But he still didn't speak. He rolled them over again, and this time, he carried her to his bathroom. He set her down in a huge, glassed-in enclosure, and then he washed her, his expression serious.

When they were both squeaky clean, he took her back to that great big bed and climbed into it with her, arranging her so she was draped over his body, and Maggy thought it was the perfect time to say the things that sat there so heavy on her tongue.

But the rain still drummed against the windows and the silence seemed sweet.

Instead, she fell asleep, curled up on Reza's chest with the fire dancing all over them both.

They came together in the night, too many times to count. She would roll, or he would shift, and it was as if the barest slide of skin against skin was too much. The first time they slid against each other he spread her out beneath him and kissed his way down her belly before settling between her legs and licking her into sobbing bliss. Another time she woke with his heat all along her back and his thigh thrust between hers. She couldn't help herself. She'd arched against all that hard, muscled heat until he'd shifted her, thrusting into her as he held her in place.

She lost track of how many times they woke and found each other in the dark. She couldn't count the number of times she fell apart, only for him to catch her there when they both fell back to earth.

The last time they woke together it was gray outside, with a hint of light across the sea. The rain had finally stopped. Reza lifted her over him and settled her on his lap, thrusting into her once again as he sat up, gathering her astride him.

It was her turn to set the pace and she took it slow, every last part of her body so tuned to him now it was as if they were one.

One body. One mind.

One heart, she thought, though she knew she shouldn't.

And the higher she climbed, the brighter that flame between them, the more she knew. What that raw thing was that took up more and more of her every time they touched. What was eating her alive from the inside out.

"One more time," Reza urged her as the sweet tension pulled tight, as she worked herself against him, hard and deep within her with his mouth against her neck. "Just one more."

And this time they broke apart together, soft and shattering.

She slumped in his lap, her forehead pressed to his, and tried to catch her breath while inside her everything was too raw. Too big, too unwieldy, *too much.*

Maggy might not have felt any of these things before. But it was like the salt in the air outside that had meant the sea was near. She knew what it was.

"Are you with me?" Reza asked, his voice low and gruff and, somehow, the sweetest thing she'd ever heard, as his hands moved gently up and down her spine as if he was bringing her back to earth with the slide of his hands over her skin.

Maggy couldn't move. She couldn't open her eyes. And she couldn't care less.

"I'm with you," she said, her mouth close to his, her head tipped into his. As close to him as it was possible to get. "I love you."

It took her another breath, long and still shuddery, to realize what she'd said.

And still one more to feel that Reza had turned to stone beneath her.

She pushed back so she could look at his face, and her heart broke. She felt it crack apart and splinter, there and then. Because he looked like a statue. Remote and inaccessible and more forbidding than she'd ever seen him before.

"Reza," she whispered. "Forget I said that. Let's just pretend—"

"No." He sounded something far darker than merely *rough* then. Much darker and much, much worse. He lifted her off of him, setting her to the side as if she was terribly fragile and required care, but then he moved out of reach. Fast. When his gaze met hers, Maggy saw nothing but blank, hard slate. "No. You cannot. That is impossible. And unacceptable besides."

CHAPTER NINE

"YOU DO NOT love me," Reza thundered at her, as if that could erase what she'd said. As if that could rewind this night. Shove it back in the bottle where he should have left it to begin with. "That is unacceptable on every level."

But there was an aching thing in his chest and he felt as if it might crack wide-open. And his body was as wrecked as if he'd gone out on a bender like a normal man might. Not that Reza needed drugs or alcohol when there was Maggy. She was infinitely more potent.

And he should never have let this happen. He knew exactly where it led. He'd been cleaning up the mess of it his whole adult life.

Maggy was still sitting in the middle of the vast bed where they'd hardly slept all night. Even now, he still wanted her. He stalked to his dressing room and threw on a pair of exercise trousers, letting them ride low on his hips. When he returned to the bedroom, she was standing by the side of the bed, buttoning herself into his shirt.

He didn't want to see how small and slender she was in his shirt. How long her legs were, naked and tempting, beneath the hem. When she was done buttoning it up, she lifted her chin and faced him, and he hated that she clearly needed to brace herself. Worse, she hugged herself around the middle as she studied him, too many things he didn't want to recognize clouding her pretty eyes and making him feel like the lowest bastard who had ever drawn breath.

Reza knew he was exactly that. But even so, he couldn't seem to ignore the part of him that urged him to go to her. To take her in his arms again. To make this right somehow, and no matter that she'd made a bad situation worse with the words she should never have said—but he couldn't do that.

"I didn't mean to say that," Maggy said, her voice quiet, though it seemed to punch into him all the same. "But that doesn't mean it isn't true."

"It cannot be true." He folded his arms over his chest and forced himself to stop admiring the way she looked in his damn shirt, as if he had as little control over himself as he'd exhibited this whole, long night. "This should never have happened." He jerked his chin at the bed between them. "Any of this."

He could see the instant she stopped feeling vulnerable—or decided to stop showing it, anyway. The exact moment that temper of hers kicked in. First there was that flash in her eyes. Then she frowned at him the way she hadn't done in some time, too busy smiling and folding her hands in her lap and learning how to exude good breeding with every breath.

"I have no idea what you're talking about." Her voice was even. Cool. "This is where all of this has been leading, surely. You didn't storm into my coffee shop in Vermont so we could end up polite and distant pen pals."

"I need a queen, not a lover," he threw her, and he

did nothing to make the hit of that any less harsh than it sounded. Standing there at the foot of the bed where he'd shown her exactly the opposite all night long. He couldn't even tell who he was more furious with—her or himself. "I have no time to dally, and certainly not with you."

For a moment, he thought he might have broken her, and a sea of self-loathing washed over him, nearly taking him from his feet.

But this was his Maggy. His tough survivor. She'd made it through twenty years of dire circumstances. She'd sailed through the past weeks. What was an unpleasant conversation at dawn? He'd seen her mouth tremble, he was sure of it, but she only pressed her lips into a firm line and kept her chin high.

Reza had the dark, uneasy notion that he was the only one at risk of falling apart here. Something that seemed far more imminent when she moved toward him, skirting the bed and coming closer than she should.

Close enough that he could smell her again. Vanilla and coconut and, beneath that, her. His Maggy. He knew her now. Her scent, her taste. He'd had his mouth and his hands on every last inch of her body. His body stirred anew, which should have been impossible after the night they'd had. But nothing was impossible when it came to Maggy. Nothing at all.

He was in so much trouble. He was far past *trouble* and into a full-blown crisis.

"You're going to have to explain to me why the fact we had sex is a problem," she said, still in that quiet way of hers, suggesting she was under control. But he could see that sheen in her eyes, telling him otherwise.

It made him feel worse. And more resolute at the same time. "Or why you freak out every time something happens between us. Shouldn't you want this?" She didn't wait for him to answer. "Why can't you have a queen *and* a lover?"

"This cannot happen," he bit out, his voice frigid, because the cold eating him from the inside out was the only thing he had. It was the only way he knew how to keep himself in one piece. "I am a king. I cannot allow anything to divert my attention from my responsibilities."

She shook her head, looking helpless for the first time in as long as he'd known her. "What are you talking about?"

"I have already told you." But it was harder now, wasn't it? He concentrated on keeping his hands to himself. And that scant bit of distance everything in him wanted to close. "I am a king. My focus must be on my people, not on the pleasures of the flesh. A king who loses his focus loses his way. Believe me."

"You're going to marry me." Her voice was fierce now, not cool at all, and there was a recalcitrant part of him that enjoyed that faint evidence that she was as shaken as he was. Reza didn't like to think what that made him. "You told me you want heirs. How did you think that would happen?"

"Not like this." He stepped back, putting distance between them the way he should have done from the start and keeping his damned hands to himself, no matter that he thought it might kill him. "I am a—"

"Stop saying that!"

He didn't know which one of them was more shocked when she shouted at him. She looked as surprised as he felt, though she couldn't have been. Reza wasn't certain anyone had ever raised a voice in his direction.

Why did it make him want to do nothing but gather her close to him again? What *was* this? Why was he still standing here, engaging in this conversation?

But he still couldn't move. He still couldn't leave her.

He was tearing himself apart.

"Stop it," she said again, her voice hoarse. "You're a king, yes. I know that. But you're also a man."

"That is the trouble," he grated out, unable to stop himself. Unable to keep himself in check the way he should. As if the tearing thing in him was a wrecking ball and he was splintering whether he liked it or not. "I must be more than a man. I must be above petty concerns. I am a creature of duty and honor, that is all. But you make me feel like a man and nothing more, Maggy, and I cannot have it."

Her face softened and that was worse. Much worse. "Reza—"

"Silence." His voice rang out, autocratic and regal. She stopped, making a faint sound, like a sob cut off before it could take root. But he was the king now. Not the man she could enchant and make into nothing more than her plaything. He had to be the goddamned king. "I should have delivered you to your brother the moment I found you. I should never have brought you here. I cannot allow *this* in my life."

"This?"

"You." He slashed a hand through the air. "I sit on a throne and hold the fate of a country in my hands. That must be my focus. That must be my *only* focus. My father split his focus and it cost him. He was blackmailed. Disgraced, if only privately. He nearly brought the country to its knees because he had a mistress he put before the crown. And his only excuse was *love*."

His voice was scathing, but she didn't back down. It was one more reason he couldn't have her. He couldn't risk it. "I don't know anything about your father, but you and I have been betrothed since I was born. You could have married someone else, but you didn't. Surely that means something."

"You died." His voice was so harsh. So cold. And he told himself he didn't care when she flinched. "And I moved on."

But Maggy had a spine of steel. She shook her head at him. "Clearly. That's what last night was about, I'm sure."

Reza ground his teeth together, and if his hands balled into fists and betrayed him, well. There was no way out of this. There was no fixing all the things he'd broken last night because he'd lost his hold on himself. There was only this, damage control and moving on.

He would not be his father, a disappointment to his wife, his son. A scandal on the throne, however hushed. A man who'd taken his own life and had left behind a son who had to clean up his mess. Reza had been twenty-four when he'd had to relocate his father's long-time mistress to one of the crown's far-off properties to keep her away from his mother and the royal court who'd despised her—and to keep her from blackmailing his father even after his death. He'd been paying for his father's mistakes—literally—ever since.

"I must marry and I must hold the throne," he told Maggy now, somehow keeping his voice in check. Somehow finding his control again. "These are the duties of every king of the Constantines across the ages.

You make me imagine that I am something more than the throne. You make me feel as if I am a man instead."

"You *are* a man." Her voice caught. "You are the best man I know."

"I am a king," he gritted out, and if his chest felt crushed, too bad. He didn't want to be the best man she knew. He didn't *want* this. He couldn't want anything like it, because he knew where it led. To a small cottage on the Isle of Skye, where a wretched old woman lived with the memories of a man who had never been hers, a man she'd tortured into taking his life, and the kingdom she'd been willing to ransom to serve her own ends. To his father's early grave, the circumstances of his death hushed up and hidden, and a cloud forever over his name and legacy. "Do you know what happens when a king believes he is a man? When he acts like he is no different from the rest? He becomes it. He thinks with his sex, his temper. He allows himself to be flattered, to be small. To think in tiny terms that benefit him, not his country."

He saw her swallow, hard. "Those are all bad things," she said quietly. "But there are other ways to be a man. It's not all sex and temper and war and pain."

"I have spent my entire life keeping myself apart from the masses for the good of my kingdom," he told her, fierce and rough. "I will not throw away what I have built on a woman. I refuse."

"Reza." His name in her mouth was a revelation, still. And he hated himself for it. "Don't you think there's another reason you feel so out of control? Maybe you feel the same things I do. Maybe this is your chance to be a king *and* a man, not one or the other. Maybe you lo—"

"Never." His voice was too harsh then. It was beyond

cold. It was nothing less than a slap—anything to keep her from saying that word. That impossible word. Love had no business here, with him. Love had nothing to do with the life he led, the kingdom he ruled. It had not one damned thing to do with that cracked feeling that was making his chest ache. "That will never happen. I will never allow it. *Never.*"

"Reza—"

But he couldn't allow her to stand there, naked beneath his shirt, all his temptations made flesh. It would be too easy to weaken, as he'd already proved. He had to end this. Now.

"I am summoning your brother," he told her, pulling the practicalities around him like a cloak. He moved around her, heading for the door, keeping his hands to himself no matter how little he wished to do so. "He will no doubt wish to carry you back to Santa Domini like the lost treasure you are. I hope that when I see you again at some or other event, we can be cordial."

"Cordial? Are you out of your mind? Reza, we—"

He looked over his shoulder. "There is no 'we.' I release you from our contract."

She looked lost, but she still stood tall. And made him feel tiny in comparison.

"What if I don't release you?"

He shrugged as if he didn't care about this. About her. "Then you will feel very foolish, I imagine, when I marry someone else. Which I will, Maggy. And soon."

And then he walked out of that bedroom before he changed his mind the way he longed to do. Before he decided she was right and he could be both a king and the kind of man he'd imagined he was last night, sunk deep inside her. Before he went to her and kissed her

mouth and took her back to his bed, the way every part
of him shouted he should do, right now.

Before he let her make him forget who he was all
over again.

Cairo Santa Domini was due to arrive on the island only
a handful of hours later.

Maggy realized that Reza must have summoned him
immediately after leaving her in his bedchamber. It suggested that the man must have leapt up from whatever
kingly thing he'd been doing and raced to fly here, all
to meet a sister he'd believed dead for twenty years.

"His Majesty expects the Santa Dominian plane to
land in two hours," one of her smiling attendants told
her when she'd made it back to her own room, still
dressed in Reza's shirt. The idea of wearing the dress
he'd taken off of her with such sweet skill made her
want to die. She'd decided it was far better to give the
staff a little show, in case they'd missed Reza carrying
her through the halls last night—

But it was better not to think about last night.

"Thank you," she replied. Because what else could
she say?

Maggy didn't know what to expect from a brother.
Especially not when he was a famous man in his own
right. Another king, no less. And she certainly didn't
know how to feel. About anything, after a night that had
scraped her raw and a morning that had left her feeling
nothing but beaten up and bloodied.

She made her way to the state-of-the-art shower in
her expansive bathroom suite and locked herself in. She
made the water so hot the steam billowed up in clouds
and first she scrubbed herself, over and over, trying to

get him off of her. His scent, his touch. The memory of his mouth against her skin. Then she sank down, her back against the wall so she could tuck her knees up beneath her chin, and she cried.

For so long she thought she'd wrung herself dry, and yet she still didn't feel any better.

When she was dressed, in a shift dress over soft leather boots and a lovely cashmere wrap she would have called *princess casual* if anyone had asked, she stood for too long at her own mirror. Remembering when he'd stood behind her.

You need to stop, that caustic voice inside her, the one that had kept her safe all this time, snapped at her. *You're only making this worse.*

She went out into the villa while her attendants saw to her packing. Maggy expected Reza to ignore her. To stay out of her way. Surely that was the least he could do.

Maggy was picking at a meal she thought she should eat, though she wasn't the least bit hungry, when Reza strode into the breakfast room.

She gaped at him. She didn't pretend otherwise. She didn't try to hide it.

And she hated herself for the little sliver of hope that wormed its way into her heart—

But this was Reza. He said nothing. He didn't take back any of the things he'd said in his bedchamber. His gray gaze raked over her as if he was looking for evidence she was still her—but then he looked away again as he helped himself to some of the food the staff had set out on a side table.

He was hungry, apparently. He was the king—and that was all he wanted to be, the goddamned king—and he couldn't have someone fix him a tray. Of course not. Of course he had to come here and torment her.

"Are you trying to torture me?" she asked him, through gritted teeth.

There was no sign of the man she knew on his set face when he turned to her. No hint of silver in his faintly astonished gaze. It was as if the Reza she knew had been replaced by a stranger.

"I cannot imagine what you mean."

Maggy pushed to her feet. "If you want to do this, I can't stop you. Believe me, I spent my whole life with my face pressed up to some or other glass, wishing I could have whatever was on the other side. I'm not doing it with you."

That muscle clenched in his jaw, which she might have seen as a sign of hope twenty-four hours ago. But that was before that scene in his bedroom. That was before he'd thrown her out, like once again, she was nothing but garbage.

She'd thought becoming a princess would change that, but it didn't. Maybe it was something in her that made her so easy to dispose of. So easy to toss aside.

"No one asked you to," he said, and she told herself she was imagining the bite in his voice. As if this was hard for him when she knew it couldn't be. Because if it was, why was he doing it?

"I'm not going to stand here and let you talk to me like a robot." She threw her linen napkin on the table and pretended it was something harder and she was aiming for his face. "You might be one. You clearly *want* to be one. And you can hide all you want. But I won't take part in it."

And yet, after all her tough talk, she just stood there.

She didn't *actually* beg him to reconsider. She didn't let him see her cry. But she might as well have.

He sat back in his chair, his mouth an unsmiling line that she wanted to taste. That was the trouble. She wanted him no matter what. No matter how little he wanted her.

"My investigators cannot be sure," he told her in his chilliest, most distant regal voice. "But they believe they've traced what happened to you."

Maggy wanted to hit him. And not with a linen napkin. But she wanted to hear this story, too. So she set her teeth and stood where she was.

"A man known to have been a member of the Santa Dominian military went on an unscheduled break not long after the car accident that killed your parents. Records trace him to London. Several weeks after that, a woman known to the British authorities after a botched drug smuggling attempt flew one-way to New York with a companion child. According to all records, the child named as that companion does not exist. The woman went underground soon after landing in New York City and was never heard from again. But three weeks later, you were discovered on that rural road in Vermont."

It shouldn't matter what the story was. She shouldn't care. "You think she was hired to throw me away across the Atlantic, far from anyone who was looking for me?"

She thought she saw a glimpse of the Reza she knew then—and it turned out, that was worse. The hint of compassion only made the cold that much more bitter when it claimed him all over again.

"I think if they wanted to throw you away, they would have left you in that car," he said softly. "I think someone took pity on an eight-year-old child. I suspect that woman was meant to care for you, not abandon you."

"Well." Maggy's voice was as cold as his. She could feel the chill of it. "That appears to be something I bring out in people. Over and over again."

Reza stared back at her and for a moment—only a moment—she was certain she could see something in his hard rain gaze. Something almost stricken. But it was gone in the next instant, leaving nothing but stone in its wake.

She told herself she was glad she felt empty inside as she walked from the room and left him there to his crown and his duty. Because the emptier she was inside, the less there was to hurt.

Maggy assured herself she was *relieved* when the Santa Dominian plane landed. During the ten minutes or so it took for the armored SUV to make it up from the airfield to the villa, she told herself what worked in her, leaving her feeling a little bit breathless, was happiness. Pure, unadulterated happiness. Because this was what she'd always wanted, wasn't it? A family. A home. And *without* having to make herself over into some Very Special Princess so she could marry a man she hardly knew.

You're just not used to all this happiness, she told herself stiffly. *That's why you feel like crying.*

Reza had never been anything but a diversion. He wasn't what she wanted. He'd been a means to an end, nothing more.

If she kept telling herself that, surely it would turn into truth.

And she was standing in the great open foyer when

the SUV carrying Cairo Santa Domini pulled up in the circular drive, her hands in fists at her sides. Alone, of course.

Because she was always alone.

Buck up, Princess, she told herself. *You always will be.*

She heard a faint noise then and glanced over to find Reza beside her. He wore an expression she couldn't decipher on his face and his eyes were much too dark.

"You don't have to be here," she told him, because she couldn't stay quiet. That made her focus too much on all that emptiness. "I'm sure you have very important king things to do. Things that men would never do, only kings."

Reza let out a small sound that she thought was a sigh of exasperation. Maybe she only wanted it to be. Then, his mouth in that flat line that still seemed to kick up all that longing inside of her, he inclined his head in that way of his. And something was wrong with her that she felt that like some kind of support. As if he was holding her when he wasn't.

When he'd made it so clear he wouldn't.

Still, something inside of her curled at that. Like a small flame. Like hope that this thing between them wasn't finished. Not yet.

Maggy jerked her head away from him, focusing on what was happening outside in the drive. She watched as if she was far, far away as a man climbed from the back of the SUV without waiting for it to stop fully or for the hovering attendants to open his door. He stopped once he was out, and didn't move again until a red-headed woman followed him from the vehicle, then stood beside him, slipping her hand into his.

And there was no denying who he was. Cairo Santa Domini, known as an exiled king and a playboy of epic proportions before he'd taken back his kingdom. Maggy had stared at his face on tabloid magazines for years. It was hard to believe he was here. And more, that a vial of blood made them family.

Whatever that meant.

The woman—Queen Brittany, Maggy knew from the internet, once a reality star and a stripper and now the most beloved queen in Europe—gazed up at the man Maggy was supposed to call her brother as if she was giving him strength.

Cairo moved again then, his strides long as he headed for the villa's glass entryway, and Maggy couldn't breathe. Her palms stung and on some distant level she knew she was digging her nails into them, but she couldn't bring herself to stop. She could hardly manage to breathe.

Beside her, Reza shifted. Then, impossibly, she felt his hand in the small of her back.

She wanted to scream at him. She wanted to ask him what the hell he was doing. But she didn't want to do anything that would take the comfort of that hand away, no matter how cruel it was. No matter how little it actually meant.

Because that was the trouble. It was nothing to him. *She* was nothing to him, no matter how much hope she might carry deep inside her.

Yet to her, that hand was everything.

It was how she managed to stand there, straight and silent, as Cairo Santa Domini and his queen came swiftly into the hall. It was how she managed to breathe, just enough, as Cairo's gaze moved from Reza to her.

Then stuck on her.

He came closer and closer, every step loud against the marble floor, and then he stopped.

Dead.

Queen Brittany murmured something, but Maggy didn't hear it. It was only when Reza replied that she realized it must have been some kind of greeting. But Cairo was silent, too busy staring at her, and Maggy found she could do nothing but stare back.

Her heart was catapulting against her chest. Her ribs ached at the assault, or maybe because she kept holding her breath.

Because he had the same eyes. The same eyes she saw in the mirror every day. Caramel colored and shaped the same. *The same eyes.*

He muttered something in what she thought was Italian.

"There was a blood test," Maggy said, bracing herself to be thrown away the way she always was. "I'll do another one if you don't believe it."

She felt Reza's hand tighten at her back, as if he wasn't throwing her away after all. Or as if he didn't want to. Her nails dug deeper into her palms.

"You look like a ghost," Cairo said, his voice rough and reverent at once. "You look just like our mother."

Maggy's breath left her in a rush. "I'm not a ghost."

"No," Cairo agreed. He dropped his queen's hand and he moved closer, then stopped again. His gaze moved all over her as if he couldn't believe she was real. As if he wanted her to be real and was afraid she wasn't, after all. Or maybe that was her and her pounding heart. "You are Magdalena. You could not possibly be anyone else."

"Call me Maggy," she whispered.

And Cairo Santa Domini smiled, so bright it seemed to haul the sun inside, lighting up the foyer and Maggy's heart besides.

"Ah, *sorrelina*," he murmured. "I always did."

And then he closed the space between them and hauled her into his arms, lifting her off the ground and holding her close. Maggy was startled. He spun her around and she caught Reza's gaze over Cairo's shoulder. Silver and gray. It punched into her.

She sneaked her arms around Cairo's shoulders, her gaze locked to Reza's, to hug her brother back.

And she told herself she didn't care when the man she loved inclined his head again, then turned away.

She concentrated on the good things. The man who set her down on her feet and returned to studying her face, his gaze as over-bright as hers felt.

Just like a brother. *Her brother.* Just like a dream.

Except this time, it wasn't a dream. It wasn't a fairy tale.

This man was her family. Which meant, at last and for good, she belonged.

And that left room for that little flicker of hope inside of her to burn bright, then glow.

CHAPTER TEN

THE THRONE ROOM in Constantine Castle was used only for special occasions these days. Coronations, of course. Special ceremonies and addresses. Mostly, it was cordoned off and used as part of the tours that the public could take through some of the less private parts of the castle.

There was absolutely no reason that Reza should have found himself there, standing before the throne like some petitioner of old.

It had been weeks since Maggy had left the villa. Weeks since the world had learned that the Santa Domini princess had lived through that car accident twenty years ago.

She was now the foremost obsession of the international tabloids, just as Reza had predicted.

And it did not help that he knew exactly what it had taken for her to smile so graciously at the cameras. How hard she had worked to appear so elegant and so beautiful, every inch of her as beautiful as her mother before her and so startlingly, obviously a Santa Domini that the fact it had taken twenty years to find her seemed like an outrage.

He told himself he only read these articles and

watched the news reports to see how and when he was mentioned. But he wasn't. And Reza did not care to speculate as to why the Santa Dominian palace did not share the fact that he had been the one to find her.

The palace said very little, in fact. It had released a statement upon her return, announcing that she was recovered after all this time and enjoying getting to know her brother and the life she'd forgotten. Cairo had given an address that had expressed his joy at having some part of his murdered family returned to him. And the world had been forced to content itself with the very few pictures the palace released over those first few days. Maggy and Cairo together, laughing at something that made their identical eyes shine. Maggy holding the Crown Prince Rafael, her young nephew, while Queen Brittany looked on.

All very heartwarming.

Yet Reza remained cold straight through.

Here in this throne room, all the ghosts of his bloodline seemed to congregate. He could feel their disapproval press against him, like the weight of the formal crown he wore only on specific occasions these days.

He stared at the throne itself.

It was only a chair, though it dated back to the fifteen hundreds. It was made of finely polished wood and it gleamed in the sunlight that poured in through the stained-glass windows and made the room into a kind of chapel. A place of power and resolve, or so Reza had been taught.

He didn't understand the part of him that wanted to burn it. Rip it apart with his hands. Make it into so much kindling—

But there was no point in this kind of maudlin self-indulgence. He had let her go, the way he should have done from the start. From the moment he'd understood that he couldn't keep his distance with her. That she made him as bad as his father.

He had made his choice.

Reza made himself turn away. He pushed his way out of the great doors, nodding at the guards who waited there. He heard them muttering into their earpieces as they followed him down the grand hall. Alerting the rest of the palace to his movements. All hail his very public life that he'd lived blamelessly all this time. Forever apologizing for his father's failures. Forever making up for his father's sins.

For the first time in his life, Reza felt as if he was drowning. As if his role here was holding his head beneath the water. As if he had no choice but to open up his mouth, suck in the sea, and sink.

Impatient with himself, he shook it off as he rounded a corner and headed for his offices. Or he tried to shake it off.

Either way, he was as controlled and expressionless as always when he walked into his office to find three of his aides and his personal secretary waiting for him.

"Sire," his secretary said, and the man's deferential tone set his teeth on edge, when it was no different than it had ever been before. "There has been a development."

"You will have to be more specific," Reza clipped out as he rounded his desk, all of the historic city laid out before him on the other side of the windows. The far-off snowcapped mountains. The gleaming alpine lakes in the distance.

But all he saw was her face.

He gritted his teeth, then focused on his staff.

"The princess, sire," his secretary continued. Carefully. "She's given her first interview."

He did not play games and ask which princess his secretary meant, though there was a part of him—the cowardly part he would excise with his own fingers if he could—that wanted to hide from whatever this was a while longer. Even inside his own head.

"I imagine it will be the first of many," he replied. Reza felt more than saw the glances his staff exchanged, and braced himself. "I assume you are bringing this particular interview to my attention for a reason?"

His secretary stood straighter. "She discusses her wedding plans, sire. In some detail."

And it took every bit of Reza's training in diplomacy to simply stand there as if nothing was the matter. As if this news did not affect him in the slightest.

If only that were true.

"Have my felicitations sent with the appropriate gift," he murmured, as if he'd already forgotten what they were talking about. Then he treated them all to the full force of his stare. "Surely such things are usually done automatically, without my input?"

"I fear I cannot do the interview justice, sire," his secretary murmured. The man thrust a tablet onto the desktop and hit the play arrow on its screen.

Reza did not want to watch this. He wanted to hurl the tablet through the window behind him. He wanted to institute beheadings and reopen the old dungeons, and he wanted to start with the staff standing before him.

He wanted anything but Maggy in front of him, laughing with one of those American television journalists with alarmingly bright white teeth.

She was too beautiful. It was worse on-screen, where her marvelous cheekbones seemed more pronounced and her lively eyes seemed warmer and more kind than he remembered. Her voice was the same, soft and faintly rough, and all he could think about was Maggy on her knees before him, sucking him deep into her mouth.

Damn her.

He'd known she would be the ruin of him. What he hadn't realized was that even when he'd removed the temptation of her from his life, he would remain ruined.

"And I'm told you plan to honor the Santa Domini royal family's traditions, despite all these years away?" the interviewer asked.

"Oh, yes," Maggy answered, sounding as if the interviewer were her best friend in the world. Reza made a mental note to give his public relations team bonuses, given the magic they'd worked with her. She looked nothing like the mouthy shopgirl he'd met. She looked like who she was—who she had always been. Magdalena Santa Domini. "I have been betrothed to the king of the Constantines since I was born. And I am happy to honor my commitments. After all, not every girl gets to wake up one morning to find she's actually a princess and, even better, she's meant for a king."

The interviewer laughed but made one of those fake noises of concern that would have annoyed Reza had he been able to do anything but stand there, frozen, that aching thing in his chest threatening to break free at last.

"But you only just found out who you are," the interviewer said. "How can you rush into something like this?"

"The king is the one who found me," Maggy said,

almost shyly, and Reza knew exactly why they'd held it back before now. For this moment. For maximum impact. He almost admired it—the Santa Dominis were nothing if not in complete control of their images. Why should Maggy be any different? "He knew who I was before I did. And we spent some time together as I adjusted to my new role." She smiled down at her lap, looking for all the world as if she was overcome with emotion. It set Reza's teeth on edge. Especially when she looked up again, now looking flushed. *Like a woman in love*, a voice inside him murmured. "I'm more than happy with my fate."

His hand shot out before he could control it, stopping the video. His heart kicked at him, making his ribs ache.

"If you continue, sire," his secretary said, even more carefully than before, "the princess claims the wedding will be in June."

"In June," Reza said. His voice sounded as if it was someone else's.

"Yes, sire."

"This June."

His secretary nodded.

Reza stared down at the tablet before him, frozen on Maggy.

He hardly knew himself any longer and it was her fault. He had spent his whole life keeping himself free of emotional entanglements, just as he'd been taught by both his mother's cold demands and his father's bad example. He was trying to rule a kingdom and Maggy was telling lies to the whole world, boxing him into corners he wouldn't be able to get out of without causing an international incident and destroying the relationship between the two kingdoms—

Reza paused then. He took a deep breath in, then let it go.

She had thrown down a gauntlet. He would pick it up.

Maggy might think she wanted the man. Reza knew better. It was high time he showed her what happened when she taunted both man *and* king.

"Have the helicopter ready in fifteen minutes." His voice was smooth. Even. As if there was none of that fire beneath it. As if he wasn't burning alive where he stood. "I believe it's time I called upon my lovely bride."

Maggy sensed him before she heard a sound.

She waited in one of the palace's grand salons, set aside for visiting heads of state and various monarchs, sitting like the picture-perfect princess Reza had made her. She'd been informed the moment his helicopter had entered Santa Dominian airspace. She'd been alerted when he'd landed.

But she didn't need anyone to come and whisper in her ear that Reza was in the palace. That he was being led straight to her. She could feel it deep in her belly. She could feel it in the electric shivers that traced patterns over her limbs and the butterflies that performed calisthenics inside of her.

And then at last he was there, striding into the grand salon as if it was his, and it all got worse.

Or better, depending on how she looked at it.

Reza moved through her brother's palace the same way he'd strode into that long-ago coffee shop. He looked elemental. Regal stone and royal temper, all the way through.

She made herself stay where she was, and no matter that he bore down upon her like a freight train.

The doors closed behind him, leaving them alone in this overwrought room of antiques with priceless artifacts scattered about on every surface. But all Maggy could see was Reza.

"I knew you'd come," she said softly when he was in front of her, standing there radiating fury and something else she couldn't quite decipher in another perfectly pressed suit. "I'm surprised it took you as long as it did."

"You should have told me you were psychic," he replied, his voice all edges and threat. Yet it rolled through her like a caress. Like his body moving over her and in her—but she had to focus. "It might have saved me the time and the trouble."

Back in the villa, that might have killed her. But she'd spent a few weeks here, in the company of her marvelously wicked sister-in-law and her sharp, funny brother, and she wasn't the same person she'd been then. Or she was more that person than she'd known how to be that awful morning after.

And she'd seen through him, at last.

"You weren't discarding me, Reza," she told him softly, not beating around the bush because she'd already lost twenty years of her real life. She didn't want to lose a moment more. "I know you might have told yourself that you were. But what you were really doing was running scared."

As she'd known he would, he turned to granite.

"I beg your pardon."

She smiled at that, and it wasn't one of her fake, princess smiles. She felt this one down deep. "I love it when you say that, so stuffy and *indignant*. But it's true. I think you know it."

"The king of the Constantines does not *run scared*, I think you will find." Reza's brows arched, but he was still right there in front of her. He hadn't walked away again. "By definition."

"Perhaps not." She raised her own brows, settling back against the sofa as if, this time, she was the one gracing a high throne with her presence. "But what about you, Reza?"

"What about me?" He frowned at her. "I don't follow."

Of course he didn't.

"You have the king thing down, I think we can all agree." And he was so much the king. Even now, standing in another man's palace, he radiated that fierce authority. Maggy could feel it deep in her belly. "Are you really going to pretend that you're not also a flesh and blood man with his own needs?"

"I am not pretending anything. But I do not have to give in to my baser instincts. I do not have to let whatever needs I might have control me."

She thought he was speaking more to himself than to her.

"But you're okay with letting your dead parents and their terrible marriage control you instead." He looked outraged, but she'd expected that. She pushed on. "I did some research into your parents these last weeks. I dug up all those rumors. The speculation that your father was so wrapped up in that woman he nearly brought the country to war. That he disgraced the crown, then took his own life. All those nasty whispers."

"They are not whispers, they are facts I have kept from the public for years." He sounded starched through, though she could see that muscle in his cheek, telling her the truth about his feelings. "And now that you know these unsavory truths, there is no need for these theatrics, is there?"

Maggy folded her hands in her lap even tighter, because she wanted to reach for him.

"I didn't have any parents," she said softly. "But I'm pretty sure the point of them is that they're supposed to protect *you*, Reza. Not make you responsible for *their* problems."

"You have no idea what you are talking about." His voice was dark. Low.

Tortured.

"If you say so," she replied in a tone that told him she disagreed. Quietly. Then inclined her head the way he liked to do. "Your Majesty. You must know best."

And she thought for a moment that she could hear his teeth grit.

The truth was, she knew him. That had been the truth she'd returned to again and again in this time away from him, nursing that flame of hope deep inside of her. She knew him because she *was* him, in all the ways that mattered. He was as alone as she'd always been. He hid it in his palaces and villas, his bespoke suits, and his ranting on about what the king could and could not do—but he was always alone. His life was a throne, nothing more.

It might shine a lot brighter than her little room in Vermont, but it was the same narrow bed and the same cold thing inside that never quite warmed. Maggy knew this better than anyone.

She knew *Reza* better than anyone, in part because he'd shown her the pain behind his mask that dreadful morning.

He had found her and rescued her from a life that had never been meant to be hers. This was her chance to rescue him in turn.

"Exactly what is it you think you are doing?" Reza asked her with soft menace, fierce danger all over his harsh face, but she couldn't allow herself to be intimidated. Not when it mattered this much. "Do you truly believe that you can announce a wedding date and I will simply honor it? Because you say so?"

"That was pretty much your original plan, if I remember it right." She shrugged. "Why shouldn't it work for me?"

"You should have told me you were barking mad," he gritted out. "I would have handled this whole thing differently."

"I'm not mad. I am mad *at* you," she retorted. She stood up then, letting her dress fall where it would. She'd chosen it carefully because it made her look like a queen and she knew it. She could see he knew it, too. "You made me into a princess. Now I want to be your queen. As promised."

His hands were clenched into fists at his sides. He looked like thunder. But he was here. He was *here*, and that was what kept her standing where she was, pretending her heart wasn't thumping and her stomach wasn't in knots.

"You cannot force me to marry you," he growled at her, as if that was the end of the matter. But he still didn't leave.

Maggy only smiled at him.

"First," she said, "it's not up to you whether you marry me or not. It's your destiny." She saw the moment he realized she was throwing his own words right back

at him. It made those hard rain eyes go silver, and that
was when she knew this would be okay. That it would
work. That the flicker of light inside of her, hopeful and
bright, had been guiding her in the right direction all
along. "And second, you silly man, haven't you realized that we're made for each other? You took a scared,
beaten-down woman and made her a princess."

"And you took a king and rendered him nothing but
a man," he bit out, but she thought he sounded less furious than before.

She'd seen that gleam of silver and she wasn't afraid
any longer. She'd already lost him, however briefly. She
wasn't doing it again. Not ever again.

Maggy moved toward him, watching that muscle
in his cheek flex as she did. She didn't stop when she
drew near. She slid her hands up on his chest and she
arched herself into him, never taking her eyes from his.

"I love you, Reza," she told him, from the very
depths of her. "I love the king in you. I love how seriously you take your duties. I love how deeply it matters to you that you take care of your people. But it was
the man who took care of me. And I love him more."

"Maggy..." he whispered, as if her name might break
him in two. "I don't know how to do this. My father—"

"You are not your father," she told him, her gaze
solemn on his. "And I have no desire to be your mistress. And, Reza, no one knows how to do it. I think
that's the point."

And she watched him break. She saw his eyes flash
silver and bright. She watched the ice crack and all that
heat pour out of him as his arms came around her, and
then he hauled her even closer.

Bringing Maggy home at last.

"You knew I would come to you," he growled at her, his mouth so close to hers. "You knew I couldn't resist."

Her eyes felt much too full. "I hoped."

"And if I marry you, then what?" he demanded. "When you strip away my control and I am rendered nothing but a man lost without you, what then?"

"Then I will come and find you wherever you're lost," she whispered. "Just as you came and found me. And I promise you, Reza, I won't let you stumble. I won't make you a worse king. I'll try my best to make you a better man."

His hands seemed uncertain as they moved up to smooth her hair back from her face, and she felt her tears spilling over when he leaned in and pressed a soft kiss on her forehead.

"I think I've loved you all my life," he told her, his voice a rough sort of velvet she'd never heard from him before. It washed through her, heat and love. "I loved you in the abstract. I mourned you. And then I saw you in that picture and I fell in love all over again."

He kissed her then, and it was a real kiss. Wild and dark and perfect, rolling through her and making her heart swell inside her chest. He kissed her again and again, as if they were making their vows here and now. As if they were fusing themselves into one.

When he pulled away again, it was her turn to reach up and cradle his face in her hands.

"When I was first found by the side of that road," she told him, "I dreamed of fairy tales. Kings and queens and palaces. Every night, for years, I would go to sleep and dream of fairy-tale stories filled with people I wanted so badly to believe were real." She smiled at him. She kissed him. "But maybe they were. Maybe they weren't dreams at all. Maybe they were the life I left behind me when that car crashed."

He whispered her name, drawing her closer.

"Reza." And her voice was a scrap of sound. "Don't you see? I've been dreaming of you my whole life. It's just that I forgot your name for a little while."

His smile then was the most beautiful thing she'd ever seen.

"I will endeavor to make certain you never do again."

"Marry me, Your Majesty," she whispered, tipping her head back and loving him with all she was, all she would be, all she'd ever dreamed she could be. Right here in his arms, at last. "Make me your queen."

That June, in a ceremony televised around the world and gushed over in all the tabloids, with her newfound family there to give her away and a brand-new country that had fallen in love with their king's lost princess, he did.

And they spent all their happily-ever-after together, making their fairy tale real.

Just as Maggy had always dreamed.

* * * * *

MILLS & BOON
MEDICAL
Pulse-Racing Passion

Set your pulse racing with dedicated, delectable doctors in the high-pressure world of medicine, where emotions run high and passion, comfort and love are the best medicine.

MILLS & BOON
True Love
Romance from the Heart

Celebrate true love with tender stories of heartfelt romance, from the rush of falling in love to the joy a new baby can bring, and a focus on the emotional heart of a relationship.